THE
HOUSE
OF
WOLVES

THE
HOUSE
OF
WOLVES

—— THE TETHER ——

JAIME GABRIEL PLÁ

Charleston, SC
www.PalmettoPublishing.com

The House of Wolves

Copyright © 2022 by Jaime Gabriel Plá

All rights reserved.

First Edition

Hardcover ISBN: 978-1-68515-445-5
Paperback ISBN: 978-1-68515-444-8

I would like to thank my parents and sister for their never-ending love and support. You are my inspiration and drive, the source of my will to build my life into the story I seek.

Thank you to William Middleton, the only lad whose mind is as twisted as my own. You're a true friend, and without you this wouldn't have been possible...so whatever happens, I blame you.

TABLE OF CONTENTS

CHAPTER 1

"What are Velka? Some might tell you that they are aliens, not dishonestly, but this is merely a superficial truth that escapes the point of such a question. The Velka are a force of nature. Immovable, unstoppable, without thought or heart or soul. Beware their storms, when their Caelicraft blot out the sky or when their soldiers swallow the land. For when their storms come, no one is safe."

—*A History of Our Invaders*, volume i, by Cornelius Valum, chief historian of the Library of Alexandria

Dorin woke up screaming with Soot drawn in his metal hand. He searched for the wyrms eating him, for their pike-like legs, their circular, teeth-filled maws. Nothing. Nothing but fresh snowy hillsides and weeds as far as the eye could see. He was hyperventilating. He needed more air. He tore off his helmet and threw it to the ground and ran his left hand, the human one, through his black, sweat-drenched hair and scratched his scalp. It reminded him of the present, that his nightmare had faded. He held the barrel of his hand cannon along his forehead, from nose to scalp, pulled back the hammer, and reset it. Again and again.

Hot.

Cold.

Salty.

Nauseous.

Dorin swallowed back down the bile that seared his throat and finally regained control of his breathing. He leaned his head back, the sun felt hot on his face. *Deep breaths. In through the nose. Out through the mouth. Fuck. Must've dozed off,* he thought.

Dorin opened his eyes and dropped his head. He reached into the backpack that he'd used as a pillow and pulled out an amber bottle. His last one. He uncapped it and drank the remnants of the harsh liquor. *Piss. Should've paced myself.* He threw the bottle out into the snow and it sank into the powder with a loud *crunch.* Dorin sat running his fingers along the barrel of his pistol, Soot. *What a piece of junk*, he thought bitterly. In four years he had never found a decent replacement, and he was getting frustrated. The trigger took far too much effort to pull, and the kick might as well have been an entire starship taking off. The only redeeming quality was the munition, high velocity molten metal, bolts accelerated and heated with electromagnetic fields. There was a reason this piece of junk was so big––it was like someone had tried to fit a Velkan Caelicraft's mass driver cannon into a handheld firearm.

Dorin cradled Soot gingerly in his hands, just staring at red glowing lines that ran down parallel to the jet-black barrel. The bolts almost looked like a flash of red lightning cutting the air from his hand to his target when he fired as the air around the shot expanded and contracted violently. Sometimes he thought the air would shatter around him. Dorin loved the sight of the metal lightning, but the sound wasn't like that of any other gun he'd ever heard. It wasn't the sound of burning light or spewing lead, it was something else. Like a massive hammer pounding in a nail with each pull of the trigger. No, it was a deeper sound than that. Like steel cracking a mountain.

Dorin loved that sound.

He looked up at the sky and fixated on the vapor trail of a ship that must have just left the atmosphere. *Too far from Alexandria. Must've been a Velkan ship.* He got up and wiped the snow that had collected on his trousers and holstered his pistol on his thigh. He put his helmet back on and pulled his hood up around it and tightened his long coat around his chest. The cloth provided little comfort against the hard, whipping cold. The place where the metal of his arm met his right shoulder burned and ached from the frozen air. Dorin snapped the fingers on his left hand, and his survival gauntlet crackled to summon a gentle flame. The fire suspended in his palm, he tended to his stump with a tender touch. He flexed his right arm, opening and closing his metal hand. He couldn't exactly feel anything with his right, but there was a strange pressure he sensed coming through the metal of the arm as his fingers gently scraped against one another. The fire melted away the stabbing pain the cold metal dealt to his fleshy shoulder.

I need to get off this miserable planet—way too cold for an amputee. Somewhere warm…with beaches…and coconuts. Mmmmm, coconuts. Dorin's mouth watered at the thought.

Dorin shouldered his pack and began the trek back to his tent at the forest's edge, just over the hill where he had been sitting. His black duster flew in the breeze, whipping to and fro. He stopped for a moment.

He heard whispers through the snow-laden holly thicket.

CRACK CRACK CRACK.

Dorin approached the frosted bushes, Soot still smoking and aimed toward the source of the sound, his pack was thrown to the floor. Behind the smoldering bushes were two Velka in the snow. One sprawled dead with a U-shaped canoe of molten metal where its head used to be. The other clutched the bullet wounds in its chest. Vapor poured out of them. Soon the molten metal of its armor sealed the holes, and the pressure built as the temperature of the artificial atmosphere within the alien's suit rose. The poor lad was paralyzed by pain, his flesh seared as the air in his suit cooked him slowly. That was the one thing Dorin hated most about Soot—a gun he would bang against rocks for fun. If he scored a head shot, anyone foolish or poor enough not to own an energy barrier would die instantly in a cloud of their own gray matter and superheated tungsten. But should Dorin miss their vitals, he might as well strap his victims to a pyre and watch them burn. It tortured them. The slugs' extreme heat refused to diminish as it cooked the target's flesh. The scout writhed before him. Pain broke his mind and surged through what was left of his body.

Dorin forced himself to drink in the consequences of his actions. He inhaled deeply and took a rusty knife from his left boot.

"Go with Okar, and journey through the stars eternal," he prayed. The dying Velka was just conscious enough to understand the prayer of its people, and Dorin saw a flash of something in its eyes. He'd seen it before, Velka had very expressive eyes. Consequences of living life in climate suits. Dorin plunged the knife upward beneath its jaw, and the Velkan scout died immediately.

He cleaned his knife, holstered Soot, and removed his helmet to better examine the corpses. They were dressed to survive on Earth's near endless permafrost. Furs accented their long dark cloaks and spurted from the joints of their armor. Dorin inspected the headless Velka. The markings of a large green snake-looking beast with wings proudly adorned the curved steel on its breastplate.

"House of Serpents. What are you doing on Earth?"

Dorin tore the banners of their house from their smoldering corpses and rummaged through their pockets to find evidence of why they'd come to his corner of the solar system. No luck. The steel that covered the bodies always made Dorin think of the alligators on Venus but also Earth's bipedal wolves. He could never make up his mind. Their heads and their ears were not unlike those of a wolf, but their snouts were wider and shorter. Generally rounder.

Their ears were covered in skintight black environmental suit latex, or something like latex. Each sported a plate of metal on the back of the ears that protected the delicate part of their body. He could tell frightened greenhorns from seasoned veterans in combat by whether the ears cowered out or flattened back to create a smooth helm. The older aliens had learned early on that an exposed ear wasn't going to remain an ear for much longer. The plating that segmented their bodies gave them a reptilian visage, but all of the designs were smooth and rounded, expressing the elegant pretensions of their people.

Velkan houses all had a flourish in their designs. The House of Wolves could be recognized by thick furs beneath their plate and similar accents to their attire. The Serpent's armor was unique in that the metal vambrace on their forearms twisted and coiled around the arm to a point on the elbows, their greaves had a similar design up to their knees. Dorin preferred the former design. The fluff made them look kinder, sweeter. He played with the point on the coiled elbow and nearly cut himself. It was hard to remember just how sharp Velkan metalwork could get.

Dorin removed the Velka's helmet and held it aloft. It looked quite nice. Certainly nicer than the dented and scarred scrap of metal he'd just tossed to the snow.

He turned a knob on the back of his left hand and the orange light that flowed from the utility mode indicator shifted to a bright cyan, then to a soothing purple—from fire to electricity to gravity effects. He warped the Velkan helm with gravitational fields emitted by his left hand—each snap of his fingers caused a warp of light and a tortured movement of metal. Soon the helmet was roughly shaped to fit his head, and he put it on. Decent for now. He made a mental note to get it fit properly later. He had worked with Velkan steel before, beautiful craftsmanship.

Dorin stood up, his silhouette became ever more Velkan as his right arm and helm matched in a smooth simplicity that reflected their origin. He looked again at the two Serpent corpses.

Hmm, Tarkus is not going to be happy about this.

Dorin made quick work packing up his camp and turned north to set off for the House of Wolves.

Dorin approached the great walls of Volthsheim—the massive gate of wood and steel, the symbol of Wolf strength. It left no question why humanity was runner-up in the struggle for societal supremacy. The walls rose high into the morning sky. The faint lines of turrets and gun towers lined the edges. The greatest city on earth. The Volthsheim walls encircled an area of over 240,000 kilometers, twenty million alien souls. The seat of the only superpower on the planet.

Until, perhaps, now.

Aside from humans, who had dozens of towns near the equator and the stronghold of Alexandria, the Wolves were the only other civilization on the planet. Velka were highly communalist, but competition *between* communities was violent and ferocious. Dorin had heard scores of horror stories from the Wolves themselves, tempests of wars raged while humans remained ignorant of the millions frozen and dead in the vacuum of space.

The houses carved up the system into different territories almost the instant they arrived. How long ago no one was quite sure. Not even the Velka.

A blue line of light burst from the seam where the gates met.

"Dorin, human freelancer," he said. "I humbly request an audience with Jarl Tarkus. It's a matter of house security."

Pressure waves shook Dorin to his teeth as an unseen speaker oscillated to life. Light shone on him as it scanned his person. A robotic chorus sounded in oppressive volume.

"Validate identity."

"Dorin, ID 21175, human freelancer operating in the wilds under authority Black R-1, authorized by First Guard Etkis Terra."

"Confirmed. Security question: What is the journey, and what is the tether?"

"Where I am going and where I have been."

The gate creaked under its colossal weight as it opened before Dorin, and he stepped inside the great city. The buildings were wooden, just like the gate, but all Velkan "wood" was fireproof and could stop the bullet of a .5K kelvin rifle. Why their metal lacked similar resilience to heat was a constant question among human academics. The gnarled, nearly impervious material was certainly organic, but the Velka made it themselves. It was forged, not found, just like their steel.

Their civilian architecture departed dramatically from the simplicity of their military gear. Each building was ornately carved, a signature the Volthsheim builders left on all their finished works. Dorin had once spent an entire day following the edifice artistry on the buttresses of a meager barracks and marveled at the mastery, the same standard expected of any Velka in their field. Decorative patterns left little plain wood exposed for the eye to see, and runes to designate building functions were carved into the face on every one of them. Each was unique except for the house sigil above their entrances. On every shop, workplace, and home was maintained the face of an animal that humans had no name for. It looked most like a wolf, with the pupils gathered into vertical predatory slits.

"Dorin! What in Okar's name are you doing back here, my friend!"

The chipper voice of a large Velka came from behind. His sonorous tone was gently digitized as it passed through the filters of the Velkan helmet. His voice was powerful, warmly familiar. The behemoth trotted quickly to Dorin and gave him a hug proportionate to his size. Most Velka were just a touch larger than a human, but this monstrosity was a prime example of the full potential lying dormant in Velkan genes. He was easily two and a half meters tall and still growing. His armor marked him as military, and his massive maroon and brown fur cloak marked him as one of the city guard. The full house sigil sown into the back distinguished his rank—the first guard.

"*Oh*, sweet God, Etkis, you're gonna kill me!"

"Sorry!" Etkis plopped him down. "What are you doing back so soon! What happened to the raids…and where'd you get that helmet?" He tapped on Dorin's helm with his massive finger.

"I didn't even make it to town. I came across some Velka on the road, from the House of Serpents."

"Mm. Well, that explains the helmet, it certainly looks like one of theirs, but are you sure? You can't make a claim like *that* without evidence."

Dorin dropped his heavy backpack and took out the banners he had stripped from the scouts he had gunned down. Etkis inspected them closely.

"Well…piss. All right. I'll get us a shuttle—I assume you're here to tell Jarl Tarkus?"

"Yeah. I can't imagine he'll be exactly thrilled to hear it, but he needs to know."

"Easy for you to say. You get to leave when he's angry." Etkis waved to a guard, a subordinate of his, and signaled for him to call them a vehicle. The Velka saluted, crossing his arms against his chest, and hustled away.

"I'm sure you can calm him down. It'll be fine," Dorin said, picking up his backpack and adjusting it so that all the weight was on his metal shoulder. Etkis scoffed.

"You're quite the optimist. I don't know if even Lady Nora will be able to keep his head on straight after this."

"That's a first," Dorin said, pensive.

"Not really. He has quite the temper."

"No, I mean that's the first time anyone's ever called me an optimist."

It was a five-hour shuttle ride to the center of the city. Dorin and Etkis flew just over the skyline, in line with hundreds of other vehicles flying and merging seamlessly with the rest of the traffic. Shuttles flew in and out of line, ebbed and weaved in harmony, almost like a dance. Dorin watched from out the window. The perfect synchronicity of it all put him in a trance and inspired curses at humanity's inability to do the same.

The buildings got larger and larger as they ventured toward the center of the city. All were still made of Velkan wood, as tall as human skyscrapers, with little more metal than rivets. Halfway along their journey, the buildings abruptly stopped, to be replaced with a large, transparent dome of silica. One of many. It went on for kilometers. Dorin could see through to the lush farmland beneath, totally alien to the frozen earth he knew. The Velka had plenty of experience with controlled atmospheres. It was what allowed them to live on almost any planet with their suits.

Volthsheim was placed on the largest deposit of fertile land on the planet, or at least that was what humanity believed. Dorin had never been sure if the Wolves had found and claimed the land or made it tenable themselves. Too much of Earth was either frozen dead or drenched in radiation. Humans just dwelled within the nuclear poison, birthed their stillborn children, and died young. But the Velka had the technology and resources to scrub the land clean. Dorin found it hard to believe that such large swaths of farmland had been left unsullied following the Phantom Fire and whatever series of wars had corrupted the earth into radioactive waste. But even these rich fields weren't enough to feed the entire population of Volthsheim. They still needed to raid. When their hunger eclipsed their mercy, they stripped other houses, the pitiful houseless, and humanity bare. They were all fair game.

They passed the farmlands, the longhouse-like residences, the labyrinthine Congress of Thought, and the skyborne shipyards to arrive at the nexus of it all. Railways, cobblestone paths, and landships converged like nerves to a brain.

The largest hall in Volthsheim. The Great Hall. The jarl's seat.

It towered above any other structure on the planet, more like a small mountain than an actual building. Trains both above ground and below pulled in and out of the station just to the south, and hundreds of Velka walked up and down the stone steps. Dorin thought he spotted one human and shuddered.

The shuttle exited the line of other flying vehicles and descended smoothly to the base of the steps. Etkis thanked their driver, and Dorin hopped out, grinning ear to ear because he didn't have to pay any fare. The benefits of flying with the military. The duo walked up the seemingly endless steps to the entrance.

Dorin checked in his backpack, helmet, knife, and pistol with the guards posted outside. No weapons were allowed, and the helmet was just another obstacle between his mouth and sweet, sweet liquor. Nobody distilled like the Velka. Nobody.

The cobblestone path that began at the doors led all the way to a tall hill at the back of the hall. The path climbed to two enormous wooden thrones. Tarkus and Nora sat in them and spoke to a much smaller and wiry Velka who knelt at their feet.

Etkis left Dorin at the entrance with two guards. Any foreigner was held under sharp scrutiny here, but this case was more of a formality than anything else. Dorin was not an official citizen of Volthsheim, but he'd long ago been accepted by the House of Wolves as an asset, if not a friend. He was more at home here than among his own people.

There were many halls within Volthsheim, but the Great Hall was unique. It defied any kind of architectural sense. The walls bent out wide into a large prism like the interior of a fine gemstone. It gave Dorin a pleasant and inviting feel of openness—the center of the walls could be easily mistaken for the horizon. The wood should in no way have been able to support its own weight. Ornate pillars were scattered within the hall that touched neither the cobblestone floor nor the wooden ceiling. Velka gathered along long tables and laughed and drank through the filters in their helmets.

There was always a large gathering here—in any hall, really. Velka rarely saw others who did not work in their field until the day came to a close and they came here to wash away fatigue with a flagon of inthol. Not that it was forbidden to cross the job barrier, it simply didn't happen. Outside the halls and family dwellings, work was all-encompassing. This is where they came to get away from their unceasing labor. Soldiers could meet builders, bakers could meet pilots.

Large, flaming hearths inspired a sense of comradery. And for those seeking a mate, a little more than that. In the corner of the hall, Dorin could see a group of male farmers competing for the attention of some female soldiers. Their masculinity-induced ignorance made them believe they were competing in tests of strength, skill, and wit—but for the shrewd, and the females were shrewd indeed, this was truly an entertainment of embarrassment. The females laughed and clapped good-naturedly, not at all impressed but still clearly having a good time.

Dorin chuckled to himself as one Velka sire, a civilian by the looks of his wool garments, tried to pick up a table with two other Velka on it and failed. Miserably. A Velka dam strode up—her armor implied military—and with less than a grunt, hoisted the table off the ground. Males and all. She did a few shoulder presses just to prove her point. But wounded pride can always be mended with a drink, and the young sire quickly forgot about his embarrassment when the dam who'd shown him up sat adjacent to him. She squeezed in close and offered him a glass for a toast. She'd patched up his fragile ego faster than any surgeon. All with gentle flirtation.

Dorin could not see the Velka's faces behind their helmets, but neither could the Velka themselves. They had developed very expressive body language, and the glowing, nearly electronic eyes that shone from their helmets conveyed a world of emotion. Not being able to see their faces used to put Dorin on edge. He felt at an uncomfortable disadvantage. But after a time, he began to appreciate the Velka's form of nonverbal communication. Especially since it was easy to read them from across the room. Dorin could always find entertainment simply watching in the Great Hall.

Dorin was used to the dangerous wilds and always sat with his back to the wall and his face toward the door—except here. He felt safe here. Only here.

Etkis approached his leaders. Dorin watched all the while as his friend whispered to them before being waved away by Tarkus. Etkis trotted down the hill back to Dorin.

"The jarl is busy speaking with the first builder right now. It won't be long, and then you can see him."

"Thank you, Etkis."

The guards saluted Etkis and returned to their posts at the jarl's approval, thankful for the end of the pointless exercise.

Dorin snickered. "I'm still not used to them saluting you."

Etkis rubbed the back of his neck. "I don't think I'll ever get used to it…"

Dorin bumped his friend with his elbow, a devilish smile on his lips. "Started abusing your power yet?"

"*Ha!* Oh, yes, yes, of course! That's the whole point, isn't it?"

"Good to know I'm corrupting you, my sweet, innocent lad."

Etkis rolled his eyes and chuckled. The two stood beside one another, watching Jarl Tarkus and Lady Nora speak with the first builder. When any noncitizen waited for an audience with the jarl, there was to be a guard on them at all times, and they had to stand at the foot of the hill where the leaders sat until they were called. Etkis shuffled uncomfortably, waiting for an end to this faux professionalism. Dorin waited just long enough so that Etkis could claim that the formality had been observed.

"Drink?"

"Always!" Etkis said, grateful to be free of the song and dance they had been performing. "You're buying."

"Ugh, right, what's the damage now?"

"With this drink? About nine hundred out of fifteen hundred gold."

"Sweet God." The two made their way to an automated dispensary. It churned out cylindrical glasses and mugs with incredible speed and precision. Velka popped gold coins into a slot and left with a drink in hand. Dorin fished in the pouches on his belt for the coins he needed. Etkis crossed his arms, dropping the game they'd been playing.

"You don't have to pay me back, you know…" Etkis said, his voice soft.

"Yes, I do. I don't like owing you." Dorin's stump burned at the concept. "I've made up my mind."

"I feel bad…"

"Don't."

Dorin and Etkis sat down together, Dorin with a mug of honey liquor marketed to Volthsheim's few human citizens and Etkis with a large cylinder of purple liquid called inthol. Both *very* alcoholic.

Dorin's attention returned to the two flirting Velka, who had moved on to touching each other's arms tenderly as they chatted and maintained eye contact. The human equivalent of ferociously making out on the table.

"So Etkis, have you met anyone recently?"

"I met a human merchant selling these imported, weird green balls of leaves. But no one wanted to buy them, so he threw a fit and left."

"It's called cabbage, God knows why he'd try and sell that here. And that's not what I meant. Have you met anyone…special?" Dorin motioned over to the two Velka he had been studying from across the hall. Their flagrant display of passion and intimacy clearly made Etkis uncomfortable, and his meek virgin gaze shifted back to the table. *Such a prude*, Dorin thought and laughed to himself.

"Oh…" Etkis mumbled. "No, not really."

"You know it'll never happen if you don't try and make it happen."

"I know."

"Come on! *First guard?* You must have people throwing themselves at you."

"You're hilarious." Etkis drank his inthol, and Dorin slapped the table in frustration.

"No really!" Dorin said. He pointed to a Velka over Etkis's shoulder, "Look, that lady over there is casting glances our way. And that one over there…and that one and that one—"

"No they're not! Stop it!"

"They're not looking at me, my boy. Either they're *aggressively* undressing you, or I've at long last entered my 'popular' phase with Velkan dams. It's so obvious. How are you not seeing this?"

Etkis fixed his eyes on his drink and fiddled his thumbs nervously. Truly he was a specimen of his people: heroic, honorable, accomplished, and *massive*. Ever since Etkis had come of mating age, he had been getting constant looks in any hall he wandered into, but the poor boy was oblivious to it all. And now that he'd been promoted to head a vocational field, it was even worse. Work was so all-consuming that courting was near impossible on duty, so most flirted here in a hall. And he had no idea how.

"I just haven't met the right one yet," Etkis said, defensive. "What's your excuse?"

"I haven't seen another human in nine months, Etkis. How could I possibly meet someone?"

"That's what happens when you spend all your time between the wilds and blacksmith. You're...young? Is twenty-three young for humans?"

"Young enough to be stupid but old enough to be bitter." Dorin laughed at his own joke, which he took far too seriously. He took a drink.

"You have your whole life ahead of you, then!" Etkis said, his voice raised in emphasis. "You need to socialize."

"I'm socializing right now."

"I don't count."

"Sure you do! Look at us, we're social butterflies, beating back our many admirers."

"Ha ha, ah yes, the legions of fans we've amassed. We could conquer the system with this kind of support!" The duo laughed at their empty table, wrapped their drinking arms around one another, and chugged down the harsh dregs that remained in their sizable cups.

"Ach! Piss, that burns!" Etkis burped. "You think we have time to get another? It goes down way easier after the nerves in your throat have died."

Dorin saw another Velka female behind Etkis eye him over. She whirled around to show off her figure in an attempt to catch his eye. *Poor hopeless woman*, Dorin thought.

"Well, you could always buy *her* a round," Dorin said, motioning over to the dam.

Etkis turned, made eye contact with her, and immediately turned back to the table, his eyes wide with embarrassment and ears pressed back flat against his head. Dorin imagined Etkis blushing furiously beneath his helmet.

"Here lies Etkis, last of his line." Dorin laughed.

Etkis grumbled in frustration, confusion, and self-consciousness. She had clearly been a gorgeous Velka to have brought Etkis to such a pitiful state.

At that moment the first builder saluted his superiors, and they descended from their perch. Dorin gave Etkis a little nudge, and they both rose to meet the jarl.

Tarkus was dressed in old military armor rather than the typical jarl finery, an homage to his previous career pursuits that he refused to abandon. He was *somehow* even bigger than Etkis and eclipsed him by another head or so. This was an advantage awarded by age, and it was obvious that one day the young Etkis would tower over his leader. He truly was a freak of nature.

Nora was smaller than her mate, but that still made her about as large as Etkis. Her wool and silk clothes draped her beautifully, and the platinum bracelets she wore on her wrists and biceps were much more befitting of her station than Tarkus's humble presentation. The beautiful designs carved into her helmet, which females of the house so often liked to relish, mesmerized Dorin every time. The intricate patterns flowed like a stream of stars in water, inscribed in runes he couldn't recognize. A true work of art, so different in spirit than the males' smooth helms. Both wore a necklace of carved sapphire, with a rune symbolizing the other's name carved into the center. The public symbol of their union.

Dorin knelt before the jarl and his mate, crossing his arms along his chest in the Velkan salute. Since he was not a citizen of the city and was not a Velka, he neither *had* to kneel nor was he exactly expected to, but these two were legends. The First Shipmaster Tarkus of the Wolven fleets, and the First Voyager Nora of the Kuiper Belt. After the death of the previous jarl, they were the only candidates anyone considered for ascension to jarldom. After Tarkus was selected, Nora challenged him to a duel of honor for the title. They fought until the sun set, and Nora finally claimed victory. Tarkus offered her the right to ascension, but for reasons known only to her, she refused, and the two declared their relationship days after. The coupling gave the House of Wolves its two greatest members joint leadership, regardless of who officially held the title. Dorin wondered what must have transpired during that battle to cause such a shift between the two. Velka communicated so much through body language; perhaps a battle conveyed more than words ever could.

"Dorin," Tarkus said, "a pleasure to see you again. I thought you were headed south for the winter?"

His respect noted, Dorin rose.

"I was lord jarl, but four days ago I was waylaid on the journey. I came across several scouts from the House of Serpents. I've brought their banners as proof."

Dorin held them out for a servant to take. A small Velka, who only came to Dorin's waist, took the banners and brought them hastily to his lord and lady.

Squires were common among the Velka as it was the final step in training for their roles in society. To be a squire to the jarl was a rare privilege.

He must be reared for leadership, Dorin thought, going back and forth between the young Velka and Etkis. Great things were always expected from the squire of the jarl.

"How did our own scouts miss this trespass!" Tarkus boomed, breaking Dorin from his thoughts.

Tarkus turned to the squire. "Fetch First Scout Rother. *Now.*" The squire wasted no time, saluting his leaders and running off.

"Do you have any notion as to why they entered our borders?" Lady Nora asked. Dorin loved listening to her speak—her voice was gently digitized, a trait all Velka shared with their helmets, but her tone was smooth, natural and cool. She was simultaneously commanding and soothing in a way that only an experienced leader could be.

"No, my lady. Unfortunately I gunned them down before I had the opportunity to question them."

"Did they have heavy armaments or explosives of any kind?"

"No, ma'am, nothing but the clothing on their backs and small arms. But they were well dressed for the weather, which means they must have acquired garments from outside Serpent territory—not many beasts on Venus I know with fur that thick. Merchants from Earth or Mars likely sold the gear to the Serpents, which means there may be a trail to find their source."

"Not an attack, then, maybe a prelude…probing for weaknesses. And they either expected to be here or *have* been here for quite some time. If the latter, it is unlikely that they are the only team within our borders."

Tarkus growled, "The House of Serpents have been making trouble on our border for years." In contrast to his mate, Tarkus had a voice of absolute authority. It was harsh and blunt but still comforting in its own way—like you knew safety could be found behind him. "Too often have they needed to be reminded of their place. We've been far too merciful as of late. Enough. They must taste the steel of consequence. But first, we need more information…"

At that moment the squire galloped up the steps with Rother trailing sluggishly behind him, a full moon brightly emblazoned on his chest. A dark scar ran across the left side of his helmet to his ear, most of which was missing. It was little more than a shredded crescent. His gray eyes swallowed the light around them and gave away nothing—no fear, no panic, no concern. The squire bowed to his lord and lady and swiftly returned to the corner in which he was stationed. Rother knelt and stood quickly. He stared Tarkus in the eye.

Rother didn't acknowledge Dorin. He looked straight past him to the jarl. Dorin could not entirely suppress his smug satisfaction.

"You sent for me, my lord jarl?" Rother asked. Tarkus spoke slowly and measuredly. His rage pressed through his words like water through a hose.

"I did, you incompetent *swine*. We have just received evidence that scouts from the House of Serpents—*the Serpents*—have penetrated our borders. But you did not bring this to me—you, whose *job* it is to detect and remove enemy agents and insurgents—but rather a freelancer of the wilds slaughtered the intruders and informed us of this trespass! How do you excuse such incompetence?"

Rother didn't move a muscle at Tarkus's challenge. The jarl's rumbling voice shook the stone floor. Still, his eyes conveyed no emotion. Dorin gritted his teeth as a shiver ran down his spine.

"My lord, it is quite possible that these scouts had just arrived on the planet when this freelancer came upon them—"

"Perhaps I should make *him* first scout then, since he clearly responds immediately to threats that, as you seem to suggest, you cannot."

Rother's fists clenched ever so slightly. *That got you,* Dorin thought as he desperately tried to hide his smile.

"My lord—"

"You've brought shame to your office!" Tarkus roared and stood and he cast a shadow that swallowed up his subordinate. Dorin's sly smile disappeared immediately. Rother knelt so fast that his armored knee clanged into the cobblestone with a loud ring. Lady Nora remained silent, studying her mate, Rother, and Dorin in equal measure.

Dorin and Etkis tensed. They shared a look between them, bonded in their panic. Rother's one good ear bowed flat in subservience, the torn one pushed back as well but stuttered and twitched at the strain. He knelt, still.

Tarkus spoke in a near whisper, intent on grinding Rother's will into dust. "Do you understand the image you've presented? To be utterly bested in your own field. Why should I not punish you, failure that you are?"

"My lord, I *have* failed you. I bear the brunt of that shame. But I shall not fail you again, and I will redeem myself upon the heads of these intruders." Rother's words were submissive, but dignified. He didn't waiver under Tarkus's ire, he spoke quickly and with the attitude of a dog rolled on his back. "I shall find and expunge every Serpent who has slithered into our midst. I swear I will not fail you again, my lord. They shall not escape my fire."

Tarkus remained standing, breathing heavily. His stare burned through Rother. He turned to Nora. Silence. Dorin saw nothing, no gesture, no nod or shake of the head, not even a glint in the eye from the regal lady. But Tarkus understood every silent syllable.

He turned back to Rother. Tarkus sat and his throne creaked beneath his great weight. His voice was cold and smooth, harsh and blunt.

"In light of your failure, your humility is apt. You *have* failed…but shall have an opportunity to redeem yourself. Be vigilant, and bring me any and all news of further intruders."

Rother looked up, about to speak, but Tarkus held up a hand. He continued, "Should any Serpent agents harm our people, you will have failed. If scouts are found by another before you or your agents, you will have failed. Furthermore, you are to assign a regiment of your most trusted fellows to enter Serpent territory on Venus and send information of a possible invasion or attack from them. Should they meet the same fate as these Serpents in our hold, they shall be honored for their sacrifice and bravery in the name of the House of Wolves—and you will again have failed. Do *not* disappoint me."

"Yes, my lord." Rother stood. "My lady," he said with a salute and a bow. Nora gave a slight wave of her finger. Rother pivoted and walked down the cobblestone path. This whole time he had not looked at Dorin once.

Tarkus muttered faintly, almost too quietly for Dorin to hear, "We should have punished that *complete unit*, sent him on a trial…"

"Hush," responded Nora immediately. "This is not the place to say such things."

Tarkus grumbled and turned his attention to Dorin.

"Dorin, thank you for bringing us this information. Your dedication to the House of Wolves is noted again. You must be rewarded." Tarkus turned to the squire and tapped his finger on the throne twice. A flash of surprise filled the young Velka's eyes before he bowed and bounded through a door behind the thrones. He returned with two items: a knife and a pistol.

"You may take whichever you prefer," Tarkus said.

Dorin looked first at the knife. He unsheathed the blade and turned it in hand. Perfectly balanced of course, the hilt made of a black Velkan wood and holds for the fingers to rest were carved into the frame. The guard and pommel both shone silver. It was larger than most human blades, about twenty centimeters from the blade's tip to the end, with a few more centimeters for the hilt. It was really more of a dagger than a knife. A stream of blue light followed the edge of the blade. It signaled the constant stream of electrons that ran down its length. It would heat anything it cut to extreme temperatures, and the metal itself was sturdier than many starship hulls. Dorin looked at the black sheath. The tip of the sheath and edgings were both plated in silver. The house sigil was etched brilliantly in a glistening sapphire at the center. He looked inside the sheath and saw a red line running down in parallel to where the edge of the blade would sit. Protons ran down it to neutralize the electrons in the blade. A work of art.

Dorin sheathed the blade and gave it to the squire before picking up the gun.

It was a smooth gray, a long barrel extending from the bullet chamber. The grip was just like the knife's, Velkan wood, with the house sigil etched into the frame. Dorin considered for a moment what this could mean—either option would have him carry a piece of the clan with him. Wherever he went, he would be a wolf. A pack member, a citizen of Volthsheim.

Dorin's heart beat faster for a moment, but he soon felt self-conscious about how long he was taking and returned his attention to the gun.

Dorin studied it, tested the weight, and fiddled with the trigger. It was so light Dorin almost couldn't feel it, and the grip felt smooth even in his metal hand. He checked the chamber, finding a large battery with a single blue light emanating from the center. An Elo weapon, the signature weapon type of the Velkan scouts, which fires an immense stream of charged electrons at the target. This gun could certainly destroy an enemy's barriers from thirty meters away with a single shot. Elegant, simple. Dorin thought back to his own pistol, Soot, in disgust. *Finally,* he thought, relishing this new weapon.

He looked back to the knife again and thought of his own rusty blade. He paused.

Mm…there will be other guns.

Dorin gave the gun back and took the knife and bowed to the lord and lady. The squire gave him a slight bow and returned to his post.

"Thank you, my lord."

Tarkus gave a soft nod. "Now, I understand you were going to raid human settlements on the border, but I have a task for you should you be interested?"

"I'm always interested."

"These Serpents…I am concerned that they may be working with the humans to the south. I would like you to travel to Alexandria and see if there is any truth to this. You will be rewarded with any information you can find, confirming or dispelling my fear. Do you accept?"

This gave Dorin pause—he had not traveled home in so long. He held the knife tight in his left hand, running his fingers along the sigil.

"I do, my lord, if I may have but one request."

"What is it?"

"I would like Etkis to come with me. He would be invaluable support should there be a greater presence of Serpents in human territory, and he can verify any information I send. I believe his word will carry more weight than a foreigner's would among some…other individuals. Your offer moves me greatly, my lord, and I am humbled." The words caught in his throat for a moment. "But I am not ready to be a citizen of Volthsheim. I'm sorry."

Tarkus said nothing. A citizen would not have been doubted, even if they were human—but a freelancer? A foreigner? Dorin could feel Etkis staring into his back, and a lead weight lumped in Dorin's throat. Tarkus took in this rejection and looked to where Rother used to be. He turned to Nora. She spoke smoothly. "A foreign informant could irk some of our people. Etkis provides accountability."

Tarkus turned to Etkis. "Could your second in command maintain your post during a leave of absence?"

Etkis raised his head. "Without a doubt, my lord."

"Very well. You will accompany the freelancer. Return when you have either confirmed a Serpent threat or have concluded that there is none."

"Yes, my lord," said Etkis with a bow.

"You're both dismissed," said Tarkus. The edge of Tarkus's voice had softened, and Dorin clenched his jaw as he turned to leave.

The rabble of the Great Hall slowly returned as Etkis and Dorin descended from the hill. Etkis spoke without turning around.

"We can take my landship whenever you are ready to leave, *freelancer*."

"Etkis, I…"

"It's your decision. I'm sure you have your reasons. I'm sure they're good ones too."

Dorin's jaw and cheeks ached from the expression he could not relieve. He looked down at the cobblestone.

Etkis stopped walking, and Dorin halted. There was a brief but weighty pause. Etkis turned slightly.

"I was being rude. This isn't about me—I'm sorry. I just don't understand… you have a home here. I know some humans have certain…opinions about joining. Are you embarrassed by us? By…" Etkis did not finish. His fingers fiddled helplessly by his sides.

"No, no, it's not that at all." Dorin approached Etkis and put his hand on his friend's immense shoulder. They looked one another in the eye.

"Okay. I won't ask, then."

They looked down at the rest of the hall. The loud rabble of laughter and the clanking of drinks enveloped them. The light was warm by the hearths' firelight, the familiar smell of inthol and honey filled the air. Etkis broke the silence.

"Come on—we have a lot to do."

CHAPTER 2

"Where do the Velka come from? Scholars, both human and Velkan, still do not know. From all my studies and interactions with the invaders, they have no historical records of what forced them from their home system, what brought them here, or exactly how long their interstellar voyage took. The only thing they seem to know for certain is that they did not leave by choice."

—*A History of Our Invaders*, volume 3, by Cornelius Valum, chief historian of the Library of Alexandria

The day dragged once they left the Great Hall. Dorin and Etkis shopped mostly in silence as they prepared what they needed for the journey. Their last conversation's awkwardness weighed like a wet blanket upon them, and Dorin had no idea how to further console his friend. His poor social skills once again came to haunt him.

They stopped by the blacksmith to ensure all their guns and armor were prepared and fit for the journey. Dorin was once again disappointed not to find a replacement for Soot. He holstered it violently and grumbled choice words of contempt for the clunky weapon. The smiths refitted his new helmet so it no longer rattled on his head, and the holes for the Velka ears were covered with plating. Dorin sold his old, rusty knife and strapped the new one to his left boot, running parallel to his shin. Dorin ensured that the House of Wolves sigil on the blade was not hidden, which would be a sign of disrespect, but not so overt as to draw trouble. Etkis noticed the choice immediately.

Etkis managed to discover a brilliant-looking Elo rifle to add to his already large collection of firearms. It had a barrel so long that from the tip to the stock, it would be near unmanageable for someone who didn't have Etkis's long arms. Dorin tried to pick it up at one point, essentially deadlifting the gun, and actually managed to pick it off the ground before dropping it after a few seconds. Etkis patted Dorin on the back at his achievement before swinging the gun over his own massive shoulder with one arm. The patronization made Dorin fume even more.

It was equally important to procure foodstuff for the long journey. Etkis made sure to purchase a conversion kit—a device designed to convert solid food into a fluid that could pass through Etkis's filters. Dorin had seen it performed only twice, both times on an expedition with Etkis into the wilds. The first time it was only a conversion of fruits, some roots, and leaves. It seemed just like blending a particularly foul smoothie. The second time Etkis processed a deer—the sound of liquifying meat and bone imprinted itself into Dorin's mind. He remembered the ungodly smell as he watched Etkis pack the strange-looking device into his duffel bag. The memory alone made Dorin green in the face.

Etkis's first words since they had left the Great Hall broke Dorin's trance of revulsion. "I've never been to Alexandria—what's it like?"

Dorin cleared his throat. "Well, it's not walled like Volthsheim. The buildings are made of stone instead of wood. And...I don't know, there are more humans."

"Oh, you don't say," Etkis retorted with a roll of his eyes. The pair slowly made their way to the train that would take them to the western side of Volthsheim's wall, toward the garage. "I mean what's the atmosphere, what do people do, what do they eat?"

"What do you care what they eat? You can't have any of it."

Etkis threw up his hand in annoyance. "You are completely missing my point! Never mind, I'll see soon enough, I suppose."

Of all the expeditions the pair had made together over the years, Dorin's old home had never been one of them. Luna, Mars, Titan, even Eris in the Kuiper Belt had been subjected to their adventures—but Alexandria had never even been so much as a topic of conversation. Etkis had never asked before, but Dorin felt sure that his friend sensed that it was a touchy subject. Etkis could read Dorin flawlessly, a stark contrast to his abilities to read the intentions of members of the opposite sex.

Dorin searched for anything to continue the conversation—the return of silence had flooded him with guilt.

"It used to be a desert."

Etkis's ears perked in surprise. "What?"

"Well, it used to be *in* a desert, I suppose. A long time ago, of course, but still."

"There used to be deserts on Earth? What, like Mars?"

"Mm, a lot warmer than Mars but just as dusty, I believe. I'm no historian, but I remember that much from my school days."

"That's incredible! It's hard to imagine anything other than snow here."

Etkis looked up at the sky. Light frost fell from the cloudless blue. The wind lapped at Dorin's coat, heralding a blizzard. It would snow and hail later, but Dorin didn't much care. Right now it was beautiful as the sun shone brightly into the twinkling snow. The air was warmer now than it had been in days, and Dorin could see Etkis smile with his eyes.

Etkis was much more jovial after that, imagination and excitement returned to him and inspired many questions about Earth's long history. Dorin felt a warm tickle in his chest that he cold could not conquer.

The garage stood as a foil to the rest of Volthsheim. The interior was all metal, and sparks flew from vehicles that the engineers worked on. It rose high above their heads, nearly rivaling the breadth of the Great Hall. Many different rafters and walkways crisscrossed overhead. Vehicles hung from great machines as they were being handled. Etkis led the way to a moderately sized landship—vents lined the entire underside of the hull, which suspended the hovercraft half a meter off the ground. The two long gun barrels that ran its length, while not immensely powerful, provided enough fire to be defensible. It had many sleek, curved lines that culminated in a long tail in the back. Just beneath the tail was a massive engine, and the engine's large power consumption more than justified the weaker cannons with its great speed.

Dorin entered the domed interior and felt like he was in a small guest room. There were windows, a large one in the front, which dropped into a cockpit, long ones running the length of the room, and a smaller one in the rear. In the room were two pairs of beds stacked one on top of the other. One had clearly been modified, as it was about two and a half times larger than all the others and was supported by immense steel girders. Dorin snickered as he tossed his pack of necessities on his own bunk. Guns hung all along the wall of Etkis's side of the room, his new Elo rifle had been placed aesthetically just behind the cockpit. Current rifles, snipers, shotguns, even a gravity cannon were counted among the armory, and Dorin could not help but feel thoroughly impressed and saddened by it. *Good God, he needs a hobby*, Dorin thought as he shook his head. He left the room to find Etkis fiddling with the cannons at the front of the landship. He spoke without moving his eyes from what he was doing.

"She's meant for a squad of four to quickly counter raids in the territory, so she'll cover the distance just fine. Got everything you need?"

"I think so," Dorin said. "How fast does she move?"

"We'll reach Alexandria in about a week's time, provided we don't make too many stops."

A new, colder voice startled Dorin. "Going to Alexandria?"

He turned around quickly, his hand hovered above Soot. Rother stood before them. His empty gray eyes conveyed nothing, and his half ear twitched subtly, a large box beneath his arm. He was around Dorin's size, much more typical in build than the titan that was Etkis. His sleek armor had distinct wear from constant battle and maintenance. The full moon that symbolized his rank shone brightly at the center of his chest. There was pride in his armor's worn-out cleanliness. Rother's gaze bored into Dorin, and Dorin stared back at him, trying to mask his discomfort. He was not as masterful over his body as Rother.

"Rother, always a pleasure. Tarkus just asked us to take a look around the city to see if there was anything *else* you had missed." Dorin snarked.

"Mm…the jarl is making bolder choices to be sending you, Dorin. He might send a legless gimp next time, judging by the fall in standards."

Dorin clenched his fists and jaw. He noticed the involuntary movement almost as quickly as Rother did. The Velka didn't move a muscle, and yet the air of satisfaction about him was palpable. He dropped the charade of ignorance.

"You're on an information-gathering mission from the jarl into foreign territory, which means you will be reporting to me. Will that be a problem?"

"Not at all." Etkis spoke immediately, before Dorin could frame a cutting reply.

"Good. Once you reach the city, you must contact our agent. She's our top spy in Alexandria. A Velka named Kya Wallace," Rother handed Etkis Kya's picture on an electronic pad. Etkis turned his head, confused. *Odd surname for a Velka*, he thought.

She was taller than Dorin, but far closer to Rother's size than Etkis's, and her helm had carved lines extending from her eyes, which made swirling floral patterns as they traveled. Her eyes were unlike any Etkis had ever seen, jet-black with brilliant white frames. Rother continued, "Only refer to her as Kya. She's our contact in Alexandria. Officially she's one of Volthsheim's exchequers, seeking out prudent investment opportunities in Alexandria. She should have a list of metal workers for you two to visit in order to maintain your cover."

"So your highly trained covert agent is…a banker?" Dorin asked, careful that his tone was more mocking than inquisitive.

Rother brushed him off. "Of a sort. Kya's never reported any Serpent activity there, but out of anyone in that city, she would have a lead. Now, we do not need the Alexandrians to know that there are multiple military agents from a foreign power investigating their city. Alibis—Etkis, you are a merchant, exploring the city to find a supplier of metals for Volthsheim and nothing beyond that." Rother handed him the box he had been carrying. "Civilian garb. Don't wear armor in Alexandria if you can help it. Dorin, you're a freelancer hired to guide him through the city. It's a common enough arrangement that you won't draw any suspicion. Be as discreet as possible, humans are dangerous in a panic. Incompetence will have dire consequences." Rother made a point to look at Dorin. "Is that understood?"

"Crystal." Dorin met Rother's eye contact. Etkis chimed in.

"If we're merchants, should we leave behind most of our weapons? I travel rather heavily armed…"

Dorin answered before Rother could, "Alexandria isn't a safe city. Everyone carries weapons of some kind or another, especially travelers going in and out of the place. A few more won't draw attention." Rother didn't say anything. Dorin felt sure that the First Scout was trying to find something to correct but had failed.

Rother directed his attention to Etkis. His gaze and voice softened ever so slightly. "They are not used to seeing many Velka there. You must be careful. They are a cruder people than you are used to—even considering present company." Dorin's jaw clenched again, his knuckles white in anger.

"I'll be careful," said Etkis with a grateful nod.

"Good. Send me a report once you've entered the city and each week thereafter. I'll leave you to it." Rother cast a look at Dorin, who returned it with equal animosity.

"Etkis."

"Rother." The First Scout left. Dorin stared angrily at nothing. Etkis broke the silence.

"You need to stop antagonizing him."

Dorin spun around, nostrils flared. "*Me?* How am I the problem here?"

"You already embarrassed him by finding those scouts, you didn't need to rub it in." Etkis returned to his work on the landship's guns.

"Of course I did," Dorin said, smug. "What's the point in succeeding if I can't rub the failure's nose in it?"

"He's supervising us on this mission, which means he'll send regular reports to the jarl. What he says may not matter to a *freelancer* like you, but it matters to me. Please try and show him some respect."

Shame returned to Dorin in a flash and his face turned red. He grumbled bitterly in concession as he carried Etkis's bag that lay at his feet, walked back into the landship, and waited for Etkis to finish fiddling with the guns. Dorin went through a hatch in the floor that led to a storage room that ran the length of the ship. At the end of it was a small shower, sectioned off from the rest of the compartment by a plastic door. Velkan suits cleaned their bodies for them. *This* was installed for human use. Dorin smiled.

He stored all of their food and essential supplies in the compartment and put his dried meats and canned fruits into a large footlocker. Dorin lined Etkis's cylinders of liquified food on the wall and gave a little shudder at the thought of what they might have once been. He put the conversion kit on the far side of the shelves, wanting to see and touch it as little as possible. He climbed out of the compartment, took his helmet off, and lay flat on his bed. He stared at the empty bedspring above him.

He would be seeing Alexandria for the first time in…he wasn't sure how long. Certainly years, but he had never bothered to track the time. The place had faded from his memory, and his thoughts journeyed through the few images he still had in his head. They felt odd, like a picture photocopied over and over again. He couldn't remember the colors of the buildings, nor what the school looked like. He couldn't remember his teacher's faces; the faces of his peers were like empty mannequins in his mind. He couldn't remember what the food had tasted like at the vendors or even at the home he had grown up in. That last thought triggered a flash of images as clear as the room that he resided in now—a knot formed in his stomach at the thought of the soft covers of his old bed, at the endless noise of chatter that filled the streets night and day entering from his bedroom window, at the smell and taste of the smoke swirling within his home…at a young Ash screaming for help from outside the burning hovel.

The door opened, and Dorin snapped back to reality. Etkis entered—a cold sweat had formed along Dorin's forehead. He draped his arm over his face to ensure that his friend would not see.

The Velka had to stoop to not collide with the ceiling. Etkis entered the cockpit and flipped the ignition. Outside there was a loud roar, the ship lifted off the ground, and Etkis pushed a button to close the sliding door that led to the garage. The engine was now only a murmur, rumbling through the ship with gentle vibrations.

A speaker over by the cockpit clicked on. "Landship T-139 cleared for exit."

Large doors opened just in front of the landship. A blast of cold air chilled the metal inside. Etkis moved the throttle, and there was a soft lurch as he and Dorin entered the now howling winds.

CHAPTER 3

*Beneath the sight of Okar, the god's companion Treya, and their children
Callva and Kior, I hereby pledge my body, my mind, and my spirit to
the House of Wolves. Though my bones may break, my mind may erode,
and my spirit may sink tethered to stone, my house shall never falter.*

—The Pledge, to be taken after the Velkan pilgrimage

Dorin's feet were up on the dashboard, and he spun the new knife in his human hand to familiarize himself with the weight. "What's her name?"

Etkis groaned, his head in one hand, with the other on the wheel. "Okar help me. It's a ship—it doesn't have a name."

"It has to have a name."

"But why! Is this a human thing?"

"No…yes? Maybe? Doesn't matter. We're giving it a name. We have to christen its maiden voyage!"

Etkis raised his head, ears perked in curiosity. "What is a 'christen'?"

"It's…a thing you do…when you…look, we're giving it a name! I vote for Lily."

"No."

"Jasmine."

"No."

"Rose."

"N…yeah, all right."

Pleased with his triumph, Dorin returned his attention to the picture of Kya. It took him a while to distinguish between Velka who were not as visually distinct as Etkis, so he studied the helmet design intently. Etkis could recognize other Velka after having looked at their picture once—such was the benefit of a lifetime of seeing your brethren behind masks—but Dorin needed more time than that.

The weather had slowed them considerably, and it was hard to tell how much longer the storm would carry on. Etkis was at the helm with a cylinder of food resting in the cupholder to his right. Finally satisfied that he could spot Kya in a crowded bar of Velka, Dorin sheathed his knife, got up, and placed the picture into Etkis's pack beneath his bed. Dorin sat back in the passenger side of the cockpit and enjoyed the sound of the wind and snow smacking against Rose's hull. The sound of nature, even in a fury, relaxed him immensely. The only thing that disturbed the tranquility was the sight of Etkis taking a drink of his liquid meal. Every time, Dorin compulsively turned away to gag.

"What do those taste like?" Dorin asked.

"Do you want to try it?" Etkis offered Dorin the glass.

"*NO!* Please, God, don't ever ask again. Just describe it. I'm curious."

"Um, I don't really know what to equate it to…"

"Is it salty?"

"What's salty?"

"Oh right…hmm…hold on, I have a plan."

Dorin went down into the storage compartment, took a few of his own food items and the conversion kit out, and returned to the cockpit.

"Dorin, don't *you* need those…to eat? I don't know how much longer this blizzard is going to last."

"It's only a few things. Besides, this is for science!"

Dorin took out a can of peaches and dropped them into the conversion kit. There was a loud whirring of gears and escaping gases, then a cylinder was released with a small amount of yellow fluid inside.

"Okay, I don't know how much the kit messes with flavor, but this is closest to what humans call 'sweet and tangy.'"

"You want me to drink this? It's only the essence of one thing."

"So?"

"It's wasteful! Do you *know* how much these cylinders cost? I need these to be a full meal with lots of nutrients. This is just irresponsible."

"Please just drink the damn thing. I'll pay you back!"

Etkis shot Dorin a look, and they both silently acknowledged Dorin's already immense debt. He took the peach juice and inserted it into his mask's filter and began to cough violently.

"*Wow*, that's strong."

"What do you think?"

"I mean, it's fine. Not exactly a round of inthol, though."

"Hmm, okay, well, this is some jerky. It's dried meat…"

Etkis tilted his head, surprised. "Just meat?"

"Yeah, humans don't eat the bone, skin, and fur of an animal like you do. We are a far cleaner people."

"I would never, ever describe you as clean."

"No idea what you mean."

Dorin plugged his nose as he inserted the meat into the kit, and an ungodly sound filled the room. Etkis did not even seem to notice the violent shredding and vacuum sounds emanating from the kit as Dorin wished for a few brief seconds that he was dead. It wasn't just like a blender; something *unnatural* had occurred in the processing, and he was sure that some eldritch magic had turned the meat into a liquid horribly more than the sum of its parts. Steeling himself for the glory of science, Dorin handed the new cylinder to Etkis.

"Now this I like! What flavor would you call this?"

"Gamy and salty. Of course this is what you like. Now this"—Dorin made great effort to keep himself from laughing—"is a very well-known human delicacy."

Dorin repeated the process and handed Etkis a green cylinder. The alien shook the entire ship as he flailed about gagging and Dorin burst into laughter.

"BLAH, OKAR KILL ME—*what is that*?"

"Cooked, canned spinach," Dorin said through gasps in his laughter.

"Ah, it tastes like a war crime! What even *is* that flavor?"

"I don't really know…bad?"

"You said it was a delicacy!"

"I know!"

"But—"

"I lied."

"I hate you so much," Etkis said and took a long gulp of his meal, which had laid untouched since the beginning of the experiment. Etkis pretended to pout, but Dorin saw the subtlest of smiles within his friend's eyes. They drove in silence for a few moments, until Dorin looked at Etkis expectantly.

"Soooo…what does *that* one taste like?"

"It doesn't really taste like any of the stuff you gave me—more like the meat than…what's wrong?"

Dorin was staring past Etkis and faintly saw an orange glow through the swirling white snow. It wasn't a bonfire, some poor travelers making camp. The glow rested too high in the air.

"Fire. I think a ranch is burning that way."

Etkis turned to look at the glow and without speaking reduced Rose's throttle and turned in the direction of the suspended lights.

"Are we near a town?" Etkis asked.

"Probably a few kilometers from Lipel. The blizzard covered any landmarks, so I can only guess."

It grew larger and larger until the silhouette of a two-story house came into focus. Etkis turned off the ignition, and both he and Dorin got out of the cockpit. Dorin opened the door, and a blast of snow and wind flooded the room. He put on his helmet and withdrew Soot from its holster. Etkis followed Dorin outside and they took cover beside a nearby tree. Dorin looked deep into the night and saw four figures standing before the house, the shape of their weapons barely visible at their sides. There was a fifth figure lying on the snow, and a sixth kneeling beside it. Dorin passed his eyes lengthwise along the scene and spotted a dark blob against a tree to the right of the house. It moved in an unnatural way. *Two people*, Dorin thought. He returned his attention to the house. Two people emerged from the front door carrying something large and heavy. The glow of the flaming building framed the figures in an evil light.

Four in front, one to the right, two coming out, so seven hostiles. House had a minimum of three individuals, one dead or unconscious, one in the center, and one to the right…need to help that one before we attend to the rest.

"I know this property," Etkis said. "These are Wolf merchants—ranchers for Volthsheim. I had to memorize all their locations when I became first guard…we should immobilize the raiders first. It's the best way to ensure the ranchers' safety."

"Agreed. Gravity cannon."

Etkis hustled back inside Rose and removed the gravity cannon from its perch on the wall, exited, and closed the door. His weapon ran the length of his massive legs.

"Take the right lane. Once it's secure, come behind and fire. I'll keep them busy," Dorin said. Etkis nodded and then retreated into the storm. He swiftly disappeared, his white armor and maroon cloak swallowed by the vicious gale. Dorin holstered Soot and walked toward the burning house.

Etkis walked slowly, hunched over, and kept sight of the house on his left. Without the reference he would lose himself in the storm, but he would also never be able to sneak up on someone without it. His size usually gave him away, but this evening was perfectly suited for what he needed to do.

He got closer and closer to the two figures Dorin had pointed to, and he began to hear a man speaking gruffly and a second, higher voice whimpering over the sound of the storm. He could not make out the words they said, but as Etkis maneuvered to the back of the man, he saw him holding a long blade with blood dripping down the length of it. He was a little larger than Dorin, most of his body still covered with large fabrics to protect from the cold. A small child lay at the foot of the tree. *A boy?* Etkis thought—it was always hard for him to tell the difference between a boy and girl when humans were young. He stalked closer and heard them speaking.

"Getting real sick of asking, kid. You wouldn't want me to ask your sister, now would you? Where did he hide the chest? You must have seen—"

Etkis grabbed the man by the throat with one hand and squeezed hard. He felt many tiny vibrations flow up his arm and into his chest, and the man dropped his blade from pain and shock as he desperately tried to breathe or scream, to no avail. Etkis pulled the man away from the tree and smothered him in the snow. Etkis finally saw his face illuminated by the glow of the firelight. He was young, younger than Dorin and Etkis both, but a long scar ran along his face. He was disfigured, not at all pleasant to look at, and Etkis imagined that humans certainly thought so as well. He looked intently at the scar. There were what looked like old burn marks on the edges of it. *A Velkan blade…*a crinkle of shame slipped into the giant's heart.

He must have lived in a raided village. The others probably did as well. Is that what drove them to this?

Blood oozed from the young man's mouth, and his hands were wrapped around Etkis's single immense one, which covered the entire width of his neck and then some. There was absolute terror in his eyes, as if a nightmare had slipped out of his dreams and was in the dark above him. The fear on his face was far greater than the fear of death—he was seeing his ultimate horror, the thing he dreaded above all else. Etkis read deep into his face—humans were so much easier to read than Velka. He saw the terror of trauma in his wrinkled brow, the years of struggle in his yellow teeth, the pleas for mercy in his watering eyes.

The child's whimper yanked Etkis out of his contemplative stupor, and he clenched his fist. Whatever this man once was, he was a savage now, a rabid animal that needed to be put down. Etkis searched his mind for a human prayer but found none.

"Go with Okar, and journey through the stars eternal," Etkis prayed. The man's eyes somehow widened even larger as his great nightmare spoke to him in a black night lit only by flame. Etkis's words of comfort were twisted into something foul. He read the man's face with regret just before he smashed in the raider's skull with a single punch of his free hand.

Etkis cleaned the blood off his hand in the snow and turned to face the child. He was trembling furiously, only a single layer of clothing to protect him from the cold. Barefooted, the weeping pup stared at Etkis and clutched his hand in agony. Blood flowed heavily from where the fingernails used to be, looking black in the brilliant glow of fire. The drops of blood froze into black splotches of paint the moment they touched snow.

They came while they were sleeping.

He approached the child slowly, tiptoeing each step and staying low to the ground. The child stared at Etkis—teeth clenched hard, bottom lip and chin trembling even more than the rest of his body. His gray eyes reflected the mass of steel before him perfectly with the backdrop flame. Etkis gazed into the reflection. His heart sank at how frightening he must have seemed.

"Hello? Can you hear me?" Etkis tried desperately to sound as soft as he could, the memory of Lady Nora's voice in his mind.

No response.

"My name is Etkis, I'm here with my friend—we're going to help you." He reached out slightly, and the child recoiled in a mixture of adrenal fear and revulsion. Etkis pulled away, confused, and saw there was still blood on his armored hand. He retracted immediately, contemplating what to do. He turned back to the man's body and removed his shoes and large coat, simultaneously scraping the already frozen blood off his white armor. He turned back to the child.

"Please put these on, you need to keep warm." He got a little closer than before, still staying low and inching his way closer to the frightened boy. The child looked at the clothes and back at his savior. Fire raged behind him, and although he crouched low to the ground, the light still carved his immense frame. His eyes glowed blue through his helmet, and the boy gazed into them. They were entirely unfamiliar, new, *alien*…and filled with nothing but kindness. He reached out and snatched the garments from the Velka's hands. He put them on and shakily stood. Etkis remained crouching low such that he was only a little taller than the boy.

"It's all right, please don't exert yourself. Is there anyone else in the house? Or only the two in the front?"

The events of that night flooded back to the child in a single second, and he opened his mouth to speak, but no sound came out. The trembling began to cease, but panic enveloped his eyes as his gasp widened to let out a silent scream. Etkis reached out and cradled the young pup in his arms.

"Shh, shh, it's all right, it's all right. I promise you'll leave here safely, and I know it's hard, but I need you to focus." Etkis looked into the child's eyes. "Please. Is there anyone else in the house that we need to save?"

The child closed his eyes and shook his head. Etkis looked at the boy, shivering now from far more than the cold, and removed his own massive cloak. He draped it around the pup, covering his entire body head to toe.

"I understand. Please wait here. I won't be long."

He stood to his full height and swung his cannon into his hands, a titan etched in orange firelight, brilliant blue eyes glowing in the frozen night. The child watched as the colossus crossed to the edge of the forest and vanished. He closed his eyes and wrapped the warm fur cloak over his face as tears streamed down his cheeks.

Dorin crossed swiftly to the men and soon their bodies came into focus. A young girl was weeping over a man who lay with his back to the ground, eyes closed and blood staining his thin shirt and the nearby snow in a deep scarlet. His chest still rose and fell. *Alive*, Dorin thought.

The two men who exited the house held a trunk between them, which they set down, tore open, and rummaged through. They clearly did not find what they were looking for as one of the two screamed and kicked the snow.

"*Where is it?* We know it's here, girl. Now you're going to answer me, or your brother is going to get the same as your—who the hell are you!" The angry man had noticed Dorin strolling up to them. The other raiders whipped around and traced their guns to his chest.

"Whoa, whoa, easy there. Sorry, didn't mean to spook you all! But I saw the fire and came over to see what all the fuss was about. Couldn't help overhearing that you were looking for something? Maybe I can offer my assistance?"

One of the raiders to the left, a middle-aged woman with a scar on her chin, looked surprised and was about to speak when she was cut off by the angry man.

"We're good, thanks. You can be on your way."

Dorin was close enough now to see that this wasn't a man but rather a very burly, very gruff woman. He cast his eyes on every one of them and analyzed what he could.

A man with silver hair stood beside the middle-aged woman. They had similar features; their brows crinkled in the exact same concerned expression. Noses different, his crooked and hers sloped, but their eyes were the same shape. Certainly related.

There was a scrawny boy to the left of the burly woman. He was missing two teeth, and he had a particularly vacant expression as his eyes darted back and forth from Dorin to the burly woman. The woman herself stood stock-still, weapon at the ready as it followed Dorin's every move. She was missing her left ear, so she angled her head to the right to better hear Dorin. Clearly the leader. *The boy's the newest member of their posse?*

The last two raiders stood above the ranchers. The first shook violently. His sleeve was stained with frozen blood. A faint stubble dotted his face, but apart from that, he had no marks on his face. He looked soft. He hadn't been here long. This raider had grown up far more sheltered than the rest. A key difference were that his teeth were still a shade of white even in the orange glow from the burning building. *Alexandrian.* His eyes could only look at Dorin once every few seconds—most of the time he was transfixed by the bleeding man and his weeping daughter. Dorin changed his mind—*this* was the newest member of the posse.

A masked figure stood to his right. The mask immediately made Dorin tense, and their weapon was casually aimed at the freelancer's throat. He did not tremble, not even from the cold. Dorin couldn't tell if it was a man or a woman— their clothing was too bulky for Dorin to decide gender without being able to see their face. On their left sleeve he saw a small star illuminated by the firelight. No one else had the mark. *The handler, definitely the most dangerous. Need to throw him first...*Dorin thought. The closest town was Lipel. Jarrod's domain. He put the pieces of the puzzle together in his mind.

"Ah, well, I'll be on my way then. I'll let Jarrod know you've got this handled."

"Wait, Jarrod?" The leader asked rapidly. The handler's head turned ever so slightly up. *That got his attention.*

"Yes," Dorin replied, shifting his eyes smoothly from handler to the leader and back again. "He's been getting a little impatient, so he wanted me to check on you." Though Dorin's voice carried to the whole posse, he turned his head more to the handler, who stiffened. All of their weapons lowered. *There we go.*

"But if you say you have this covered, you have it covered. We look forward to seeing you in…say, an hour? Lipel's not far, even with the blizzard, so that's enough time, I think. Oh, before I forget—" Dorin looked at the newest member, who tore his eyes away from the bleeding man and his daughter, both of whom still lay motionless in the center. "Jarrod wanted me to let you know, your family in Alexandria send their regards."

It was a gamble. Maybe he hated his family, maybe he was estranged, maybe he didn't have a family at all. But Dorin took his chances. The young man's face drained of what little color remained. He turned to his leader.

"Ika, he can help us! We need the—"

"Shut your mouth, Pyter!"

Dorin maneuvered to the left of the group such that he was facing the right edge of the forest but all of their backs were to it. It wouldn't be long now.

"Look, Ika," Dorin said casually, "I'm not looking to take much of the reward. Maybe five percent would do? I think that's quite generous."

She looked flustered and turned to her handler. The masked figure remained silent, focus broken, eyes fixed on the snow before them.

"Well, I suppose…"

"Perfect. What do you know so far?"

"Well, the money is supposed to be in a chest, but we've looked everywhere and haven't found—"

The masked figure spoke with a deep and hoarse voice. "What sector did you say you were from?" He looked at Dorin. His composure had returned. *Uh oh…*

"The Northern sector, closest to Volthsheim. I'm sure you've noticed where my helmet—"

"Really? Me too. I don't think we've ever met. What was your name again?"

"D-Donald…" *What is the matter with me?*

"…Donald?"

"Yeah…is there a problem?" *Of course there is! Donald is a stupid name! *Who is named Donald*?*

"Well, that all depends, *Donald*…if Jarrod sent you, then I'm sure he told you who was involved."

"Not really. He doesn't much care about a bunch of freelancers." Dorin gestured to the rest of the posse, who looked both vaguely insulted and relieved.

"No, no, Donald." There was venom on his tongue. "What's *my* name?"

…Great.

The posse all raised their weapons at once. Two blue lights shone tall in the black behind them.

A boom—like a starship taking off compressed into a single second. An oscillating tone filled their ears, a ringing pitch that always seemed to rise with no end. Deep pressure pushed through the air into the eardrums, through the brain, and down the skeleton. The world became heavy, the snow compacted. Everyone crashed to their knees as the air crushed them into submission. The raiders all tried to move. They screamed and panicked in their confusion as to what was happening. The daughter lay flat over her wounded father—neither tried to get up. The handler did everything in his power to raise his gun, desperate to kill the man who was responsible, but his strength failed him entirely. Flesh and bone couldn't move in this kind of gravity. But oil and steel?

Dorin drew Soot. The barrel moved slowly but surely and found its target. The leader. His metal arm creaked under strain, and her head vanished. The gore sank straight down to the earth and packed with the snow. Her body crumpled. Then the vacant boy. Then the old man and his sister. They all got the same. Dorin shot the Alexandrian boy straight in his shoulder. He screamed bloody murder as his right arm hit the ground before he did, his wound cauterized.

Dorin shot the handler's gun. The steel barrel split like wood hewn by an axe, and Soot's molten slug caked the upper mass of the weapon. Completely useless. Dorin fired once more into the air.

The tone from the gravity cannon ceased. The invisible hand that had pushed everything down had relinquished its grip. Dorin kept Soot pointed at the handler with his metal hand, his aim focused and immoveable. The handler looked wildly, confused, but soon fixed his eyes on the massive black and red pistol. Dorin rolled out his body, flexing his stiff muscles and moving to get the feeling back. He waved at the blue eyes at the edge of the forest, and Etkis vanished again. Dorin walked to the handler—Soot still smoked threateningly. The blizzard raged and the red-hot barrel vaporized every snow flake into superheated steam.

"What were you here for?" Dorin asked.

The handler's voice was no longer deep and hoarse but thin and reedy, "They…they owed money. Jarrod wanted it, just like you said! Please, I'm sorry, just let me go, and you'll never hear from me again—"

"Shut up." Dorin stayed transfixed on the masked man. Made sense—the freelancers certainly thought so, but how could he be sure? He raised his voice. "Etkis, hurry over! Kid, are you all right?"

The daughter spoke, and her father grunted weakly, "Y-yes, but my dad…"

"I know—just hang on. We'll help him soon."

Slowly, through the sound of the wind, Dorin heard crunching snow. Etkis thundered closer, entirely visible. His gravity cannon was sloped over his shoulder and he cradled something in his cloak. The daughter gave an audible gasp. The handler turned slightly to see the encroaching Velka and seized in terror, his body contracted in shock and fear. His odds grew ever more hopeless.

"It's okay, he's with me," Dorin said to the shaking girl. "You all right, Etkis?"

"Yes, but I'm worried about the little one. I think he was frostbitten when I found him, we need to get him warm."

The young girl began to hyperventilate. "Do you mean Nook? Is he okay? *Nook, is that you?*"

A weak, timid voice sounded back, "Lola? It's me…"

Etkis approached the girl, who was now far more worried about her little brother than afraid of the huge Velka. Nook could've been a baby by the way he was wrapped in Etkis's cloak and cradled in his immense arms. He dropped Nook next to his sister, and she held him tight, a moment of respite suspended in time. She snapped back to her unconscious father. *"Please, can you help him?"*

Etkis looked at the man's wounds and examined the cut across the belly. He looked at Dorin, pleading for a solution.

"We need to get him into town, to a doctor," Dorin said. "That's the best we can hope for. Etkis, come here. I need your help." Dorin turned back to the raider. "Take off your mask," he commanded. The shivering man complied.

He was gray haired, with black eyes and a pointed nose. Mucus ran down his nose, and tears trailed his cheeks. Dorin thought him a sniveling rat. "Why are you here?" Dorin asked again. Etkis stared at the man, studied every feature, every detail of his face and body.

"I told you, they missed a payment, and the boss wanted his due, that's all! Please—"

"He's lying."

Etkis's response was crisp and immediate. He turned back to the children. The handler looked as though he had been shot, sickly pale as his head jerked stiffly from Etkis to Dorin.

"Well, that clears up things a bit. Thank you."

"W…no! No, I'm telling you the truth! That's all—"

"Etkis, take them back to Rose, and that boy there too." Dorin motioned his head over to Pyter, the one-armed raider lying in the snow. His wound had been seared shut by the heat from Soot's slug. "I think that poor kid just made a bad decision—he's paid for it. Whether he pays any more depends on if the old man makes it."

The handler was practically quaking now, desperate to lengthen his shortening life span, *"Please, you have to believe me!"*

"All right, Dorin, but don't be too long. We have to leave in the next few minutes, otherwise neither of them will make it. Get the information you need, and let's go."

"Heard."

"Come now, little ones…" Etkis helped Nook and Lola to their feet and picked up both their father and Pyter. They all marched toward the woods where Rose hid. Soot had cooled in the blizzard and now only the tip radiated orange. Dorin shifted the gun into his human hand and walked closer to the handler.

"Now—why do you want to lie to me?" Dorin asked.

"I…I wasn't!"

"I'm sure you're a good liar to humans. I almost believed you myself. But you're not fooling my friend, Velka are very good at reading people. Now, what did Jarrod send you here for?"

"I...I..."

Dorin reached over to the rat's side with his metal arm and found a rib with his thumb. He barely had to press at all to hear it snap like a twig.

"Ah, stop! Please stop! Stop! I'm sorry! Please...he'll kill me."

Dorin jabbed Soot's barrel in the man's eye, "And I won't?" he asked. Dorin could smell the rat's seared skin and burning eyelashes.

"But—"

"Either you die here and now, forgotten in a blizzard, or you try to get as far away from Jarrod as possible. Live a few hours. Your call."

The handler ran through his options, and knew he was trapped. He sagged his head, "Jarrod wanted their trading permits!"

"Why?"

"Something about entering Volthsheim quietly! That's all I know, I swear!"

Dorin looked into the rat's beady eyes. He fingered the trigger as the man began to weep.

Dorin lowered his weapon. "Good, thank you. You can go." Dorin stood up and grabbed a gun that one of the raiders had used and examined it.

"Really?"

"Really. Go." Dorin didn't look at him as he fiddled with the firearm. He studied it intently.

The handler didn't move for a few moments, frozen still in disbelief. He recomposed himself and stumbled away from Dorin. He ran in the opposite direction of Rose. Tears of joy streamed down his face. He had made it—it didn't seem possible. He couldn't help himself and smiled like a child as bright euphoria filled him.

CRACK.

The bolt passed through his leg and shattered his femur. He let out a yell and rocketed to the snow. He couldn't move; his body denied him—but he would not be denied. The man forced his torso up and crawled with his forearms and carved through the thick snow. He left a trail of frozen black behind him and he coughed violently as the orange glow of the fire he had started bathed him in a distant warmth. He felt only pain and the joyful tears turned sour from agony. His broken rib pierced a lung. He crawled, and he began to gasp for air. He wheezed, still crawling. Blood filled a dry mouth. Crawling. He reached out his hand and silently begged for someone to help, someone to find him, *anyone.*

And then he died.

Dorin stood still with Soot pointed at the murdered man and the raider's gun pointed down in his human hand. Finally, he holstered the smoking gun, not blinking once at the corpse in the snow. He looked back to the raider's weapon. The symbol of the House of Serpents was branded just above the grip.

Etkis is just gonna love this…

Dorin turned his back on the carnage as the house collapsed into burning tinder.

CHAPTER 4

*You couldn't get me out of this city if you paid me. I mean, what else is out
there? Onyx wolves, mammoths, Velka, starvation, plague, raiders, and
who knows what else. People can whine about the Velka all they want,
but a bullet's a bullet, no matter who fires it. Kills you all the same.*

—The Alexandrian Post, Interview with Deputy Daniel Cheung, 3.12.1100

Lipel had a single hospital with a single room, with a single doctor, that stood
beside the largest of the town's thirteen taverns. Etkis sat on the porch beside Rose. He couldn't fit through the door without tearing a Velka-shaped hole
in the edging. Dorin brought Lola outside as the doctor cursed after he pricked
his hand with the needle, again.

"What's your name, kid?" Dorin asked. Lola was despondent. Etkis gave
Dorin a smack in the arm.

"I'm very sorry for what has happened, and we will keep you safe," Etkis said.
"You're Volthsheim merchants, which means that the city can help you even more
than we can. But I need your family name to let them know what's happened."

"Roarer. My name is Lola Roarer."

"Thank you. I'll let the city know what's happened. Be with your family now."

Lola nodded to Etkis and went back inside. Etkis sighed, exhausted.

"Volthsheim merchants raided by a Serpent-backed mobster. What a
nightmare."

Dorin leaned against the wood beam of the terrace. "If anything, it's convenient. We were already going to Alexandria to look into the Serpent's activity. This is just another reason to look into it."

"Nothing about this is convenient," Etkis snapped. He went into Rose to relay the message back to Volthsheim. The doctor came out onto the porch, his false tooth shining in the sunlight.

"The boy's missin' three fingernails on his right and, 's got some frostbite on 's feet. The pappy's in bad shape. Gots a knife wound in his belly."

"You don't say," Dorin said, the words dry on his tongue.

"Mhmm, sure does," the doctor replied, proud of his deduction. "And that otha' boy's just missin' his whole arm. Clean shot that was. Didn't have to do much with him."

Dorin grunted.

"Now I've gotta go get some antibiotics for dem folks."

"You already got some."

"Huh?"

Dorin pointed inside to the open cabinet filled with drugs.

"Oh, ugh, those don' work for what we need. Need some more antibiotics, for the pain, ya understand."

"Then don't we need painkillers?" Dorin said, flat.

"Y-yes, that's what I meant. Painkillers. Strong ones. Real strong ones."

"Mm."

"Yes."

"Mhmm."

"Only one place to get those."

"Yup." Dorin didn't take his eyes off the doctor. The pungent smell of alcohol fell from the old man's mouth. Without another word the doctor walked off into the tavern next door.

Dorin glanced inside the hospital.

Lola cradled Nook in the corner, his hand heavily bandaged, both wrapped in Etkis's cloak. The maroon and brown fur cuddled their faces as the wolf sigil etched in the back embraced them. Mr. Roarer lay on the only mattress in the room with crooked stitches along his gut.

The one-armed boy had only just been seen to—his crimes put him lowest on the order of patients. Soot had seared the wound shut, and the brevity of his exposure to the elements kept any sickness from creeping into the black flesh. He was unconscious, of course, as was Mr. Roarer. The doctor's office only had one gurney, so the raider lay on a makeshift bed of chairs in the back of the room. The room was silent. The children lay in shallow sleep, exhausted from the day's events and too frightened to rest well.

Etkis walked out of Rose and to the porch. Dorin spoke without turning his head.

"What if we went after Jarrod? We're in Lipel already, and he's been in contact with the Serpents. We should find out why."

"I'd rather not go looking for a fight. Rother will investigate quietly. Trust me, he's good at this."

"Fine."

"Where's the doctor?" Etkis asked after looking inside the hospital.

"Tavern."

"Irresponsible swine…" Etkis muttered.

"Sent the message?"

"Yeah," Etkis replied, still irritated. "I don't know how long it'll take for Volthsheim to send a letter to the Roarers. The town doesn't have any radio towers, and Rose's channel is for military use only. Human civilians…yeah, they can't use it."

"People around here are probably used to waiting for news. It won't be an issue. What do you think they'll say?"

"Volthsheim traders are insured through the city, so usually we would reimburse them for any property damage or stolen goods and then send scouts to hunt down the raiders. But since these swine headed fools were after their permits… I don't know. That's an attempt at infiltrating the city. There's bound to be a change in protocol."

Etkis sat down on the porch and the wood strained to bear his weight. Dorin sat beside him, leaning back on his hands. "Is that your department?"

"If there were an army of raiders amassing outside the city walls, it would be. But Rother is better at espionage so he'll spearhead the investigation."

Dorin kicked at the snow with his boot. "Do you think it would've worked?"

"Stealing the permit? Absolutely not."

"Not a chance? Velkan security's not *that* good."

Etkis twiddled his thumbs. "The permit is useless. It's a block of wood."

Dorin stopped playing with the snow. "Then how do you know who to let in?"

"Well...you know how humans track cattle?"

"Yeeees..."

"That."

"...I don't..."

"The physical permit is useless. We...*they* secretly put a chip in the merchants, and that's what lets them through the walls."

Dorin stood, shocked. "*WHAT?*"

Etkis put his hands up and pushed them down, "*Shush!* Someone will hear you! I could be marked a traitor just for telling you this, so you've gotta keep quiet."

Dorin tried and failed to whisper. "*People agree to this?*"

Etkis coughed, uncomfortable.

Dorin tilted his head. "Wait a minute...*am I...*"

Etkis coughed again.

"*You didn't?*"

"Not me personally—"

"*Etkis!*"

"*What?* Every human let into the city has to be branded like that—"

"*BRANDED?*"

"That's just what we—*they* call it!"

Dorin sat back down, checking his body for any small lumps he might not have noticed before. "What the actual fuck."

"With merchants, it lets us know if someone has been robbed and if the thief is trying to enter the city. With people like you, it's a way of designating allies."

"That's..."

"I know." Etkis turned away. "But it works," he said in ashamed defense.

Dorin removed his helmet and felt the cold breeze rush against his face as he set it aside. They sat gazing at the snow in silence. The blizzard had ceased brooding an hour ago, and the fresh snow glistened in the dawn light. Dorin was consumed in thought…

Why would a gang leader try to sneak into the city? Volthsheim would never trade with Jarrod or any of his fronts. He just wanted another revenue stream? Doubtful—there's no way Jarrod would think that a stolen permit would've worked more than once. Even if he didn't know about the chip, security is too tight in and around the city. Maybe he wanted agents in the city to warn him of attacks? Well, it's the same issue. They'd be discovered too quickly. There aren't enough humans to blend in. And a merchant from Volthsheim walks under the guarantee of a thousand Wolf guns. Nobody touches them. Say what you will about Rother, but his nuclear attitude is effective. So whatever reason Jarrod had must have justified taking that kind of risk… the Serpents must have offered him something big.

"Hey, Dorin?"

Dorin jumped when Etkis broke the snowy silence. "Yeah?"

"What do humans believe happens after they die?"

Dorin looked at Etkis in surprise. Etkis faced toward the horizon, his eyes uncharacteristically empty.

"Depends on the religion."

"Right, there's more than one. How many are there?"

"A lot."

"Is there a general consensus on what happens?"

Dorin chuckled. "Our religions don't really agree on much. Some think we're reborn in a different life. Some think we live in eternal bliss…"

"Good…that sounds nice."

"And some think we suffer for all eternity," Dorin said with a snicker. Etkis's head whipped to Dorin, horrified.

"*What?*"

"Oh yeah, it's a big thing—called hell. Fire, brimstone, never ending torment. Lots of people believe in it."

Etkis shook his head. "I like eternal bliss more."

"Heaven. And it's a package deal too, so you go to one or the other. Same religion."

"Okar help me…you tell that to children?"

Dorin smiled. "Oh, especially to children."

"How can you do that to them?"

"How could we resist! Childhood trauma helps fill the void."

"Why are humans so sadistic?"

"We are an angry and bitter people."

"That's not projecting…" Etkis muttered under his breath. Dorin's jaw twitched in irritation—Etkis rubbed his knees in panic. He didn't mean for Dorin to hear.

"All right, then…any others?" Etkis said, his voice higher than usual.

"Some, like me, believe nothing happens at all—no offense." Etkis gave a little wave of his hand.

"What do you say when someone is about to die?" Etkis asked. "Does it all depend on the religion?" Dorin began to understand what his friend was asking.

"Pretty much. I don't know what you would say to someone before a…violent end."

Etkis watched the edge of the sun begin to dance along the curve of the earth. An out of place warm breeze blew past. Dorin wondered for the first time whether or not his friend could feel it through the armor.

They sat together silently, looking on from the doctor's shack. Rays of sunlight pierced through the leaves of the forest, making elaborate shadows far along the snowy prairie. It was a beautiful day—the hours after a blizzard were always the loveliest. Dorin felt bitter as the short-lived warm breeze died. Dorin snapped the fingers on his human hand, and his survival gauntlet summoned a small flame. Dorin held it close to where his metal arm met his shoulder, relishing in the small relief the warmth provided. Etkis sat beside him, melancholy in thought.

In the distance, at the fringe of the forest, a plume of powdery snow rose high and caught their attention. A figure came into focus, and as they drew nearer, the burgundy sunlight illuminated them. A Velka riding a rover, similar to Rose, only much smaller. It had no dome and was built for one. The guns, the vents keeping it aloft, and the engine in the back were all similar. The Velka slowed down as they approached the town, and Dorin and Etkis moved to greet them. The carvings on the Velka's helmet designated her as female, and the half-moon on her breastplate indicated that she was of a middle rank among the scout regiment. She dismounted and retrieved a folded yellow letter from her satchel. She ran to them and crossed her arms in front of her chest to salute Etkis.

"First Guard Terra, sir, Scout Hiru of sector 34, ID number 98801, reporting. First Scout Itha requested that I deliver this to you, for the human merchants Roarer. It is not sealed, sir. I've also been instructed to assist with any medical attention for the human family."

"Thank you—what is your name?"

The scout's ears perked up in surprise. A first-name basis was a sign of friendship among Velka, and requesting it was a clear sign of care and respect. Highly unusual for someone of Etkis's rank to display toward anything lower than the head of another vocational field. Unorthodox, even if he was so young. She'd heard that Etkis liked to get to know his troops better than most Velka, but other regiments as well?

"Toa, sir…Scout Toa Hiru."

"Toa Hiru—thank you. Your swift envoy is sincerely appreciated, and I will let First Scout Rother know so as well."

The scout's fingers fluttered a little bit, reflecting her beating heart. Naturally, Etkis did not notice.

"I—thank you, sir." She paused for a small moment, forgetting herself. She suddenly remembered why she hadn't moved. "My orders are to stay until I receive a response from the family. Etkis. First Guard Terra. Sir." She added the last bit hastily.

"Of course, they're right in there." Etkis gestured behind him to the shack. "Do check on Mr. Roarer, will you? His condition is rather grave…I am concerned. Do what you can for him. The children are sleeping right now, I believe. Please try not to wake them. They need their rest. Also, the man in the back is one of the raiders. He is to be held here under guard until he regains consciousness. He may then be questioned and transferred at Rother's discretion."

"As you say. Sir." She saluted again. Her eyes darted along his frame as he began to read the letter. She turned to go until she noticed Dorin for the first time. She gave him a little nod—to which he only smirked. Her eyes widened and ears bent back. She looked down, hands now rubbing together in embarrassment, and went inside the little shack. In a moment she was gone—Dorin was surprised by the restraint she had shown by not casting back a single look of longing as she walked away.

"You don't even have to try, do you?" Dorin asked, still smirking.

"Try to what?" Etkis asked without looking away from the letter.

"Ugh, never mind—what does the letter say? 'Sorry for your inconvenience'? 'We have many home defense solutions available for purchase'? Rother's quite the capitalist."

Etkis scoffed and handed the letter to Dorin. The handwriting was beautiful, the calligraphy was slanted, and each letter curved into the next. Each word was ornate but utterly clear.

Pretentious little irksome prick, Dorin thought as he became irritated with Rother through this nonverbal exchange addressed to someone else. He began reading:

Dear Roarer Family,

I hope this letter finds you all in better health than I fear. I am First Scout Rother Itha, overseer of all terrestrial intelligence and corresponding security outside the walls of Volthsheim. I have been informed by my colleague, First Guard Etkis Terra, of the tragic events that led to your family's current plight. I personally take full responsibility for the crimes of these savage men, and you have my most sincere apologies for the events that have transpired. Since you are traders of Volthsheim, your safety is an extension of our own, and an attack upon you is an attack upon us all. I promise you, I will make it a personal priority that those responsible for this attack will be found and justly punished.

To the matter of your home and safety—there are several options that you have before you. The first is to receive full compensation for the unfortunate destruction of your home as per the insurance you have as respected traders of Volthsheim and all her holdings. You would be assigned a dedicated scout to monitor your property at all times, should these villains make another attempt on your property and your lives. The second is to deny this assistance and become entirely independent—should you feel that our failure to ensure your safety cannot be acquitted. I will understand if you feel this way, and there will be no consequences from the House of Wolves for this decision. However, I implore you to allow me to absolve this failure in my duty. The third option is that I have requested and been granted permission from our jarl, His Lordship Tarkus Lupine, to invite you to live within the walls of Volthsheim among our people. You will still receive compensation for your suffering, and you will also be given a home in the agricultural district of our fair city, to continue your profession as ranchers, should you so desire. You will be safe here—our security is overseen by your acquaintance First Guard Etkis Terra, whose expertise and competence in this regard are unparalleled. It is my hope that you choose the latter option and allow us to redeem ourselves in your eyes.

Regardless of your decision, those responsible for your pain will be brought to justice. You have my word.

Sincerely, and with most concern,

First Scout Rother Itha, authorized by Their Lordships Jarl Tarkus Lupine and Lady Nora Lupine

Dorin stared at the words, reading them over and over. He looked at Etkis, back at the letter, and back at Etkis again. He desperately searched for a reason to be angry or to criticize Rother but found none. It took what felt like a millennium to speak.

"They'll be allowed to live in the city…"

"That's what it says."

"That's huge…I can't believe it."

"You should give Rother more credit."

That rubbed Dorin the wrong way—being wrong was always a punch in the stomach. Dorin never expected this level of generosity from the Wolves, and from *Rother*? He couldn't believe it. Etkis nudged him on the shoulder.

"If you wouldn't mind, please go in and let Lola know. I would but…you know. The door."

"Don't make me do it."

"What? Why?"

"*Rother…*" Dorin shuddered.

"Don't be a child."

Dorin grumbled and turned to the little shack, then stopped and turned back.

"The letter doesn't say why they were attacked. Is there a reason?"

"It's become a military matter, a security breach. They don't need to know."

Dorin nodded and went into the building. Toa was fixing the inept stitching and replacing the bandages on Mr. Roarer's stomach. The doctor still hadn't returned from the tavern. Dorin went to the sleeping children. He gave Lola a nudge with his foot.

"Hey, kid."

Lola stirred and looked at Dorin. She tensed, uncomfortable in his presence. He cleared his throat.

"Volthsheim responded and sent this letter—you know how to read, right?"

Lola scowled, insulted. "Yes, I can read, mister."

"Okay, that's…that's good." He cleared his throat again. "The old man is out of it, and you're the second oldest, so you gotta decide what you're doing."

"Decide what? You haven't told me anything yet."

"Just read the thing." Dorin tossed her the letter. She began to read and her hands began to tremble.

"We could live in…in the city?" she asked.

"Well, that's one option, if you want—" Lola jumped and gave Dorin a massive hug. The sudden human contact made Dorin feel nauseous.

"Yup, all right, that's enough of that," Dorin said while he wiggled out of her embrace.

"Nook! Nook!" Lola shook her brother awake. He turned to her sleepy-eyed and grunted an inaudible question.

"We're going to live in the city of Wolves! In Volthsheim!"

Nook didn't move for a second, but the shock soon wore off. He smiled, and his lethargy vanished.

"We are?"

"Yes, yes, look!" Lola showed him the letter, and they read together. The children laughed and tears streamed fully down Lola's face. The last few days almost seemed worth it to them now. Lola ran to the porch as Nook trailed behind her. Etkis had his back turned when she hugged him. Nook followed suit. Etkis turned to them in surprise but soon hugged them back. Dorin smiled at the scene, only a little heartbroken that he didn't know how to share in their celebration.

"We can't just keep waiting here," Dorin said.

Dorin and Etkis looked through the doorway into the shack. The children were now in a far deeper sleep as they slumped against one another, still wrapped in Etkis's cloak. Color had begun to return to Mr. Roarer's face as he slipped in and out of sleep. Toa was changing his bandages again, cleaning the wound silently and efficiently. The marked improvement in medical care had calmed the children immensely. The doctor himself had slithered in and out of the shack for the past two days, always insisting that there were more "antibiotics" or "bandages" that he needed. He always came back empty-handed with the smell of alcohol on his breath.

The raider boy was flanked by two Alexandrian deputies. The official position was that these men were an extension of human law, reflections of mankind's renewed efforts to tame the wilds. But every born and bred Alexandrian knew what they really were—mercenaries bought and paid for by Volthsheim. They secured Velkan interests in human territory, Alexandrian in name only. A single bureaucratic step away from direct military occupation.

The raider boy stared at the wall. He'd come to a day or so ago and hadn't said a thing.

"Etkis, they'll be fine," Dorin said. "Toa will arrange to take them to Volthsheim tomorrow. We don't need to be here for that."

"I know…"

Dorin looked at his friend, whose eyes passed from the children to their father.

"I'll see if I can replenish our supplies in town, but when I get back, we need to leave. All right?"

"Yeah. All right." Etkis didn't take his eyes off the family as Dorin left. He put his helmet on and journeyed deeper into Lipel.

Lipel was the sort of town that Dorin preferred to avoid. Volthsheim was fireproof. Lipel was not. Each building looked more like a tinderbox to Dorin, ready to be set aflame. It was one of the larger human settlements outside of Alexandria, perhaps two thousand people or so. No one could reasonably call it bustling, but to Dorin every space and building felt crowded. Any space with more than three human beings felt crowded to Dorin, but there was an undeniable claustrophobia in every room.

Ugh…people, Dorin thought, disgusted. He glared at the individuals, who looked far more like him than the company he preferred. Too many, too close. The reasons why he never missed Alexandria flooded back to him in waves— their smell, their pettiness, their horrendous proximity. Dorin needed alcohol to survive the onslaught of human contact. Luckily this wasn't difficult, as the human propensity for substance-based liver damage was one of the few that Dorin appreciated. He needed a drink before he braved the "crowded" goods store. He walked to the tavern closest to the goods store, shuddering at the number of people he needed to traverse in order to make it to the bar.

Ten people in a ninety square meter room—no one could possibly cross this place without gagging.

Dorin shuffled uncomfortably as he made ridiculous maneuvers with his body as he did everything in his power to avoid making physical contact with the objects of his hate. Some patrons stared at this ridiculous display of misanthropy, thinking that this metal-armed man had perhaps a contagious disease or a unique form of brain damage that made him travel in serpentine patterns. They shuffled away in their chairs, and Dorin thanked a merciful God that he did not believe in. He made it to the bar, hastily removed a few coins from a pouch on his belt, and slapped them on the counter. The bartender, a middle-aged man whose number of teeth matched the paltry number of brain cells in his head, waddled pigeon-toed over to Dorin. This was the only human being Dorin was willing to tolerate right now due to the promise of alcohol, and the bartender took the money as he stared at the metal hand that poked out from Dorin's sleeve.

"Honey liquor, please, good sir." Dorin fought with every fiber of his being to sound pleasant.

"We don't have that here…sir." The bartender's eyes darted back and forth from Dorin's peculiar metal hand poking out the sleeve and his even more peculiar helmet.

"Humph, mead then."

"Don't have that either." He kept staring.

Dorin inhaled deeply, "Okay, rum then."

"Don't have th—"

"Oh, for God's sake, what *do* you have?"

"Well, uh…we have vodka…"

"And?"

"That's it."

"Goddamn it. Just say that then! Fine, one. Please."

With the speed of a professional alcoholic, the bartender retrieved a shot glass and poured a clear liquid into it. It smelled like shame and bad decisions—a familiar and brutal stench. Dorin removed his helmet, took the glass with his metal hand, and swallowed the drink. It was awful, utterly devoid of any positive qualities save for the preposterous alcohol content. He set the glass down. His eyes watered. He felt fire in his throat, and it took the edge off. Dorin opened his eyes. The bartender was still staring.

Staring.

"Do you fucking mind?" Dorin snapped. The bartender turned pale and took the glass from the counter and shuffled away, eyes to the floor. Dorin put his helmet back on, the extra distance from him and the other people in the room provided comfort.

Dorin stepped outside the tavern but swore and stopped on the porch. Three men stood in the snow waiting. Guns at hips. Hands at guns. They all wore a star on their sleeves. The same as the handler. The middle goon, a blond man with bright blue eyes, spoke for the posse in a thick country accent.

"'Scuse me, but ya wouldn't happen to be the fella that's buddies with a big Velka, would ya?"

Each man stood half a head over Dorin, at least. The one on the left had a toothpick in his mouth, while the one on the right was sweating despite the cold. The leader eyed Dorin up and down, stopping once on Soot at his side, once on his metal hand that poked out the sleeve, and landed at his helmet.

"You already know." Dorin growled. "Drop the game. If Jarrod wanted a corpse, we wouldn't be having words. What's he want?"

The blond man laughed. His blue eyes made Dorin uncomfortable…*but why?*

"He doesn' 'ppreciate interference in his business affairs. He asked us ta see that it don' happen again. But we need some help with your friend. Boss said you'd help us with that."

"Did he? Not a shrewd businessman—he should've done his research first." Dorin's right hand hovered over Soot, ready to draw.

"Oh, he has."

Dink.

The sound of metal hitting metal. A sharp electric shock ran up Dorin's steel arm, filled his body, and the arm went limp. He whipped around, and there stood the bartender, red in the face, holding a bizarre-looking pistol.

Before Jarrod's men could unholster their guns, Dorin raised and snapped the fingers on his left hand. His survival gauntlet wasn't meant for combat, but it was enough. A jet of flame seared the bartender's eyes. The scream jolted everyone in the tavern. The fluids in his eyes boiled. Dorin wrapped his arm around his neck and pirouetted, switching places with the man. A hail of bullets shredded the bartender as Dorin dove behind a wall. His metal arm was still limp from the shock. Dorin awkwardly cross-drew Soot from his hip and bound to the right-side window. He popped out, braced, and Soot boomed three times—the sweating man gargled weakly, and his clothes caught fire. The recoil made his aim flail. Brutal pain ran up his left arm as Dorin's shoulder screamed for mercy. After all these years of training and strengthening his body, Dorin could fire Soot in his human hand without breaking any bones—but he could certainly still feel the damage. Adrenaline numbed the pain for now.

Patrons screamed as they dove for cover in what looked to be familiar locations for them.

The two remaining men tracked Dorin well and spent bullets on the window frame. Wood chunks vomited over Dorin's shoulder. He dropped and cursed viciously. He wasted three shots on a single person. Reloading would be too difficult with only one arm, especially with two opponents and no backup.

Three bolts gone, five left.

Dorin leaned against the window and peered out. They were gone. Dorin scanned the field. He saw the edge of a toothpick poking out from behind one of the porch's wooden beams. He leaned from cover and took the shot. He hit nothing but the beam. However, the impact launched hot splinters into the lackey's face. Dorin heard screaming and saw the man huddled on the floor. His face was covered by blood-soaked fingers. The man stumbled and ducked behind the building. The beam smoldered and sprouted flame.

Piss. The last thing he needed was a bar fire. He fired two more shots at the beam, and it burst. Blazing wood sizzled out in the snow. The dead hitman still lay burning in the middle of the road.

Two bolts left.

Dorin looked around for the last hitman but saw nothing. He was too far to see footprints in the snow. Dorin took to the bar for cover. One patron's nerves snapped, and he screamed and made a break for the door. *Poor fool*, Dorin thought. He waited for the blond man to shoot the poor bastard the second he left the saloon.

Nothing happened. The patron fled, but no shots were heard, and no screams or words were uttered. *Strange…*He constructed a mental map of his surroundings.

The front road, the porch, the tavern itself. Two lanes ran on either side of the tavern. The blinded man fled to the left. The blonde should've gone to the right. It only made sense. But he's not waiting out front. He would've shot at me and then at the patron. Where is he? Dorin returned to the map—*front, left, right, back*—

Back.

There was a click from behind the bar wall.

The wall erupted into bullets and fractured lumber. Dorin rolled away, a shot tunneled into the wood where his heart used to be. Glass and clear, high-proof alcohol flew every which way. Patrons flooded out of the bar, wailing as bullets whizzed out of the back of the tavern. Two were caught in a hailstorm of high-speed detritus and lead. Dorin aimed Soot at where the shots came from but stopped—this much alcohol might as well have been gasoline in this ligneous death trap.

Dorin got up, jumped through the window and into the snow. A shot flew past his head from the left—the blood-covered hitman clutched his right eye as he fired. His aim was skewed by blood and pain. His next two shots went wild.

Dorin sent a shot of metal lightning straight into his face. A gust of orange fire and crimson blood colored the sleet and snow.

One bolt left.

Dorin ran to the dead man, whirled, and pointed Soot behind him. Directly at the spot where he had been standing a moment before. The blond man burst from the right side of the tavern to where he had heard Soot's distinct shots. Dorin fired.

In that moment Dorin realized what he had seen in this man's eyes that had made him so uncomfortable—he was a professional. The blond hit man dropped so hard and so fast that snow flew in the air as Soot's red lightning rocketed above him. He aimed and fired at Dorin from the ground and chips of wall flew beside where Dorin hid.

Out.

Piss.

Dorin holstered Soot and removed his new Wolf knife. Speed was his only option. He ran from cover and threw his knife at the hit man, who was still on the floor. The throw was masterful; the knife landed straight where the blond man had been. He rolled out of the way and staggered to get up—but Dorin had bought himself enough time. He was close enough now.

A snap of his left hand, and a small fire ignited. The blond man screamed as his gun hand burst into flame. Dorin grabbed his knife off the floor. He ran and went for the kill. The blade entered just below the rib cage. Starving electrons along the blade sizzled the flesh and seared all they consumed. Dorin cut up, slicing the hit man's heart in half. The dead man fell into a torrent of steamed blood. His blue eyes turned pale.

Dorin breathed heavily as he stared at his handiwork—three dead men, a destroyed tavern, and three hundred gold pieces' worth of spilled liquor.

Not bad for six minutes' work, Dorin thought as he leaned on his knees, desperately trying not to throw up inside his helmet from fear and adrenaline.

Dorin swallowed back the rancid vodka, which burned his throat anew, then cleaned and sheathed the knife. He ran to the bartender's corpse and moved it to find the pistol he had used, taking it in his left hand. He'd have to examine it later. Jarrod would send another team soon enough. The pain in his left shoulder began to rear its head as the adrenaline subsided. Dorin swore and wondered if Soot had bruised the bone. He could feel his metal arm coming back to life as his fingers once again obeyed his command. The limb was fully functional by the time he had run to the doctor's hut, where Etkis stood waiting. There was fear and confusion in his eyes.

"What happened? I heard Soot––I was worried!"

Dorin leaned on the hospital wall. His chest burned, and he sucked in air hard. "I'm fine. Listen, have Toa take the Roarers to Volthsheim now. Grab a weapon, and give her Rose, and then have her come back with a unit of scouts. We may need them."

"Why? What's happening?"

Having caught his breath, Dorin stood straight and reloaded Soot. "Jarrod's men attacked me. He's not happy with us 'interfering with his business affairs.' He'll be after the Roarers too—that's for sure. We need them gone."

"So much for not looking for a fight. And what are we doing?"

"We're going hunting."

CHAPTER 5

Two biologists were hung until dead at Opahaw, fifty leagues southwest of
Volthsheim, by the local human villagers. The cause of this conflict is still unclear,
but I recommend immediate annihilation of the village. Put down the beasts
responsible, burn their homes, and drive the rest to their refuge across the sea.

—First Scout Rother Itha's Report to Jarl Tarkus Lupine, 9.13.1100

Dorin took a handful of snow and packed it around his bruised left shoulder. He squeezed his lips together tight until the cold eased the pain in his bones. Soot had done more damage than he'd hoped but less than he feared. He sighed, threw down the remaining snow, and put his shirt back on. The helmet slid over his face and brought a tinge of warmth to his cheeks. Dorin kicked his empty tin can of apricots off the doctor's porch, and it tumbled down the stairs. He doubted whether the drunkard would even notice that syrup slathered the steps. Etkis was busy talking shop with Toa, and Dorin couldn't be bothered to sift through the jargon of Velkan bureaucracy right now. Instead, without thinking, he clicked his tongue and went to pick a fight. He slid along the side of the building into the alley and found the two Alexandrian deputies with their horses and the raider boy tied to the hitching posts. The deputies, one lean, the other alarmingly rotund, argued fiercely over which of them had the bigger hat until they noticed the freelancer approaching. The fat one spoke first.

"Eh, what do you want, chump?"

Dorin shrugged. "Just wanted to say hello. Taking the welp back home?"

"Not your concern. This is official Alexandrian business."

Dorin cocked his head. "Do you deputies usually step in *after* someone's done all the work for you? I haven't heard a single 'thank you' yet."

The deputy spat in the snow. His face was slick and greasy, unpleasant to look at but oh so punchable. The other deputy, his face so lean you could be forgiven for mistaking him for a starving urchin, said nothing. He swallowed a dry throat, and that was all. The fat one stepped forward. His double chin bounced while he spoke. "You've got some nerve on you for a slave. Freelancer working for the house? I ought to gut you right now, damn traitor that you are."

"The word 'hypocrisy' is lost on you, isn't it, *deputy*? Who is it that pays your bills again?" Dorin asked. The deputy turned beet red, furious at anything he didn't immediately understand.

"Are you mocking me?"

"Oooo, nothing gets past you, does it, bud?" Dorin said dryly. The deputy drew a knife and held it a finger's length away from the freelancer's heart.

"You'd best remember your place, slave," he whispered. "Now I suggest you get back to your cur and—"

The moment the slur came out the deputy's mouth, Dorin grabbed the knife and the wrist attached to it with a steel hand. The fat man squealed like a frightened piglet and struggled impotently, flesh against metal. He pushed on Dorin's hand with his entire, enormous girth but to no avail. The steel pushed ever onward. Dorin moved slowly. He made sure the deputy could feel every second of his powerlessness. He pushed the man's own hand back on him, the knife edge getting closer and closer to his gut. Dorin manhandled him, so that the Deputy had his back to the wall, and the knife, still in the man's own hand, raised up to rest between his chins.

Dorin whispered, *"Call him that again."*

The Deputy gargled unintelligibly through panic and fear. His partner stood mouth agape at the scene before him. He began to draw his pistol but stopped at a single look from Dorin. The moment the pistol left that holster, the lad knew his end would come. The pistol sank back into its hole like a rat fleeing from a terrier. The lad took a few steps back with his hands outstretched. Dorin squeezed tighter, and the deputy cried in pain, his wrist just a few newtons away from snapping in twain.

Dorin muttered through bared teeth, *"Go on. Call him 'cur' again."*

The knife drew a red, dripping line along its edge. Dorin's prey winced in pain and shook his head, "No! No, please—I'm sorry! I didn't mean nothing by it! Please…"

The freelancer scoffed and released his grip. The deputy gasped for air and was left delirious from adrenaline. Dorin snatched the knife and crushed the blade to small and sharp pieces. "Glad we have an understanding," he said. "Now both of you do me a favor—step away for a minute. I want to talk to your charge."

The lean deputy didn't wait for his partner. He scurried off to the front of the hospital where Etkis talked with Toa. The fat one glared at Dorin one last time but lost the last of his nerve in less than a second. He fell in line behind his more cowardly, but far wiser, companion.

Dorin turned his attention to the raider boy. This entire time the poor kid had gawked at the freelancer as though he were death itself, cold and metal and brutal. Dorin crouched, and the child winced, preparing himself for the pain that would certainly come. Tears rolled down his face. Dorin reached around to his belt and pulled out a canteen.

"Here," Dorin said. "It's warm."

The boy hesitated, but his chapped and broken lips told Dorin this was just fear futilely writhing against a need. He held the canteen softly to the boy's mouth, and he drank the water in long gulps. The fear on his face turned into sweet relief.

Dorin capped the empty canteen. "They'll take you home soon. Do you know what that means?"

The boy furrowed his brow, unsure if this was a trick question or not. "My family and me…we're to be exiled."

Dorin nodded. "Or killed, but probably exiled. You really screwed your family over with that stunt, you know? Moving out of Alexandria and into some backwater town like this won't be a picnic."

The kid gritted his teeth. "Why? How is this fair? My folks came to Alexandria because they were raided by the Wolves, and now because I did the same damn thing, we get thrown back to the devils? *Explain that to me!*"

"Lower your voice."

The raider swiftly remembered his fear and bit his tongue. New tears welled in his eyes, tears of frustration and impotent anger.

Dorin sighed. "The world's not a game. There's no referee calling foul ball when a human village gets raided." There wasn't anything he could say to calm the raider's rage at the injustice, the inequality of being the lowest ranked of two species on a planet. But he could beat some realism into him. That might just save his life. "You're from Alexandria. You've seen Velka ships at the spaceport, right? Did any of their mass driver cannons scream, 'Fair and equal treatment' to you? You made a choice, and you knew the potential consequences. Don't plead the victim when things work out the way you knew they could but didn't want them to."

The raider boy opened his mouth to protest, but Dorin cut him off. "Now, it's Velkan tradition that when someone commits a crime against the house, to take a body part, a permanent reminder of the transgression. But after that the crime is to be forgotten, ignored. I'm going to give you that same opportunity. I've taken care of the first part. Now for the second."

Dorin reached into his belt and pulled out a long bar of solid silver. The raider gazed upon it as though it were an angel.

"Got this last year when we raided Yuntan out east and put down the child trafficking cunt who lived there. Your family needs it more than I do. Take it. Head southeast from Alexandria, follow the Lodda River about forty leagues. There are fertile and warm lands down there and plenty of bison to herd and fish to…well, fish. Build a ranch there, and your family can live good lives away from the Velka to the north and from raiders to the east. There aren't any towns like this down there. It'll be isolated, but being exiled doesn't forbid you from trading with Alexandria. You can get all the supplies you'll ever need and live quietly and peacefully."

The boy looked more confused than ever. Dorin slipped the silver into the kid's inner jacket pocket and stood to leave without another word when the kid spoke.

"Why? Why are you doing this?"

"You fucked up. You paid for it. Doesn't need to ruin the rest of your life too."

"But this is more than that. People kill for this kind of money."

Dorin turned, his voice sharp. He needed the boy to understand. "What I gave you isn't money—it's a new life. A fresh start. If you intend to be long in this world, never get them confused. I wouldn't have killed for money as a kid, but I'd have killed for this." The boy didn't have an answer, he only sunk his head in thought. Dorin whispered, "I don't think you're a bad kid. We all do things to provide for the ones we love, things we aren't proud of. I've just given you a means of doing that without pulling a trigger. Use it well."

Dorin walked off without a second glance. His boots crunched in the snow. He felt numb, as if in a waking dream that he had only then woken from. Dorin squeezed his hands together to make sure he did indeed still have control over his own body. He began to play back the last few minutes in a vain attempt at understanding what on Earth had driven him to such foolishness.

Toa set Mr. Roarer gently onto Etkis's large bed inside Rose. Mr. Roarer was finally lucid enough to say thank you—Toa looked at him, confused. She had rarely spoken to humans, and those conversations were rarely pleasant. "Very good, sir," she responded, unsure if that was the right thing to say. Etkis entered and removed an Elo shotgun from his wall. He removed a new cloak from the storage compartment, identical to the first, and fastened it around his shoulders. Finally, he removed two metal and glass cylinders from the storage compartment and closed it. Suspended inside each contraption were glowing blue orbs. As Etkis finished, Mr. Roarer spoke. "Excuse me, mister?" Etkis turned to him and Toa gave a surprised look. He gave her a nod. She saluted and left the room.

"Mr. Roarer, how are you feeling?" Etkis asked as he knelt beside the bed.

"Better, thank you. It's nice to finally make your acquaintance, mister."

"Call me Etkis, please."

Mr. Roarer chuckled weakly and winced at the pain. "All right, Etkis. I just wanted to give you my thanks, face-to-face. You not only saved my life but also my children's lives. And you and your folk have given us a new home in the safest place on Earth—I don't know how I can repay you."

"It was our duty to intervene. No thanks are necessary, Mr. Roarer."

"Call me Jim, please."

Etkis laughed. "All right, Jim. You don't need to thank us…but you're welcome. Stay safe." He stood.

"I wanted to thank that young man too, but I haven't seen him. Could you—"

"I'll pass it along. Goodbye, Jim. Callva's speed, and may Okar watch over your journey."

Jim smiled, and Etkis tried to return the expression but was unsure if Jim could understand his body language the way Dorin did. Outside, Toa waited for him.

"Was there a problem, sir?"

"No, not at all. He just wanted to say thank you. Humans are more sentimental than we are. It's a trait I admire—please, indulge their gratitude."

"I…yes, sir."

She returned to Rose, and the engines soon gave a soft roar. Lola and Nook walked over with Nook still draped in Etkis's old cloak. It carved a snowy trench as it dragged long behind him. They stopped and Nook looked at Etkis's feet. "Goodbye, mista'…um…thank you for…" Etkis knelt down and set his possessions on the ground. The snow crunched as he moved. He put his massive hand on the pup's shoulder.

"It's all right, Nook. Be safe. Lola, watch after your younger brother, won't you?"

She gave a timid smile and nodded. Nook moved to give Etkis back his old cloak.

"Keep it," Etkis said. "A gift." Nook tried to hide his delight as he again clutched the warm fur.

"Speaking of, we made you a gift, Mr. Etkis, sir!" Lola exclaimed. She reached into her pocket and took out a small doll. It was crafted from bandages they had found in the hospital shack, stark white and made in Etkis's image. The only color on it came from the two blue stones sewn in for the eyes—where they got the stones, he would never be sure. He cradled the idol in his hand and his heart beat wildly.

"I don't know what to say…thank you." He held the little doll protectively to his breast.

"We'll never forget you, sir," Lola said. "Please come see us when you return to the city?"

"It would be my honor."

The children gave him one last hug, which he returned with an immense arm. The other held the doll to his chest.

They boarded Rose, and the landship sped away. The plumes of snow it trailed glowed orange from the light of the setting sun. Etkis looked again at the little effigy and played with its miniature features with his thumb. He tied the doll to his gun and turned to the porch. Dorin skulked in the shadow the roofing provided.

"Mr. Roarer wanted to say thank you," Etkis said.

"That's nice of him."

"You could've seen him—"

"Yes, I could've."

Etkis's ear twitched, irritated. "He wanted to thank you in person."

"And I'm sure he would've meant it too."

Etkis scowled.

"Now if he was really grateful, he'd have lined our pockets," Dorin said, picking at his teeth. "But at least the sniveling urchins are out of our hair, right?"

"Dorin, what in Okar's name is your problem!" Etkis said, fuming.

"This piece of jerky's been stuck in my teeth since the brats woke up and it's driving me nuts! Do you have a needle?" Dorin said with the interest of an Alzheimer's patient halfway through an epic poem.

"They wanted to thank you for saving their lives, and you talk about them like they're trying to con you! What's wrong with 'you're welcome' or 'no trouble' or 'my pleasure'?"

"Wh…ohhhhhh, you mean problem *with the people*."

"Yes, you glob of spunk!" Etkis shouted in fury.

"What?" Dorin asked in utter confusion.

"*You heard what I said.* And they have names!"

"So does my gun, but you don't hear me talking to it."

"*They're people*, you swine-headed ape!"

"*Fuck people!* And screw you! I'm not obligated to—"

"Okar help me! I don't care that you didn't want to see them! You should have, but I know who you are. That's not the problem—don't you *ever* disrespect them around me again! They lost everything they had—their home was burned down. Nook had his fingernails ripped out! Jim got *eviscerated*! If it wasn't for us, they'd have ended up like…how can *you* not sympathize, you elitist unit!"

Dorin looked at Etkis wide-eyed. They didn't fight often, and rarely with this kind of anger. He held up his hands in capitulation.

"Etkis, I didn't need to be so snide—"

"Rude."

"Yes, rude. I'm sorry."

Etkis frowned, ears down and out, shoulders slumped. "I shouldn't have yelled at you."

"I deserved it," Dorin said with a strained laugh. "But you'll learn, just like I did. Their gratitude stretches only as far as is convenient to them. The moment it isn't, when you need them to put something on the line for you, their appreciation will fall apart into salt and sand. I didn't need to hear it."

"If they're so conniving, why did you save them? You saw the fire. I never had to ask for help. You didn't think twice."

"They might've had money…"

"You're lying."

Dorin clenched his jaw, resentful of Etkis's insight. "I…I just did."

Etkis sighed and turned to the road. The frigid black night finally swarmed the town. Torches lit the street, but apart from them, Etkis's eyes were the only source of light. Two blue suns suspended meters in the air framed his body in ethereal light.

"Where do we start?" Etkis asked.

"Gang leaders are political officials in these towns—the largest house. He's gotten word by now that I wasted the hit squad, so he'll be expecting retaliation. There'll be plenty of guards inside so we should hit them from two sides. I'll penetrate them from the front. You smash the back."

Etkis cringed. "You met this guy before?"

"No, but I know of him. He's the biggest gang leader outside of Alexandria. I filled a few contracts for him back in the old days with…" a lump formed in Dorin's throat. Etkis gave a sad nod. "Back when I was a freelancer."

"You're still a freelancer," Etkis said.

"I work for the Wolves now."

"But you're not a citizen, so you're still a—"

"Can we not do this now? Please?"

Etkis looked down with embarrassed anxiety. "Sorry. I know we talked about it. And…yeah. Um…I'm sorry."

"It's okay," Dorin said. The wet blanket of shame returned to haunt him. There was an awkward silence. The wind groaned. It was the only sound.

"Why didn't Jarrod attack us here, before the Roarers left?" Etkis asked, desperate to change the subject.

"Same reason he sent men after me, not you—you're *way* more of a deterrent than you think."

Etkis snorted in abashed discomfort.

Dorin rubbed his hands together in excitement. "Did you get the shields?" he asked.

"Yes." Etkis handed Dorin one of the cylinders he had retrieved from Rose. They both placed the batteries on the small of their backs and the magnet within clung to their armor. It took up a third of Dorin's back but could hardly be noticed on Etkis.

"*Ha ha, yes!*" Dorin shouted. "I've never had one of these before!" Dorin reached around his back and flipped a switch and his barrier turned on. There was a faint, barely visible blue hue around his body now. "*I'm invincible.* Hit me. Etkis, hit me!"

"I'm not going to––"

"*Hiiiiiit meeeeee!*"

Etkis groaned and smacked Dorin in the back and he face-planted in the snow. Dorin raised his head, spitting out snow, furious. "What the hell! I thought I had the barrier on?"

"You do." Etkis grabbed Dorin by scruff and lifted him to his feet with one arm. He patted down his friend like a parent pats down their delinquent child.

"But the barrier will only stop something with sufficient velocity, like bullets. Otherwise air couldn't pass through, and breathing is pretty important. That's why a lot of Velka use blades—the barriers ignore them. Elo weapons overload the barriers, but you'll be safe for a shot or two. And don't turn the barrier on until you absolutely need it—you'll drain the battery."

"…These kind of suck, don't they?"

"I mean they still stop *bullets*. If it doesn't meet your *illustrious* standards, I can keep it—"

"*No*, no, nononono, it's great, thank you."

They walked down the street and spotted Jarrod's house—a monument to his ego. It was fashioned after Alexandrian architecture, but failed to capture the beauty—like a young boy mimicking his father. Dorin thought it would've been cute if the attempt hadn't been so sincere. Marble was rare in the wilds, so the walls were supplemented with segmented lines of wood. Statues of swans marked the entrance to the property.

They stalked into the black alley of a nearby building.

"Four guards at the entrance, two by the door, and two on the balcony," Dorin said. "I'll take them out and you go around. Remember, *smash their back door*."

"Gross."

"You won't be able to fit, a problem I often have. Improvise. Penetrate on my signal."

Etkis gagged. "What's the signal?"

"Gunfire."

Etkis rolled his eyes and vanished into the night. Dorin looked back at Jarrod's symbol of arrogance. It stood just beside the bank. *Of course it does.* The roof was the same height as Jarrod's house, and that put it just above the balcony. *Perfect.*

Dorin rushed from alley to alley to the back of the bank. He took out his knife and sunk it deep into the wall—his left shoulder screamed in pain. Soot's bludgeoning had left its mark. Dorin clenched his jaw tight as he tried to ignore the pain. His metal hand grabbed the wall itself. He carved tiny divots in the wood beneath his steel fingers. He scaled the building, slowly, quietly. Metal on marble would've been far too loud. His hand would have pulped the stone to dust, like mulch at his fingertips. Everyone in the house would hear. But this soft cedar dampened the sound of every thrust of his knife and grasp of his hand. He reached the roof and massaged his wound. He looked over the edge to the men standing watch on the balcony.

Dorin hopped to Jarrod's roof and lowered himself to the balcony. In a flash he threw his knife into one man's face and snapped the other's neck. They both died before they knew what had happened. Dorin retrieved the blade and turned around to the door that led to the balcony. No windows, no way of knowing what was on the other side. Dorin thought of entering a room with an unknown number of hostile gunmen. *With the shield I could do it…I could definitely do it.* Dorin felt the phantom ache of the million bullet holes he would receive, panicked, and turned to look over the railing. The last two sentries shivered and grumbled about the cold.

"Goddamn, I hate winter. So fucking cold."

"Stop bitching, it's always cold."

"But it's *more* cold. You ever think of getting to Venus? Can you imagine? *Beaches!*"

"We have beaches on Earth."

"A shore covered in snow is not a beach."

Dorin climbed down from the balcony and landed behind the two guards. Silent as any predator.

"Think of it! Swimming, drinking, that's a life worth living!" The man stared into the middle distance and a line of drool ran down the corner of his mouth. "They have coconuts…"

Dorin wrapped his metal arm around the whining sentry and threw his knife at the second. The blade pierced his jugular and sank down to the hilt. His blood simmered and boiled. He desperately fumbled for anything to hold onto to stay standing, to no avail. He slumped to the floor, dead.

"You're right, a life without coconuts isn't a life worth living," Dorin whispered to the panicking sentry. His chokehold kept this prisoner from making any noise beyond a muffled gargle.

"Now, is there a secret knock? A password? Anything?" The sentry shook his head, his face turned purple.

"Nothing? Really? Your security is egregious, you know that?" The guard gave a horrified nod.

"Welp, all right, thanks." Dorin squeezed tighter, and the man fell unconscious. *A man who loves coconuts is worthy of life.* Dorin dragged the two guards out of sight and pulled out his knife and blood hosed from the dead man's neck. He cleaned and sheathed his blade, drew Soot, and came to the door. There were small windows running parallel to the doorframe that allowed him to take note of the layout. A large greeting room, three doors on the bottom floor. There weren't any guards in there. *Well, maybe in the bathroom.* There was a staircase by the front door that likely led to the bedroom. Dorin counted the bodyguards about the greeting room and at the second-floor walkway.

One, two, three four...fifteenish gunmen. Piiiiiss.

Dorin searched his mind for a strategy that didn't involve brute-forcing his way through all those bodyguards but came up short. All he could do was thin the number before braving the fire. He and Etkis would have to be enough.

Dorin took a deep breath, reached around, and flipped the switch on the battery attached to his back. A soft hum filled his ears, and a blue, nearly translucent field enveloped him. Dorin knocked on the door. "Hey, guys, when's the next shift change? It's freezing out here!" He aimed Soot against the door. Eye level.

"Bill, I swear to fuck," someone said from behind the door. "If you ever get a coconut, I'll shove it—"

The doorknob turned.

Etkis moved through the ankle-deep snow, far from Jarrod's gilded mansion, hidden in the black. He had a straight shot to the back of the wall from here. All he had to do now was wait. He knelt in the fresh snow and played with the cold powder, his gun in the other hand.

He looked at the house and felt a twist in his chest, and he swallowed bile back down. He hated it when the job got personal. Other Velka—it never got

personal to them. Etkis closed his eyes and breathed deep. "Okar, give me purpose. Kior, give me focus. Treya, give me will." He clenched his gun and the
wood grip creaked beneath his fingers. He was a soldier, a warrior, and he knew
his duty. His duty was violence.

He opened his eyes. The target flooded into his vision. How many people
were in there? *Not enough.* Etkis looked down at the Roarers' doll. Its tiny blue
eyes curved in a smile.

"Okar, take them with you, to journey through the—" He stopped. His
thoughts slipped back to what Dorin had told him. "May they journey to heav-
en…may they live again. May they find peace…" None of it felt right, like half of
an answer torn out of someone else's book. What did they believe, these faceless
men? What did they want? Duty commanded that he kill them, but he didn't
want them to suffer. He searched for a prayer, a saying, something to help their
souls pass on.

"May they…may they die without regret."

A shot from the house rang through the valley. Dorin's gun, Soot, unmistakable. It sent a tremor down Etkis's spine. He spent his youth in Earth's frozen
wastes; the cold was home. But that sound made him shiver. The echo was so per-
cussive that it held as more gunfire cracked beneath the blanket roar. Etkis still
felt the thunder in his ears, in his bones, an unnatural sound even to a soldier. An
evil sound. The sound of death taking pleasure in his work.

That was the signal.

He stood, reached behind his back, and the barrier hummed to life. He started running. The earth tore with every stride.

The door was shredded by an onslaught of hot lead—all that was left was a nub
of wood at the base. A bullet smashed against the barrier, and a blast of frigid air
hit Dorin in the flank. He patted his side to find the bullet hole, but there was
none. "I will never doubt you again, Etkis," he said out loud. The barrier stopped
another bullet several centimeters from his forehead.

A sound from afar—rumbling. Growing louder. Like a stampede. Dorin peaked through the shattered window.

The back wall exploded into an avalanche of flying stone and lumber; some bodyguards were smashed by the hail of debris. The second-floor walkway above the impact crumbled and falling stones smashed into Etkis's shoulders—he brushed them off with a twitch. He fired the shotgun and a hail of diffracted light crashed into the nearest man. He burst into superheated dust.

"Aaaaaaahhhhhh!" The scream came from Etkis's right.

A massive bodyguard, one of the largest men Dorin had ever seen, charged at Etkis. He fired his machine gun wildly. The bullets pelted off of the barriers. A flash of white—Etkis bore his foot through the man's chest—ribs snapped like twigs—and launched this idiot against the wall. He burst like a grape on impact.

Every guard immediately threw down their weapons and ran for the door. They passed Dorin without a second glance.

Dorin walked, shaking, into the destroyed house. Etkis wasn't winded in the slightest. "Not enough…" he muttered. "You all right?" He asked Dorin.

"I'm fine. How many did you get?"

"Four, why?"

"Ah. You see, I got five!" Dorin said. He puffed out his chest. His insecurity was palpable. "Four outside."

Etkis took a deep breath, "Good job, Dorin."

"And then the one by the door."

"You did the *goodest job*. Happy?"

Dorin tilted his head, surprised at the tone. "What's wrong?"

"I…" Etkis stopped himself. "No jokes right now. Please."

"…No one's going to miss them, Etkis," Dorin said.

"You don't know that."

"Yes, I do. I was in their shoes, and the only one who would've missed me put a bullet in my back."

Etkis grunted, then gasped in panic and checked his gun—the doll was still there, intact. He sighed with relief.

"Okay, now, Jarrod…actually, hold on, I want to check something," Dorin said. He went to the bathroom and opened the door gently.

A horrified young man raised his hands, his pants around his ankles. He squeaked like a kitchen mouse, "I surrender…"

"We figured. Go on," Dorin said. He had never seen a man concurrently wipe, pull up his pants, and sprint away at such speed. He was sure the lad's record would never be broken.

Dorin ascended the stairs while Etkis stood guard at the bottom. *Well, this worked fine the first time.* He knocked on the bedroom door.

CHAPTER 6

Open file > Human Leadership > Warlords > Unconfirmed: Jarrod.
Threat level: Gamma. Confirmed crimes: 0. Suspected crimes against
human vassals include, but are not limited to, 359 counts of conspiracy
to commit murder, 132 counts of political maneuvering, 567 counts of
theft, 67 counts of arson, 32 counts of hiring unsanctioned freelancers,
12 counts of poaching, 209 counts of assault, and 54 counts torture. Only
suspected crimes against Volthsheim are 1,089 counts of tax evasion.

Update: 1 Suspected Count of Insurrection. Elevate to Threat level: Beta.

—Volthsheim database, restricted for head of military fields only

"Hold on, now, I'm coming out. Don't shoot," Jarrod said from behind the door, a light huskiness in his voice. Dorin moved aside as the door opened, Soot pointed straight at the gangster's heart. Jarrod was not at all what Dorin had expected. The infamous kingpin was renowned for brutality, and the pretentious house made Dorin think of fat, green-bellied politicians in Alexandria. He'd built an image of a bald, certainly smelly, manatee-shaped man, keen to send goons out to do his bidding as he cowered behind a desk. Dorin's old contracts for him were usually assassinations, with the occasional blackmail of various political figures in small towns who took a stand or criminals who posed a threat. He thought Jarrod sat back and reaped the fruits of other people's harvests, just like the despots in Alexandria. Instead, he was handsome. A middle-aged man with immaculate blond hair and brilliant blue eyes. Arms and chest rippled beneath a loose-fitting Y-neck shirt that betrayed a powerful, dangerous physique. A sharp line of facial hair made his square jaw even more pronounced. Scarred hands and neck marked his life a hard one, a life of struggling for power. Power he had earned. Though Dorin was slightly taller and his gun aimed at Jarrod's heart, he couldn't help but feel small.

"Pleasure to meet you. My name is Jarrod," he said with arms raised. He was calm. It put Dorin on edge.

"Hi," Dorin said. He shook his head. *Did I just have a seizure? What is wrong with me?*

"Downstairs, I presume?" Jarrod asked.

Dorin nodded like an idiot.

Jarrod strolled down the staircase with the grace of a dancer and took an apathetic glance at his destroyed home to calculate the damages. Satisfied with an estimate, he turned to Etkis and smiled brilliantly. In contrast to everyone else Dorin had met in Lipel, Jarrod's teeth were white as snow.

"Well, hello! My, you're quite the specimen, aren't you? As you may have guessed, my name is Jarrod. I'd love to know yours."

"Etkis Terra, first guard for the House of Wolves…pleased to meet you?" Etkis responded as he cast a look of utter confusion to Dorin.

"First Guard Etkis, an honor," Jarrod said, reaching out his hand. Etkis shook it, clearly unsure what was happening, when Jarrod's complete greeting finally dawned on him. Etkis clenched his fist at Jarrod's familiarity; the use of his first name was a sign of friendship that made his blood boil. Etkis reminded himself that humans didn't think such things, but something about Jarrod made Etkis think that this man knew exactly what he was doing. Jarrod quickly proved Etkis right.

"Oh, I apologize," the kingpin said, "that's not how your people make new acquaintances, is it? Treya bless your home, as you have blessed mine. Did I get that right?"

Etkis cast a sideways glance at the gaping hole in the wall he had made. "Yes, actually…that's usually for guests, though."

"Well, perfect—what are you if not my guests?"

"Captors," Dorin interjected, desperately trying to sound intimidating rather than like a mentally damaged yokel.

"Come now, there's no need for such hostilities," Jarrod said, smooth as before.

"There isn't? You tried to kill the Roarers. You tried to kill my friend," Etkis said coldly. Jarrod looked up at the Velka, his body language cold but his voice sympathetic. Etkis found it extremely confounding.

"It was just business, gentlemen. I was hired by a third party to acquire something very important from that unfortunate family, and was committed to fulfilling that contract. As for you two fine gentlemen, you thwarted my efforts, and therefore I thought it prudent to take steps to ensure that my operations would never be interfered with again. However, I gave orders to capture mister...um?"

"Dorin."

"Dorin...have we met before?"

"No. Worked for you once or twice, though."

"Ah, yes, I recall now! You did that contract in Mercia, what, five, six years ago? Excellent work there, young man. Where's your partner? I mean the young woman, not our Velkan friend here. What was her name? Allie? Amy?"

"Ash...her name was Ashton."

Etkis froze and looked at Dorin, who began to tremble. They never spoke about Ashton. Just saying her name made Dorin's stump burn as it met his steel arm, his heart panic, his lungs fight for air. A hot iron had pierced his chest, and his vision became blurry. *Can't think about that now...about her now.*

"Dorin?" Etkis asked, great care in his voice.

"I'm fine. Her name was Ash...she's gone now." Dorin thought for a moment he might shoot himself in the foot to distract from the pain in his chest. He took a deep breath and found a comforting resolution. "Etkis is my partner now."

Dorin and Etkis shared a glance. It said everything Dorin needed to hear.

"Ah, well, a pleasure to officially meet you, Dorin. To continue with my narrative, I gave orders to capture Mr. Dorin here alive——hence the portable EMP that one of my men used, as I'm sure you noticed." Dorin reached in his pocket and pulled out the bizarre-looking pistol the bartender had used. "That's the one," Jarrod said with pride. "I'm sorry to hear that the entire episode turned into such a violent affair. My apologies."

"You seem real broken up about it. Actually, you look a lot like one of those guys…blonde hair and such."

"My cousin. No hard feelings, good sir—he was an utter ass. Couldn't stand him, personally. But nonetheless, I did try to capture you, to discover your identities and in order to find out how to take out this magnificent fellow here." Jarrod gestured to Etkis, who shuffled, uncomfortable from the compliment. "Clearly, I miscalculated. But in every mistake, there is opportunity." Jarrod slowly reached for his pocket, "May I?" Dorin hesitated, then nodded. Jarrod retrieved a long cigar and a lighter. *Good God, that must've cost a fortune,* Dorin thought. Jarrod lit the cigar and puffed on it with reverence. He took a second out of his pocket and offered it to Dorin.

"No thank you. I'm…Amish," Dorin said. Jarrod raised a single eyebrow and pocketed the cigar. Etkis looked at Dorin as though the latter had turned into a fish. *Unless Etkis's size forty-eight boot is in my mouth, there is no excuse for what just happened.*

"Now," Jarrod continued, only laughing a little, "I suspect you've come here with questions, for which I have answers." He threaded his words slowly through a drag of his cigar. He began to stroll over to a cabinet beneath the stairs that Dorin hadn't noticed before. He raised Soot.

"It's all right," Jarrod said as he raised his hands even higher. He very slowly opened the cabinet, reached in, and pulled out a cylinder of purple liquid. Etkis's eyes widened in surprise—inthol was almost impossible to acquire outside of a Velka house. "I'd be a very poor host if I didn't cater to my guests," Jarrod said, handing Etkis the cylinder.

"I'm on duty."

"Whatever you feel comfortable with, my friend. It is yours to keep." Etkis tensed at the word "friend". His jaw locked and his flesh screamed for retribution. *Control,* he thought. Jarrod took a seat on a pile of rubble and took a drag of his cigar. "Now, your questions?"

"That third party you mentioned, House of Serpents?" Etkis asked.

"The very same—they came to me seeking attire that would keep their agents safe in Earth's weather. After that they began arming me and many other fellow businessmen and offered us a contract. To discover a way to infiltrate your fair city, first guard. And if we fail that, we cause enough chaos to keep your guard busy for years. A shame what can happen to a city when its military is stretched thin, don't you agree?"

Dorin cocked back Soot's hammer. Etkis put his hand on Dorin's shoulder. "Businessmen?" he asked. "You mean criminals. Gangs and kingpins."

"We're still businessmen, first guard. We merely happen to peddle bullets and blood rather than pedestrian wares." Jarrod gestured to Dorin with the cigar. "As I'm sure *you're* aware."

"You're not making a great case for yourself. Organized crime doesn't exist in Velka society," Dorin said, jaw clenched and lips tight.

"Oh, I know," Jarrod responded. "'The house before the self. The spirit before the body.' That's what your gods say, correct? It makes doing business with your fine people extremely difficult," he said with a gesture to Etkis. "This is my first contract with a Velka house, and until now it's been extremely profitable. I'm eager for it not to be the last, but I'm not partial as to with whom. Therefore, I would like to offer you my services."

"Services?" Etkis asked in disbelief.

"Indeed. Earth is a small place and getting smaller all the time. I can't imagine there'll be enough room for you *and* your new neighbors."

"Neighbors?"

"Services…" Jarrod rubbed his thumb and forefinger together.

"Don't test me, Jarrod," Etkis said. His voice rumbled and the gravel and rubble shook beneath Jarrod's feet. Jarrod mulled over his options.

"A kingpin in Alexandria sold me that inthol," Jarrod said, pointing to the cylinder in Etkis's hand. "They haven't been getting it from you, have they?" Jarrod asked. Etkis growled and looked into the viscous purple liquid. A serpent was stamped at the base.

Dorin spoke up, "Linel's the head of the Alexandrian circuit, a dangerous fuck. He's Tarkus with no morals. I *really* don't wanna deal with him, but we don't have a ton of options. He's a 'businessman,' so we can talk business. Let's kill Jarrod, find Linel, simple."

"Linel?" Jarrod smiled. "You haven't been there for some time, have you, young man?"

The color fled from Dorin's olive skin. "A name," he demanded.

"Put the gun away," Jarrod said to Dorin.

Dorin snarled. "You cuck, you're not in a position to—"

"Do it," Etkis said, not taking his eyes off Jarrod.

Dorin whipped to his friend. "Etkis, what the f—"

"A little broken man in his little broken castle. He's not a threat. Not to me."

"But—"

"Do you know the kingpin's name?"

"I…no, but we can figure it out!"

"You can learn right now," Jarrod said, cigar in hand.

Dorin hesitated, then holstered Soot. Jarrod dragged on the cigar, long and slow. The tobacco tasted like the survival he crawled toward. "His name is Pompeii. I bought that EMP from him. Quality Serpent ware."

"Why would you buy from your competition?" Dorin asked.

"Because information is more valuable than gold. I've learned a lot by playing weak and dumb with those obtuse proletariats. People are a lot more willing to talk when they think they have all the power." He took another drag on the cigar. "Now gentlemen, back to my offer. I am at your mercy now. I have no illusions of that––but I believe I have proven here that I am more valuable to you and your cause as a living friend than a dead enemy. I am willing to pay penance for my slights against you. It is only fair."

"Against us? What about the Roarers? You nearly killed them!" Etkis boomed. For the first time, for just a moment, Dorin saw Jarrod's hands tremble in fear and mortality flash in his eyes. He smiled again.

"Yes, you are right, and I will accept your justice—but let me keep my life, and I can offer you my exemplary services nearly free of charge."

"Nearly?"

"Operational expenses, my friend."

"I'm not your friend," Etkis snapped.

"Good sir"—Jarrod self-corrected without missing a beat— "I operate at my best when I can focus on the task at hand rather than how much it will cost me."

"He's full of it, Etkis. Let me shoot him," Dorin said.

Etkis didn't move as he considered the offer.

"Not convinced, I see," Jarrod said, his voice cold and alluring. "Well, I have one more tidbit of information, if you're interested."

"What is it?" Etkis asked without hesitation.

"Do we have a deal?"

"Depends on the information."

Jarrod took a long drag on his cigar and leaned forward. Smoke rose from his mouth as he spoke. "The House of Serpents has a new jarl."

"You're lying," Etkis said, panic in his voice.

"Am I?"

Etkis narrowed his eyes. No one moved as he read the muscles of Jarrod's face and body and listened to his heartbeat with his lupine ears. After a moment, Etkis grunted in frustration.

"Piss, no, you're not. Xylon is dead? When did this happen? How?"

"When? Two years ago. How? I'm not entirely sure, but the new jarl is named Loka."

"Never heard of her. You have no idea how this happened?"

"All I know is that the coup involved—"

"Coup? What is that?"

Jarrod furrowed his brow and tilted his head, surprised for the first time in quite a while. "A coup d'état? It's an illegal, and violent, seizure of power—you've never heard the word before?"

Etkis shuffled, insecure. He shook his head.

"Interesting…" The gangster said, enraptured in thought for just a moment. He swiftly returned his attention to Etkis. "The coup involved the former first shipmaster of the Serpent fleet—Jormar, the Dragon. Heard of him?"

"Yeah…him I've heard of."

Dorin looked to Etkis questioningly. "Later," Etkis said.

"He's on Earth," Jarrod said, all luster emptied from his voice.

Even though Etkis was a meter away and his chest was layered in thick armor, Dorin could hear his friend's heart begin to race.

"That…I…you're sure?"

"He's not someone you forget. I believe Jormar is leading the Serpent campaign on Earth, overseeing the operation, but at a certain point, I can only speculate. What I *do* know is that he is working closely with Pompeii down in Alexandria. That's where I saw him, at Pompeii's compound."

Etkis didn't move, attention shattered.

"Etkis?" Dorin asked.

Etkis didn't hear him immediately, as if Dorin were shouting across a long chasm. He stirred after a moment. His body shook, but he was completely numb. Etkis stepped away, lost in thought. He looked down to the doll Lola and Nook had made him and cradled it in his hand. His heart sank—there was a speckle of blood on the tip of the doll's ear, bleach white tinged red.

Dawn encroached on the land, and faint sunlight poured into the ruined house. A bead of sweat ran down Jarrod's temple.

"Okar forgive me," Etkis whispered to the little doll. He spoke up. "Scouts will be here soon. They'll take you to Volthsheim, and you'll be punished." Etkis turned to Jarrod. "*And* the house gets a body part. Maybe a hand, or an eye, or both. It's our way. Think of it as 'an operational expense.'" Jarrod turned slightly pale.

"But you'll live," Etkis said, hate and guilt in his voice, "and we'll own you."

Jarrod hesitated for a second, then gave Etkis a strained smile. "Sounds like a plan, friend."

"Call me friend one more time and I'll tear your heart from your still living body."

Jarrod's smile vanished. Sweat fully lined his brow. "Yes, sir, Mr. Terra."

CHAPTER 7

*...storms ravaging the eastern shores. In local news, a fire burned
down a small residence in the miner district. The fire brigade arrived
three hours after the fire burned itself out. One reported dead and one
missing. In other news, fresh potatoes will be coming to market...*

—The Alexandrian Post, 7.12.1100

"Are you okay?"

"I'm fine," I say. My eyes burn. The tears leave cold streaks down my cheeks.

"Good. Come on, then, let's go."

I look up at Ash. She's distorted through my watering eyes. How old are we? Fourteen? Who can remember? "Go? Go where? The house is burned to the ground."

"We'll leave the city, move out into the wilds!"

"Now?"

"Yes now! Why are you being so difficult? I thought this is what you wanted?"

"Not like this...I thought—"

"What? That Mommy Dearest would kiss you goodbye, with a little suitcase in hand, and she'd wait for you to come home to tuck you in at night? She's dead, D. Get over it. My parents have been dead for years, and it's only up from—stop crying."

"It's my fault."

She doesn't respond. I'm gonna throw up. Please, please say something! "These things happen," she finally says. Nothing else.

Oh...

"I should've checked the hearth to make sure the grate was closed," I say through stifled sobs. "She always said to check, and her knees made it hard to go down the stairs, so it should've been me—"

"It's only your fault if you tell yourself it is. Sera shouldn't have lit a fire and then gone to bed. That was a dumb thing to do."

"She trusted me to check—"

Ash stood up and slapped her hands against her thighs. She's taller than me then—it drives me crazy. "Well, you didn't! If she had done it herself then maybe she would still be alive! D? D, come on, I'm sorry. I...baby, come on, it'll work out."

"No, it won't."

"Sure it will! We just need to get out of the city, and then we can start out fresh—doing work on a ranch, our own land, just like we talked about! Right? Doesn't that sound good, D?"

I sniffle, but it does help. Just a bit. "Yeah...yeah it does."

"That's my man. Now let's pull ourselves up—that's it."

I stand up from the grimy alleyway. The street beside us bustles with people. Children play in the corner square. Townsfolk walk by in every direction, apathetic to the two teenagers covered in soot and filth. A man passes us in the alley. He doesn't look once.

"We'll need money," I say as my nose runs heavily. "Everything Mom and I had burned in the fire. What about your rainy-day fund?"

"Gone. I had to use it to pay off Linel."

"What? Why?"

"Because I had to! Look, it's fine. We'll just find some work. There's plenty out there for people like us."

"People like us? What do you...no."

"D—"

"Ash, no. I don't want us to have bounties on our heads for the rest of our lives."

"You can't get what you want without taking some risks, Dorin."

"Dorin? Dorin!"

"Huh…what?" Dorin snapped back to reality. His helmet lay beside him, his hood down behind his black hair. He had been playing with Soot in the pale morning light; the black and red gun carved a clear silhouette against the white backdrop. He had no idea for how long.

"Are you okay?" Etkis asked.

"I'm fine," Dorin said. He squeezed Soot. His tongue pressed hard against his teeth.

"You don't seem fine…Ashton?"

"Yeah."

"Wanna talk about it?"

"Not really—thanks, though."

Etkis nodded and sat next to Dorin, massive shotgun still in hand. The Wolven scouts had arrived, Toa and a dozen others. Shackles clinked on Jarrod's wrists, and the scouts yanked him onto one of their landships. Jarrod winked at Dorin when he got into the landship, and Dorin clenched his fist.

Toa walked over to the pair. "First Guard Ter—um, Etkis, sir. First Scout Itha wishes to speak with you as soon as you are able." She maintained an unusually straight posture and looked over his head, desperate to maintain professionalism with her impossibly sexy superior.

"Thank you, Toa. How are the Roarers?" Etkis asked.

"Safe inside the city, sir. They send their…" She paused, unsure what the word meant, "They send their regards," she finished.

"That's very kind of them. You brought Rose back?"

"Rose?"

Dorin snickered and Etkis shook his head. "Pardon me, landship T-139."

"Oh, yes, sir. Just over there." She pointed.

"Thank you. If that is all, you are dismissed."

Toa nodded but lingered for a moment. She silently prayed for Etkis to say something, anything to her. She wanted him to take her in his arms and carry her into his home. To link their airs and relish in each other's bodies. She imagined their life together—it was beautiful. Full of love, children, and status. He would hold her, call her his star, and care for her as they grew old together. All he needed to do was ask, say anything to satisfy her bounding heart.

He didn't, of course. She rejoined the rest of her regiment.

"Rose—Okar help me, I sound like a human," Etkis said once Toa was out of earshot.

"Don't you dare say that, you're a lovely person! Think of your reputation," Dorin chimed with a smile.

"Ha ha, if I lose my reputation because I'm too human, then I don't want it," Etkis said. "We didn't even make it to Alexandria before our first report. What a week…"

Etkis stood up stiffly and stretched out his body, cracked his neck, and rolled his shoulders.

"Are we still going?" Dorin asked, timid. Etkis noticed the unusual tone. "We found evidence of Serpents working with humans. Why go to Alexandria?"

"There's a difference in magnitude between Serpents working with crime lords in the fringes of human territory and them working with the largest human city in the system. But you're right, we've confirmed their intentions, and we have a vague time frame—they must have been at this for a while for Jarrod to know what he does. We'll get orders about what to do next. But with *Jormar* involved…" Etkis's eyes curled in concern. "I can't imagine we wouldn't go."

Dorin felt his lips tighten. The closer he got to the city, the more real it felt, the more memories flooded back to him. The pressure of their resurgence gored his mind. He realized that his return had felt so surreal when he first accepted the contract. Now it was different—they could reach the outskirts of the slums by the end of the day. His body reacted to the thought, retracting in mortal fear and revulsion. His skin crawled, his lips felt numb, his stomach knotted.

"It's okay," Etkis said. He knelt, and Dorin realized he had been staring into space as his friend came into focus. Etkis spoke with a melody of empathy and the lyric of compassion.

"It's been a long time. It's got to be a different place now—and you're a different man." He put his hand on Dorin's shoulder. Dorin felt the lump in his throat and the tremor of his chin, the water in his eyes. He couldn't meet his friend's gaze—he closed his eyes and nodded. He turned away and breathed deeply.

"Why don't you stay here, take a minute? I'll deal with Rother," Etkis said.

"Okay…"

"Don't worry. I'll put him in his place for you."

Dorin sneered softly. "Tell him he's a glob of spunk."

"*Ha*, Okar save me. I should never have taught you that word."

"What does it mean, anyway?"

"Yikes…ask me after a few drinks. I'll buy next time, how about that? Forget your debt for a night. I am a merciful creditor."

Dorin laughed harder. "All right, thanks. And…thank you." He finally met Etkis's gaze again. He saw Etkis eye a smile, and he allowed himself the comfort of his company. Etkis stood and walked into Rose. Dorin's face began to hurt, the laugh so contrary to his heart. He fiddled with Soot in his right hand, metal on metal. He focused on it. He closed his eyes and rested the cool barrel on his forehead. He pulled the hammer back and reset it. Back and forth, over and over. His heart steadied. He breathed deep. The pain in his jaw ebbed, and the muscles slackened. Back and forth, over and over. He felt safe again.

"Etkis, it's pleasant to see you unharmed," Rother said. His thin voice sounded robotic through both the filters of his helmet and the transmission channel. His gray eyes drank light, ghostlike through the monitor.

"Thank you, Rother, sorry to keep you so busy," Etkis responded, his voice still sonorous through the channel.

"Where's Dorin? Indulging in swine no doubt."

"First Scout, I'm surprised. To begin our official debriefing with an insult? I can't imagine Jarl Tarkus would approve of such a breach of etiquette, considering your recent *blunders*," Etkis said. The threat vibrated the metal speakers.

"…I was being unprofessional," Rother said. His stone demeanor betrayed a hint of discomfort.

"Yes. What have you found on your end?"

"We've found small terrestrial deposits of firearms branded with serpents. Several human raiders were caught retrieving them. It's nothing that could threaten the walls but enough to harm small convoys."

Etkis sighed. "That's consistent with what Jarrod told me."

"Jarrod?"

"A crime lord I'm sending you—he's trading information for his life. Jarrod's responsible for the raid on the Roarers and should be punished accordingly."

"Roarers?"

"Yes—the ranchers…you wrote them a letter?"

"Ah! Peasants? Yes."

Etkis grumbled indistinctly. His ears twitched, irritated.

"I understand you're concerned for their well-being," Rother continued. "They've been branded and put to work safely within Volthsheim."

"…They're not cattle."

"Mhmm. Well done capturing Jarrod. His antics cost us a great many resources. Be assured"—the edge of Rother's voice peaked upward and his fingers tightened around an invisible knife—"he'll be punished thus."

"Thank you." Etkis sighed. "Jarrod will be working as an informant under your authority—given Jarl Tarkus's approval. Watch him close, he's wily. Have you trapped more Serpent scouts?"

"Four teams of two at the moment. We're still finding more. Operating within human networks as means to evade us—those aren't Velkan tactics. But they *are* Serpents after all. Now that we're aware of their strategy, we've had success hunting them down. If the Jarl heeds my advice, he'll bleed human settlements to uncover Serpent agents and contacts. They'll give us information we want, or their homes will be razed, fields salted, and the Serpent collaborators will die just the same—humans have abused the freedom they've been granted. There are consequences."

"And how do you suggest we do that?" Etkis's tone was cautious.

"Commit to greater raids. More frequent, more firepower. If man abuses *our* steel, then they pay with *their* blood."

Etkis flashed to the raiders at the ranch. The one he murdered—his scared, grossly scarred face.

"What if humans are conspiring *because* of these raids? Pressure from the Wolves would chase them right into Serpent arms. If the Serpents have promised cooperation and ending raids, man's best interest is to support them. The steel, food, and lumber, they aren't ours—if they were, then we wouldn't pillage them!"

Rother's muted gray eyes contorted in confusion. His voice was devoid of any passion. "The ability to take is the power of ownership. Utilizing resources, without the power to retain them, is a privilege. Velka, the Wolves, we control every resource from Volthsheim to the shattered surface of Luna. Until our house is bested in the crucible of war, the right to own is ours alone."

Etkis sighed and rubbed the back of his neck. *Stubborn, intransigent, typical. When was I like that?* There was a time when Etkis knew an absolute certainty: the authority of the House of Wolves. Wolves had conquered Earth and Luna, charted more of the asteroid and Kuiper belts than any House, returned the Serpent genocide of the House of Stone in kind and given the forlorn Velka a home. Humans? They hardly existed. Their population sat below ten million. Nothing but an inconvenience that the House of Wolves tolerated. Their lives were a privilege. Like Rother's resources. Because even for Etkis, there was a time when he too thought that the power to take or protect, even a life, was ownership of the thing. The thing that is human life. Since he was a pup, he was barely conscious of their presence—like exotic birds that picked at green budding sprouts during the short weeks of summer and returned to their roosts far away, Etkis didn't know where, through the brutal months of winter. Whatever the species was before the Velkan advent, their legacy was a ruined biosphere and millennia of degradation and death. The slowest extinction of any animal on record. Etkis didn't care. Man didn't matter. *What changed?* Etkis asked himself, the answer clear. His memory flooded with images from the first time he met Dorin atop Luna's dunes. Droplets of his blood coagulated around motes of gray dust that fell so slow in a sixth of Earth's gravity, his right arm ravaged by beasts and a traitor's bullet in the shoulder. Still standing. *The bags under his eyes, the pain in his shoulder, phantom hands wrapped around his throat—he never left the Sea of Tranquility.* But Etkis couldn't help but feel a guilty twinge of joy for that day, the day his life changed. The first human he had ever met—his best friend.

Now? Now he was different. He felt it, so did everyone else. Rother, Tarkus, even Lady Nora. He saw it in their eyes. He lived in a social divide. Desired for his skill and body but little else. Velka wanted him for what he could do, not for who he was.

Tarkus will agree with Rother. He'll never sacrifice the security of his people for the autonomy of others. It's his duty as jarl. I understand. But the consequences will be the opposite of the intention, I'm sure. Lady Nora…perhaps she would listen? Tarkus would certainly hear me out but not listen. Nora has the temperament to understand and the reputation to make a difference.

"I disagree with your proposition. It's in our best interest to incentivize humans to work with us, rather than the Serpents. We cannot do that by tightening our grip. If we deliver on the promises made by the Serpents, ending raiding and protecting human caravans, then the risk of working with the Serpents will convey no more reward. They'll be willing to help us."

"Etkis…" Rother sighed and leaned back in his chair. "Do you know what a blood eagle is?"

"No…why?"

"It's an execution. Tie the victim, prostrate, and flay their skin from their back. Break and separate the ribs from the spine, with a cleaver or hatchet."

Etkis's stomach turned.

"Pry out the ribs and pull the lungs out from behind. At this point there's a small but nonzero chance the victim is still alive. Then the body is nailed to a board, and the lungs are spread like a pair of wings. The blood eagle is a human invention. I've seen it, deep in the backwoods. A man had stolen a horse."

"Rother, I…"

"Have you seen a man hung, drawn, and quartered?"

"No."

"The victim is hung by the neck from a length of rope, just long enough so they must stand on the tips of their toes but not enough to cause strangulation. They are vivisected, innards pulled through the incision. And then castrated."

"Castrated?"

"A human term for detaching genitals from a living man with a knife, scissors, again perhaps a hatchet. The torturer burns the bits in front of the victim to break what little remains of their will. And finally they are killed…laid flat on the back with ropes tied from each limb to a separate horse. And then the executioner starts the horses."

Etkis felt faint, his balance failed him, he had to sit down.

"What about a Catherine wheel?"

"That's enough."

"I've seen them all. Never by Velkan hands, although I'll make a point that I've seen it done to our brothers and sisters by *men*. You are young, new to your station. You spend your time with children and kindly farmers, to whom I've also extended protection—but I face what these people offer their kin and what they'd do in turn to us."

"We're not above reproach—we commit executions."

"We do, but it is logical, and with deference and respect. Even the greatest failures end with a bullet to the head or the opportunity of redemption through trial. But the humans? They make it long and demand suffering to relish in. And you think they torture the deserving? Murderers, rapists, traitors, and war criminals? The knife, the rope, the saw, it never ends there. They mutilate women for adultery. They torture heretics and deviants. They slaughter their own en masse by skin color, place of birth, and the gods they worship. There is nothing logical about it…it doesn't make any sense, Etkis. It's not just…the pain they inflict isn't justified by whatever crime could have been committed. When I was a recruit, I saw a village burn a human pup alive. Why? She was a witch, of course. She cursed their crops and the fields were fallow. It didn't occur to those *savages* that the Earth is made of *ice* and *crops fail*. They needed something, someone to blame. Did they hold their leaders accountable for stripping the soil, harvesting the largest foodstuffs, and leaving the smallest yields for next year's bounty? Did they search for new sciences or techniques to save their crops? No. They took that small, weak, innocent child and burned her skin black as she screamed for her mother. They chose a little girl *because* she was helpless. *Because it made them feel tall.*" Rother closed his ghostly eyes and clenched his fists. The memory was all-consuming, enthralling in its horror, a living monster that still visited him at night after years of waning empathy. In a single moment, Rother was again a pup, seeing the beauty of the world blighted and rotten. His voice trembled. He almost whispered, "I can still hear her screams, locked in my head." He opened his eyes, the ghosts now revenants, vengeful in their hate. "And you want to play with them, let them into our lives? Our walls? What will they do to *our* small, *our* weak, *our* innocent? I cannot imagine…you are a guardian, Etkis. It is why you were chosen to protect our people. I respect you for it. Truly, I do. But you want to protect the humans, and it is a mistake. You're a nearly three-meter-tall behemoth, Etkis. The reason you think so highly of these creatures is because they fear you. They're on their best behavior around the Wolf who could kill them with a single swing of the arm. But among the small? Humph. You cannot save them from themselves. You'll learn, just like I did because trust me, I tried. Their morals only stretch as far as convenience."

Etkis sat in silence, alien bile crept up his throat and tiny muscular convulsions shook his seat. Velka would kill. They'd kill for honor, for resources, by accident. Etkis had done more than his fair share; his trade was by definition violent. But he couldn't deny that when he collaborated with men, he inevitably left feeling…disturbed. There was always, *always* an incident where violence was taken too far. Nook's fingertips, ragged and flesh-torn, flashed in his mind. Fingernails ripped out by raiders and left pooling blood into the snow. He'd killed them not ten days ago. He was nauseous. His armor bore down on him and felt like a cuirass of lead. His shoulders crept toward the floor under the force of his pauldrons. He gripped his gun, and the Velkan hardwood creaked against his strength. Light cloth draped over his hand, and he looked down. The effigy the Roarers had made for him bounced against the length of his gun, arcing in motion with his twitching muscles. He reached out and held it—and stopped trembling.

"They have the capacity to be better if we give them the opportunity." Etkis faced the monitor again, his voice resolute. "All peoples are capable of wickedness, ours included. But give any Velka or human the chance to change and better themselves, they will." Etkis straightened his body. "Dorin has proven this many times. He is a better man now than he was when I met him. I'm better for knowing him, and so is the House of Wolves"

"Dorin is a viper, a *snake*," Rother said. His calm voice dripped with revulsion. "He has fooled you, the jarl, Lady Nora, and many others. He is not like you—he doesn't fight for justice and he doesn't use his power or privilege to protect. The bullets he fires, the lives he takes, are for his own perverse pleasure and to improve his position. He is a vain, spiteful creature devoid of honor. He'll shoot you in the back the moment it best suits him because *that's* what he's learned. Because *that's* the nature of his kind."

Etkis didn't respond immediately, not with words. Rother's instinct was to flee. A thousand millennia of evolutionary impulse screamed at him to find a dark hole, to hide and cower until some great archetypical predator had passed him by. Every synapse fired in agreement to take action, to invoke a fear response inherited from his earliest ancestors. He conquered the natural instinct before certain death and willed himself still.

"Are you willing to defend your insults, Rother?"

"You'd duel me over a savage?"

"If you'd kindly use his name. And yes. I would."

There was a leaden silence. Rother narrowed his eyes and shook his head. "You are first guard. You have as much authority to make proposals to the jarl as I do. If you desire to spoil your reputation for…for *Dorin*, and for his people, fine. I cannot stop you. But Tarkus will."

"I appreciate the advice."

Rother sighed, turned away from the monitor, and plugged a food cylinder into his filter. There was a gentle sound of *whirring* of organic matter passing through his helmet. When Rother was sated, he sat in thought, perturbed. The air was thick as concrete.

"Your mission was intelligence—I infer that 'Jarrod' provided?"

"He did, disconcerting information…you sent a team to Venus, yes?"

"The jarl ordered it."

"Have you heard anything peculiar?"

"The strangest thing is the climate: Venus is far drier than it was the decades before the travel ban. Climates don't change that quickly. Why?"

"Have they heard about a new jarl?"

"Of course not. If Xylon were dead, the Serpents would make a declaration to the other houses."

"Jarrod claims Xylon died two years back."

Rother tilted his head. "He's lying."

"I'm sure he isn't."

Rother's ears perked up. The shredded one twitched compulsively. He produced an electronic pad and stylus and began writing feverishly.

"If that's true, most of the Serpent's population are entirely unaware. I'm not sure what to make of it. What else did Jarrod tell you?"

"The new jarl is called Loka, but I've never heard her name before. Have you?"

"It's crossed my desk. She has a full crest, special, black operations. My counterpart. Very young, very capable—she has an unprecedented position for her age." Rother squeezed the stylus.

"Every scout took the same vow. No one will ever know of our feats; we live and die in the shadows of quiet shame and anonymity. Power is for the great and *the weightless.* My ilk and I could taint the entire house from the jarl's seat." Rother's gaze slipped away from the monitor. He stared at nothing. The full consequence of Loka's jarldom crept upon him. He whispered, "My entire scout family knows the chance that our deeds may weigh our spirits down, too heavy to journey with Okar through the ether. When Okar calls the spirit to join his voyage through the stars, the scouts bear the weight of iniquity so that the house may ascend. Loka—how could she? Her entire house could be ruined, tied down by her crimes. Okar would never accept such a heavy spirit as jarl. For *anyone* in our position to ascend as jarl is not merely unprecedented. It's horrific. And for no one to know?"

"It was not a typical succession. It was a coup."

Rother's gaze snapped to Etkis—his cold eyes collapsed, his visage waned, ears pressed flat against his head as if prepared for battle, breath shallow and quick. Etkis sat back. He'd never seen an expression by anyone from his home. Rother was looking at him like he was an enemy of the house.

Rother's voice was careful. His tone betrayed to Etkis that should he answer unfavorably, Rother would resort to violence. "Where in Okar's name did you hear that word?"

"Jarrod told me. It means—"

"*I know what it means.* Never say it again. If you introduce the idea of a coup, even passively, into the house, I will kill you in your sleep. And when I do, both our spirits will sink into Earth's molten core." He relaxed slightly. "Man's ideological cancer dies with us, Etkis."

Etkis felt a lump in his throat, afraid he'd been poisoned without knowing, "I'm sorry. I didn't...I understand. I thought it was just a word."

Rother scoffed. "A human word is never just a word." Rother dropped his head and his hand covered his visor. "I never wanted this for you, for anyone, really. I'm sorry. Now you share my weight."

Etkis had never known Rother to show sympathy or care, and this total change in decorum comforted and frightened Etkis in equal measure. He felt a sudden bond with Rother but one that filled him with dread. The bond of two brothers walking hand in hand into damnation. "There's something else," Etkis said. "Jormar is on Earth."

Rother dropped his notepad and stylus onto his desk with a loud thud. He leaned his head in his hands and swore viciously under his breath. "Oh, of course he is!"

CHAPTER 8

"And so, to declare his love, Okar commanded the void to pull the stars in a necklace for Treya, who held it aloft for all to see. Treya left Okar to wait for three galactic cycles before returning with an answer, and the god bore the stars around her breast in tender acceptance of Okar's love. The king bowed his head and embraced the privilege of his new reason for living."

—Velkan joining ritual, Odyssey of Stars, *Book of Inception*

"If I were getting Etkis a gift, it would be one of two things," Dorin said. He sat on the front porch of Jarrod's house and traced arcs in the air with his Velkan knife. Four scouts surrounded him. They hung on his every word. "Top of the list is a .5K kelvin sniper rifle, adjustable scope with interchangeable ballistic or energy-based munitions. In maroon if you can find it. Or red, always red with that boy. He spent an hour molesting the House of Waves first weapon-smith during the Summit of the Houses last year on Titan, that poor frightened man. Been trying to find one since."

Dorin put the tip of the knife to his lips and paused in thought. "Or triple-filtered inthol, honey base. Buy imported from the House of Blades on Mars—he'd never admit it to barkeeps in Volthsheim, but your house never quite figured out how to layer honey with the iodine, or so he tells me," Dorin said. The scouts nodded vigorously—gift giving was an important step in Velkan courtship. Toa rubbed her hands together compulsively. Dorin thought about little flies, rubbing their feet in nervous longing after landing near a sweet bun. Iyl, Vikor, and Yimir took notes on data pads. Iyl switched from daydreaming to writing to going back into her own little world cyclically. Vikor had the rifle on his pad's database, looking over his shoulder as if he were a hawk guarding his kill. Yimir counted his gold to see if either of the items were within his meager scout budget.

"Now remember, he's incredibly shy but equally sweet. The moment you approach him in the Great Hall, he may enter rigor mortis or he may scatter like a frightened puppy. A massive, *massive* puppy. Be patient and remain calm. He's infinitely more scared of you talking to him than the other way around. Patience and persistence are key. A food cylinder might help. If you've ever seen a farm-hand calm a horse with oats, you'll know what to do."

"Is it true you two killed a naga on Eris?" Iyl asked, her ears perked at attention. Dorin allowed himself a moment of satisfaction. He loved it when his and Etkis's exploits became legend.

"Killed? No. We *hunted* it—I tracked it beneath the surface with my *exceptional* skills and laid a trap of smoked rikle. When the Naga emerged, Etkis tackled it and wrestled it to the ground. It was incredible—the beast was five meters long, I tell you, and strong enough to crush a landship with a single stroke of its tail! It tried to hit Etkis, and it did, but he was stronger—he tanked the blow and suplexed the monster! It crashed onto the stone, dust everywhere, and he pinned it down with all his might. I wanted to kill it, take its skull as a trophy. But Etkis said no. He's softhearted that way. Once the beast calmed, submitted to his authority, he let it go. Victory was the only glory he needed. What a humble, *powerful* fellow he is." The four scouts muttered among themselves and Dorin buried a chuckle. *You're welcome, Etkis,* Dorin thought. *You may not die a virgin after all.*

"He cannot be that strong. It's impossible…isn't it?" Yimir asked. His fingers tapped the back of his data pad.

"Impossible for *you*, maybe. But you haven't seen him in action. That hole?" Dorin pointed over to where Etkis had broken into Jarrod's mansion. "You would think that was a breach charge or a concussion grenade, right?" They all nodded. "Wrong. Etkis ran into it, and it *exploded*."

Toa audibly moaned.

"Dorin!" Etkis peaked out from inside Rose and waved him over. "Time to go!"

"Coming!" Dorin turned back to his adoring crowd, whose eyes were bulging at their entering hero. "I know you all want to come too, but be patient. I've given you all the advice I can. This is only a chance for you. I can guarantee nothing! No one has succeeded in what you are attempting to accomplish, but maybe one of you will be the first. Maybe, soon, you will be *coming* with Etkis in a very different manner."

Toa moaned again.

"Thank you, Mr. Dorin, sir. We will never forget you! Thank you for this opportunity!" Vikor said with a vigorous handshake—Iyl shook Dorin's other hand at the same time. Yimir looked like he was going to cry over his gold purse. Its emptiness reflected his shattered hopes and dreams.

"No, no, thank *you*. Treya's blessing in your…endeavors. And Callva's speed, friends," Dorin said. He bounded over to Rose and shut the door behind him. He hustled over to the cockpit, threw his helmet onto his bed, and sat beside Etkis. His friend turned on the ignition, and the soft hum of the engine filled the room, and Rose lifted half a meter off the ground, the vents underneath kept it suspended off the earth. Dorin beamed at him. Etkis looked back suspiciously, but said nothing of it.

"We're going to Alexandria—are you all right with that?" Etkis asked.

Dorin exhaled and suppressed the urge to clench his jaw again. He stayed outwardly relaxed, with only the small scream inside his head. "Yep, I'm good. I had my moment. I'm good now. How's Rother? Still a *glob of spunk*?"

Etkis sighed, still perturbed. "Today, yeah."

"*Yes! Finally you understand!* What happened?"

"We…discussed our philosophical differences," Etkis said. "He wants to commit to more raids on the border. I suggested the opposite. We submitted our proposals to Tarkus. He and Nora will review both and discuss it."

"More raids make sense."

"Okar help me—not you too."

"I've made a lot of money off those raids, and if war is coming, then the house should stock up on food and raw materials. Besides, we know the Serpents are working with human gangs. A show of force will put them in their place." Dorin punched his hand for emphasis.

"Or strengthen their resolve to fight the tyrannical power stealing their gold, livestock, and harvests." Etkis leaned his head back on the seat, eyes closed, exhausted. "The logistics of the mission are the same. Same alibis, reporting under Rother, the works. Only now we have a lead, this Pompeii person. And we need to find out why and where Jormar is on Earth."

"*Jormar the Dragon.*" Dorin snorted. "A little dramatic."

"Velka give honorifics to members of other houses after they achieve a great feat. Jormar deserves that title, in a way…"

"What did Jormar do to earn something with that much pizazz?"

"He committed the genocide of the House of Stone on Mercury."

"Oh…" Dorin cleared his throat, unsure what to say. "Not what I'd call a 'feat,' exactly."

"It was a feat of fear. I remember when it happened. I was a pup. He broke their navy and rained solar fire down on the planet and turned the dirt to glass. Twelve million dead." Etkis took out a data pad and shuffled it to a photo of Tarkus standing before a kneeling Velka, before handing it to Dorin. Judging from the scale, Jormar was a little bigger than Etkis but much older, more like Tarkus. His magenta eyes glowed like a neon sign. They were a stunning color, yet Dorin felt disturbed. They seemed so quietly violent, kneeling before Tarkus seemed to physically hurt him. Jormar's ears were torn in different places, and parts of his fingers were missing. The Serpent sigil was emblazoned proudly on his chest plate, and the crown of horns that adorned his head denoted his status—first shipmaster of the Serpent fleet. "He is the worst of what my people have to offer…" Etkis said.

"What happened? After Mercury?"

"He followed the few Stones that remained when they sought sanctuary on Earth. Tarkus was only a fleet commander at the time, but he smashed Jormar on his way to Luna and drove him back to Venus—we received tribute from the Serpents, but they stopped paying after about a decade. No one's seen Jormar since that battle. We all assumed he'd been sent on a trial or outright exiled after his defeat. If he had won, I don't know if Earth would still be habitable."

"He came here? How do I not know about this?"

"There are a lot of things humans don't know."

"Fuck…where are the Stones now?"

"The survivors were adopted into the House of Wolves, they're either on Earth, Luna, or are voyagers in the asteroid and Kuiper belts. There aren't many of them—I've never met any, not one." Dorin handed Etkis back the data pad.

"If Tarkus defeated Jormar, what's his title?" Dorin asked.

"The Iron Wall."

"Lord. I don't have to call him that, do I?"

"Absolutely not! We never call our own by a title if they have them––it's egotistical."

Dorin scoffed. "Because sitting on a throne in the largest building on the planet is so modest."

Etkis put the data pad away. "If Tarkus went around Volthsheim calling himself 'The Iron Wall,' he'd sound like a complete unit! Even now that he's jarl, no one does it."

"When you get a title, I'm *only* going to use it. Once you capture Jormar, you'll be sure to be gifted with one! But more importantly, *I'll* get a title! Let's get going—where do we start once we get to Alexandria?"

"We find Rother's agent, Kya."

"Kya…" Dorin struggled to remember the name. "Oh piss, that's right! What's she look like?"

"You don't remember?

"A lot's happened since we left Volthsheim! I just need to remind myself."

"I'm surprised. She's pretty memorable."

Dorin snapped to Etkis, an evil smirk was on his lips. His eyebrows waggled suspiciously. "Really now?" His narrowed eyes and crooked, upturned smile filled the massive alien's stomach with an iron ball of anxiety. Etkis had long ago been conditioned to associate *that face* with plotting, scheming. From his perspective the plans made behind that mischievous expression came at the cost of Etkis's comfort and social dignity, and often involved the most terrifying of creatures: women.

Etkis side-eyed Dorin with a mixture of annoyance and panic. "Don't."

"I'm not implying anything, Etkis. Nothing. Nothing at all. Etkis, look at me." He did. "*Nothing at all.*" Dorin's lie was smooth; they generally were. But Etkis knew, and the iron in his gut stored itself for later.

Etkis rolled his eyes. "She's about your height, maybe ten centimeters taller." Dorin giggled—she was nowhere near his height. But since he was over two and a half meters tall, such differences in size meant little to Etkis. He continued, "Her helmet has a floral, swirling pattern of lines carved between her eyes and ears." Etkis drew a mock pattern over his helmet with his finger.

"What color are her eyes?" Dorin asked.

"Black with a white outline."

"You remember all that, huh?"

"Yes, it's my job!"

"Right. No other reason."

Etkis grunted and shuffled in his seat. The cockpit moved slightly. He slammed into reverse, and Rose lurched back so hard Dorin slammed into the dashboard.

"Agh, Etkis!"

"Seatbelt please," the Velka said dryly. He turned Rose around and glided down Lipel's only road. The engine blew snow behind them into large columns. They sped through the town, wood buildings blurring beside them, and made it to the forest within minutes. They sat in silence for a while as Dorin rubbed his bruised nose.

"You seemed to be having fun back there with the scouts," Etkis said in a misguided and desperate attempt to avoid another conversation about Kya or female prospects in general. "It's good to see you socializing! What were you all talking about?"

Dorin inhaled deeply, beyond pleased that Etkis's attempt to escape the frying pan had landed him straight into the fire. "Romance."

"Really? You?"

"I'm very romantic, thank you! When I walk by women, they swoon. Men *stiffen.* We talked about how to get noticed by someone you…admire."

"That's really sweet! I'm glad you're opening up, and…you didn't."

"Oh, but I did."

Etkis sighed. "How many?"

"Four. Toa too!"

"Really? Huh, I never would have guessed."

"I know, and it breaks my heart to know you're *this* stupid."

"I really wish you wouldn't do that." Etkis grumbled.

"Why not, you dense lug? I'm building the *legend*! The first guard, defender of the House of Wolves, hunter of the great Naga on the frozen asteroid Eris."

"The baby one? Adorable—nature is incredible!"

"No, no, I told them about a five-meter monster, which of course you wrestled to the ground."

"But that never...why would you tell them that?"

"Because no one's gonna froth their loins over you carrying a tiny lizard-monkey three klicks back to its nest. Besides, now they're *foaming* for you."

Etkis shuddered. "Stop it! Treya guide me this is humiliating!"

"Being hit on is embarrassing?"

"Yes! I don't know what to do...I just stand there and sweat like a swine-headed fool!"

"One day, if through nothing else but by sheer osmosis, you'll learn how to use my incredible charm, Etkis. I know it's difficult to match such astonishing charisma, but I believe in you. For now you can leech off me, my precious, romantically challenged remora. Oh yeah, there were a couple of males swooning over you too by the way."

"Really? Huh, that's flattering. *Wait, that means...*oh no, how do I tell them that I'm not...you know, interested?"

"I dunno. You should be open-minded, Etkis. You'll do great."

Etkis groaned in chagrin and gripped the steering wheel hard and the leather squeaked against his hands. He wallowed in a panic so uncomfortable he thought he'd enter a coma through sheer anxiety. Dorin silently cackled in the seat beside him. Etkis tapped on the wheel with his thumbs, nervous.

"Dorin, have you ever...like...I know you make jokes about it all the time, but have you ever...done...*that* with someone?"

"Done what?"

"You know..."

Dorin narrowed his eyes and scrunched his eyebrows, not entirely sure if he was really having this conversation, "Have I ever...fucked?"

"No, I mean se—wait!" Etkis snapped to Dorin, eyes wide, "Is that what that word means?"

Dorin cackled and slapped his thigh. "Fucking is sex, yeah! What did you think it meant?"

"I don't know! You use it in so many contexts, I've been confused for so long!"

"You could've asked me what it meant!"

"It seemed like it should be obvious…I didn't wanna seem silly."

"God—well yes, that's what it means, and yes, I've had *the sex*."

"Can you not…ugh, all right, well, what's it like?" Etkis asked, embarrassed at his own curiosity.

"Etkis, we're different species. I don't even know how Velka *FUCK*."

"Stop!" He begged. "I'm not asking physically. I mean, like, what's it *feel* like? To be with someone like that."

"Like plunging your pork sword into warm gruel. Tight gruel."

"Dorin, that's disgusting."

"But oh so satisfying…"

Reading Velkan facial expressions was tricky. The helmet covered everything, save for the long, wolflike ears. But a well-trained eye, Dorin's eye, would find all the information they needed from the undulating shape of their large expressive eyes. Etkis's eyes were squirming between disgust and shameful fascination.

"*I was serious*—never mind! Okar, you're so unhelpful."

"…I thought it was funny."

"I know you did."

The day was serene. No blizzards or storms—only the gentle sound of wind caressed the ship as it sped through forested tundra and ice-sculpted prairie. Dorin and Etkis took turns sleeping and driving. The last few days had finally caught up to them.

The sun set an hour ago. Etkis lay asleep in his bed. He'd removed his armor and wore only his environment suit and helmet. Dorin was at the wheel and rubbed his eyes to keep himself awake. Over the hill side, he could finally see it.

The lights stretched from the shore to the eastern "mountain range," piercing the night. Twisted monoliths of bent iron and torn metal let light through massive holes in their silhouettes that alluded to their true nature. Not mountains at all, despite what the locals called them. They were enormous ancient and broken starships. The mountainous corpses were human designs from a time when man held the resources to construct ships of such size and caliber. Built for a war between peoples that no one could remember. For reasons that died with them. The ships and their masters were a long time dead.

The great river Nodda, too large and swift to freeze, broke into many veins that snaked for kilometers inland. One of these veins flowed through the city and into the ocean. The tributaries would've been invisible in the darkness if it hadn't been for the reflection of orange lights dancing on the water. More lights blinked on the edge of the horizon beyond the city; boats large and small snaked back and forth and blinked in and out of existence in the rolling black. Buildings rose high from the banks of the river, to the center of the city over to the mountain range and encircled the salt-lake Vatriout just to the south. They merged with the silhouette of the dead ships. The full moon framed it all perfectly in cold, harsh silver. Overhead, shadows occasionally obscured the opulent moonlight. The dark blots came from starships that entered and exited the atmosphere and cracked the silence with supersonic shockwaves, all funneled through the city's spaceport on the other side of the mountain range—humanity's last connection to the stellar void. On land other vehicles—landships, speeders, and armored rovers—crowded the lanes into the city's ports. Headlights added noise in the cacophony of artificial stars. Faint flickering spread far along the meadows to the base of the hill that Dorin and Etkis were now on. The slums. Dorin's old home. The yellow, sodium glow looked sickly, like a pulsating infection.

They had made it. Alexandria. The last vestige of human power in the system.

Dorin gagged.

"Etkis, wake up. We're here. *Etkis!*"

Etkis woke up with a start and slammed his head on the base of the top bunk with a loud thud. "*Ugh, piss*, what did you say?" Etkis asked. He rubbed his head and staggered out of bed.

"We're here," Dorin said. Etkis hurriedly dressed himself in the civilian clothes that Rother provided. He pulled blue trousers, a green tunic, and a long brown coat with wool on the lining over his frame, with some difficulty. A golden tree with exposed roots sewn at the chest was stretched near to the point of bursting. The symbol of the Wolven merchants. Etkis fastened the fine leather boots to his feet and groaned as he stood up. Everything was too tight. The final addition to his garb was the Roarer's white doll. He tied the little white effigy to his belt. Etkis sat in the passenger seat beside Dorin and took in the sight.

"It's beautiful…" he said. "How many people live here?"

"When I was here, there were half a million or so Velka living here."

"Well, okay—and humans?"

"Five million. But it looks like the city's expanded. I don't remember most of this…refuse. Probably more."

"More than the rest of the planet! Amazing…"

"Mm."

The pair sped down the hill on Rose and came to the edge of the slums. Lanterns lit the front of brick and marble houses. The white stones were dull and pale compared to the pure white snow pleasantly yellowed by the firelight. Dirt-encrusted children ran amok in the street. They kicked a ball between themselves and laughed—the game distracted them from their screaming stomachs. The adults held a far different attitude––the gift of youth no longer distracted them from their inescapable poverty. They sat and leaned on their homes and smoked cheap cigarettes with a bottle or two in hand.

Rose stalled between the dozens of other vehicles journeying from the slums into the ports. They had made it deep into the slums and began to see small stands where poor merchants desperately peddled their wares. Molded fish, poached pheasants, and potatoes lined their stands. Some sold metal homewares such as pots and pans, while others peddled farm tools.

"Why is this part of the city so…poor?" Etkis focused on a child sitting on a dilapidated stoop with mismatched shoes and a coat far too large for him. His face was hollow, cheeks sunken in and nose blue. The only way he knew the child was alive was from an occasional cough that shook his body.

"What did you expect? A parade? These are the slums. It's always been like this. People who work with their hands, or those who don't work at all, live here. Small farmers, lunar miners, refugees."

"Refugees?"

"People fleeing from raids out in the wilds. If they lose too much, they'll come here."

"Oh," Etkis said. His chest tightened. "Why doesn't anyone help them? They need food, clothing."

"This isn't Volthsheim, Etkis. Why would anyone spend their pittance of time and money to feed people they don't know?"

"Civic duty?"

"That's funny," Dorin said, grim.

Etkis shook his head. He struggled to understand how humans allowed this happen to their brethren. Soon a revelation hit him. "Is this where you grew up?"

"Yeah. With my mom. Never knew my dad."

"What was her name?"

"...Sera," Dorin said. His lips curled, and he gritted his teeth together. He hadn't said her name in years. The image of a beautiful, tired woman with wavy black hair came to his mind. Hazel eyes. Freckles dotted her face. She had two scars, one on her eyebrow and the other on her jaw. Dorin never learned where she'd got them from—he had never wanted to ask. A lead weight lodged itself in his gut, and he squeezed his lips together.

Dorin made a hard right turn at the next corner, and a few pedestrians jumped out of the way to avoid being hit. They yelled justified profanity at the landship, and Etkis stuck his head out the window and shouted an apology behind them.

"Dorin! What are you doing?" The Velka asked.

"I have to make a stop."

It had been years and hundreds of empty bottles since Dorin had been down these roads, but he made each turn without hesitation or confusion. The old memories had soured, but they guided him to exactly where he wanted to go. He turned off the ignition and opened the door. Dorin had one foot out of the ship when Etkis stood up to leave as well. Dorin spoke without turning.

"Do me favor, Etkis—stay here," Dorin said.

"Are you sure?"

"Yes," he said without warmth or pause.

Dorin hopped out. He turned the corner and stood before a line of identical brick houses broken by a single gaping grave. The brick remained scorched but intact. It had trapped the heat and made the entire building a furnace. All the other elements had collapsed years ago, some during the fire and some after. The door had been stripped by looters long ago. Dorin walked through the bare threshold and looked at the scene with fresh eyes.

Pale blue light poured into the hovel from holes in the brickwork, the open doorway, smashed windows, the collapsed ceiling. Dorin could see his breath in the early night chill. His old home was far smaller than he remembered. The stairs jutted nearly straight up, and the kitchen and living room had no clear beginning and end—there was no delineation between the two in the wreck. The second story had caved in during the fire. Splintered black wood was scattered on the floor. Snow had dropped through the uncovered windows and the holes in the ceiling. It mixed with the aging soot to paint a fluffy black tapestry within the hovel. Dorin shuffled past the wreckage in the center of the room to the fireplace. He knelt and shoved the ashen snow aside to look at the scars on the floor. The heart of the fire. He saw plainly where the log had fallen out, where the flames had begun. Nothing had changed. No one had the time, money, or desire to rebuild here. To heal it. To bury it.

He had seen what he'd wanted to. All that remained was to look for what he didn't want to find. He was less than a meter away from the answers to a question he didn't want to ask but couldn't refuse to let lie. He walked over to the wreckage in the center and threw aside enormous panels of wood with ease as they crumbled in his metal grip. The pit in his stomach was drawn from a black premonition. Dorin sought an answer that he already had, one that he knew in his heart the moment the charred building came into view. Each piece of debris he cleared only dug this pit deeper and deeper into his body, until it became a nauseating borehole in his gut. He vomited. A charred and broken bone lay on the floor.

Dorin screamed, stood, and paced. He punched the wall. His human hand tore against the brick, and his steel fist pulverized it into powder. Two circles, one of blood and one of shattered stone, hung on the wall. He couldn't breathe. Tears rolled down his face. His hands trembled, and he shook them to regain control. He drew Soot and pulled the hammer down and reset it. He tried every tool in his arsenal, but the panic didn't abate. He couldn't keep standing. Dorin fell, and Soot crashed through a charcoal pile of detritus. He couldn't breathe. He couldn't stop crying. He held his head in his hands and begged for it all to stop.

"Dorin?" Etkis asked timidly. He had stuck his head inside the house to look for his friend. When he saw Dorin on the floor, he rushed to his side and held him. The tiny figure writhed as he clutched him closer. Dorin tried to scream, to yell at his friend, but hardly anything came out through his sobs. He slammed his fists in a feeble resistance of his friend's embrace.

"I…I…I t-told you…t-to stay…"

"I know, I'm sorry…" Etkis whispered. The Velka was still, arms around Dorin, and eventually the little will Dorin had to be angry eroded away. He stopped trying to push Etkis away and just cried. He had nothing left.

The silver light and shadows changed their lengths while they stayed there. Dorin regained his lucidity. His voice was hoarse from crying.

"She's…she's still here," he whispered. Etkis perked one ear in confusion. "Will you help me?" Etkis saw the small bone in the debris.

"You don't have to ask," he said.

Etkis helped Dorin stumble to his feet. The man swayed with his head sagging and walked with his feet barely lifting off the ground. Etkis was scared that his friend couldn't even support his own weight, but they trudged on nonetheless. Dorin got a shovel from Rose as Etkis cleared the flooring. Etkis found every scattered piece and set them to the side with the greatest respect he could muster. Dorin tried to dig but could only impotently scratch at the bare earth. His body had no more strength left to offer him. Etkis helped Dorin to the corner where he could sit. The Velka took the shovel and dug a swift and deep crater in the center of the house. He placed each individual bone in the hole and filled it back up with the icy soil.

Etkis walked over to Dorin and wiped the dirt off his trousers and took a deep breath. He was unsure what to say. "I...I don't know how this works for humans. Do you say something or—"

"Let's just go," Dorin muttered. "This was a bad idea."

Etkis saw Dorin rub his forehead, purse his lips, tighten his grip on the steering wheel. He had offered to drive, but Dorin had insisted otherwise. "I need the distraction," he had said. From that point on, he hadn't said anything. They spent hours in traffic, moving a few meters every twenty minutes or so. Etkis considered for a moment to ask about Ashton but thought better of it.

"I never met my parents—did I ever tell you that?" Etkis asked. Dorin didn't take his eyes off the road.

"Once or twice, but you never said what happened to them."

"Nothing happened, or at least I don't think so. When Velka are born, we're nursed in a hospital with an artificial atmosphere for years. We don't allow parents into the hospitals––logistically it's too difficult because the atmosphere has to be so strictly maintained. We learn and play in the hospital, and we're only released when we're big enough for suits. It's a big deal, your first suit. It's your first step to becoming a part of the house. I remember mine. The nurse told me how proud of me she was. I didn't know her name. I had never met her before. She just said that to every pup as they left the hospital. After that we either go straight to preliminary training programs, like boarding school, or our parents take us in. But I'd never met them and they'd never met me. I was seven...they would've been strangers."

Dorin furrowed his brow. "They were still your parents. They didn't even want to meet you?"

"Some do. They make the effort and build a relationship, but I think it's different from humans and their parents. There's that disconnect of not...I don't know. Maybe I'm talking nonsense. My parents never made that choice, so how would I know? Most Velka choose to focus more on their duties to the house than raising children. Velka pups are given a family tree as soon as we can read, but that's the most familial contact we get during those early quarantine years. I have no siblings. My parents are named Astra and Nonim, I think, voyagers in the asteroid belt. I have one cousin named Vitor—he's a builder—and I'm distantly related to the Velka who invented inthol. That's all about my family I've ever known."

"Quite the legacy…have you ever tried to meet your parents?"

"Once, right after I got flagged for military training. I was on my first training mission, and I was in a unit with this Velka named Triti. She was a few years older than me, but we always had the same path. I followed her through basic, secondary, and finally military, like what you'd call a sister. She looked out for me, taught me the ins and outs, protected me when I got picked on."

Dorin finally looked at Etkis, a surprised expression on his face, "*You* got bullied?"

"Ha, constantly! Like a fisherman pummeled by a gaggle of geese!" Etkis said, a smile in his eyes. Dorin laughed––Velkan idioms were always far more fun than the drag human equivalent. It was the first time he had smiled since they had arrived in Alexandria.

"I wasn't always big, Dorin, but I was always different…anyway, I was in the unit with Triti, conducting a training exercise outside of Volthsheim, and we were caught dead in the open by a group of human villagers. They thought we were raiders, I think, and they opened fire while we were eating. Most bullets can't pierce Velkan armor, the gaps in the armor, sure, but that's not usually fatal. But Kior has a cruel sense of divine irony. Triti took a bullet straight through the visor and out the back of her skull. She died instantly."

Dorin chewed on his tongue, unsure of what to say. Etkis closed his eyes and slowed his breathing. His voice was heavy and labored. "We killed all the villagers, down to the children. Even those that didn't attack, the ones that hid in their homes. I remember their begging and crying when we burst down their doors. I'll always regret that. How we…how *I* lost control. We came back to the city, burned our dead, and went on. The next day it was the same classes, the same routine. I felt like I was the only one who noticed she was gone. Angry, scared, and lost. I didn't have anyone, no one to look after me anymore, no one I loved. I decided I wanted to see my parents."

"You don't need someone to look after you, Etkis. You're very independent," Dorin said. His misguided compliment landed flat.

"I didn't need someone to look after me...I wanted connection. I thought I could blame them. Or maybe I thought they could replace her? I just wanted to do *something*. Only Lady Nora and Tarkus have current deployment records...so I broke in. Lady Nora caught me red-handed shifting through their files. Okar help me, I was ashamed. She just talked to me, asked me what I was doing. I screamed at first, then I cried. Humph, I swear Tarkus would've killed me if Nora hadn't calmed him down."

"Did you at least learn where they were, your parents?"

"No, Astra and Nonim are quite common names. I didn't even know what to look for...I was just rifling through papers. Velka choose their surnames when they enter their profession so it's not familial. A lost cause in the first place. But Lady Nora started checking up on me after that. She came to my marksmanship competition, to my military termination ceremony. She saw me off on my pilgrimage, where I met you. After you and I pranced around the system for a year, she offered me the squireship to the jarl. I admire her. I look up to her. She's my friend and my mentor...but I know it's not quite what you had. I'm...curious about her, your mother."

Dorin said nothing. His jaw hurt from holding in the memory. He squeezed the wheel and the shredded skin on his knuckles bled anew. Etkis spoke softly.

"I'm sorry...I can't imagine. But I'm also happy for you, Dorin. You had something most of my people will never have. You had a family, one who loved you. And she'd be proud of who you are now."

"Family isn't just who you're born with Etkis. It's also a choice."

CHAPTER 9

*Nearly every culture in every era in history developed alcohol
of some kind. Why? To escape? To cope with the fragility of our
lives? 'Course not! It's because booze is fucking delicious!*

—UNKNOWN, RECORDING FROM AN ALCOHOLICS ANONYMOUS MEETING, 12.31.1099

They spent the rest of the drive in relative silence. Etkis became more upset at the poverty of the slums. Soon he stopped staring out the window altogether. Dorin stared straight ahead. He didn't give the starving populace a second glance. Eventually they managed to park in the Alexandrian port, just outside of the slums. Beyond the port stood the merchant's quarter, the lower middle class of the city, which connected to the wharf. Dorin put Rose in park, but before he could move, he felt a heavy weight on his shoulder. Etkis's hand gripped him.

"Are you sure you feel ready for this? We can take a day, just let Rother know we arrived tomorrow?"

"Etkis, you don't need to worry about me. I'm fine," Dorin said. A lie, of course, but Etkis had begun to learn the human decorum of leaving such obvious falsehoods alone. The Velka clenched his jaw and nodded.

Dorin smiled, his forced body language alarmed Etkis. He saw through the holes in the mask. After all, he lived his whole life behind one himself. "I'd rather just get to it," Dorin said. "The sooner we finish, the sooner we leave."

Dorin patted Etkis on the back and hopped out of the cockpit. Etkis lumbered after him. Dorin loaded Soot, holstered it, and was halfway out the door when he noticed Etkis staring at his gun wall, paralyzed by indecision. Dorin sighed and sat down on the doorframe. This always took forever.

"What about the Elo rifle I got back in Volthsheim? It has a really nice weight to it, and it has a solid range."

"Etkis, we're going to be in buildings and alleys. What range do you need? You don't have *any* pistols?" Dorin asked. He snagged his helmet off his bunk and played with it absently, inspecting the scratches he had earned in the short time since he'd gotten it.

"I do, but their sights are all finicky, and I'm not as good at shooting from the hip as you are. *Oh*, we should go to the blacksmith while we're here! Wouldn't that be fun? I want to see some human wares!"

"They're called weaponsmiths here, and sure, if you want."

"The shotgun feels like too much. Is it too much?"

"It's *fine*. Just pick something!"

"Well, there's this DE rifle I've been meaning to use. It makes a dark energy laser that…ah, no, I might hit someone else. Okay, the Elo shotgun!"

"Thank fu—"

"No, no, definitely too much."

"*Ugggggggggh!*"

"What about the gravity gun? It saved us back with the Roarers, and it's so pretty! Oh, but wait, we might be indoors. No."

Dorin bonked his head in frustration on the doorframe. He looked out the door into the lot they'd parked and searched up and down the roadway. Travelers lived out of their vehicles and were parked as far as he could see. Many had set up fires in front of their mobile homes, cooked fish and jabbered on about their journeys. But try as he might, Dorin couldn't find a single lawman wandering the lot. He had expected Alexandria's poor excuse for a police force to come and at least inspect them before allowing them to stay in the squalid district, but no one had come. Not even the Alexandrian deputies. *The standards have *somehow* fallen.*

"How are we supposed to find this contact of yours?" Dorin asked.

"Rother will send us a message with her location within the hour, standard. She has to stay inconspicuous. For *some reason* she doesn't want two heavily armed persons strolling up to her front door…what about the current rifle? If I turn the voltage down, I can reduce any collateral damage."

"*Sure! Just take it, please!* I need a drink."

"Oh, no, liquified people are a health hazard in a city this dense."

"More of a health hazard than *regular* death?"

"Of course! Much harder to clean. Someone might slip."

"Jesus God."

"*Oh, I know!*" Etkis knelt down and reached under his bed. He pulled out a massive Velkan hatchet and dagger. Dorin's insecurity squirmed at the sight. A dagger and tomahawk to Etkis were a sword and battle axe to Dorin. Both had the signature blue line following their bladed edges, which the Velka were so famed for. The dagger had a jet-black pommel and a brown wood grip with depressions carved in for fingerholds. Etkis slid it into a black sheath attached to his thigh. Just like Dorin's, the clan sigil was carved in silver at the center of the sheath. The hatchet was surprisingly intricate. Runes ran up and down the length of the wood, and a stretch of black leather framed the base. An intricate carving of a shooting star followed the blade's length. Dorin wondered if he had the strength to swing it at all.

"Since when have you had those?" Dorin asked.

"It was an impulse buy from last year, a gift for myself when I became first guard, but I've regretted it ever since! I never thought I'd use them. This is great!"

"You know a *gun* might be nice."

"This is perfect! I can have these and then get a new human weapon tomorrow at the blacksmiths——I mean, weaponsmith. *Ah*, I'm so excited!"

"Three weapons, and you thought the shotgun was too much. Can we please go get a drink now?"

"I'm ready. Let's—"

The console in the cockpit beeped loudly and a bright white light flashed from the monitor next to Rother's call sign.

"*Are you kidding me!*" Dorin shouted. "No, no, no, no, nooooope, we are getting a drink before we meet this lady. I cannot walk through these streets sober."

"Have you ever considered that drinking to cope with your issues might not be healthy?"

"Literally never. Come on, let's go."

"Sorry, Dorin."

"Why do you hate me?"

Etkis scoffed and rolled his eyes. He lowered the tomahawk to his side and the magnets in his belt snagged onto it with a loud *clank*. He walked over to the console and opened the file while Dorin was opining on the advantages of having one or two drinks before a firefight.

"It calms the nerves, improves confidence and performance in many ways. Especially when *courting* Etkis. Toa met you for twelve seconds and was ready to do shameful things to your body. We'll spend days with this lady! Can you imagine the sexual passion you'd inspire in Kya with a little liquid luck? Believe me, Etkis, sobriety is the enemy."

Etkis waved a hand dismissively.

"Please, Etkis, liver damage calls to me!"

"…Huh. Looks like you'll get that drink after all—Kya wants us to meet her at a bar."

Dorin tossed his helmet on the bed and quietly pumped his fist. "I like her already."

"*This* is the place?" Dorin asked. He couldn't believe his luck. They stood in front of a bar. A dive, in every sense of the word. Loud rabble came from within. Occasional shouts and smashing glass rang through the open windows and the saloon doors. A drunkard unzipped his fly and leaned on the wall with his forehead and stared down as the urine pooled on his boots. "Bella" hung above the terrace in neon lettering.

"Looks like it." Etkis said. Three men with guns walked into the bar and cast a look his way. He waved meekly, and they spat on the ground. "Friendly crowd. Not what I expected from one of Rother's agents."

"It's beautiful…" Dorin said, grinning from ear to ear. A nugget of nostalgia welled within him. "Etkis, humanity deserves to be collectively shot—but this is the one thing they've achieved above your people. A dive bar is the single greatest place on Earth."

They walked in, but Etkis had to turn sideways to fit and still scraped paint off the doorframe. The wood caught and tore a small hole in his new tunic. Etkis groaned. *No one will notice another mild degradation in this…establishment,* he thought. The dive was larger than the outside suggested but was still cramped. Their feet stuck to the floor, and the pungent smell of cheap liquor and cigarette smoke leaked from the walls and tables. A poker game went on in the corner, with a clear loser. He stood in a rage, hand at his hip, breaking the cardinal rule of gambling. A woman beside him pistol-whipped him in the face, smooth and practiced. Blood splattered along the table, adding to the tapestry of dried fluids marring the green fabric, and he fell to the floor unconscious. The other poker players pounced on him; his breach made him fair game, and they took whatever money he had left on him. The woman collected her winnings and ran out of the bar. She bumped into Dorin on her way out. The other players stripped the unconscious man of his clothes. His leather jacket and boots would fetch a decent price over in the slums.

The bartender was half-asleep. He drifted from staring at the wall and pouring drinks. Only the frequency of requests kept him awake. Two Velka sat at opposite ends of the bar, a male and female. They drank a bubbling orange liquid Etkis had never seen before. Dorin began to walk over to the female Velka.

"What are you doing? That's not her," Etkis whispered.

"It's not? Her helmet has the same patterns—"

"No, it doesn't, what are you talking about? Kya's helmet has lily patterns. Those are daffodils."

"Been staring at her photo a lot, huh?"

Etkis scrambled for words in his defense. "Lilies are a beautiful and distinct flower! Six petals, star-shaped. Although hers only have five petals…"

"Such detail."

"I love botany, and I won't apologize for it."

The female turned her head to reveal her blue eyes—Kya had black eyes with a stark white outline.

Dorin clicked his tongue, "Piss, you're right. Then where is she?" He looked around but saw no other Velka in the joint. Two patrons started a fight at a table. Broken glass flew in the air and plinked off Etkis's helmet and he wondered how the bar could pull a profit at such consistent loss of tableware.

"I don't—"

The back door of the bar burst open, and out came a Velka dam holding a burly bearded man by the hair. She slammed his head against the blood-soaked poker table with her long pistol pushed against his temple. She wore a long leather duster coat, metal pauldrons on her shoulders, and a worn tunic with silver trim peaked out from her coat. The image of a gold coin was woven into the tunic, the symbol of the Volthsheim bankers, the exchequers. Only one coin, the lowest rank. Cotton pants and leather boots strapped to her feet. Her garb screamed both human and Velka.

"Now, what do you say, Laurence?" the dam asked, a gentle rasp in her voice.

"I—I'm sorry, ma'am!" he said. Tears streamed down his bruised and swollen face. He had taken a massive beating.

"That's good, Laurence! Now, are you going to see Natalie again tonight?"

"No, no, ma'am!"

"Are you *ever* going to see her again?"

"N…" He hesitated, just slightly. The Velka slammed the butt of her pistol against his hand. Etkis could hear the tiny cracks of his bones over Laurence's screams. "*Fuck, Kya!*" he shouted. She hit him again, and his squeals turned to whimpers.

"Hey, Etkis, you think that's her?" Dorin asked.

"Mhmm," Etkis squeaked back.

"What was that?" Kya asked Laurence smoothly.

"N-n-n-o, ma'am, I ain't never gonna see her again!" Laurence said.

"And what happens if you do?" She twisted his hair and he winced bitterly.

"You're gonna cut off my bits and throw them in a fire!" He wailed.

"That's right! Sizzling like cocktail weenies on a barbeque. Good, Laurence." She hoisted him off the table, let go of his hair, and holstered her pistol. "Glad we have an understanding." She dusted him off. He remained paralyzed in fear as she brushed her hand along his vest, and he winced with every gentle swipe of her hand. "Get home to your wife. I'm sure Abby misses you."

"W-what do I tell her?"

"The truth, I imagine, unless you want two beatings tonight."

"Yes, ma'am." Laurence limped off cradling his broken hand and blood pouring from his nose. He scuttled past Dorin and Etkis without a word.

"Friends!" Kya shouted from across the bar, Dorin and Etkis turned to her in shock. "So glad you could make it! Mac—*Mac!*" The bartender shot up with a jolt, his tired eyes entirely attentive. "Get my friends here something to drink, put them on my tab. Come on, I've got a table!" Dorin and Etkis shuffled over to her side of the bar and looked for an empty table. There were none. Kya walked over to a large booth. A greasy man in a white coat was accompanied by two beautiful young women and two muscular men with guns at their hips. The man in the coat smiled grossly, and his eyes and hands darted up and down the ladies' frames. The ladies smiled back in kind. They were well paid to hide their disgust.

"Beat it, Phil. I got business," Kya said to the greasy man.

"Kya!" Phil's smile vanished. His greasy face turned red. "This, uh...this ain't the best time."

"Don't start talking to me about time, Phil. You're already a week late, and my generosity is wearing thin. Get out and get my money, or you'll have a bullet-sized problem in your head. I hope these ladies double as doctors."

He nodded, sweat dripped from his double chin, and his posse filed out of the booth. One of his bodyguards, a scarred, huge black man with platinum teeth, smiled at Kya. "Hey, lady! How you doin'?"

"Vern!" Kya responded. They shook hands and gave each other a warm hug. Kya continued, "Sorry I didn't see you! How's Maria?"

"Ah, she's good, thanks. Took her first step this week!"

"*No*—really? Congratulations! Sorry I gotta bust you out like this. Have some business I need to take care of."

"Ah, it's all good, K. I know how it is."

Phil cast a vile glance at Vern and grumbled something under his breath. Kya snapped to him, hands on her hips.

"*What was that, Phil?*" Kya shouted.

"N-nothing, ma'am!" Phil said in a panic.

"That's what I thought. Scram, you ogre. Hey, Vern, give my love to Carmen!"

"For sure. She's still waiting for you to come over for dinner."

"I'll find some time. See you later, Vern."

"See ya, K." They waved goodbye, and Vern left behind the rest of his posse. Kya sat down, put her arms over the seat, and closed her eyes and sighed deeply, her ears splayed out sideways, and she relished for a moment in the comfort. Etkis and Dorin still stood like idiots, no idea what to do or say about what they had just seen. One of Kya's ears perked up, she didn't hear them sit down. She opened her eyes and pointed to the booth opposite her. Dorin and Etkis sat down––the table leaned toward Kya as Etkis's chest pushed against it. Dorin was smushed a little against the wall to make enough room for Etkis.

"Ahem…hello, my name is Etkis, this is Dorin. Pleasure to meet—"

"So good to see you both again! What are you doing in town?" Kya said loudly. Etkis looked at her confused.

The bartender came over with two cylinders, a shot glass and a bottle of bourbon. He set them on the table.

"Um…looking to buy some metals for Volthsheim? Right?" Etkis looked to Dorin for confirmation, but he was busy chugging straight from the bottle, the shot glass untouched. The bartender turned and left. They were alone. Kya leaned in and kept an eye on the rest of the bar to ensure their privacy.

"Sorry about that," she whispered. "It's better we already know each other. You two are old friends of mine from the city, you're just making a social call while you're here on business. I happen to know some contacts that you can talk to, copper, steel, titanium, the works. I'm your middleman, so you'll be seeing a lot of me. That's how the front of this operation goes—got it?"

Dorin laid down the bottle. "Sure thing," he said through a smile, followed by a contented burp.

"Good…so hi, I'm Kya, good to meet you. Etkis and…Dory, right?"

"*Dorin*. You have terrific taste in bars, by the way," Dorin said with a quick glance around the establishment.

"I had something to take care of here first."

"No, no, I mean it. The *ambience* reminds me of nights I can't remember." Dorin looked at the fresh stain of blood on the poker table. "And we saw," Dorin said with a laugh. "I thought you were a banker?"

"I am—doesn't pay as well as you'd imagine." Kya leaned on the table, eyes on the rest of the bar. Her expert eyes scanned for any prying ears. "'Each according to their ability, each according to their needs', or however it goes. But sometimes your need is greater than Volthsheim exchequers calculate, so here I am, earning a living wage."

Dorin put his foot up on the booth seat. "What are you, some kind of PI?"

"Independent contractor."

"Good for keeping a low profile."

"Humph. In this city, it's the Velka no one knows who are suspicious." She scratched the back of her ear and stretched her neck. Dorin thought she must have been awake for far too long. She continued, "What does Rother want?"

"He hasn't told you?" Etkis asked, surprised.

"The *gremlin* doesn't tell me anything," Kya said, annoyed. Dorin smiled and added the insult to his mental list of adjectives for Rother. At that moment Kya's ears flipped up and back against her head, her body tensed, and her head turned at a subtle angle. "What is this? Another checkup?" she asked, suddenly defensive. "...Why's he sending the first guard and a human hitman to talk to me? I sent him the manifest, so what's the problem?"

Etkis had one ear up and the other out. He turned to Dorin, who took another swig of bourbon, and back to Kya. "Um...nnnnno," he said, confused. "We have no idea what you're talking about—what checkup and what manifest?"

"Don't screw with me. You expect me to believe that? Look at you two—like this isn't some sort of message."

Dorin plopped the bottle back on the table. "Rother didn't pick us, Tarkus did. You'd think I'd play lapdog to that"—he scrolled down the mental list—"pissant?" Kya chuckled, but no tension left her shoulders. She was still tightened like a spring. Dorin continued, "We're not here to hurt you, so just calm down. Stow yours and I will mine, deal?"

Etkis looked at Dorin, not understanding, then peered under the table. Both Kya and Dorin had their guns drawn, still low at the hip, aimed at the other's nethers. Kya mulled over the proposition and holstered the gun. Dorin did the same.

"Okay. Pocketed," Kya said.

"Do we look like hitmen?" Etkis asked, his honor lightly bruised.

"Not at all," she quickly said to Etkis, then turned to face Dorin. "Just you, Dory. No hard feelings. Torn clothes, five o'clock shadow, metal arm to boot. And you seemed as at home in a grungy saloon as the rest of us thugs. Anyone grinning that wide to be in a place like this isn't exactly a person of well repute." Dorin smiled and raised his bottle. Kya scoffed—it wasn't meant as a compliment. She took a deep breath and scanned the bar again. No one was listening, she was sure. "What's this about, then?" she asked, her tone less violent.

"This is about the House of Serpents," Dorin said.

Kya's ears perked up in attention, her eyes widened, and her fingers scraped the table into a fist.

"Tell me everything."

"Okar piss on their graves!" Kya muttered and slammed her fist on the table. Etkis winced at the blasphemy. Kya whispered, half to herself, half to the duo across from her. She was hunched over the table. "Pompeii, huh? Piss. What else did Jarrod tell you?"

"Jormar is on Earth," Etkis said.

Kya shot up with her hands pressed against the table. "*What?*"

"Jormar may be the impetus behind this campaign against our house on Earth. Jarrod said he saw him at Pompeii's compound."

"That can't be right..." Kya took a long chug of her drink and the orange liquid drained to half. She dropped her head into her free hand, her fingers covered her visor. She shook her head, her brain abuzz with thought and alcohol. "Explains a few things. Pompeii's been hiring every able body he can find, but no one seems to know why. I thought it was just protection in case Tarkus ever wanted to raid Alexandria itself, but a two-pronged attack makes more sense. No army of men and women with rifles and pistols could stop a Caelicraft's gravity cannon—but a coordinated assault between them and Serpent forces? A true threat." Kya drank again, and the liquid fire took the edge off. She slowed her breath. "Location's easy. Pompeii owns the city and wants everyone to know it. His compound is east of the mountains, beside the spaceport. Hopefully the reasoning behind the convenient placement of his base and the spaceport is obvious. We have a couple of options—go in loud or quiet. I'll let Rother know the location, but if we go in with strike teams and shock troops, we could be walking straight into a trap. Half the city could burn, and Jormar and his Serpents may still escape through the spaceport. That's our last resort. The better option is we're invited inside and can confirm Jormar's presence and cripple their defenses. *Then* we call in the Wolves. Dorin, you're our ticket in. First things first, we find a contact of Pompeii's—not too hard, they're everywhere, but they're awful choosy about who they invite into the compound. I'll mention Dorin is looking for work. You'll have to get their guard down somehow."

Dorin nodded, head tilted back while he milked the last morsel of bourbon out of a half-liter jug.

"What about me?" Etkis asked.

"You're confirming Dorin's cover. He's your guide through the city. You're a dumb, helpless drone who has to do shopping for Volthsheim. Seem easy?"

"Well, when you put it like that…but what about when the operation starts?"

"I imagine you'll lead the strike teams when Dorin calls us in, but that's up to Tarkus. Until then you're just a Volthsheim merchant looking to buy some garbage human wares so you can take them back home to make quality materials. Be condescending, people will buy it more."

Etkis's ears flattened in concern and panic—Dorin snorted beside him and nudged his friend with his elbow. Dorin chugged again.

"If we pull this off, we can burn out this invasion before it ever starts," Kya said, her voice resonant with hate and pride. She chugged what little remained of her drink and ordered another. She moved to drink again but stopped, her gaze unfocused. "If we fail…let's not think about that."

Etkis said nothing. He'd never failed an operation before. He'd hardly failed anything before that didn't involve his incompetent courtships. He looked to Dorin for comfort or support and could only scowl as his friend collapsed with his forehead on the table. The freelancer forced his head up, and he swayed as though on the bow of a ship in a storm.

"Right, let's go, then. Get this over with. The train for the"—*hiccup*—"for the spaceport runs every hour. We can still catch the next one."

Kya squinted her eyes. "What are you on about? You can't just go to Pompeii's compound. We have to build your cover first, and that alone will take a week."

Dorin burst into laughter and slapped the table, and everyone in the bar looked their way. Both Kya and Etkis reeled in alarm, though the former in a far more hostile manner.

"You're adorable, Kya—"

"Excuse me?"

"But I'm not spending weeks here, lady. You do what you like, but I'm going straight there." Dorin tried to stand to leave but swayed and sat back down. Kya stuck her finger in Dorin's face but recoiled when he tried to bite it. She grabbed him by the collar and brought him nose to nose over the table.

"Listen, you prick, you do something *that* stupid, and this whole operation goes up in flames, but more importantly to me, my life will too. I live here. This is my home. I have a lot of friends and loved ones around Alexandria, and if you put me in danger, you put them in danger, and that I won't allow. If you jeopardize this operation, I'll put a bullet in you myself, and I doubt Rother will put up much of a fuss."

Dorin grabbed Kya's hand with his right, and the steel strangled her grip loose. She winced in pain, and the two locked eyes. Dorin's drunken gaze had an uncomfortable sharpness to it, a learned adaptation to killing and surviving too often with more alcohol than blood in his system. Kya returned the fury in kind and placed her hand on her pistol and could sense he did the same.

Etkis put his hand on Dorin's shoulder, a polite but immovable request to de-escalate. Dorin scowled through a burp and side-eyed his friend. Etkis spoke softly. "I agree with Kya. It's a better plan. Patience is key, and it's been a long time since you've been here. She knows Alexandria better than either of us, and that includes how to approach the leadership here."

Dorin tsked and let Kya go. Her ears perked in surprise––she didn't expect the man to back down so easily. She looked at Etkis. What did someone have to do to hold such respect and influence over another? Kya leaned back in her seat and put both hands on the table. An offering of peace. Dorin didn't acknowledge it, but she was sure he noticed. He drank the last dregs of his bourbon and slapped it on the table.

"I'm gonna need another bottle…" Dorin said, barely intelligible.

"Piss off, you're gonna bankrupt me," Kya said, annoyed.

Etkis grumbled. "I'll pay for it. I promised I'd buy you a drink." He fished around one of his pouches for some gold coins and gave them to his drunkard friend.

"Ah, thank you, Etkis, you're a treasure." Dorin slurred his words. He stood on the booth seat to be eye level with the Velka. He hugged Etkis's head. "You big hunk of…meat." Etkis began to speak but chose to say nothing. Before he could move to let Dorin out of the booth, the man clambered over him to escape the table. He tripped over his own feet and fell face-first on the floor. He shot up, nose bloody, unshaken. "And hey, *you*, later you still gotta tell me what *'spunk'* means!" he shouted. Every other Velka in the joint turned their head, shocked by the sudden profanity. Kya burst into laughter. Etkis slapped his forehead, ears pressed down and out in shame. Dorin stumbled over to the bar. He leaned his full weight onto the counter. He needed it to stay standing.

"Sorry about that," Etkis said, looking up. "He's not the most professional, but I promise he's very good at what he does."

"For as much of an ass as he is, he's doing a much better job of blending in than you are," Kya said.

Etkis shot up, ears forward. "What? How?"

"First, you're right, that's not what anyone would think an agent would do. Rother makes sure we put on a show in front of you lot—professional, orderly. But a show is all it is. Just look at Dorin—too dumb, a great disguise, so long as he doesn't waggle his tongue too much. Second of all, you haven't touched your drink once."

"Wh—I'm on duty!"

"No, you're not. You're just some Wolf who wandered into a bar with his two friends and who needs a drink after a few long days on the road." She traced the edge of her glass with her finger. Her voice resonated the air with intent. "Besides, I bought it for you. It's rude not to drink."

Etkis's heart skipped a beat, and he began to think about things he didn't intend. Her ears carried a gentle feminine curve that highlighted the floral patterns etched into her helmet, and her duster coat and tunic couldn't hide her body's curves. Kya leaned back, her head slightly down and eyes up, evoking a confidence that Etkis could only dream of. Her eyes were beautiful, black as the void, their outline white as snow. He felt himself fall into her, hypnotized, pulled in by her gaze. The only sound was her lightly rasped voice, which massaged the air, a blanket that enveloped him as he fell further and further into the warm darkness. Etkis felt a strange detachment from his usual romantically incompetent self. The amber light, powerful smells, and light rabble ambience inside the bar inspired a certain attraction he could hardly understand but couldn't deny. Maybe Dorin was right—there was something oddly mystic in this dive, something that drew him to emotions and desires that he rarely indulged.

Etkis's trance snapped in two when he realized he hadn't said or done anything for a solid minute, and his self-conscious panic knew only one solution. He slammed the drink into his filter and coughed almost immediately.

"*Blech! Okar help me—what is that?*"

Kya slapped the table. "*Ha!* City boy."

"This isn't like any inthol I've ever had!"

"It's not inthol. It's a substitute the humans make, called vindol."

"Spunk of a name."

"Oh, it's awful—with twice the alcohol of inthol. *I love it.*" Kya took a long drink. Etkis, desperate to impress, tried to match her pull but coughed after about two seconds as the flavor seared his tongue and throat.

"Why is it so tangy?" he asked in a high-pitched tone.

"So what?"

"Tangy? You know, like the flavor of a peach."

"Flavor? What are you on about?"

"Never mind." Etkis cleared his throat and turned his head to look in any other direction. His skin felt hot beneath his helmet for his self-assessed breach of professional etiquette, an assessment Kya didn't share. He tried to return to a sense of normalcy. "When do we head to the compound?" he asked. "Tomorrow night?"

"No, it'll take a few days to establish our cover. People need to think you're just here to buy stuff. I'll let you know when. Until then you and the drunkard need to play metal merchants."

"But I don't know anything about metalworking…"

"This'll be a learning experience, then."

Etkis chugged and coughed again, Kya laughed. She traced her eyes along his body. His broad shoulders and chest commanded space, and his arms bulged with even the smallest movement. *He's built like a mountain*, she thought. But what caught her attention more was the stillness he evoked, a quiet humility in his posture and movements. He had no desire to boast, to draw attention, or to make others feel small. A rarity indeed. Etkis looked over to Dorin in concern. His ears sloped up, sharp, proud, yet elegant and beautiful. His luminescent blue eyes were filled with amusement and worry in two enormous but equal measures. There was such kindness in his eyes. Kya lingered on them.

"So how'd someone like *you* meet someone like *Dory*?" she asked.

"Dorin."

"I know. How'd you two meet? Not a lot of humans Tarkus and Rother would trust for this kind of assignment—we're lucky to have him. If you can keep him behaving, that is."

"Ha, well, Tarkus trusts him…Rother, not so much. He and Dorin have a… tumultuous history. Before I met him, Dorin was a freelancer and worked for a lot of the human gangs in the wilds and syndicates on Earth, in the asteroid belt and Mars. I don't think Rother's really over that."

"Huh, maybe he's not so bad then. Anyone who gets under Rother's skin is in my good books. Before you met him, though? What changed?"

"It's not my place to say, but he's changed a lot since then. He works for the Wolves now."

Kya snorted and drank more vindol. "Not much of a freelancer if you're exclusive."

"Yeah…" Etkis glanced at her briefly but looked away again, still embarrassed. "Tarkus offered him citizenship, and he said no."

"What! Really?" Kya shouted in a whisper. Etkis nodded. Kya stumbled for words. "When was this?"

"Right before we left Volthsheim—he's the one who found and killed the Serpent scouts, and for his service, he was…given the opportunity."

"*He* found them?" She pointed to the drunkard with her drink in hand. "Not Rother?"

"Ha ha, no. Tarkus was pissed about that, nearly sent Rother on a trial."

"Wish I could've seen it," Kya muttered, half laughing. Her tone turned bitter. "But to say no? Ungrateful little swine."

Etkis turned to her, resolute and defiant. His voice rose high in dispute. "He just wasn't ready!"

"Not ready for what? Food, safety, and a steady income? Do you know how many of my friends here would kill for citizenship to Volthsheim? And to throw it away?"

"He's a complicated man!"

With those words, Dorin fell to the floor. His second bottle of bourbon spilled across the counter and dripped onto his face. The bartender looked like he was going to shoot himself.

"I'em fn, wherenins Etkis—*Euuuetiks*, lts go, ts tme to go hme," Dorin said, half-conscious. The bartender looked to Etkis and Kya in a desperate plea for help. Etkis sighed.

"Okar save me…I'll take him back to our landship. We're in lot D-48, space 102, when you need to find us. Where will you be?"

"Nowhere you need to know," Kya said. Etkis thought to press the matter, but something in the back of his mind advised against it.

"Okay, then." Etkis stood and the table tumbled back to even ground with a soft *bang*. He stopped and turned back to her. "It's good to meet you, Kya. We'll see you tomorrow?"

She chuckled softly. She noticed his drink—empty.

"You will."

CHAPTER 10

Every war, every battle, every hardship our people inflicted upon our brethren
in all of our recorded history has been for the acquisition of, or competition
for, resources. Yet today I stand with awe, disgust, and horror at the death of a
culture. Mercury is nothing now. A shattered ring around Sol. There is nothing
to salvage, nothing to be gained from this genocide. I sought answers in every
book of the divine Odyssey of Stars, every rational philosopher, and yet still
cannot comprehend the actions of Jormar the Dragon. To think we are capable
of such evil…is this the privilege of Okar's chosen? Are these the rights of power?

—Report from Lady Nora Lupine, then Nora Qatar,
first voyager of the Kuiper Belt, reassigned for
reconnaissance against the Serpent fleet, 1.15.1102

Jormar. She repeated the name, over and over again in her head. The pain
that went with the name still felt numb. The alcohol was wearing off, and her
heart began to race. *Jormar.* She suppressed the thought and kept her heart steady.

Kya walked the cobblestone street. Gray sunlight peeked over the marble
buildings and brick apartments—5:00 a.m. Only the drunk and the hungry were
up at this hour. She reached her apartment building and stopped to check if anyone was tailing her. *No one this week—good.* She was too tired to play her charade
any longer than she absolutely had to. The last nineteen hours had finally caught
up to her. She opened the door and climbed up the steps two at a time to the top
floor and entered her apartment. Half a dozen locks lined the opposite side of the
door. She turned them all.

The apartment was messy, not dirty. Furniture littered without much care, but no garbage lay on the floor. She went to the window on the side of the apartment facing the street, opened it, and stuck her head out. She hadn't noticed anyone following her, but she could never be too careful. She needed to be seen.

After a few minutes, she closed the window and went to the bedroom door. Large, metal, airtight. A Velka's bedroom, designed to hold in the same atmosphere as their suits and to keep the rest out. The only place they removed their suits. She opened the door and closed it behind her. The room was bare save for a bed with messy sheets and a large air unit attached to the wall; the machine converted Earth's air to Velkan atmosphere. She walked over to the unit and pulled it out of the wall. It was a fake. Hadn't worked since she bought it.

The hole in her wall led to the top of the adjacent building, only slightly lower than her own. She climbed through the hole and replaced the filter. It looked normal from the outside.

Jormar. Her heart sprinted again in her chest. She felt dizzy as past and present collided in her nauseous mind. Hearing his name for the first time was odd, as if it hadn't really happened. Like being poisoned, and she hadn't felt it until now. She slapped herself in the helmet and the metallic ring brought her back. She couldn't deal with this now.

Kya stalked the rooftops, staying low and in the long morning shadows. The buildings were built tightly linked together—she'd been very careful when scouting out the apartment. Jumping alleys would've called far too much attention. She made it to a fire escape several hundred meters away, scaled down to the street, and hustled to the wharf.

The ocean lapped against the wooden pier. Boats bobbed up and down on the low tide, their bells rang out loud in time with the waves. She dropped to a house beneath the main road against the ocean. A small boat was tied down near it. A mailbox was attached to the house, a name carved beneath the address: "Residence of Doctor Oliver Wallace." She checked around one last time—no one. No tails, no bystanders. She opened the door and walked in.

It was a small dwelling, clean and tidy, charming with rustic affectation. She sat down on the couch and let out a long sigh of relief. Finally, home. She looked at the clock on the wall—6:00 a.m.

"Hey, Sunshine! Another late night?" a gentle voice asked from the kitchen. Kya closed her eyes. Her anxious heart thawed at her father's voice.

"Mhmm. Took care of Laurence, I'll get the rest of the pay from Natalie this afternoon."

"Is Laurence still with us?"

"He'll be fine, just needed to be set straight. Another midlife crisis—Abby will keep him in line."

"That's good to hear."

"Ran into Phil and Vern too."

"Oh, how was Vern! How's his little girl…um…" Her father paused. Kya heard him snap his fingers in frustration as he tried to draw the name.

"Maria. She's good—took her first steps."

"That's lovely!"

"And then Phil should pay me by the end of the day. That should cover the rent."

"Don't worry about that now. You need to eat." Kya heard the whirling gears of a conversion unit turning food into a liquid meal.

"I need to sleep is what I need to do."

"One, then the other. Come now."

Kya groaned and got up from the couch. She entered the kitchen, a small man half her size with white hair, pink skin, and green eyes handed her a food cylinder. He scurried from the fridge to the stove and to the pot of tea with the energy of a man half his age. Kya drank the food in a long gulp. She hadn't realized just how hungry she was.

"Thank you," Kya said. Her eyes contorted in affectionate suspicion. "Don't tell me you were waiting up?"

"I worry!"

"You know I'm fine."

"No, I don't know that, which is why I worry. Besides, I'm old. I'm up at the crack of dawn anyway."

Kya leaned her back against the wall and tapped on the food cylinder with her fingers. She watched her father toil at the stove, and she cracked her jaw. Kya cleared her throat. "I met with Rother's spooks."

Ollie's head snapped toward her, wrinkled brow scrunched. "You did? Why didn't you tell me?"

"*I didn't want you to worry*. Not till I knew what was what."

Ollie rolled his eyes. "Oh well, thank you, I feel so much better!" He sighed and turned off the stove. He faced her, all attention on the conversation. "What happened? Not another checkup, was it?"

"No, a new assignment. He sent help, or Tarkus did, I guess. Had to meet with them."

"*Tarkus*? That can't be good, if he's directly involved."

"It's the House of Serpents. They're on Earth, setting the stage for an invasion."

The old man's worried brow fell. He closed his open mouth and put a hand on Kya's arm.

"Are you all right?" he asked.

"Of course I am. I just…this will be taking up a lot of my time, and I don't know how it's going to go down. If things go south…"

Ollie shook his head and stepped away. "Sweetheart, we've talked about this."

Kya set her food cylinder on the counter and followed him to the sink, where he'd begun cleaning dishes already washed an hour ago. Her voice rose in desperation. "Volthsheim is the safest place on the planet! It's supposed to be beautiful, and the humans there have a very strong community—"

"No, no, I won't hear of it."

"There'll be an adjustment period, but I can talk to Rother and—"

"*Ha!* You think I want Rother checking up on me every day, making sure I'm keeping my filthy monkey nose down and out of the way? No thank you. I've lived in this city all my life—this is my home, and I'll be damned if I abandon it to become a second-class citizen across the world."

"That's not even his job, and the new first guard is a very nice fellow!"

Ollie scoffed. "To Velka, you mean."

"To humans."

"You don't know that."

"I—"

"No." He cut her off.

"Pabbi—"

"No! I won't be looked at like an animal walking down the street every day!"

"Pabbi, please!" Childhood dread boiled up in a sea of anxiety. She couldn't lose him too. Not to her old demons. "Jormar is on Earth," she muttered. The words were quiet, but her father heard them as if she had screamed.

Ollie stopped dead. He set the plate down and stared at his daughter, hoping that he'd misheard. "What?"

"He's here, he's involved. I don't know how, why, or what he's doing here but I'm scared and I don't know what to do if he finds me, or what he'll do to you! He's working with Pompeii which is just *fucking PERFECT* so now he's linking arms with the most well-connected person in the city and I have to find *both* of them before they fucking kill me and Tarkus sends two fucking *amateurs*, I'm so screwed and I don't know what to do! Pabbi please *please* just go!"

Ollie stood helpless as panic finally broke his girl. Her body convulsed with every wracked sob. He wrapped his arms around her, and she clung to him, desperate not to drown in her sea of fear.

"Okay…I'll go. I'll go," He whispered.

Her breath steadied, the pressure in her chest abated. "Thank you, Pabbi."

"Here, let's get you to bed. You've had a long night."

Ollie helped Kya to her bedroom. The door had the same atmospheric sealing as the one in her fake apartment. The only difference was a small plaque on the front with "KYAS ROOM" written in crayon and child's drawings littering the edges. Scribbles of a home she had nearly forgotten—red and yellow jagged lines formed an old Velkan house. Inside was a room full of old toys, books, and knickknacks. A record of her journey to adulthood that Ollie could never bear to part with. She sat down on her bed, hyperventilating. He grabbed a small wooden wolf he had whittled years ago and placed it in her hands. She could feel it's bumps and curves through her suit, the smooth wood, the tiny ears and nose. An anchor.

"It's all right. Breathe." He knelt in front of her and demonstrated. He inhaled deeply through his nose, out through his mouth. "Breathing in, I know that I am breathing in. Breathing out, I know that I am breathing out. Say it with me, dear. Breathing in, I notice my breath has become deeper. Breathing out—"

"I notice that my breath has become slower." She finished with a sniffle. She closed her eyes. They spoke in unison.

"Breathing in, I calm myself. Breathing out, I feel at ease. I smile. I release. I dwell in the present moment. I feel it is a wonderful moment. I contemplate the coming and going of the waves. I contemplate the coming and going of the water."

Kya let out a long sigh. Ollie touched her cheek, his hand familiar with the cold metal. She opened her eyes.

"Better?" He asked.

"Mhmm," she muttered.

Ollie stood and went over to the air unit and turned it on. A small red light blinked atop it. He left her food cylinder on her nightstand and went for the door.

"Sleep well, Sunshine. I love you."

"You too, Pabbi."

Ollie closed the door, leaving the room dark save for the blinking red in the corner. Kya stared at the banner on her side of the door. The red and black cloth with an onyx star at the center appeared with each flash of light. The red stopped blinking—the air was converted. She unhinged her helmet, a rush of gas was released, and she removed it. She didn't take her eyes off the banner, now bathed in dark red.

The oldest thing she owned, all that was left from a time long dead.

The banner of the House of Stone.

CHAPTER 11

How do you retain power? Fear? Blood? Wars of attrition? All useful, but expensive. My preference? Food. Feed your followers, and starve your dissidents. They'll rebel eventually, sure, but you try and fight a rebellion on two hundred calories a day.

—Volthsheim database, scout archives, recorded audio from Linel, Warlord of Alexandria, 5.12.1073

Midsummer. The snow is half slush. Elk and squirrels rustle behind me, a herd of bison and mammoth graze the prairie to the east. Mercia is a few kilometers north. Villagers walk the streets. It's 7:00 a.m. They line up at town hall, single file. The doors will open soon. Election day, Jarrod had it in his sights. We're waiting for Bonnie, the mayor. She'd been cracking down on Jarrod's "protection services." She had to go.

Our tent at the edge of the wood. We're in our final firing position, have been for half an hour. The sniper rifle in my hands felt so warm, the wood grip formed perfectly against my hands. Ash lies next to me with her own gun. Her red hair is cut short, tied in a bun. I try not to look at her. I never stay angry when I do. I keep looking through the scope.

"You're still mad," she says. "What do you want from me?"

Fuck that pisses me off. "An apology."

"I'll make it up to you!"

"That's not an apology! What are we supposed to do after this? We're not back to square one, we're back to square 'go fuck yourself.' *We. Are. Screwed*."

"You're so dramatic, it's not that bad."

"Is that a joke? Oh god, you don't still think you're funny, do you?"

"I am very funny, that's offensive."

"We finish here, and every last coin goes to Linel. Then how much more do we need to pay off? What? Four more jobs? Six? We were so close, but no, you could double it all, you said."

"Okay."

"Just one more hand, you said."

"Okay! How was I supposed to know he owned Copen? It's days away from Alexandria."

"The point is not that the money went to Linel, Ashton, the point is you lost *all of it*! I can't believe you."

"D, it'll be fine. We can figure this out," she says. She reaches out to my shoulder, and I shrug her off.

Typical.

Through the scope I see the target. Midforties. Blond hair. Purple coat. She smiles and talks to the voters, they laugh. She's charming. She goes to the back of the line.

"Target identified. Back of the line."

"Confirmed. Take the shot when you're ready."

Me. Always me. She says it's because I'm a better shot. I've never been convinced. I think she just doesn't like the responsibility—if the job falls apart, it's on whoever fired the first shot. So it's always on me.

I never complain. But I should. Maybe next time.

I feel the wind and adjust my aim. I exhale. The reticle is off her body but the bullet will find her brain stem, I'm sure. I feel the trigger. I begin to squeeze—

A child runs up to Bonnie. A small beanie obscures their face, I can't tell if it's a boy or a girl. Bonnie picks her child up and gives them a kiss. They smile at each other, and my heart seizes.

"What's wrong?" Ash asks. She hadn't been looking down the scope. "Oh," she says, before I have the chance to speak. She saw.

"You said school was still in on election day…"

"It is. Maybe the kid's sick or something. Ah well, doesn't matter."

I turn to her, mouth agape. "Doesn't matter?"

"Why should it?"

I look at her in shock. She looks back at me—utter confusion. She genuinely doesn't understand the issue.

But she's right. It shouldn't matter. We need the money, and backing out of a job halfway through is bad for your health. At this point, it's us or them. We need to do it. I need to do it. No other way.

I look down the sight. Heart beating out of my chest. I can feel the pounding pulse in my neck, in my wrists and hands. Mouth dry. I inhale. I see Bonnie look at her child and smile. The kid takes off the beanie—a boy. I exhale. Bonnie kisses his forehead. I squeeze the trigger.

The sound rings out. One second. Two—then the bullet hit. A blizzard of blood. Bonnie falls down and the boy drops from her arms. Townsfolk turn and scream as they realize what just happened. I can't hear them from here but I know what they're shouting. Ash opens fire, indiscriminate, hardly aimed. People burst red and crumple in the crowd. Blood mixed with slush; swaths of crimson paint the street. Jarrod needed more than an assassination––he needed a message. No one will defy him after this—at least not for a few more years. Then we'll go again.

I only pulled the trigger once but it was enough. The boy gets up, so scared, so confused, face and clothes splattered in his mother's blood. I can see it from here, the fear, the panic. So familiar…

I can see his mouth open wide as he shouts for his mother. He didn't understand she was right next to him, face down in the snow. He realizes. He shakes her body. Nothing. He weeps. He wails in the street. No one takes him, no one runs out to protect him from the bullets, from the sight of his mother's corpse. He's alone. From now on, alone. I can't watch anymore.

I put the rifle down. I'm going to pass out. I'm going to throw up. Ashton scoots next to me, rubs my back and cradles my head, her fingers run through my hair. She buries her face in my neck. Her hands smell like gunpowder.

"You did so good, baby, we're one step closer. I'm so proud of my man." She can sense my panic. She kisses me, her soft lips on mine.

Don't cry. She'll laugh again.

"I promise I'll make it up to you, D. Just a few more jobs, I promise, and we'll be square. Then we can start saving up for the ranch again. How about you keep the

cash this time, huh? It's safer with you." She smiles—so beautiful. I nod. My stomach churns again. Don't cry.

"I love you, Dorin," she says. I believe her. I'm not a bad man—how can I be? If I hadn't shot that mother in the street, we'd be dead by next week. I have to protect us.

"I love you too, Ashton," I say. She smiles. We kiss.

I'm not a bad man.

I'm not a bad man…

Dorin sat up gasping, his face and body covered in sweat. He searched for corpses but saw only the metal gray interior of the landship. He looked around, and his senses came back to him in a wave. He was in his bed on Rose, curled in stark white sheets. He was down to his boxers. His shirt, pants, and coat all hung from the top bunk, freshly cleaned, but the smell of alcohol still stuck to the cloth and leather. Soot hung safely in its holster from a bedpost. Etkis was sleeping. He sported only his helmet and black bodysuit. His merchant clothes were set beside the bed. He lay face down and snored like a bear in hibernation.

A piercing headache hit Dorin and his left shoulder screamed. Last night became horrifically clear, and the hangover amplified the pain in his injury. He ran out the front door and threw up in the lot. Cold snow stung his feet. Tears streamed down his eyes as hot, vile bile seared the back of his throat. His head shook with every heave and tremor, worsening his migraine. He massaged his human arm with his metal hand but the freezing steel provided little comfort to his throbbing flesh. It had gotten worse, not better, over the last few days.

Dorin stood up after he finished regurgitating bourbon, each of the five rounds came up in reverse order. An old man and woman stared at him from across the way, from the front of their rover. Dorin's nose flared. He opened his mouth to shout a quip but was interrupted by another onslaught of putrid regret.

Shower first, then insults, Dorin thought. He staggered back inside and closed the door behind him, careful not to wake Etkis. Dorin went down to the storage compartment and over to the tiny shower at the end of the walkway. He undressed, turned the handle, and stepped into the cold running water. His head still pounded, but his stomach was quelled in shock from the cold. The water turned warm, then hot. He let it run down his hair and neck and back. The steaming water soaked away the thoughts of his nightmare, the memory that had woken him. The heat soothed his purple shoulder, his pulsing temples, his aching stump. He stayed until the water ran cool again.

Dorin stepped out, clean. He grabbed a towel, dry clothes, and a bag of dried deer meat from storage and readied himself. He pulled himself up each rung of the ladder, swinging with only his metal arm as his left hung limp and pathetic at his side. Etkis was still asleep. Dorin tiptoed over to his bunk, a strip of meat hanging out the side of his mouth, and found his boots beside the bed. He began to put them on when there was a loud knock at the door. The sound brutalized Dorin's migraine anew. He scarfed down the meat, rushed to the door, one boot on, desperate to end the agonizing sound, and opened it.

"Dory, you look just peachy," Kya said. The vomit that caked the snow next to her told her everything.

"Har har. Kya," Dorin whispered, "keep it down. Etkis is still asleep."

"I'm walking on four hours sleep, he'll live. Come on, wakey wakey time. We have to go 'shopping.'" Kya pushed Dorin aside and walked inside Rose. A step in, she saw Etkis lying on the bed asleep. She stopped, stared, and snorted. "He sleeps…naked?"

"What? He's not naked, he still has the suit on."

"To us, that's naked." Kya tried everything in her power to keep from laughing. "Okar, I can't believe this…does he not own pajamas? Is there not a conversion unit in here? What is happening!" She tried to respect his privacy. Her eyes darted from the ceiling back to Etkis, temptation drawing her gaze over and over. The black suit framed his muscular body perfectly. *Okar, and I thought he was huge last night…*for a single, guilty second, Kya wondered what Etkis and Dorin did in the hovercraft when they were all alone.

"I do not have the energy for this," Dorin said. *"Etkis, wake up!"*

Etkis shot up and hit his head on the top bunk with a loud gong sound. He fell off the bed and groaned.

"*Piss, ow*—are we under attack? What happened?" He shouted. His hand rocketed beneath his bed, and he retrieved his hatchet. Etkis stood up, eyes wide, ears back, ready to fight. He and Kya made eye contact.

"Kya? Wha—*AH!*" He realized the state he was in and grabbed the sheet from his bed to cover his body. It only went from his chest to his thighs.

Kya let him hang in silence for a moment. She took it all in. Her voice was as enthralling as ever. "Good, you're awake. We have to go and build our cover story. Shopping and such, like we discussed. Meet me outside once you're dressed—unless you're ready now? Either works for me." Her gaze danced down Etkis. Etkis babbled.

"N-n-n-no, I'll...the clothes on body are good! Minute, then walk...yes."

"Hm," She muttered softly. "Well, hurry up, then, city boy. I don't like to be kept waiting." She pivoted and walked out the door, her eyes curved into a devilish smile. Etkis trembled in complete silence.

"That was fun. Let me know when you're ready," Dorin said. He plopped on the bed and covered his eyes to nurse his head. Etkis nodded and desperately wished for an execution.

Hundreds bustled in the city plaza dressed in ragged yet clean clothes that marked the city's middle class. The streets were plowed free of snow, and the remaining white filled in the gaps between cobblestones. Snow was dumped into large piles on the corners of the plaza, and a large fountain roared in the center. Icy mist refracted sunlight into a kaleidoscope of color as it billowed from the crashing water.

Dorin shook his head, the sheer idea of a fountain baffled him. "Only in Alexandria would people choose to make it colder in the *dead of fucking winter* for the sake of vanity."

Kya rolled her eyes. "It's a historical monument. Fuck me, do you ever stop whining?"

"Not when I'm awake."

Kya laughed despite herself. Etkis turned his head, fascinated by the bizarre waste of precious water. "It's beautiful…but why build it?"

Dorin ignored him as he laid down along the edge of the fountain and put his arm over his eyes in a classic hangover position. Kya held her head high, pride in her voice. "It's a dedication to our greatest diplomatic achievement! Built on the bicentennial of the Alexandria's independence." Her posture slumped as her pride gave to realism. "Or you know…*supposed* independence."

Etkis rubbed the back of his neck. "We don't like to use the 'I' word back home. And I actually meant, what does it do? The fountain?"

"What do you mean? It spits water."

"Right, but is that all it does? What's it do for the people here?"

"It's pretty."

Etkis scratched his head, struggling to understand why anything would be built without some kind of a practical function. "Okay, but…do people drink out of it?"

"You're not supposed to," Dorin chimed. He stuck his face in a slurped as obnoxiously as he could. Kya ran over to him and yanked him to his feet.

"Stop that! Okar help me, you are like a literal child!"

Dorin tried to stick out his tongue but a wave of nausea instead made him cough up the water he'd just drank. A few chucks of his breakfast hit the ground too. Kya turned to Etkis in utter disbelief.

Etkis shrugged, embarrassed. "You said to blend in…"

Kya groaned and led Dorin and Etkis away to the street corner to the meeting she had set. A pair of independent contractors greeted the trio and led them into their office to discuss business. Their smiles widened the longer the meeting went on, their hearts bounded at the idea of having such a large contract with a buyer as financially stable as Volthsheim. One trader after another, hour after hour. Dorin was ever determined to be as much of a jackass as possible—he pretended to write sales information in a notebook as he harassed the merchants, and Etkis apologized profusely, the only sincerity among a slew of lies.

For two days they roamed the Alexandrian markets and conned merchants with the same false promises with different ornamentation. Dorin had no idea how much steel should cost compared to aluminum or copper or any other metal they browsed, so he fabricated the largest numbers he could fathom paying. He played a sadistic game that made him chuckle, the merchants salivate, and Etkis grimace. Kya was often silent during the proceedings, only making the initial introductions and polite farewells.

Etkis couldn't help but feel disappointed with Alexandria. The more he saw of the city, the more it shocked and horrified him. He winced at the sight of roped pigs trotting in line behind sellers, fresh off their tundra ranches. They were filthy and abhorrent animals to the Velka. Etkis had never actually seen one before, but they were every bit as disgusting as he had been told by his peers. Dorin made a point to buy some slices of bacon and chewed the crunchy meat loudly and proudly. Kya averted her eyes, and Etkis nearly hurled in his helmet.

The true horror Etkis witnessed was poverty. Homeless crowded the corners of every marketplace. They begged for spare coins or food. Few in Alexandria had anything 'to spare.' Some vagrants had the fortune of shoes; those that didn't had blue flesh and absent toes. The first homeless man Etkis tried to talk to screamed and ran into a labyrinthine alleyway, terrified at the behemoth before him. From that point on, Etkis was sure to have gold coins in hand on approach, like breadcrumbs to pigeons. He spent a near fortune on charity. They smiled and thanked him and blessed him in the name of foreign gods the Velka didn't recognize. Dorin scoffed. He was sure that paupers would only buy drinks to warm their throats and bellies. He was too jaded to believe sob stories and fairy tales about their starving children. Etkis didn't know the city. Dorin did. Kya remained silent but watched intently when Etkis knelt to give the hopeless a token of care.

Etkis forgot some of the melancholy, and his excitement returned when he found a merchant selling small, green leaf balls. "Look, Dorin, I found the cabbage! It's the same kind that the man who came to Volthsheim was selling! So strange, so mystical," Etkis said in excitement and wonder. Such plants were extinct on Earth; they had to have been imported from either Mars or Titan.

That, or they were smuggled in from Venus, Dorin thought. *Nah. Cabbage isn't exactly worth the risk of breaking the embargo. Wolves aren't lenient when it comes to smuggling.* The freelancer inspected the green ball closer. His eyes went wide, and he laughed.

"That's lettuce!" Dorin said with mocking glee. Etkis turned his head to the side, baffled.

"What? What's lettuce?"

"Different vegetable."

"But…but they look the same."

"I don't know what to tell you, buddy."

"Madness…absolute madness." Etkis handed the merchant back the lettuce, his eyes curved down and shoulders slumped. They visited different vendors selling iron, steel, aluminum and other such metals for the rest of the afternoon, and again Etkis desperately qualified their deceptions.

"I cannot guarantee that the city will contact you, we have to weigh all of the vendors…" Etkis said.

"Even a chance is worth much, sir! I promise you our product will exceed competitive standards as well as your expectations!" the seller said. Leather moccasins were wrapped around his feet. Old burn marks covered his hands and forearms. An old man in the corner and young children all worked the shop—they all looked quite similar. Etkis swallowed. None of the family was well-fed. The vendor's cheeks were especially sunken in, but his eyes glowed with hope. Hope for a better future. Hope in a lie.

"I…I'll be sure to pass it along." Etkis shook the man's hand one last time and left as quickly as he could. The owner went to shake Dorin's hand as well, but Dorin turned and left without a word.

The owner whispered, almost too quietly for Etkis to hear, "Thank you, Kya. This means a lot—might be able to get the kids their own place if this works out!"

"You got it, Vinny," she said. "I'll talk to you later."

The trio walked back to the center of the plaza beside the fountain. Dorin sat down on the fountain steps and nursed his head against his hand. His helmet provided some protection from the sun, but it was still too bright for the constant hangover that he had managed to maintain since arriving in Alexandria three days ago.

"That's nine vendors," Dorin said, exhausted. "Are we done? I need a drink."

"That's the last thing you need," Kya said. "But that's enough for today. We'll pick up in a different part of town tomorrow—maybe two more runs, and we should be good." Kya looked toward the northeast corner of the market. A man with a long green overcoat drank from a bottle and leaned against a wall. He'd been in the plaza for as long as they had. She tried to determine if the man was armed or not, but he was too far away. *Fair bet, though.* She looked to the west. A young woman sat on a bench reading a tattered book. She was definitely armed.

"Hey, Etkis," Dorin said, "why don't we swing by the weaponsmiths, check out *human* wares? My boredom has reached critical mass, and I need a break."

"Sounds fun—sure!" Etkis said, giddy. Kya chuckled at the massive warrior bouncing up and down like an excited puppy shown a ball. She hazarded a glance to the northeast wall, then to the western bench. The man and woman were both gone.

Etkis barely squeezed through the weaponsmith's door. The wooden frame made a loud squeaking sound as the lumber bent against his mass. He took in the shop. It was nothing like the grand forges and machines of Volthsheim, slamming hammers and whirling gears. He'd envisioned tiny humans at the helm of great, foreign machines working away like little elves. He'd imagined them trading goods, laughing and passionately debating the merits and detriments of different firearms, shields, and other armaments. He couldn't have been more disappointed.

The store was tiny and yet still the largest gun store in this part of Alexandria. Etkis hunched to barely fit inside, and he could almost reach either side of the walls with his arm length. The store was indeed full, but everyone was miserable. They worked their way uniformly from ogling the most expensive guns to the still fine but cheaper weapons further down the aisle. Then to the midpriced tools, then to generics and knock offs, and so on. Their faces fell the farther they went, at the same rate that both price and quality dropped, until they stood disheartened in front of rusted scrap they could barely afford. One man in front of the cashier couldn't cash up enough even for the discount bin and begged to be put on layaway. He was ass-ended out an open window by a guard.

Etkis browsed the handguns and pistols, which were too small for him to fire. There were no weapons for Velkan hands. The market didn't exist. There simply was no demand for human-made Velkan weapons. Volthsheim produced better, cheaper, lighter, and more reliable tools for its citizens that the humans in Alexandria could only long for. Kya went to a cleaning station and gave one of the workers a coin. She disassembled her long pistol. The wide and fat magazine slid onto a cleaning cloth at the workbench, and a second later the slide and recoil spring lay neatly beside them. She ran a copper-bristled rod through the barrel, greased each mechanism, and coated the metal in gun oil. Dorin went to the front of the shop to speak with the owner.

"Greetings, good sir," Dorin said through a forced smile. His misanthropy almost caught the words in his throat. "How are you this fine day?"

"Drop it, young man—what do you want?" the owner said. His old face was covered with ash and grease and his voice was hoarse from years of smoking. His bushy moustache bounced on his lip as he spoke.

"Thank god," Dorin said, relieved to be free of the shackles of common courtesy. "I need one-hundred one-K kelvin rounds," Dorin took out Soot and placed it on the table. "Custom size." The smith shifted his head and waited for a punch line that never came. He laughed nervously.

"A thousand kelvin? Are you burning down a building? Why would you need those?"

"That's what this guy takes," Dorin said and gestured to Soot.

The weaponsmith was flabbergasted but intrigued. He picked up Soot, nearly dropped it, then hefted it with both hands to control the gun's weight. After a few playful spins of the cylinder, he plucked out a large, brass shell and examined the ammunition.

"Guns that take this kind of heat are bigger than a person—or strapped on a tank. Where'd you find this thing?"

"Luna."

"The moon? What the piss was it doing there?"

"Waxing poetic and writing the novel of a generation—*what do you think it was doing there?*" Dorin didn't quite yell at the man but emphasized the smith's stupidity with his "outside voice." Dorin continued, "Someone had it, they died, and I found it."

The smith struggled to bring the hammer down and gave up. He looked at the grip—it fit in his hand perfectly. "It's definitely made for humans, but I've never seen anything like this before. How do you even fire this thing?"

The mustachioed man was mock aiming down Soot's sight when a thought crossed his mind. He glanced at Etkis and Kya, the only two Velka in the shop. His already sweaty brow became soaked enough to drown a sailor. His eyes flicked from them to Dorin. He leaned in close so that only Dorin would hear. "Does it pierce Velkan plate?"

"If you gave it to someone mentally deficient enough to shoot at one, it might. Blows human heads off all the same."

The smith licked his sweaty lips and swallowed. He held the cartridge up to his eye. It too was heavier than it appeared, and it looked damn heavy. He felt like he was holding an ingot; the thing must have weighed half a kilogram. It was warm, hot even. The heat poured out of the red-tipped eye of the round like a flashlight of fire.

"Who made this?" the smith asked.

"The ammo, Volthsheim. The gun, not sure, but it's gotta be them. Never seen a human gun like it."

"Maybe, some of it. But the EM rails—Velka don't use electromagnets in their guns. There's a lot less recoil using gravitational fields, so they never bother. Their ballistic weapons opt for pure kinetic impact—but this amount of heat? From a hand cannon? Hate to say it, it's not like any gun I've ever seen, and it sure as hell isn't from Volthsheim." The smith's impassioned curiosity vanished into impotent shame. The smith put the bolt down. "I don't really know where I'd begin...the bullet's so compact..."

For as little Dorin thought of his own kind, he still thought they had the means to complete what he saw as a simple task. For once, his expectations were too high. Dorin snatched Soot out of the weaponsmith's hand and held it to his chest, protective. *Shouldn't be surprised*, he thought, and put the bolt back into his bandolier.

"Wait!" shouted the smith. "I'll pay you for that gun!"

"You couldn't afford it, pal."

"I'll trade you, then! Anything I've got—hell, *all* I've got! Everything in this shop is yours for that piece!"

Dorin scrunched his nose, single eyebrow raised. He turned his head back to the man. "Generous. Why?"

"Look, that gun of yours? It's terrible. Utter garbage."

"Yup."

"I don't know anyone that could fire it. Even if they did, it'd mince their fingers to sausage. But this is the single most advanced piece of human technology I've ever seen. Velkan guns fire electrons with batteries or fire projectiles through gravitational fields. This does neither."

"You're a scientist now, are you?"

"Listen to me!" The old man snarled. Dorin raised his brows, surprised at the tone. The smith was louder than he intended to be and looked back to Etkis and Kya. Neither had taken notice. He whispered, emphatic, "That thing is human made, no question. If I gave it to Pompeii, they could—"

Dorin stopped listening as a wave of thoughts crashed into him all at once. *Does he know Pompeii?*

Dorin mulled over the circumstances as the stone of anxiety in his stomach grew and grew in size. He looked at the smith. The man's eyes flashed from Dorin to Kya to Etkis and an oily sweat lined his face. His mustache trembled, and his fingers scraped the counter as he spoke. *Does it pierce Velkan plate?* he asked. He offered everything he has for it. No real freelancer would turn him down. Dorin suppressed a grimace and breathed deep. He squeezed Soot and turned back to the mustachioed man. *If I walk away now, he'll wonder why. Ugh, I really fucked this up.* "I'm intrigued. What's your name?"

"Cormac."

"Let's talk, Cormac. But not here. I'll meet you in the alley behind your shop. Don't want certain ears listening." Dorin tilted his head toward Kya and Etkis. Cormac smiled through crooked teeth. He walked out the back.

Dorin groaned and grit his teeth as he walked away from the counter. Etkis noticed the anger burning from his friend. "Dorin? What's wrong?"

"Stay here." Dorin walked out the front door and stopped at the corner of the building, where the walls turned into the alley. He leaned around the corner and saw Cormac waiting. Dorin drew his knife from his boot and hid it in his sleeve, careful not to burn himself on the blade. He walked into the alley with arms outstretched.

"Cormac! All right, tell me what you're thinking." Dorin stood a little over a meter away from the smith. He needed to close the distance slowly. Anything else would've been suspicious.

"Simple. You sell the gun to me, and I reverse engineer it. I sell the technology to Pompeii."

Dorin cocked his head and paced in front of Cormac. "Why wouldn't I go and meet with Pompeii myself? Cut you out entirely? I'm sure he has plenty of engineers who could do the job."

"*Ha*, you think Pompeii's going to meet with just any freelancer? And no, I could count the number of smiths who could work that piece on one hand. And I'm the best."

Dorin paced back and forth, back and forth. With each lap he closed the distance a few centimeters. Bit by bit. "How convenient for you. But I've met Pompeii a few times, you see, worked for him once or twice. We're acquainted. He'll see me if I make enough noise."

Cormac smiled hideously, and for the first time, Dorin noticed a sadistic glint in the man's eye. He'd taken the smith for just another Alexandrian, desperate to rise above his station, far too confident in his abilities. But now Dorin felt something sinister from this small man. Cormac spoke slow and smooth.

"You're a good liar, son. But you tipped your hand. You've never laid eyes on the boss."

Dorin stopped pacing. *What did I say? Damn it.* He put his hands up, "Okay, okay, you got me. But if this gun's as valuable as you imply, then I want a cut of your profits. Deal?" Dorin was close now, just a few more steps. He prepped the knife behind his back, with a firm but loose grip on the handle.

Cormac leaned his head back, smug. "I keep the shop and split the profits with you seventy to thirty. Sold."

They shook hands. Dorin gripped the knife and prepared to strike.

Etkis called from the end of the alley.

"Dorin! What are you doing?"

Dorin turned to see his friend's eyes fixed on the knife he held. Cormac and Dorin were more alike than the freelancer realized. At the moment his head turned, Cormac pulled a wrench from his tool belt and slammed it serendipitously into the only bit of flesh left on the metal half of Dorin's body—it hammered into the soft back of his knee. Dorin screamed and buckled while Cormac snagged Soot out of its holster and ran for it. Dorin sheathed his knife, staggered up, and swore hideously.

He hobbled after the old man, but he was shockingly spry for his age. He ran into the crowd at the other end of the alley, and he weaved back and forth through the ocean of people like any practiced thief. Dorin followed and knocked down more than a few pedestrians to keep up with Cormac. He knew Etkis would be stalled far behind him, unwilling to trample the dozens of people necessary to catch the bastard quickly.

Cormac passed a group of homeless and saw an opportunity. He stuck his hand into a pouch on his hip and threw a fistful of coins on the floor behind him. The poor dove for the gold, like greased hogs to the trough, each piece worth a day's full belly. The swarm blocked Dorin's path, and he shoved and pressed against the bodies. Cormac laughed, thrilled, and turned to keep running, sure of his escape.

A gloved fist rocketed from the shadows as he passed the next alley and clocked him across the face. Cormac was dragged into the dark. Pedestrians continued to walk by unfazed.

Just another Tuesday to them.

Dorin finally made it through the crowd and turned into the alleyway.

Kya had Cormac pinned to the ground with her knee on his back and gun to his temple. His nose was bloody, a bruise grew from where she'd punched him, and her hand covered his eyes. *Must've gone around the back before Cormac made off with Soot...she was listening to our entire conversation*, Dorin thought, both annoyed and impressed at her competence. Before Dorin could speak, she put her finger up to her filter. Dorin understood. A Velka's voice was unmistakable, so any utterance would give her away. And she was too well-known in the area to risk saying her name. "Huh, clever. Didn't know you had it in you," Dorin snarked. Kya gave him the finger.

Kya wrenched Soot from Cormac's grasp and tossed it to Dorin. The freelancer put the gun back in its holster, snug. Dorin proceeded to do what he did best and kicked an old man in the dirt. He walked over and threw his weight behind it and crashed the tip of his foot into Cormac's ribs. The smith sputtered and squealed as the air was knocked out of him.

"That's for stealing my gun."

He kicked again.

"And that's for the wrench!"

Another kick. For fun.

Dorin leaned on the alley wall and massaged the back of his right leg, where he was sure a nice fresh bruise was forming.

Cormac spoke with a trembling voice, Kya's gun ever present to his head, "Okay, okay, I'm sorry! Look, you have it back now! There's no need for this to get any more bloody. How about I introduce you to Pompeii? You'd be rich with that piece, I'm sure!" Dorin looked at Kya, questioning. She shrugged. *Well, she doesn't care how I handle this. But Etkis will…I should probably just kill him and be done with it. The more people who know about Soot, the worse off we'll be.* Dorin heard the telltale signs of Etkis's approach—thundering footsteps and frightened gasps from the townsfolk.

The Velka rounded the corner to see the rest of his group surrounding a beaten old man in the dirt.

"What in Okar's name was all that?" Etkis said. Cormac began frantically shouting, begging for his life.

"You, Mr. Wolf, please! Help me! They're gonna kill me, please!"

"*Shut. It,*" Dorin muttered to Cormac, followed by another kick. Dorin walked over to Etkis and pulled him by the arm to the street, farther from the alley entrance, where Cormac had no chance of hearing. "I thought I told you to wait inside?" Dorin asked.

Etkis shrugged. "There seemed to be a problem, so I wanted to help."

"I told you to stay *because* there was a problem!"

Etkis lowered his head, embarrassed. Dorin took a deep breath, unable to stay angry at the earnest lummox. He put his hands on his hips and kicked the snow beneath his feet in a slow and steady rhythm.

"Sorry about all that," Dorin said. He clicked his tongue. "I fucked up, so I had to deal with this guy, then I fucked up *again*, and now Kya's got him, so it's fine. I just need to cut his throat, and then we can go get drinks."

Etkis shook his head. "Wait, what? Why? He stole your gun, and now you have it back. Kick him in the ribs a few times if you need some justice!"

"Way ahead of you."

"You don't think death is a little disproportionate?"

Dorin sighed and took off his helmet. He knew Etkis would have a hard time accepting something like this. He looked around to make sure no pedestrian lingered to listen in. Dorin leaned in, and Etkis squatted down so they were near eye level. "He wanted to buy Soot," Dorin said, "take it apart and sell the blueprints to Pompeii. He offered me everything he owned for this one gun. This one garbage, impossible to fire gun. Now, explain to me what sane freelancer, part of a profession built around identities that begin and end with the fastest way to score gold, would say no to a deal like that?"

"I don't…I guess they wouldn't."

"And what would be the only rational reason not to go for it?"

"If you didn't want Pompeii to get the blueprints…yeah, I see the problem."

Dorin drew Soot and shook it for emphasis. "You've seen what this thing does to people, Velka included. If by some miracle that cocksucker could actually reverse engineer this thing and *make it usable*, Pompeii could slaughter *battalions* of Wolves. Think about it, those blueprints would give human terrorists the ability to punch way above their weight class. Soot's one of a kind, and it needs to stay that way."

Etkis nodded, and Dorin holstered Soot. He started back into the alley.

Etkis interrupted again. "But do you have to kill him?"

Dorin groaned and walked back. "God, Etkis, yes I do! He's not some animal we've cornered, and he's not a kid on the street. He says he knows Pompeii, which makes him part of a network of *literal* interplanetary criminals. You can't keep doing this!"

"Me? You're the one who spared the raider back at the Roarers' ranch!"

Dorin put his hands on his hips, fumbled for words, and blew a raspberry. "Th...I...*pfffft*, totally different circumstances. Doesn't count."

"Of course it does! You let him live because you could see that he'd made mistakes in his life and he wasn't a bad kid. You punished him, sure, but you gave him a second chance. He reminded you of yourself."

"*Ha!*" Dorin looked down and kicked the snow, harder now, avoiding Etkis's eye contact. "Okay there, *Freud*, whatever you say."

"I don't know who that is. But I'm right. I've seen how people in this city live, and you know it far better than I do. This guy saw an opportunity to climb out of the pit, and he took it, whatever the cost. It was a mistake, and he should pay his due, but it doesn't make him a monster. Just like that boy at the ranch."

"I should've killed that raider. There. Is that what you want me to say?"

"Not at all. I'd never been prouder of you."

"*Uggggggh!*" Dorin threw his arms up in frustration. He hated making Etkis proud. Every time it built new standards he had to maintain. Standards he felt in his gut he'd eventually ruin.

Etkis put his hand on Dorin's shoulder. "Mercy is never something to regret, Dorin. Kindness begets kindness."

"Yeah, yeah." Dorin squeezed the bridge of his nose, frustrated. He sighed. "Well, we can't just let him go. He needs to leave town. We need to scare him."

"Seems easy enough. You horrify bartenders across the tundra! What's a little old man?"

Dorin scoffed. "Hilarious. Well, thanks to you and your *huge mouth*, he now knows that the Wolf who I came into the store with has seen an assault."

Etkis sucked in air through his filter. He hadn't thought about their cover story at all throughout this entire event. Dorin went on, scolding him. "And I'm supposed to be just another freelancer for you Wolves, so there's no way you wouldn't report me."

Etkis's ears flattened out and he tapped his fingers together. "Yeah...my bad. Sorry."

Dorin sighed. "It's fine. I need to put on a little song and dance for him now. Come on."

Dorin put his helmet back on, and they walked back into the alley where Kya and Cormac were waiting. Kya still had him pinned, hand over his eyes, gun to head. Cormac had been trying to bribe his captor with anything he could think of, but the longer the silence went on for, and the longer the gun stayed pinned to his brain, the more panicked he became. By the time Dorin and Etkis returned, Corman was a weeping, snot covered mess. Kya saw the duo enter the alley, and she extended her gun arm out in exasperation. *Where have you been?* her expression implied. Dorin and Etkis had been talking far longer than she expected.

"I know, but the Wolf says let him go. You wanna argue with him, be my guest," Dorin said. Kya gave the two a questioning look but soon figured out the charade. Dorin pushed Kya out of the way and took her position pinning their charge to the floor. "We'll handle it. Wait for us." She stood and walked out of the alley. *She'll be listening*, Dorin thought. He drew his knife and pulled Cormac up to his feet. His steel hand wrapped his throat. He put the blade next to Cormac's eye, the blue light threatening. Cormac stared at it. The only thing going through his mind was the phantom sensation of fluids boiling in his eye.

Dorin spoke, agitated. "All right, you slippery little prick, listen up. Today is the single luckiest day of your life. See the Wolf?" He gestured with his head to Etkis. Cormac looked up at the enormous alien and nodded meekly. Dorin went on.

"He gets queasy at the sight of dead rats, so you're gonna leave town. Tonight. And you won't come back, ever. If I see you again, I'll stick you with enough holes that your skeleton will be repurposed as a cheese grater. Got it?"

Cormac nodded again, words unable to come out of his mouth. Dorin flexed his mechanical muscles and picked up the little man by the throat and Cormac's hands grasped the metal limb in panic. Dorin placed the edge of the knife so close to the man's face he burned off a portion of his bushy mustache.

"I didn't catch that. What did you say?" Dorin asked.

Cormac stammered through the choke——his words came out with the paltry air his windpipe could provide. *"L-leave t-town! D-don't come back! Go-got it!"*

Dorin dropped the man, who landed and coughed with his whole body. Dorin sheathed his knife. "Good, I'm glad we have an understanding. Now thank the Wolf. If it weren't for him, you'd be leaving town through the bottom of the river."

Cormac staggered to his feet, his face red, eyes watering. He staggered over to Etkis, got on his knees, and bowed his head, "Thank you, Mr. Wolf, thank you so much!"

Etkis's eyes curved into a gentle half-moon smile. He knelt down and fished a few coins out of his pouch. "I imagine leaving the city will be expensive. Here, take this, sir." Etkis handed Cormac several gold coins, the last Etkis had on him. Dorin rolled his eyes.

The old man stared, mouth agape, at the gold and at the Velka. "Th-thank you, Mr. Wolf."

"What's your name, sir?"

"I…Cormac…my name is Cormac, Mr. Wolf."

"Hello, Cormac. Travel safely. Callva's speed."

Cormac bowed his head again and muttered, "Thank you, thank you" as he hobbled away massaging his throat. Once he left the alley, Kya returned.

"Well…that was interesting. Excellent work, Dory, putting yourself in a position that not only jeopardized you but the entire operation while implicating Etkis and me in a single stroke. Very well done. Masterful really," she said, hands at her hips.

"Fuck you, Kya! Sorry I'm not clairvoyant! I just wanted bullets, how was I supposed to know he was a cutthroat?" Dorin shouted.

"That's not the problem. You tried to go off and kill the man in a back alley without giving Etkis or me so much as an inkling. Thank Okar you're not nearly as quiet as you think you are, or he'd have gotten away. You're welcome for that, by the way, you reckless little prick."

Dorin snarled and approached Kya, but Etkis grabbed him by the collar and held him off the ground. Dorin flailed and kicked in midair trying to put his fist through Kya's stupid face but soon calmed at the impotence of it all. Etkis brought Dorin eye to eye. "Calm down. It's okay to be mad, but a fight isn't solving anything." Dorin grumbled indistinctly as he was set down. Kya snorted, smug, but Etkis turned to her as well. "And *you* don't need to be insulting anyone. The matter was solved and no one was hurt—"

"*No one?*" Dorin shouted and pointed to where Cormac had hit him with the wrench.

"*Almost* no one was hurt." Etkis corrected himself without missing a beat. "Dorin doesn't need you to point out his mistakes, Kya. He knows."

Kya began to retort but stopped herself. She crossed her arms and looked away in what Dorin could only describe as modest embarrassment. "So long as he knows," she muttered.

Dorin swore again to himself, leaned against the alley wall, and massaged his leg. He slammed his fist into the brickwork and bits of stone tumbled to the floor like hail. "*I. Hate. This. Fucking. City.* Can we go home yet, *please*?"

Etkis twitched his ears. "Come on now, it's not that…well…it's not *all* bad!"

Dorin pushed himself to standing. "Everyone in this city wants to kill me, rob me, or kill me so they can rob me! Of course no one hits *you* with a wrench, so everything's just dandy! *Ugh*, I need a drink."

Etkis grunted, uncomfortable. He looked at Kya, and she shrugged. "I know just the place."

Dorin sat down in the wood chair with a wince. It had been two days, and his leg still hurt, but his left shoulder had turned from a dark aubergine to a sickly red and yellow. Progress. The trio were back at Bella, the bar where they had first met. They had returned every night since Dorin and Etkis had arrived in Alexandria. Kya insisted that it was important to maintain a consistent cover—stiffs on the job who needed to relax after a long day's work. Her third round of vindol implied a different, simpler answer. The bar was packed with human and Velka alike. Another game of poker brewed with potential violence, and the rest of the bar was full of hearty laughter and foul drink. It was early enough in the night that people weren't swaying and toppling over tables but late enough that hands began to shake and alcohol spilled from glasses onto the mahogany floor. Dorin, Kya, and Etkis were all exhausted from a long day of fake shopping. Dorin ate what he referred to as a human "delicacy" of breaded fish and deep-fried potatoes. Etkis and Kya thought it looked exactly like chicken feed, but they said nothing. Dorin's helmet sat on the table beside his plate. After his third shot, Kya and Etkis had both barred him from ordering any more alcohol. He pouted in unusual silence and stared at his glass of water, lips twisted in spite. Etkis and Kya each had a food cylinder, while Kya was surrounded by empty glasses of Vindol with a fresh one in hand. She offered Etkis a round, which he refused as politely but firmly as he could.

"Do you think the tail is promising?" Dorin asked, french fry half out of his mouth. Kya looked at him, ears perked and surprised.

"Tail?" Etkis asked.

"We've had a few people following us all week. I thought it would take longer than that for Pompeii to put folk on us, but you won't hear me complaining."

"I didn't even notice," Etkis muttered.

"I say we find one of Pompeii's people and get the message out: handsome hitman available for hire. Thoughts?" Dorin asked Kya. He reached for his drink and swallowed the liquid but had forgotten that it was water. He slammed it down, disappointed.

"Wouldn't 'cripple for hire' be more accurate?" She asked with a none-too-subtle gesture at his metal arm. Etkis snorted; Dorin tightened his lips. Etkis looked at the ceiling pretending to have seen a bird. "But I'm impressed, Dorin," Kya continued. "I thought you were just a drunken imbecile."

"I can be a sober one too."

Kya chuckled. "I see that. I'll put the word out tomorrow morning that you're looking for work, but we should wait another few days before you actually approach anyone, let our cover really sink in."

"Feels excessive…"

"Patience is a virtue, Dory," Kya said. "Just relax, enjoy the city for a little while longer. I'll work it all out."

Dorin gritted his teeth. He looked over to Etkis, and a sudden idea brought an evil smile to his lips. "Since we're here *another* day, tomorrow we can finally visit the *brothels*, Etkis—your dreams have finally come true!" Dorin had never seen anyone freeze all motor functions like Etkis did just then. That included literal corpses.

"…Brothels?" Kya asked, her tone careful. Etkis's beating heart shifted from "extremely nervous" to "please let me die."

"*No!* No, no, no! I've never—that's not an activity that I would ever—I mean, look, I would do that…the physical act, I mean! But not with a mistress lady of the night! Not with a lad of the night either! I enjoy the female body, just not… you know…prostitutes." Etkis fumbled.

"Oh, good," Kya said. Her lovely voice betrayed a subtle smile behind her helmet. She leaned in. "Don't bother paying anyone for that, city boy. Build like yours? Trust me, dams and sires alike will be *begging* you for just a night! The hookers might just pay *you* for your services!" Dorin cackled and slapped the table. Etkis dropped his head into his hands and wondered if there had ever been a recorded death from sheer panic among his people. He didn't mind being the first.

"Well, Etkis," Dorin said through a fistful of chips, "I think Kya's right for once. The professionals aren't nearly as good as you'd hope. The lesson? Always lower your expectations, buddy. Disappointment is life's most sobering punishment. Now, sexy coworkers? Those have a much more consistent track record. 'In what?' you might ask?" Etkis fled into a small corner of his mind and tried to put his head under the table. Of course it couldn't fit. "Etkis? Buddy, look at me," Dorin said. Etkis peeked through his fingers. Dorin put his hand on his friend's shoulder. "Orgasms. I'm talking about orgasms."

Etkis slammed his head into the table, and splinters of wood flew every which way. Dorin quickly stole a glass of Vindol from an unsupervised table and gave it to Etkis, who instantly began chugging. Kya and Dorin clinked their glasses and laughed heartily.

Dorin stood, his eyes watering. "I'm gonna take a leak. Don't steal my chips." Dorin patted Etkis on the back and whispered, "And remember, Etkis, *sobriety is the enemy*." Etkis moved to say something, his eyes furious, but instead he finished his drink in one last go and immediately ordered another. Dorin ran straight to the bar rather than the bathroom, swerving to avoid touching any patrons, leaving the two Velka alone. Before he was out of earshot, he called over his shoulder, hitting his hands together in emphasis, "Frequency *and* magnitude, Etkis! Consistency!"

"He's fun," Kya said.

"He's a real riot," growled Etkis, his voice low and bassy with anger.

"I see why you keep him around. Very good for your reputation."

"Ugh."

Dorin slammed a copper coin on the countertop and motioned for a drink. The bartender poured him a double, and he chugged every last drop. He closed his eyes and let the liquid fire slow his beating heart. He turned and looked around the dive. Drinking, laughing, games, dancing, and singing. The clatter of plates and glasses on wooden tables, the stomping of feet. Too much. All of it at once. The level of input hurt Dorin's eyes. He closed them and shook his head, waiting for the alcohol to ease his burden.

When he opened his eyes, Dorin focused on one trio sitting at a table in the corner, farthest away from a dance party in the back. They spoke in hushed whispers, and from what Dorin saw, they were clearly well versed in covering up illicit dealings. He saw a small bag of coins change hands beneath the table and then a cylinder of purple liquid. Inthol. Jarrod implied he'd gotten his bottle from Alexandria. And there was the proof. Dorin snickered. *Kya wasn't kidding, Pompeii's people really are everywhere…sorry, Kya, patience can suck it.* He approached the men, cracking his fingers with his thumb.

"Greeting, my smelly compatriots," he said. They all turned to him, their faces confused but threatening.

"You got a problem?" the one across the table asked. They were all about Dorin's size, well-muscled, scarred, and all armed. Typical goons.

"Problem? No, quite the opposite, my yellow-toothed friend." He put his hands on the table and leaned in close. "I'm looking for work, and I heard that Pompeii is hiring for something big. I'd like to talk to him about that. *Personally.* Was wondering if you three lads could make an introduction," Dorin said. The goons stared at this stranger's metal hand, and they opened and closed their own to air out the sweat building in their palms.

"Don't know what you mean," one said.

Dorin slammed his boot on the table, and the men flinched. Dorin drew his knife and plunged it into the wood. It offered no resistance to the knife's combination of sharpness and heat; it parted as easily as a warm knife parts butter. The blue lines that ran along the blade's edge left no question as to its craftsmanship—Velkan weaponry was prized in Alexandria. They stared, mouths agape at the blade, then looked back at Dorin.

"I don't want to hurt you boys. Well, I *say* that—my point is I don't need to. Just give your boss a message, that he wants to hire me. Otherwise, I'll have to send a different kind of message to get Pompeii's attention. A bloody one." The three men all stood.

"Piss off," the biggest one said.

"Always the same dance," Dorin said with a smile. Dorin stomped down on the table as hard as he could. It flew into the man across from him, who grunted in pain and clutched his bruised gut.

The two other thugs charged Dorin. Neither drew guns—escalation was unnecessary against a single man. They couldn't have been more wrong. Dorin ducked and weaved between all their punches and parried with his steel appendage. Every blocked punch cracked bone as flesh yielded to metal. Dorin only launched a few well-placed hits with his human hand to the trachea and face. Their blood sprayed onto his brow, jaw, and stubble. In seconds the two attackers collapsed to the floor, their throats crushed, noses broken, hands and forearms fractured. The last man standing charged over the table with a drawn knife. Dorin thought it was a cute attempt. He parried a cut and broke the goon's elbow with an arm bar. The limb bent forty-five degrees in the wrong direction. He dropped to his knees, mouth wide, screaming, and Dorin kicked out his teeth. The pitter-patter of hard calcium phosphate echoed on the wood floor. It was over. The whole ordeal had taken less than twenty seconds.

The three men writhed on the floor. Dorin panted slightly, standing above them all. Blood dripped down his cheek and clothes, and he could hear the quiet crimson drops drip down upon the floor. In that moment he realized that he was surrounded by silence. He turned. Everyone stared at him. No one spoke. Etkis stood, hatchet drawn but unused. Kya stood too but had her hands to her head in horror. Dorin turned back to the thugs, who regrouped around the table. Dorin walked over to them, steady. He tried to wipe the drops of blood off his face with his sleeve, but instead it just smeared to a glossy sheen of scarlet. The thugs all kept their distance and backed away from him. Dorin pulled his knife out of the table with a sizzle of burnt wood.

"Deliver my message," he said. "And tell Pompeii I'm disappointed—Jarrod had tougher goons in a backwater town than you chumps." Dorin put his boot back on the table and sheathed his blade. "I think the king deserves a professional."

CHAPTER 12

New file > Human Leadership > Warlords > Unconfirmed: Alias: Pompeii.
Height, unknown. Age, unknown. Physical description, unknown.
Suspected of inciting an insurrection, conspiracy with adversarial house,
unsanctioned assassination of Warlord Linel. Special note: undetected
by scout regiment for unknown duration. Threat level: triple alpha.

—Volthsheim database, restricted for head of military fields only

"Sober imbecile in-fucking-deed!" Kya shouted. Plumes of frozen air tumbled from her filter with every word. She paced back and forth, and a deep trench of snow formed around her feet. They had quickly made their escape from the bar after Kya had tossed a small bag of coins to the owner for damages. They'd sheltered in a black back alley, several blocks away from the dive. The alleyway was darker still as it was juxtaposed against bright burning amber lights that flooded the street. Snow floated gently from the sky. Dorin leaned against the breeze-block alley wall, arms folded across his chest to protect himself from the cold. His shoulder hurt anew. The bone had been put under far too much stress after the fight in the bar. Etkis stood beside him, barely able to fit in the width of the ally, his head down, listening intently.

"Calm down," Dorin said. "We needed Pompeii's attention, and now he knows that I'm a capable hire. He can't ignore his own men getting beaten to butter in the middle of his territory. He'll have to take notice."

Kya kept pacing, waving her hands in furious emphasis. "Yes, Dorin, he will take notice—but instead of showing up in a suit and tie for your job interview, you've kicked down the boss's front door and slammed your dick on top of the desk and screamed, '*I'm here, bitch, sign me up!*' If he does or doesn't hire you, he'll *definitely* remember you! And by extension *me*. Because, *unfortunately*, we're associated with each other."

Dorin raised his voice to match Kya, a mistake he didn't appreciate. "Every day we wait, the Serpents flood more weapons into Wolf territory, human gangs become a greater threat, and Rother climbs farther up our asses!"

Kya finally stopped pacing. "They know I'm connected to you—do you understand the position you've put me in? You leave when all this is over, but I have to live here! What contacts am I going to be able to make after this? No one will trust my judgment now!"

Dorin lowered his voice. "I've saved us days' worth of nauseating conversations with metal vendors. So, really, you should be thanking me. *You're welcome.*"

Kya thrust her fist into Dorin's stomach. Air exploded out of his mouth, and his stomach cramped and yanked his solar plexus deep under the sternum, his knees buckled, and he fell. It had been a long time since he'd been well and truly gut punched—he had to focus on keeping dinner from spilling out his mouth. Kya lifted her arm to throw another punch, but Etkis grabbed and pulled her off Dorin. She thrashed against his arms, and he released her, his hands up and open.

"That's enough, he gets the point," Etkis said.

Dorin wheezed, hands on his stomach. "Actually, I didn't quite catch it. Could you try again?"

"Shut up," Etkis said with a little kick to Dorin's foot. "Kya, we'll figure it out. We've saved a lot of time on…introductions—"

"*Introductions?*" she screamed.

"I know, not ideal, but it's true." He lowered his hands and leaned in, and the snow crunched beneath his shifting weight. "The sooner we eliminate Jormar and Pompeii as a threat, the sooner this all goes away."

Kya balled her hands into fists, her ears flattened over her helmet. She grunted furiously, and a blast of white air flew from her filter. "*Idiots,*" she spat. She turned and stormed away, cursing violently under her breath with every stride.

"Thanks for that—she's got a fantastic straight," Dorin said. He sat back against the wall with his arms still cradled his throbbing gut.

"That was a real swine-headed move, Dorin," Etkis said. His voice was calm but was weighted with deep disapproval and a hint of shame. "You couldn't talk to us about that stunt first?"

"I saw an opportunity, and I took it! I don't understand the problem."

"You're not doing this alone. You can't just do what seems best in the moment without considering the consequences to everyone else! You really screwed her over."

Dorin sighed. He struggled to his feet and rested his head back against the stone wall. His stomach throbbed and shoulder burned. The pain in his arm made him fiercely regret the bar fight, just not in the way Kya and Etkis meant. Dorin opened his eyes and looked up. The narrow passage up became a funnel, a long horizontal strip of the luminous stars. The night was unusually clear, and he could see the rim of the Milky Way stretch across his entire field of view. The moon shone straight above; its transition from full to waning could barely be noticed.

"Remember that time on Phobos, when we saw a comet? We hopped on our ship and followed it just because we could. We landed on it and watched Mars fly back into the distance at forty kilometers a second, the red disappeared into a haze of crystal dust. We didn't wonder what the consequences were, how stupid it was to land on a speeding ball of ice headed straight into the asteroid belt. We did it because it was fun. It was dangerous. An adventure…I miss that feeling."

Etkis squatted down in front of his friend, "Next time ask. Okay?"

"Okay."

"And go apologize to Kya."

"Oh, come on!"

Etkis tilted his head.

"Fine," Dorin grunted. Another wave of nausea hit, and he had to lean on his knees. "But I won't be happy about it."

"Deal…you're not moving."

"Yeah, no, Jesus pissing Christ, she hits like a meteor. Just give me a second."

Kya fumed down the street toward her apartment. Her hand never ventured far from her pistol's grip. She turned slightly to look behind her. *Three tails...piss*, she thought. There were only a few hours of darkness left, and she would need them to make her escape back home to Oliver's. Kya made it to her building and hopped up the stairs two at a time to get to the door. She entered the dark room, shut and bolted the heavy door. The apartment was too high for the streetlights to shine through, but bright blue moonlight shone down onto her mismatched furniture in long columns from the two windows. It was jet-black save for the prisms of light. Kya took a long, deep breath and leaned her forehead against the door. *Safe.*

"Kya, is it?"

Kya spun and drew her pistol in an instant. Kya couldn't see the intruder's face, but it was a woman's voice, with no digitized inflection, so it must have been a human. "You can put the gun down, I'm unarmed," she said.

"Sure you are," Kya said. Her gun stayed put, her finger on the trigger. The stranger didn't seem to mind at all, and Kya knew why. If she killed this intruder, Pompeii would surely kill Dorin and Etkis. The mission would be scrapped. And Kya wouldn't live to see the end of the week.

The stranger chuckled. "I like them savvy. You have no idea how many *curs* fall for that."

Kya twitched at the slur, but her gun remained steady. *Pompeii's known for swift retaliation, but this is just ridiculous.* A silhouette moved on the sofa chair at the far end of the room, hair to the shoulders, muscular frame, but Kya could see no more. "Did Pompeii send you?" she asked. She didn't reach for the light switch—doing so would've been a declaration of war against the hitman. If she didn't want to be seen, fine. It wasn't worth the risk.

"Something like that," the stranger replied. "I'm familiar with your PI work, you have quite the reputation! You rough up your marks more than a little, huge fan of that, and your info is always on point. I love that kind of reliability."

Kya searched for subtext in the woman's voice but found none. She wasn't monotone, there were clear inflections in her voice, but it was cold, empty, almost devoid of sincerity. Just like Rother. A chill ran up Kya's spine.

"I enjoy what I do," Kya said.

"We have that in common…do you know why I'm here?"

"I have a notion. Those poor chumps at the bar? Friends of yours?"

"Tools of mine, and yes, partially. It forced me to come here myself."

"Yourself? You're…"

"Pompeii, at your service. Before you ask, the moment you kill me triggers several contingencies that result in the murder of fifty-seven people, all your friends, two of which are the freelancer and Velka you've been in contact with."

Kya fought the impulse to pull the trigger. She couldn't be sure if this woman was indeed Pompeii, she couldn't tell if this woman was lying without seeing her face, but something about her compelled belief. The conviction in her voice, the promise of violence in the air. Every instinct told her to believe. To be afraid.

"I believe you," Kya said. Pompeii leaned forward on the couch.

"I've been watching you for some time. Do you know how many Velka live in Alexandria?"

"I haven't counted."

"I have—647,398. Most are here on contract to trade goods that Alexandrians provide for Volthsheim, over sixty percent of which is lunar ore for interstellar fuel. Twenty percent is metal and other bulk infrastructure goods. Ten percent are foods that humans can't consume but Velka can, and ten percent are here for banking—loaning money to humans with interest. And that's where you fall in."

"Is there a point you're coming to, or do you just like to hear yourself speak?"

Pompeii leaned back in the chair and scratched at the armrest. "You're unique, Kya. No human has ever seen a Velkan child outside of your fortress cities, and certainly not in Alexandria. And yet some people have told me that you've been around this city since you were a little bitch about knee-high. Now how does that make sense?"

"It doesn't. You should check your sources." Kya felt blood rush through her heart to her limbs. She fought the natural instinct to flee or murder.

"I did—*thoroughly*. You should keep fewer, better friends."

Kya felt her throat go dry and her jaw squeeze tight. *Who could she be talking about?* Kya thought. *What did she do to them?* Though Kya couldn't see her, she knew Pompeii was smiling.

"You've been here for, what? Two decades now? I know for a fact that you're aware of what happened twenty years ago, about three hundred thousand kilometers in the air, just beside Luna."

Kya felt terror, but she held it in. When she spoke, her voice was hard as stone. "How do you know about that?" she asked.

"A recent acquaintance of mine had firsthand experience. Very interesting stories. He said your people fought bravely to the last man—or the last woman, in this case."

Jormar, Kya thought. The terror grew, an apocalypse to her sanity—but she held her tongue. The only reason she knew about him was because of Dorin and Etkis's intel. To reveal her knowledge would tip her hand.

"My theory," Pompeii said, "is that an escape pod crashed in the harbor in the middle of the night—people might have mistaken it for spaceship debris or a meteorite, but instead it was a little. Velka. Pup. How close am I?"

"…Close."

"*Yes!*" she shouted in delight, the first real sign of emotion from this dark figure. "Tell me, why do you choose to live in the poorest region of the entire solar system? You could've lived anywhere, but you chose to stay here. Where you grew up, among me and mine. I like to think we've accepted you and that you've found happiness here. A life. A family. More than you have with the Wolves. And we need your help."

Kya sneered. "You threaten my friends, and now you ask for my help? You're a real piece of work, aren't you?"

"Just because I'm a bastard doesn't mean everyone else is! Think about them. The thousands of men, women, and children fleeing here in terror from the Wolves. Everyday people come here seeking shelter from the raids. They seek my protection. But what I know that they don't is that Alexandria isn't safe. Our 'independence' is a farce, a political posture to appease the other Velka houses. That's all it is. One day soon we'll be raided too. They've herded all the cattle to a single pen, and now they can take everything they need. You know what they're capable of. If we used every single ship we have and fitted it with a mass driver cannon, would we stand a chance against a single Wolf Caelicraft?"

"…No."

"No. We'd get stomped. That's why we need the Serpents. The way the House of Stone needed the Wolves, now humanity needs the House of Serpents. It's the only way for my people to survive the coming storm. Surely you can understand that?" Pompeii's voice changed ever so slightly. Kya thought it sounded almost pleading. "I need your help to save the lives of your adopted family."

A surge of panic. *Was that just a turn of phrase?* Kya thought. *Or does she know about Ollie? I can't very well ask. It's true that the raids have been worse than ever, but the Wolves would never attack Alexandria...right?*

"What do you need?" Kya asked. *Better to play along for now.*

"Simple information. You have some friends in town, a man with a metal arm and an uncomfortably large Velkan Wolf. Tell me about them."

Kya relaxed her tight shoulders. "Velka's an old friend of mine. A merchant from Volthsheim, as I'm sure you've heard. I suggest you find better people––I spotted them pretty quickly this afternoon. And the day before. And the day before that..."

"Idiots," Pompeii spat.

Kya continued, "The human is some freelancer hired for protection and guidance. He asked me to start fishing for his next contract, so I was going to see if you were hiring. But turns out he wanted your...personal attention. Sorry about the bar, wasn't my idea."

"This metal man, does he have a problem with me?"

Kya snickered. "Not at all. He just likes the attention."

"Humph, he must think highly of himself. But he beat up three men by his lonesome, and if you vouch for him, he just might have a place in our higher ranks. Names?"

"Etkis, merchant, midrank, and freelancer's named Dorin."

Click.

Kya's pulse quickened. Pompeii had pulled back the hammer of an unseen gun, no question. "What's wrong?" She asked. No response—there was silence. Kya thought back to the last time she was in this apartment. She searched her mind to see if there was any clue that she had left behind that might lead this woman to Ollie but found none. If she was to die here, she needed to be sure her Pabbi was safe.

Pompeii took out an envelope and held it up in the moonlight for Kya to see. "This will get him through the door. Compound, by the spaceport. Tell him to be there at eight p.m.," she said. She tossed the envelope onto the black floor. "Etkis, no connection to the Wolf guards or scouts?"

Kya felt the muscles around her jaw tighten. "None."

The figure in the dark began to walk toward the door, toward Kya. She moved simultaneously to maintain the distance between her and the figure, circling around the dark apartment. In the shifting light, Kya tried to discover this woman's face—but all she could see were flashes of bright red hair. The stranger put her hand on the doorknob and turned it but stopped.

"Dorin...I heard his *right* arm is the metal one. Is that true?"

Kya turned her head to the odd question. "Yes...why?"

"Huh...get some sleep, Kya." The door opened and shut—Pompeii was gone.

Kya dropped her aim and ran to the radio stashed beneath the kitchen sink. Her shoulder ached from holding the gun, and she let it fall next to the console. She dialed in the familiar frequency and clicked the button. She held the wireless mic in her hand as she scoured the apartment for cameras or listening devices. Nothing.

"Ollie? Ollie, are you there?"

Silence. Kya felt her stomach drop. She gripped the microphone hard. A tired voice answered.

"Hello? Kya? What's wrong?"

Kya leaned her back against the wall, hand to her chest, and realized she hadn't been breathing. Deep gasps of air filled her chest. "Nothing, Pabbi, everything's okay. Did you message Rother?"

"Scouts are picking me up tomorrow...are you sure everything's alright? You sound out of breath."

"Everything's fine, I promise. Go back to sleep. I love you."

"Love you too, Sunshine." The microphone clicked, and Kya dropped it to the floor. She walked over to the couch and collapsed. She plunged her head into her hands.

That was too damn close. She sat up, shut her eyes, closed and opened her hands, over and over again. She began to repeat her mantra to herself. "Breathing in, I notice my breath has become deeper. Breathing out, I notice that my breath has become slower…" She went on, repeating the meditation until the blood pulsing in her neck to her ears slowed, her breaths became easier. She opened her eyes. The moon had changed position in the sky, but she had no idea what time it was. *Pompeii's a fool. How could she think that I'd betray the Wolves? Arrogant…he's right about the way man is treated, though. Ollie never wanted to go to Volthsheim for a reason. I know too many good folk who've come here because they lost everything. It's been policy to leave Alexandria for so long, but I've never really thought about why. What's stopping them?*

Knock, knock.

Kya jumped. *What now?* She retrieved her pistol and walked to the door. She placed it with the barrel facing the wood at the center of mass.

"Who is it?" she asked. She felt the trigger.

"The drunken imbecile, open up."

Kya groaned and opened the door a crack to see Dorin standing in the hallway with his helmet beneath his arm. The harsh fluorescent light made his skin look sick and pale.

"What is it! Wait—how'd you find my apartment?" she asked, not at all masking her contempt. Dorin looked past her into the room.

"Why are you just in the dark?"

"*Dorin. What. Do. You. Want?*"

Dorin looked away for a second and chewed on his tongue, and thought for a moment about leaving. *She reeeeally doesn't wanna talk.* The memory of Etkis's shameful stare kept him fixed.

"Look," he said, avoiding eye contact, "I know we have different methods in this case, and *maybe* I went about things in a rash or impulsive way and *maybe* I should've talked to you and Etkis about it first." He turned to her. "*But* I also saved us time, I'm sure we'll hear from this Pompeii twat within the day…but I recognize that the consequences for you are more severe and I didn't think about that and *maybe*…for you the risks did outweigh the reward. And I didn't think about that. So yeah. There."

Kya narrowed her eyes. "Is this an apology?"

"Sort of. Kind of. Yes."

Kya twitched her ears and tapped on the door with her thumb, waiting for the magic words. Dorin rolled his eyes and inhaled deeply. "I am sorry. I apologize. I offer my pride as recompense for my dishonorable conduct, the whole lot! Please, can I stop? This is really uncomfortable for me."

Despite herself, Kya began to chuckle, and soon Dorin smiled too.

"Thank you. Yes, it was stupid and selfish and all those things. But…thank you."

"You've got a good arm—this was better than getting slugged again. But just barely."

Kya thought for a moment and realized her pistol was still in her hand. She looked back into the black apartment. She'd left the letter in one of the patches of blue light that came from the windows.

"I should be honest," Dorin said. Kya turned back at him in surprise. His head was down, and he twisted his foot against the lanolin carpet. "I didn't want to come here, to apologize. I'm not…good, that way. I'd have gone back to my bunk and stared at the wall in angst until I died if you let me. I meant what I said, but I'm only here because Etkis asked me to come. So here I am."

"So here you are…" Kya squeezed her pistol in her hand; the wood grip squeaked from the friction. She holstered it.

"You don't need to wait until tomorrow," she said. Dorin scrunched his brow, puzzled. Kya opened the door wide. "Your 'plan' worked. You're in."

CHAPTER 13

The House of Wolves own humanity, naturally. No one disputes this. But is it not then their responsibility to see to the well-being of their vassals? To exert their incomparable power against a dying breed? And for what? Their meager resources? When a pup disrespects their elder, are they beaten within an inch of their life? Of course not. They are disciplined, and shown the error of their ways.

—Her Lordship Jarl Myrr Notoko of the House of Waves, Summit of the Houses, 2.27.500

Etkis sat in Rose with his hand over his eyes, his jaw tight. He squeezed his fist and focused on the cloth doll tied to his belt. He could've sworn the little blue eyes mocked him. He was alone in the cockpit with the monitor on. The console's cold blue light reflected off the metal interior to make a prison of monotone color. A warm and powerful voice came through the speakers. Lady Nora was on the screen, her tone sympathetic but unyielding.

"I'm sorry, Etkis, but it's necessary," she said.

"How? Shooting down fleeing aircraft would limit casualties and accomplish the same goal."

"We can't risk our warships, Etkis. If a single Serpent aircraft were to leave the Alexandria spaceport, we'd be putting our navy at risk. Each ship is a key node in the web of power we've spun around Volthsheim, Earth, Luna. For now the balance favors us, not the Serpents. And to your point, what would become of Alexandria if the Serpents gained control? Human casualties would not be *limited*."

"They'll hate us for this."

"Fine. They can hate us. They can be right to hate us. But they have to respect us."

Etkis shook his head. Lady Nora continued—her tone shifted to reflect a small offer of consolation.

"Tarkus and I have decided against increasing raids on human settlements. I agreed with your recommendation. We can avoid that carnage."

Etkis threw a hand up, frustrated, "Small solace now. This will make raids seem like a snowflake in an avalanche."

"We do what we can walking on the edge of a knife, Etkis. Brief Dorin and Kya on the mission. Rother has sent his scouts. You will rendezvous with them and your guards over the edge of the mountains. Kya will know a route to ensure that you aren't seen."

"Yes, my lady."

She lingered for a moment. Etkis felt her empathy, struggle, and commitment through the monitor. He nodded in affection—she understood. The screen went black. The sun budded on the horizon. He leaned back and closed his eyes. *The Roarers…the merchants…the children in the slums*, Etkis thought. A vice gripped his throat and diaphragm, and he wished he could stop feeling. The door slid open with a loud clunk. Dorin ran in, followed slowly by Kya.

"Etkis, you won't believe this! *It worked! I'm a genius!* Pompeii's invited me to her compound!"

Etkis whipped around to face them. "Wait, what? It's only been a few hours!"

Kya shrugged. Etkis shook his head. "Piss, all right. I don't want you to go in alone, but I also sure as hell didn't want you beating Pompeii's guards into bloody steaks, so screw it. We have our orders. We're to meet some scouts and some of my guards over the mountains, in the forest by the compound. We're not to be seen—Kya, do you know a good route?"

"Depends on how you feel about sewers."

"Great…*sewage*. We'll jam their communications once Dorin gives us the signal that the vehicle bay's blocked off. I don't have a plan for how you do that exactly, any explosive will be taken off you before you make it inside…but you need to cut off their exit."

Dorin blew a raspberry. "Half-assed and half-planned is how I approach *every* job, I'll figure it out. What's the signal?" He held an imaginary assault rifle and shot it into the sky in aggressive pantomime. Etkis narrowed his eyes, keenly aware of Dorin's usual tactic.

"*Not gunfire,*" Etkis said. "Find a south-facing room, flick the lights in Morse code. We'll break in and capture or kill all targets. They won't have a chance to escape on foot...hopefully they'll just surrender instead of dying en masse. Sardines in a bucket or however the saying goes. Once you've given the signal, Kya and I will shoot a flare...the Wolf fleet will destroy the spaceport."

"What!" Kya shouted. "The port draws in over *half* of Alexandria's economy! You'll cripple us, and we barely get by as is!"

Dorin turned to Kya, his nose scrunched in disgust. "It'll cripple *them*, you mean. And good. Uppity peasants."

Kya shoved Dorin and he threw off her hands with his metal arm. "This is my home too!" she yelled. "These are your people! How can you turn your back on them? On us?"

"Easily. When you're born an urchin, raised as an orphan, and die betrayed, you tend to abandon the shit that got you from A to Z."

Kya shuffled her feet, uncomfortable. She had a pit in her stomach that forced her to contend with the fact that she knew exactly what he meant. *If Pabbi hadn't found me back then...*

Dorin went on. "You're my people now. You and Etkis. And I'm"—Dorin forced the next word—"*sorry* that you're in this position. But we have a responsibility to the house, to ensure its safety at any cost."

"Oh please, you didn't even want citizenship to the house when it was offered to you!"

Dorin scrunched his eyebrows, "How..." He looked to Etkis, who in turn looked at the floor, "Damn it, Etkis!"

Kya put her finger on Dorin's chest. "Just because you're angry and spiteful doesn't mean you get to burn the world with impunity. No one gets to be that selfish." Dorin twisted his lips in anger but didn't retort. There was a leaden silence. Etkis waited until he was sure they were finished. This needed to be resolved between them. He couldn't interfere.

"I don't like it either, Kya. I said as much. But the jarl has decided. We can't take the risk that there's any hidden Serpent warships or munitions. And under the cover of night, with communications cut and no way for them to quickly get to the port, we can remove the threat with no risk to ourselves and to the house. Hopefully we can help them rebuild it once this is over."

"After countless deaths and punching a hole in the economy! These people don't have a safety net, Etkis, they don't have a house looking after them. If we break their spaceport, they'll starve before we 'build them another one.'"

"I was just trying to be positive…we bomb the port, then we move in. That's the mission."

Dorin spoke, giddy. "Sweet, sweet justice for the amount of times I've been stopped at customs. *What have you got in that bag, sir? There's a five-drink limit on flights, sir.* I've wanted to kill that place for a long time! Now if only we could blow up the moon too, my bucket list would be complete!"

Etkis smacked Dorin in the head, and Dorin proceeded to rub his new bruise. *I've got a nice collection going,* he thought. Kya had a deep desire to punch him square in the face, which Dorin sensed and so immediately backtracked.

"I'm…sorry. That was inappropriate." Dorin coughed uncomfortably. "…When are we leaving?"

Kya rolled her eyes and fumed. In a way, Pompeii had predicted something like this. This wasn't a raid, but it might as well have been. In fact, it was worse. Much worse. She felt like a fool for not listening. "If we want to make it there by your meet time Dorin, Etkis and I need to leave now. Dorin, you can head over in the afternoon. Take the trains––it'll help you to take normal public transit. Etkis, we should arm ourselves now. There's a sewer hatch just across the lot we can use."

Etkis pulled his weaponry off Rose's arms rack. He sheathed the knife and clipped his hatchet to his waist. The Roarers' little doll bounced on his hip, attached to his belt. Etkis grabbed a current rifle from the wall. Two large capacitors bulged near twin exhaust ports where human guns would sport their action. The Velkan electrical weapon could dump enough voltage through the air to exceed even robust insulator's breakdown rating and would arc even through thick rubber. It would blow through the snow piles and ice sheets that littered

Alexandria like a flamethrower through tissue paper. The Serpents wouldn't be ready for it. It would melt through unbarriered humans and boil Velka alike in their suits. He grabbed his armor and stuffed all his equipment in a large sack. The last thing he grabbed, solemnly, was a flare.

Kya grabbed a bandolier and slung it across her chest. She filled the empty holds with grenade after grenade, then snagged Etkis's new Elo rifle off the wall and heaved the long heavy weapon with both hands. The gun Dorin could barely lift was swung around her shoulder like any other gun, and the freelancer twisted his mouth in insecure spite. Kya's long-barreled ballistic pistol was ever-present at her hip. She felt like she could conquer the world with this much firepower. If Pompeii wanted her corpse, she'd better send a goddamned division. She and Etkis attached their barriers, the large cylindrical batteries magnetically connected to the smalls of their backs.

Dorin donned his helmet and drew Soot. He inspected the gun, rolled the massive cylinder, and counted all eight bolts. He stuck warm slugs into his own waistline bandolier, in the few slots that were empty. He holstered his hand cannon with a twirl.

Etkis came over to him and put his hand on Dorin's shoulder. This operation would put Lipel to shame. Neither knew if someone out in the compound carried a bullet or energy cartridge with their name or the name of their best friend. For Dorin it was an uncharacteristic moment of sobriety. He put his small, human hand over his friend's.

"You too," Dorin said, his usual facetious tone absent. Etkis tapped on Dorin's helmet, right on the visor.

"Keep your head down, Velka visors—"

"I've heard."

Etkis left without another word. He remembered his foster sister Triti and prayed Dorin would not share her fate. Kya walked straight past Dorin, still angry, but before she could leave, he spoke up.

"May Okar give you purpose, Kior give you focus, Callva give you will."

Kya stopped, shocked at the prayer of duty for her people. She'd never heard any human, not even her own father, recite it. She took a deep breath, her anger and compassion battling in her heart.

"I still want to punch you in the face, you know."

Dorin shrugged with a smile. "It's a common affliction."

"Ha, I bet."

Dorin chewed on his tongue, regretting his careless words earlier, "I'm sorry…again. I owe you a round of inthol once this is over."

Kya's ears twitched, the apology sincere. She nodded, a smile filled her eyes. "Damn straight, you do…don't get shot, Dorin." And she was gone.

Etkis changed into his armor as soon as they entered the sewers and thanked Okar to be back in familiar garb again. Kya turned her back to let him change in privacy, the urge to look powerful in her bones. When he finished, Etkis threw the clothes and sack together in a pile and incinerated them with a touch of his tomahawk. The two headed west, toward the spaceport. They talked the whole way through the damp sewers. Every question Etkis asked was pleasantly personal, didn't dig too deep into her life, and at the same time was politely interested in her day-to-day affairs. He was shut down each time by a witty comment—the telltale mark of someone who wanted to change the subject.

"Which province of Volthsheim did you grow up in?" Etkis asked. "My early years were Province Nine, but military training was over in Twelve."

"I grew up in a magical area, free of responsibilities and oceans of liquor. It's only for *the specials*, you understand. That's why you've never heard of it."

"Ah, yes, yes, naturally. You *are* special. This mystical land have a name?"

"If you have to ask, you're not ready to know."

He dropped it after that. Kya had no trouble asking about Etkis's personal life, and he found in her a surprisingly empathetic confidant. He told her about his journey to Alexandria in detail beyond a military briefing, mixed in with the occasional joke at Dorin's expense. She asked him about the doll that Etkis had tied to his belt.

"It was a gift," he said. "The ranchers gave it to me after Dorin and I saved them from raiders. The Roarers. I hope they're doing well."

"I don't see the resemblance—it doesn't look anything like Dorin…it's far too pretty."

Etkis felt his heart dance a little, unsure if the flirtation he felt was intentional or not. "Hilarious. Dorin didn't get to know them, that's why they didn't make him one. Wish they did, though, would've been good for him."

Kya cleared her throat, uncomfortable. "Dorin told me you made him apologize. About what happened last night."

"…Oh. I take it he did, then?"

"Yes. Poorly."

"Sounds about right." They laughed together. Kya squeezed the rifle in her hand. The sincerity made her feel uneasy, but pleasantly so.

"You didn't need to do that," she said after a moment, "but I wanted to say thank you."

Etkis gave a little wave of his hand. "You don't need to thank me. He was being an asshat, and he needs a nudge in the direction of minimized asshattery from time to time."

"You really care about him, then? You're always trying to look out for him."

"Of course. Is that odd?"

Kya shrugged. "In a way. Most Wolves I've talked to see humans as…"

"Cattle?"

"Yeah."

Etkis played with the stark white doll in his hand. He was surprised at how easy it was becoming to talk and spend time with Kya. She was a constant flirt but always in good humor. She made blood surge through Etkis's heart. He never reciprocated, of course, not that he didn't want to; he was too uncomfortable to do so. They weren't in the Great Hall of Volthsheim, after all. It was a scandal to fraternize in the line of duty. Not that Kya gave a damn.

Kya and Etkis had gone into the sewers at the crack of dawn and emerged at the edge of twilight. Etkis struggled to clamber out of the manhole, his broad shoulders caught on the metal rim. He spent thirty seconds on the ladder trying to get his limbs and armor out of the manhole—Kya waited silently below for him to figure it out.

"*I am so sick of this!*" He growled, sweaty, humiliated, and miserable. "I miss Volthsheim, where doors are made for properly sized citizens."

"Yes, yes, what a hard life you live."

Etkis pushed his pauldrons hard against the steel-concrete rim, and bits of gray broke with a loud crack and flew into the snow. Once out, he held the sewer grate open as Kya passed through. He set it down gently. The cover now sat tilted on the broken concrete. Kya looked at the spaceport beyond Pompeii's compound.

"It'll be gone by tomorrow morning," she said. "You have no idea what this'll do to them—to us. I hope I don't have any friends there tonight…"

Etkis stayed crouched, facing away from her. He couldn't look her in the eye right now.

"I'm sorry. You don't have to believe me, but I tried to convince them not to do it."

"…It's something you would do."

Etkis stood and came beside Kya. A transport ship descended from Luna and landed on the cement tarmac. Dozens of people exited the craft and loaded into a car that would take them to the train station.

Etkis offered a meek capitulation. "At least those poor workers won't have to die."

Kya spoke without looking at him, her voice measured. "Humanity might begin attacking after this. What are we going to do about that?"

"We'll convince them to stand down."

"If they don't?"

"It won't come to that."

"And if it does?"

Etkis swallowed a dry throat. He couldn't entertain the possibility. "They're the native people of this system, of this world. Every Velka owes them a debt from the day they're born. We won't kill them, we're better than that. We'll find another way."

"Easy to say in peacetime. I hope we keep to it."

The air was leaden with their solemn duty. A moment of silence. Etkis kicked the snow. "I know we're not your favorite people right now, but once this is over, you should come to Volthsheim. You don't have to stay, but Dorin would love to get drunk with you!"

"Ha ha, he would, huh? What the hell, he owes me a drink anyway."

"Okar help me—he owes you too now? Welp, we can bankrupt him together. If I can still stand, I'll have failed."

Kya laughed, and they both began to walk through the woods, searching for the advance team of scouts and guards.

"I've never met a Wolf guard," Kya said, "other than you, anyway. Introduce me when we meet them."

"Of course! I've only met a few scouts—I think Toa's been sent here along with some of the others who picked up Jarrod."

"I've worked with Toa a few times, she's a sweetheart." Kya said. She side-eyed Etkis, her tone sly. "Is she your partner?"

"How could she be my partner? I'm not a scout..." The realization dawned on him, and the crushing responsibility of forming a response stuck words in his mouth and made him trip over his own massive boots. "*Oh, you mean*—no, no. Not at all. Nothing romantic. Not that I wouldn't, she's very beautiful—"

"Uh huh."

"But you know, I don't know her. And that's unprofessional."

"You don't date military types? Shame."

Etkis swore. Every possible response seemed laden with unintended meaning. "That's not what I meant!" he said, desperate to backtrack.

"Why don't you ask Toa out when you get back to the city, then? Afraid she'll say no?"

"Not at all."

"Wow."

"No, wait! That's not—I'll shut up." His bulk wilted in despair.

"No, no, it's okay," Kya said through a laugh. "I'm sure she'd say yes too. Not a lot of folk could resist all of *that*."

"...Thanks," Etkis said. The temperature of his skin peaked inside his suit to dangerous levels.

"Dorin and I can applaud from afar. You two could have a lot of fun together! She loves flowers, by the way."

Etkis swallowed, his throat dry. This was his time. Now or never. Etkis remembered Dorin's words of comfort from years ago on an alcohol-fueled night filled with romantic failures comparable to piloting a starship into the sun. Etkis didn't just crash and burn. He ignited on entry and melted into hot plasma—and he didn't even have the luxury of dying. Etkis remembered Dorin's look of bemusement and utterly anticipated disappointment when he said, "Every dog has his day, my boy."

Etkis breathed deep in determined consternation. *Etkis, *you* are the dog. Today is your day!*

His skin was so hot beneath his suit he thought he might combust. "Well... what do *you* like?"

Kya's voice caught in her throat. "Wh...I..."

A voice from off in the woods called to them in a low whisper, "First Guard Terra? Sir, we are ready at your command."

Sunlight shone horizontal in the late evening. Trees separated the light just enough so that gold rays could penetrate the thicket. The snow was orange with the setting sun. Toa Hiru and several of the other scouts who apprehended Jarrod appeared from the dark woods with two dozen other Velka. Half bore different symbols of the moon on their chest, while the other half were adorned with pieces of the House of Wolves sigil. Scouts and guards, from veteran to recruit. They all crossed their arms across their chests in the Velkan salute.

"Scout Hiru! Ahem...a pleasure to see you again," Etkis said.

"I bet it is," Kya muttered. Etkis bumped Kya affectionately in the arm but couldn't help but feel disappointed at the deflection.

"How do you want to approach the compound, sir?" Toa asked. She didn't look at Kya at all. Etkis for once understood why. He tried not to think about it, and he knelt to be at eye level with them all.

"We stay in the thicket until nightfall, then we station near the edge of the woods. Dorin is our man inside. When he's ready, he'll give us the signal. At the signal, turn on the communications jammer. Then I need Scout Hiru to head over the ridge and shoot a flare so that our warships can launch their attack. After the flare we storm the compound. I'll be the vanguard. Stay behind me for as long as you can. In my experience humans tend to surrender after a good show of force. Serpents will likely die fighting. I'd like to take them alive, if possible, but don't put yourselves at extreme risk to do so. Put them down if you have to. If you see Jormar, don't approach him alone. Surround him and cripple him with explosives, or call for me. Together we can bring him down. I don't expect him to come alive, but it would be helpful if he did. Rother and I have questions about their jarl."

Dorin rode the train through Alexandria in the late evening. He had spent the bulk of the day drinking and cleaning Soot, his two most calming hobbies. As the sun began to drop west, he hopped onto the train line. Alexandria, even motion-blurred out of the speeding train's windows, disgusted him. He suppressed his gag reflex at regular intervals. Sometimes a poor unwitting stranger would sit next to him in the crowded car. Dorin stared at them unblinking like a lidless reptile until they got up and left. Such was his way around mankind.

The train had emptied, save for the lunar miners, once it had passed through the tunnel beneath the ancient, dead starships that made up the Alexandrian "mountain range." The smell of space travel and dust filled the car and triggered memories of his old home. His mother always smelled like that when she returned from work. Ashton used to say it smelled like brimstone, but Dorin thought it smelled more like burnt steak. Like a safe, warm meal. He clenched his jaw at the thought. When the car finally stopped on the other side of the mountains, Dorin ran out to escape the people and the memory. He walked through the station for no more than a minute, then a strange valet with a bushy white goatee walked up to him. Dorin handed him the letter that Kya had gotten from Pompeii. The man didn't even read it.

"Pardon me, sir—my master is expecting you," he said.

Dorin followed him to a small rover a fraction the size of Rose. He got in the back seat. In the seat pockets were bottles of honey liquor, just like the kind in Volthsheim. Dorin threw off his helmet and grabbed the bottle, uncorked it, and swallowed mouthfuls at a time. He'd missed the taste so much—he hadn't realized how much he had longed for Volthsheim. The massive steel walls and warm hearths in the Great Hall. The taste of this sweet, burning liquid gave him a smile from cheek to cheek. *Pompeii is a lady of fine taste!* he thought. The valet took the wheel, and they sped down a road. The rover rumbled over the snow-covered stones. Before long they came to a large metal gate with guards at either side. It opened slowly; the poorly oiled hinges squeaked horribly. A cheap imitation of Volthsheim's walls. The compound itself was as lavish as any human being on the planet could afford. It was everything that Jarrod had aspired to project. Ornate statues scattered around the grounds. The walls were tall, solid marble. The white stone blended into the snow. Lanterns turned on as twilight faded and amber light bled into the coming dark. *Linel's old home,* Dorin thought. He'd mopped floors here as a boy. That was how he'd met the crime lord. From what he remembered, there was a bookcase with hinges tucked out of view in the study upstairs. He didn't know why back then, but now he was sure. It was the escape tunnel.

Dorin was let out of the car, the valet held the door open with a bow. He stepped out and climbed the marble steps to the compound doors—colossal slabs of wood and steel like an ancient castle straight out of a storybook. A cacophony of voices erupted from the building as soon as the doors parted. Men and women of every size and background filled the building, every one of them with a firearm or two of incredible quality. Elo rifles, spear cannons, radiation pistols, and a host of other foul instruments of murder and mayhem. Velkan weapons all. Serpent weapons. Dorin tapped his hand against Soot. Dorin didn't see a single Velka in the crowd. *Strange, thought there'd at least be one...maybe in a different room.*

The main hall was well lit with candles, lanterns, and a chandelier up above. The wind howled behind Dorin—the blizzard called from a kilometer away. The doors shut behind him with a heavy thud. A butler dressed in a white suit with black lapels walked over to him.

"Right this way, sir," he said. His voice was posh, exactly what Dorin expected. He followed and took note of the layout. He saw the door to the study at the other end of the staircase, facing the southern window. *Perfect.* He was led to the dining room, full of just as many soldiers as the main hall. It was a long room with a table fit to seat over fifty people. Toward the close end of the table, where he was invited to sit, was a mixture of bright, delicious looking foods. Succulent meats, colorful vegetables, steaming soups. But above them all was a tall bowl of freshly cut coconuts.

"Is…is that?" Dorin muttered. Saliva built beneath his tongue. He dove past the butler and threw off his helmet, which crashed to the marble floor with a loud ring. Many people stared at him and scrunched their noses in disgust and shock. Dorin ignored the roast duck, the Beef Wellington, the tiramisu and scarfed down piece after piece of sweet coconut, the milky taste fresh in his mouth. They could've been picked fresh from the tropics of Venus. Tears welled in his eyes. It was everything he'd always dreamed of. A tall woman in a wool trench coat walked over to Dorin, her brown hair tied in a bun, a machine gun in hand.

"Freelancer, I'm Catherine. I'm in charge of security here."

"Dorin," he said through a mouthful of coconut, milk ran out of the corners of his mouth. "Pleased to meet you."

Catherine took out a bag of coins and plopped them onto the table. "You start now, yeah?"

"Keep the coconut coming, and I'll do whatever you want."

"Good. The main hall and the dining hall are yours, set yourself up where you want. Just be ready to shoot."

Dorin kept eating, he needed to appear consistent. But he got an uneasy feeling. He didn't expect to be given such freedom; it was too generous. He paid more attention to the other soldiers. None were eating. A few were giving him odd looks beyond his poor table manners.

"Expecting trouble?" Dorin asked. He made direct eye contact with her.

"No, we're getting ready to move out. Boss wants phase two begun by morning." Catherine met his gaze, unflinching. Dorin tried to look for some kind of tell but found none. Either she was an exceptional liar, or she knew nothing. *Piss, I wish Etkis was here. He'd suss her out in a second.*

"Sounds good. Thanks for the meal," Dorin said. He picked up one last piece of coconut and grabbed his helmet off the floor. As nonchalantly as he could, he walked out the door and strolled through the hall. He checked every door he could find, checked down every hall and every floor. Not a single Velkan Serpent. *How have I not seen a single one yet? Where's Jormar?*

Catherine stared at him from downstairs. He waved to her as obnoxiously as he could. Most normal people would've sighed, rolled their eyes, or just plain left. But Catherine just waved back with an empty smile on her lips. *Thaaaaaat's fucking weird.* Dorin hustled inside the study and shut the door behind him. *Something's definitely off. Need to work fast.*

He went to the window first and knocked on it with his metal hand. Bulletproof. He smiled. Soot would blow it apart in one shot. That would be his exit. He hustled over to the bookcase and examined it. Sure enough, small steel hinges were on one side. Pompeii's escape tunnel, he was sure. Dorin tried to open the bookcase but it was too heavy. *Good. Once I jam this closed, they definitely won't be able to force it open with anything less than a grenade. That'll buy the Wolf ships enough time.* He searched for a button to open the secret door, then he started pulling books. Nothing. Dorin began to look around the room for clues.

It was like he remembered. Red leather furniture, a red rug, and a dark brown coffee table. The hearth crackled with fire opposite the windowsill. Atop the shelf of the hearth were three items. An antique Colt .45 that Dorin picked up and accidentally crushed in his metal hand—he was too used to Soot. Neatly placed on the mantle was a single piece of pure lunar fuel, probably the most expensive thing in the entire building. He shoved it in his pocket.

Finally he inspected the skull of Earth's massive onyx wolves, beasts that could walk on four or two legs, climb with retractable claws, and worst of all, had thumbs for throwing stones. It was the most ferocious animal on the planet. Dorin lifted the mouth open. It was hard even with his metal hand. He reached in and felt around until he found a switch—he pulled it. The bookcase opened like a door into a nuclear reactor. Dorin set down the skull and rushed over. Inside was a long, black, steel hallway. The sound of engines and metalwork echoed from the gaping maw, he had no idea how long it went for. Dorin looked at the back end of the bookcase. There was a metal panel held with screws. He stripped it with his steel hand and went to work on the wires.

Dorin hadn't the faintest knowledge about electrical engineering, but he figured at least some of the wires were important. He lined them all up perfectly so that they were in a column and measured the thickness of the bookcase. His knife was longer.

Dorin ran back to the wolf skull and flipped the switch again. The bookcase shut, and Dorin took out his knife. He plunged it where the wires had been on the other side and sliced up. The sound of sizzling wood, copper, and rubber bubbled from the tip of his blade. *"Ha ha!"* he whispered. Dorin ran back to the skull one last time and to review his handiwork. He flipped the switch. Nothing. *I am a literal genius. Time to call in the cavalry.* Dorin walked over to the light switch. The study door opened. Dorin blew a raspberry. *Piss.* He tried to cover.

"Hm, weird! Can't see anything outside, thought I'd get a better view from up here. Blizzard's really picking up. I think I'll head back—" Dorin turned around.

Before him was a boy, maybe sixteen. Curly brown hair. Perfect teeth. *One arm.* At the sight of Dorin, he turned beet red, tears welled in his eyes and began to overflow down his cheeks. He turned to the open door. It covered whoever was there.

"Yeah, that's him. He's the one. He helped the Wolf," the boy said. Dorin felt cold and clammy, as if he were already dead.

"You..." Dorin muttered. "You're that boy from the ranch. The Roarers'. You're the one I let live. Why..."

"We all make mistakes, D," said the person behind the door with mocking familiarity.

Dorin had imagined this moment so many times.

What he'd do.

What he'd say.

All of it vanished.

From behind the door, followed by two Velka from the House of Serpents, walked a tall red-haired woman with a pistol on either thigh. Scars covered her exposed arms, her navy-blue tank top expensive but worn. She smiled. Another scar curved down from her right eyebrow. Her green eyes were bright in the orange firelight of the hearth.

"For example," she said, "all these years, every time I replayed what happened in my head, I always thought I'd shot you on the left, not the right. Every time I saw your face when I went to sleep, I saw it splattered in blood from the wrong side. And now I see you, standing here, alive, and with the wrong arm missing. I can't tell you how much that fucks with my head."

Dorin stood there motionless, his helmet still on, his arms at his sides. The Serpent bodyguards moved to encircle him, but she put her arms out to stop them. She walked closer to Dorin, step by step, her arms wide by her hips. She continued.

"I couldn't believe it was really you, ya know? I still can't believe it. When Kya said your name, I knew she had no idea, and I didn't know much either. I just wanted—needed to see you. To see you alive." Tears welled in her eyes and flowed down her cheeks. Her eyes were bloodshot and her lips quivered. "I'm so proud of you. You're stronger than I ever knew." She wiped the tears away as if they burned her skin. She inhaled and squeezed her fists. "But then, this morning, the kid came to my door and told me about a metal-armed man who helped the House of Wolves kill freelancers at a ranch outside of Lipel. I guess it's true. Is it too much to hope that you're here alone? That you're not here to spy for the Wolves?"

Dorin didn't answer. She smiled, disappointed and resigned. She was close now. A meter away. "Dorin...don't worry. I'll protect you. You're not one of them, and Jormar knows that. I made sure he knew." Her eyebrows rose. She remembered something. She snapped her fingers, and a butler came in with a hefty bag of gold. She took it, and the butler left. She held it out to Dorin. "I can finally pay you back! For the gambling, for...everything else. Take it. I have more, if you'd like? It's only fair." Dorin didn't reach for the gold. He didn't move at all. Her smile faded. Her eyebrows scrunched in confusion. She stopped walking toward him. She'd never felt so uncertain. "Please—just give me a chance. Things can be like they were, but now we're on top! Wouldn't that be good...I know you must hate me, baby. You should. What I did on Luna...I wouldn't...if there had been any other choice, I'd have made it. You deserve answers. Just come with us, and I'll tell you—"

Soot's smoking barrel screeched like a reaper. Dorin pulled the fastest quick draw he'd ever managed, and red lightning bludgeoned her straight through the bag of gold and in the throat and blew her across the room. She smashed against the wall, then tumbled to the floor, molten gold pieces splattered and hardened on the floor. The Alexandrian boy ran out of the room screaming bloody murder; Soot's cracking bolts brought back his terrifying memory. Both Velkan Serpents charged straight at Dorin. He managed to fire one more shot to the right. It caught the soldier in the hip, burned straight through his armor, and he dropped to the floor and began to scream as his bone marrow began to ignite.

The other guard knocked Soot out of Dorin's hand. The Velka unsheathed a wicked scimitar with a cut toward the neck. Dorin somersaulted back, the blade only cut air, and drew his knife. Dorin ducked blows to the head and tried to thrust to the flank but missed. He slammed his right fist into the forearm. The blow would've shattered any human's bone, but the Serpent threw off the punch with a single parry, armor heavily dented but flesh unscathed. They dodged and parried and threw punch after kick. Dorin managed to pin the Serpent's sword arm and twist the weapon out of his hands. They broke apart, dove in, Dorin thrust cut at the throat but instead took a punch straight in the kidneys and fell to his knees, mouth full of blood. The Velka went to stomp on him in the head—Dorin rolled and threw his knife. The Velka bent backwards and narrowly dodged impalement in the head, the knife sank into the wall and stayed there. Dorin dove and grabbed the Velka by the head and skewered his steel thumb into the hard glass visor. They fell to the floor, Dorin on top, whizzing atmosphere poured out the hole with such force that blood sprang out as if from a pressurized hose.

The Serpent screamed and flailed, hitting Dorin in the helmet and neck. Dorin pulled out his hand and blood shot out with even greater force onto the marble floor. The Serpent's suit began to close around the hole to keep in the escaping atmosphere. He grabbed the Velka's filter and squeezed as hard as he could, broke through the metal and pulled. The Velka tried to hold its mouth to keep in the air, but there was nothing to be done. His movements slowed, and eventually he passed out, blessed to die in his sleep. The other guard, the one Dorin had shot, was still shrieking and was doomed to die in a few minutes. Immolated slowly. Soon the blood in his veins would begin to boil.

Dorin panted heavily and walked slowly over to his knife. Before he could pull it out, his own head was slammed into the wall. Cracked marble fell to the floor. His helmet visor cracked. His assailant hadn't drawn her guns.

Soot's molten bolt dripped from the point of impact, sliding off Pompeii's strained barrier just in front of her throat. Dorin hadn't noticed the faint blue hue until now. The energy shield flickered blue and finally failed—the molten metal plopped to the floor. Dorin grabbed the knife from the wall and tried to cut her. He tried to punch her. He tried everything he knew how to do. But she knew him. She had taught him all his tricks, after all.

She stayed on his left to avoid his steel arm, not delivering a single attack. Dorin slowed, his muscles screamed with effort, every gasp of air burned. Finally she engaged and kicked the back of his knee out and punched him in his hemorrhaging kidney. Knee to the stomach. Elbow to the nape. Heel kick to diaphragm. Dorin landed on his back and the force propelled blood out his mouth and all over the interior of his helmet. Thick scarlet drops dribbled out the filter, down the sides of the helmet and pattered to the floor. Through red smears over cracked visor glass, he couldn't see anything. Dorin forced himself to his side, then to a knee, and tore off his helmet. He looked at her. Her hands lowered from her fighting stance. For the first time in four years, they saw each other as they were. Him on his knees, her with bloody fists. She smiled. He screamed. Dorin committed to a final desperate rush. He wanted his knife sunk to the hilt, no, to the pommel inside her. He bayed like a hound after prey and didn't even hear himself. Dorin lunged at her trachea.

She sidestepped the blade in a pirouette and slammed her elbow into his left shoulder. The bone had been brutalized when he had fired Soot in Lipel with his human hand, weakened in the bar brawl, and now it gave. It popped straight out of the socket and he went down. His eyes barely stayed open. He heard footsteps and her voice shouting.

"Boy! Launch a flare. If the Wolves are here, Jormar will have found them by now. It's time." Dorin saw her black combat boots kneel next to him and flip him over. "Rest now. Don't worry."

Dorin spoke through bubbled blood and half consciousness. "Ash…don't hurt them. Please."

CHAPTER 14

My brothers and sisters, it is my greatest privilege to accept this honor, this symbol
of your faith in me. I hope only that Kior guides me to be worthy of your faith.
As long as there is strength in my flesh, I shall bear your shield. As long as there
is air in my breast, I shall maintain vigil upon our walls. And until my spirit
ascends with Okar or sinks below tethered to stone, I shall never falter in my duty.

—DRAPING CEREMONY, CONFIRMATION OF FIRST GUARD ETKIS TERRA, 1.1.1123

Etkis knelt beside Kya, his shield of a shoulder kept her out of the wind. The
blizzard slammed into him hard from the east. Visibility dropped even
through their augmented Velkan HUDs. The troop could still just see lights
twinkling from the compound through the dark and snow. Yellow orbs refracted
off of windows were their only azimuth, and the blinking glow was their only
guide through the torrent of ice. The regiment was silent and low. Etkis closed his
eyes, raised his chin to the stars, obscured by roiling clouds and whipping snow.
Kya remained silent as the platoon muttered in unison, "Okar take them with
you, to journey through the stars eternal." Etkis opened his eyes and added, "May
they die without regret."

The troops sat together to keep warm. Their vigil might be long, and the
night was cold. Kya shivered and nudged closer to Etkis until they were shoulder
to shoulder. He coughed uncomfortably. The silence suffocated him. He leaned
over to whisper in her ear, just loud enough to be heard over the blizzard but quiet
enough so that the others couldn't hear.

"Can I ask you a personal question?"

"Now?"

"I mean…"

Kya sighed. She'd been asking him questions all day and now felt a faint obligation. "Depends."

"I noticed that you didn't pray with the rest of the company. I've never met a Velka who doesn't. I'm curious why."

"Why would I?"

"Those Velka down there are doing their duty, just like you and me. They deserve to ascend with Okar for completing that duty. I'd hope they would pray the same for me."

Kya chuckled. Her words dripped with resigned apathy. "Etkis…there isn't an enlightened way to die. Everyone we kill, everyone we bury is the same. Flesh returned to the dirt. If you want to believe their spirits 'ascend,' that's your business, but I don't want to be so deluded."

"You don't believe in Okar? Callva? Kior? Treya?"

"If there really are eternal, cosmic beings watching over us, I doubt they very much care what we do. Good folk are punished. Bad folk rewarded. The universe is indifferent, and if the gods exist, so are they. It's just us down here, trying to make things just a little bit better. Prayers aren't for the dead, Etkis. They're for the living."

"For the living…" Etkis studied the doll on his belt. The small blue stones for eyes. The pointed ears. The nubby little arms. A memory of the children he saved. But he'd forgotten the blights that covered the doll's face until now as he studied it. Brown marks from the raid on Jarrod's house. The speckle of blood on the ear. Another memory of men he murdered.

CRACK. CRACK.

Two bright red flashes emanated from the compound's top floor.

Kya had been around firearms since she was a child. Her resume was a laundry list of alleyway fights, dirty deals gone wrong, and justice killings. She could tell you the make and model of most human weapons from pitch and timbre alone.

She'd never heard anything like this before. Not from human arms or even Velkan ordnance.

It was definitely the rapport of light arms fire. Despite that, from all the messes and scrapes she'd been in, it sounded the *least* dissimilar from the Serpent shipborne batteries that had bombed Mercury into the third asteroid belt in the system. "What the piss was that?" she exclaimed.

"*Soot,*" snarled Etkis. "Damn it, Dorin. That's his gun. But only two shots? Something's gone wrong." He turned back to the rest of his regiment. "Turn on the jammer. I don't want them calling in reinforcements or air support."

A scout took out a steel box and flipped a switch. They hid it in a bush and came back. "Done," they said.

"Good," Etkis said. He turned to his guards. "We need a perimeter around the estate, the advanced team—we're going in hard and fast. Kya, we'll find Dorin and—"

Etkis stopped when the black night vanished—a bright green flare shot up from compound grounds and burned the forest with twisted, ghoulish shadows.

"That can't be good." Kya whispered. Etkis wasn't sure what it meant until he turned around. A figure deeper in the forest leveled a gun. Etkis moved to fire his own, but it was too late. The gravity gun shrieked from deep within the woods, and the entire troop collapsed. A fifteen-meter radius of snow was compacted into a solid sheet. Trees failed to support their own weight, splintered, and toppled. Several Wolves were crushed under fragmented lumber ten times its usual weight. Blood splattered from beneath the bark. The surviving Wolves shouted in confusion, but soon understood what was happening. In a moment the Serpents would line up their shots and execute those who'd survived the first salvo.

Kya lay facedown in the hardened snow and pushed against the ground. She rose a few centimeters before she slammed back to submission by gravity. She tried to search for her executioner. She peaked from the corner of her eye and craned her head as far as she was able. It wasn't far. But Kya only saw Etkis. He was the only one left standing.

Etkis was nearly a head and shoulder taller than any of his fellows and twice as heavy.

Any other Velka of his mass would be drowning in their own blood.

His muscles screamed at the strain, his ligaments and tendons were on the verge of tearing themselves apart. He thought his chassis would rend his shoulders from his body. He thought he'd give in. But he stood firm. Etkis tried to raise his gun but it was too heavy. It fell and sunk into the ground. He grabbed the tomahawk from his belt with both hands and brought it behind his head. His shoulders were nearly stripped from the scapula. The muscles in his chest bulged and threatened to pull the meat off his ribs. Snow and dirt, ice and stone, yielded beneath his feet and he sunk further into the earth. His target was clear.

The Serpent assailant deep in the woods shook in horror. All he saw was a towering goliath on two feet who had no right to stand. Burning blue eyes like neutron stars locked onto him. They were prepared to send death his way. He couldn't move without disrupting the gravity prison he'd created. He feared for his life but took a deep breath and thought rationally. *Even if this monster could throw that axe,* the Serpent thought, *he'll never hit me. He'd have to adjust for two changes in trajectory in midair. Impossible.*

Etkis could barely think as his heart struggled to push oxygen into the arteries in his brain. He couldn't just wing this one, there were too many variables. As a connoisseur of gravity weapons, he knew his enemy's specs. *Ten times Earth gravity. Fifteen-meter radius. I'm dead center. I'll have to throw this thing the equivalent of one hundred and fifty pissing meters just to clear the gravity field. Then…* The axe was pulling him backward to the earth. He fought it and the gun that was trying to pin him to the tundra and stayed upright. *Then another thirty meters in regular gravity.*

He had another second in him. Maybe.

Fuck.

So he just threw it.

Etkis launched his ax with all his might. The blade's edge was a disc of blue plasma—it flew with the force of a starship engine. It cleaved the Serpent, his gun, and the trees behind him dead in half. The gun clattered to the ground, and gravity decreased. Etkis collapsed. Air rushed to fill his starved lungs. There were black spots in his vision, and his muscles shook from the trauma. Kya rolled over, drew her pistol, and unloaded on two Serpents. Rounds exited their heads. *"Return fire!"* she shouted.

Beams of burning light flew to and from the dark forest. Toa dove for the current rifle Etkis had left in the snow, and Kya threw flame grenade after flame grenade. They burst in the woods, the cold wood ignited like kindling, and the Serpents were illuminated like dark phantoms in a backdrop of fire. The air filled with volatile ions from the fire and smoke. Conductivity rose dramatically. Toa fired the gun, cracking thunder sounded. The white current hit a Serpent and arced across half a dozen more. The surge of thousands of volts blew apart their barriers and burnt them black and dead.

Kya retrieved the long Elo rifle she'd gotten from Etkis's armory and began sniping the retreating Serpents. Each shot left a smoldering crater through the gaps in Velkan plate.

In the blaze, from deep within enemy lines, a new Velka emerged. Bigger than the others. Far bigger. It swung a massive blade like a conductor's baton, and the chorus of Serpents regrouped behind it. Toa aimed the arc caster and fired. Her aim was true, and she saw a burst of electricity—the barriers erupted in plasma gas and died. But the figure only winced and kept walking. It was simply too big to kill. There wasn't enough voltage, even from Etkis's gun. Toa screamed commands, and the Wolves focused their fire. Staccatos of energy bolts, slugs, and assorted metals bounced pathetically off the armor. Kya and Toa helped Etkis back to his feet as the titan cut scouts and guards down like a scythe through barley.

Etkis's vision ebbed and flowed, until it finally returned. To his horror. He saw his brave brothers and sisters gutted and shot. Some he'd known for years, some he had met a few weeks ago. They were all his failure, his weight to carry.

"Sir, we need to go!" Toa shouted. Etkis shook his head, free from his stupor. He called to his squad, the survivors.

"Head toward the compound! Toa, run to the spaceport and launch—"

An ax caught Toa in the chest, and she flew backward, blood spurted from the wound. He and Kya rushed to her. His own tomahawk was buried halfway to the haft in her armor. Kya carefully pulled out the blade and gushing red flowed from shoulder to hip. Toa's hands trembled over the gash, her stark white armor smattered with scarlet gore. She tried to speak, but her words were unintelligible.

The suit closed around the wound, but even the miraculous Velkan medical systems couldn't put blood back *in* her body. Etkis looked to see who'd given him back his blade.

It stood over the crumpled remains of burning conifers, over three meters tall. Shoulders as broad as his own. A greatsword thrust deep into the chest of a Velkan Wolf.

Before a tempest of fire and swirling snow stood Jormar the Dragon.

He whipped the Wolf off his blade as easily as a youngster would snap a towel. The scout flew off the sword in two pieces, which landed in syncopated thumps in the snow. He spread his legs apart and sank into a wide fighting stance. The greatsword was poised over his shoulder, gripped between both massive hands. Blood and viscera dripped down Jormar's forearms. The coiled steel vambrace guided the dark red fluid to the tip of his elbows, from where it trickled to the earth. They locked eyes. The Dragon didn't move.

A challenge.

Etkis swallowed, the smell of burning timber and death brutalized him even through his air filters. He took his hatchet in one hand, his dagger in the other. He felt something unfamiliar in his chest. In his throat. In his palms and fingers. He'd been scared many times in his life like anyone else, but almost always for the sake of others. He feared for the safety of his friends, for the threats to his house. But he'd so rarely been scared for himself he didn't even recognize the emotion. He couldn't remember ever being truly scared of someone before. Afraid for his life.

He felt nauseous—unwilling to accept the provocation. Phantom pain snaked through his body as if his flesh were preparing itself for punishment. Like a premonition, he felt his bones splinter and blood fill his helmet to the point where he could hardly breath through the bubbling liquid. He thought of running or crawling away. He imagined Jormar standing above him and stomping on his head until it burst like a ripe melon. He thought of begging for his life. A deep guilt rose to drown his deafening panic.

Etkis turned to Kya to command a retreat but stopped himself. She was frozen, terrified. Almost like she'd stepped into a nightmare. Etkis looked to Toa, bleeding on the floor. To his troops, fighting for their lives. To the compound, where Dorin was captured...or worse.

They all put their lives on the line, every battle, not knowing which would be their last. And now, faced with the same prospect, how could he do any less?

Etkis punched himself in the head to drive the thoughts away. If he was going to die, he'd die proud. He'd die protecting. He charged without a word, billows of snow rooster-tailed behind each heel.

Kya still couldn't move, her long rifle slung over her shoulder and pistol holstered. Motionless. Petrified. When Etkis ran to fight his foe, she didn't see him. She didn't see the snow or the night.

Etkis's faint outline in the whirling gray blizzard was the silhouette of her father in the blistering Mercury sunset. It was a recreation, a shadowy evocation of the nightmare that had haunted her for these past two decades. Again a hero fought the Dragon. Valiantly. And again it didn't matter.

Etkis caught the greatsword in a parry, the blow carried the weight that had given Jormar his title. The force drove Etkis back and his boots left two long trenches in the snow. Etkis grunted and bound the greatsword's foible up and around his head. He swiped at Jormar's hands with his tomahawk. The enormous sword crashed to the ground as Jormar pulled his hand free of the ax blade's path. Etkis swiped and cut, each hacking slash the consequence of thousands of hours of training. They were strategic and surgical, fast and fueled by fear. The violence was aimed at limb and head but pierced only air. Jormar ducked and weaved around each slash. He was graceful. He danced with Etkis until it was clear that he was leading the deadly waltz, and Etkis was forced to follow.

Jormar traced long curves in the snow with every evasion and each masterful maneuver. He weaseled his way inside Etkis's guard. Despite Jormar's bulk, he threw nearly a dozen swift punches. Each blow dented armor and bruised the flesh and bone underneath. Kya could hear the impacts, like a power hammer striking with machine speed and ferocity on a soft billet. Jormar slammed Etkis in the throat with a forearm shiver. Etkis dropped his weapons and clutched his windpipe. Jormar grabbed an arm and broke it at the elbow.

Etkis fell to his knees. His head forward, presented for an execution. Jormar retrieved his greatsword.

It was the same. Jormar had dismantled Etkis just how he had systematically slain her father. She was now fully grown, but Kya's mind regressed for a moment at the hands of her childhood nightmare.

But this wasn't a nightmare. This was real. A real moment, not a cruel memory she had no power over. This time she wasn't a helpless child.

Kya stripped an incendiary grenade from her belt and hurled it with every ounce of resentment and courage she could summon. Her pride and friendship with Etkis had enabled her, ennobled her, with this moment of agency. Kya's inner strength leveraged the explosive into the air, and her fear catalyzed the reaction in her muscles into a pitch unlike any she'd ever thrown before.

The grenade rocketed to the Dragon's head.

Jormar plucked the grenade half a meter from his face.

Kya couldn't believe what she'd seen. Her demon stared back at her, and she knew she'd been marked as his new prey.

His arm cocked like a snake and began to throw it back.

His fingertips were barely touching it when the grenade exploded into flame.

The object of her nightmares screamed. A fireball engulfed his hand and forearm. Jormar thrust his arm into the snow but only pulled a blackened stump out of the white frost. He snarled and locked onto Kya. She was next. He began to stand when Etkis got him in a hold from behind, his good arm around the neck and his broken arm stuffed limp beneath the armpit. Etkis linked his hands together and screamed as he torqued his fractured arm taut. He lifted the Dragon high into the air, eclipsing the moonlight, and slammed him back to the planet in a suplex that punched through the permafrost layer and splintered the granite beneath like a meteor strike. Etkis's eyes were squeezed shut. *Okar, please.* Jormar wasn't moving, but Etkis kept him pinned on the neck and kept shoving him into the rock. *Okar, please, please, please stay down.* Jormar was limp as a fish, breathing, but knocked out cold. The Serpents were just as stunned at Etkis, but after a second, they moved in to support their leader. A harpoon hit Etkis in the head, but it bounced off his barrier. It snapped him back to his senses.

"Retreat!" Etkis shouted, voice still hoarse from his injury. He retrieved his hatchet and attached it to his belt. Kya hoisted Toa up and sprinted to the compound. Three Wolf guards held their ground to give their comrades a chance

to escape. Etkis grabbed three wounded Wolves and piled them onto his good shoulder and fled. He kept running and didn't turn around once. He didn't need to. He heard everything. The gunfire and shouts of his trusted clansmen slowly faded until they ceased entirely. Etkis sobbed silently, his failure complete, his shame total. "Okar take you, my brothers, my sisters, to journey through the stars eternal…" His thoughts flashed back to what Kya had said.

For the living…

"I'm so sorry," he bubbled and wept.

Etkis made it to the compound gate, where Kya waited for him. Toa was still on her back. Etkis kicked the gate down. The steel lock burst apart like glass. The human freelancers near the front doors opened fire and their bullets made little piles of snow jump into the air. Kya shot them all through the eye in a second. They slumped to the ground.

"Go to the back door," Etkis said. "We need somewhere to hide the wounded."

They worked around the compound until they'd found a large wooden door. It was tilted down, and Etkis hoped it led to a cellar or granary, something out of the way without a back entrance. Kya burned through the lock with the solar edge of her Velkan knife and threw open the doors. She and Etkis went inside and shut the doors behind them.

The cellar was dark and damp and lit by a few weak lanterns. Kya laid Toa down, and Etkis dropped the three soldiers he'd been carrying on his back as carefully as he could. Of the three wounded, only one of them was a guard. The only one still conscious. The cuisse over his thigh had been punctured by a large arrow. Etkis felt the arrow gently and could tell the broadhead had touched the other side of the armor, but hadn't pierced through. He unbuckled the armor and removed the metal, carefully as to not touch the arrow threaded through the steel. He grabbed the shaft and looked to his subordinate.

Etkis coughed, his traumatized throat tore on every word. "Are you ready, my brother?"

The guard shook his head. "No, but do it anyway."

Etkis pushed and the broadhead escaped the flesh. The guard covered his filter to stifle the scream with small success. Etkis broke the shaft and pulled the two pieces of the arrow out of the Wolf's leg. The guard rolled his eyes in pain, and his suit closed around the wound.

Etkis wasted no time as he then tended to a scout. He'd passed out—his chest rose and fell slightly but erratically. He'd been left with more plasma burns than skin on his left arm, but Etkis was more concerned about infection or loss of atmosphere. He was in a critical condition. The last Velka had died in his arms. Etkis laid him down flat on the floor, crossed the arms along the chest in the Velkan salute, and placed his own palm to his fallen soldier's head.

Etkis tore pieces off his cloak as pillows for Toa and the unconscious soldier. Kya panted and reloaded her guns.

"Are you okay?" she asked. Etkis sounded sixty years older, his voice hoarse from his injury.

"I led my entire squadron into a trap that almost killed us all. I'm far from okay."

"I meant your arm…"

Etkis looked at his mangled limb as if he'd forgotten about it. His fight-or-flight response and suit-induced opioids had numbed the pain significantly. "Oh, right," he said, "should probably do something about that, huh?"

"Probably," Kya said. She found a barrel in the cellar and pried the curved boards off for a splint. She tore even more pieces of Etkis's diminishing cloak and slung the wounded appendage tight to her comrade's chest. There was a heavy silence. The muggy cellar air was cold and thick. Etkis spoke in a whisper, his voice defeated, "…Thank you. For saving my life."

Kya stopped working for a moment, unsure what to say. She finished the first knot and tightened it gingerly around his fractured arm. "You too."

Etkis looked at Toa. Her eyes were barely open.

"Toa? You still with us?" Etkis asked. The blood loss and drug-induced stupor slurred her speech.

"Yup—A-Okay, sir. Sorry, I mean *Etkis*. I might just take a lil' nap, if that's okay."

"Not a chance, scout. Stay awake. Stay with us. We're gonna get you back to Volthsheim yet. Think of...um...flowers. Daffodils and lilies. Orchids and gardenias."

"Mmmm, I didn't know you liked flowers, sir—so do I."

"You can show me your favorites once we get you back safe and sound, how about that?"

Toa tried to nod. Her eyes narrowed even further. She shivered and mumbled incoherently, "I feel all tingly, sir."

Kya finished tying Etkis's sling, and she took off her long human overcoat and draped it over Toa like a blanket over a sleeping pup. She removed her vam-braces, pauldrons, and cuirass and tore the thick fur on the inside of the plate and piled it beneath Toa to keep her warm. Etkis did the same. Kya had to help him due to his injuries and piled the thick fur around the unconscious scout he'd saved. He walked over to his guard and knelt.

"We bungled this pretty bad, sir," the guard said. "I'm sorry. We should've seen them surrounding us."

"You did your jobs beautifully. It is I who failed tonight. I'll see to it you make it home. What's your name?"

"Guard Ragar of the third regiment, ID number 7145—"

"I know all that, but what's your name? The name you have in the Great Hall, among the safety of friendship and warmth?"

"...Murik. Murik Ragar. My friends call me Murray, sir."

Etkis's eyes curved into half-moons, his smile evident. "Murray—I like that. I have a favor to ask of you, Murray. Do you think you can watch over your com-rades? Kya and I must leave to continue the mission, and you're the only one able to care for your fallen brother and sister. Can you do that for me?"

Murray drew his sidearm from his hip and winced. "With every bullet I have and every breath in my chest, they shall not come to harm, sir. I'll make you proud."

"You already have." Etkis stood up and walked further into the hall. He mo-tioned Kya over. They whispered.

"How are we getting them out of here?" Kya asked. Etkis rubbed his throat, his voice returning to its normal pitch.

"We're not—not yet. Reinforcements will only arrive once we launch the flare to initiate the airstrike. Our communications are severed with the jammer, but so are theirs. They won't know we survived the ambush for a little while, which means I have the element of surprise for once. I'm going to find Dorin… you need to get over the hill and launch the flare."

Kya took a step back, a pit in her stomach. "Etkis…I don't—"

"I know, and I'm sorry to ask you to do it. But we're the only two left. They'd be able to spot me over the ridge easily, and if they did, I don't think I could handle the remaining Serpents with one arm. It has to be you."

"…Fuck. Okay." Kya turned to leave, but Etkis stopped her with a hand to the shoulder. He turned her around and wrapped his arm around her in a tender embrace. "Please be safe," he whispered. "I don't want to lose anyone else today."

Kya's pulse quickened. She didn't know what else to do but wrap her arms around him. "I will. You too. And find Dorin. I still want that drink."

Etkis laughed. "Will do." They separated. Kya walked over to Toa and pulled the flare out from her belt.

"Gonna borrow this for a little while, Toa. Don't you worry, I'll bring it right back."

"You'd better," Toa responded, her words barely intelligible. "It's pretty, like a blooming freesia. I've always wanted one in my garden."

Kya touched her hand to Toa's head. She found herself praying for her life. *Stupid*, she thought, but finished the prayer anyway. *Prayers are for the living, and she's not dead yet.* She stood, holstered the flare around her waist, and hoisted up her Elo rifle. She walked to the cellar door and pushed the door open. The blizzard was coming down even harder now.

"I'll see you fuckers soon," she said over her shoulder and left. Etkis drew his hatchet and ventured into the black catacombs.

CHAPTER 15

Torture is a human invention designed to induce cooperation either mentally, physically, or spiritually through the generation of physical or mental anguish. Leaving aside the vile spiritual implications of such methods, the practical issue with this measure is that the victim will say anything for the pain to stop. It compromises any information that would be obtained. But the fact is that this practice has endured, through genocide and religion and apocalypse. This leaves us with one of two implications. That sometimes it works, or worse, they enjoy it.

—Volthsheim database, *Foray into Human Conflict*, by First Bellum Intepretor Bitom Voluski, head of the War division for the Ministry of Human Interpretation.

Dorin woke in a cold cell that reeked of mildew. Sickly yellow light dribbled in from the hall on the other side of the steel bars. His vision was still blurred, his mind hazy. He was bound to a chair; his metal arm was strapped with steel plates and half inch bolts appropriate to keep the superhuman cyborg limb from splitting the restraints. A shooting pain from his left shoulder drove the fogginess from his mind. He swore viciously and hoped it was just dislocated. His other wounds and aches reared their viscous heads as well. He swore he'd need a new kidney tomorrow.

Dorin looked around and saw his survival gauntlet and knife outside his cell on a wood desk. No sign of Soot. He instinctively pulled his arm to his forehead to scratch at a dried and cracked spot of blood but only heard the screech of titanium on hard forged steel. His arm was thoroughly pinned. The bindings were too many and too strong. After a second or two of pointless flailing, a prison guard came over to his cell.

"Ma'am, he's awake," he said.

Ash walked in front of the cell carrying a bright lantern and opened it. She had on a stylishly embroidered fur coat and gloves, the kind she and Dorin would never have been able to afford before. It was far colder here than in the building up above. She smiled and spoke to the prison guard. "Open it." The man pulled out a ring of jingling keys and unlocked the cell. Ashton pulled a stool from the other side of the bars and sat in front of Dorin. She set the lantern down and began to pull off her gloves and put them in her coat pocket. She half turned her head to speak to the guard. "Leave us. No disturbances." The guard left. Ash breathed into her hands and rubbed them together as the footsteps echoed through the hall. She stared at Dorin for a few seconds, studying his face. He sat motionless—his anger barely contained.

"How are you feeling?" she asked. Her voice was gentle.

"Dandy," Dorin spat.

"Your beard's coming in a lot better," she said and reached to touch his short stubble. Dorin leaned his head away from her hand, his nose scrunched in hate. Ash stopped and retracted, hurt. She swallowed and forced a smile. "You gonna finally grow it out? I know you always wanted to."

He didn't respond.

Ashton bit her lip and shifted in her seat closer to Dorin.

"I'm sorry that I had to hurt you. I hate it. I hate that we're fighting and hurting you made me feel sick to my stomach. You know I don't like to."

"Never stopped you before."

"...I'd thought I'd lost you."

"*Lost me?* That's rich."

Ash pursed her lips. Dorin clicked his tongue.

"So 'Ash' became '*Pompeii*' huh?" He said, mocking her. "Fuck, you still think you're funny, don't you?"

She chuckled, "I'm very funny, thank you. Do you know what happened at Pompeii?"

"I'm sure you'll tell me."

"Pompeii was a city, maybe five millennia ago. One day people were going about their business when a volcano erupted and buried *everyone*. It didn't just destroy them. It didn't just kill them. It *preserved* them. Can you imagine the power it takes to stop time, completely, and hold it there for generations? For thousands of years, those people were buried in ash—and they're still sitting petrified at the moment of their deaths. The power to cement a legacy utterly—that's a beautiful thing, don't you think? Not a single person is alive today who knew any of those people, who saw the eruption, who saw the tsunami of ash and smoke. I can't tell you the awe that place inspires, frozen in time. I'll take you there someday, you'll love it! A snapshot of history preserved for all to see. I'll never forget what I saw there. That's going to be me. We're going to leave a mark on this Earth that'll last long after we're gone. Just like Pompeii."

"Fitting name, since *everyone died there*. Just you wait. For once in your parasitic life, you'll have to face the consequences of your actions."

Ashton scrunched her eyebrows and leaned back. Her jaw was tight, her cheeks pushed in, her nostrils flared. She had to take a moment to bury her seething anger. "We'll be leaving soon," she said. "Jormar will finish killing the Wolves soon enough."

"You don't know that," Dorin snapped.

"I do. Once he's done, we'll move out. How'd you know about the secret room in the study?"

"Mopped floors for Linel back in the day."

It took a moment for Ash's memory to come back to her. She nodded. "Ah, that's right. Piss. I bet you didn't leave a way for us to open it, then? Well, we'll get it open eventually, in pieces if we have to. But in the meantime, we need to ask you some questions, okay? I need you to tell me how you get into Volthsheim. Jarrod wanted to steal a permit from some ranchers to get into the city—stupid. A stolen permit is never going to work more than once. But you walk in no problem, don't you? How do you open the gates? Is there a passcode? A phrase? What?"

Dorin responded with a rancid glob of blood and saliva onto her face. She recoiled and kicked the stool she'd been on against the wall. She paced back and forth, wiping her face repeatedly, even far after the spit was gone. Eventually she brought her hands off her face, and she breathed in deep, doing everything in her power to calm herself. After a few seconds, she was able to speak again.

"Dorin...I'm really, *really* trying here! No one's coming to get you out."

"If you're so sure my friends are dead, then what's the rush? You want to evacuate anyway, so why even bother with the escape hatch? Just walk across the lot to the car, put me in, and drive off. Why do this now? Are you still afraid to go outside because Wolves might still be on the prowl?"

Ashton clenched her lips together tight and flat. Dorin whispered to her.

"You're a coward. You've always been a coward."

Ash leaned in and punched Dorin in the face. More blood dribbled out of his mouth. He spat on the ground and made eye contact with her. Ashton looked as though she were about to scream, but her visage soon collapsed into one of regret.

There was a knock on the cell bars, Ashton spun around. "*I said no dis—*"

A Velka, no taller than Dorin, with emerald eyes, waited outside the bars. The carvings on her helmet implied she was female. Snow was still packed into crevices in her armor. She must've come from the blizzard raging outside. Dorin noticed a subtle tremor in her fingers, movement of the throat, uncentered body-weight. He could only notice these things after years of watching and analyzing the Velkan body language. This Velka was nervous, perhaps even frightened of something. And she didn't want Dorin to know.

Behind her was a short, stubby old man with a bushy mustache. He eyed Dorin evilly. Dorin thought he looked familiar.

Ashton bit her tongue when she realized who she was speaking to. "Yui... what is it?"

The Velka only motioned with her head for Ash to come out. She complied, and the two went farther in the hall, where Dorin couldn't see. He could barely make out every other word. The old man kept his eye on Dorin all the while. He strained to listen.

Ashton whispered as though she were strangling every syllable. "*What do you mean 'unconscious'?*"

Dorin couldn't hear the response, only murmurs. The old man held something that caught his attention. An enormous pistol.

Soot! Dorin narrowed his eyes, the realization of who this man was made his jaw lock tight. *Cormac...*

Dorin wanted to lunge at the man and steal back his weapon. It looked as though the mustachioed bastard had failed in his attempt to disassemble it. It had taken Dorin months to figure out how to fieldstrip the piece just to clean it, there was no way someone could perform the intricate procedure in an hour. But that hadn't stopped Cormac from trying. Dorin made a mental note to beat him senseless. Yui's voice brought him back out of his thoughts. Their voices were growing louder.

"Why not kill him? He's caused enough problems."

Ash snapped back, "No."

"He's of no value. I can do it if you'd like?"

"*No!* Just...I need more time."

"We don't have time. We're leaving for Beta site and so should you. I'll put a bullet in his head and be done with it."

Dorin felt his stomach climb into his throat, his lips sweaty and cold. He heard a scuffle outside. Cormac kept smiling and studying Dorin, like a cat admiring a mouse before pouncing. He heard Ashton's voice.

"*No!* Please! I—he knows too much about Volthsheim. I need him to tell me how to get past the gates."

Cormac turned his head sharply toward the two down the hall. His eyes shifted between them and Dorin. Yui, the Velka, sounded intrigued.

"...He can get you past the gates?"

"Yes," Ash replied.

Yui sighed loudly. "Fine. He lives. Pompeii, they need you upstairs to get the escape door open. Don't go outside unless it's through that door...we'll have more company soon. I must go rejoin my unit. Do not tarry."

Dorin heard footsteps recede into the distance. Cormac smiled at his boss.

"Well played, ma'am. Quite the bluff," he said, his tone curious. He was probing. Ash understood. Her tone shifted. Subtle and violent.

"No one goes in there without my express orders, got it? If I come back and there's a single scratch on his head—"

"Won't be any more than the ones you gave him, ma'am."

Dorin couldn't see Ashton's reaction, but Cormac had clearly stepped over the line by the way he stood up straighter and his smile wavered. He cleared his throat. "As you say, ma'am."

She didn't answer, but Dorin heard her leave. Cormac waited until she was well out of earshot. He called out, "Pyter! Luca! Come!"

He grabbed the knife and survival gauntlet from the table and hustled into the cell. He hid behind the wall and looked at Dorin and put his finger to his lips. Dorin scrunched his eyebrows, confused.

The prison guard returned, and two men followed behind. Cormac took Dorin's knife, went around the wall, and sank it deep into the prison guard's neck. Steam trickled out of the wound and the blade sizzled flesh. Both other men shouted in surprise, Dorin's mouth lay agape, and the old man dragged the corpse into the corner of the cell. He drew out the knife and boiling blood jumped out of the hole.

He reset the stool Ashton had kicked and sat. He set the knife and survival gauntlet down next to him but held Soot obsessively.

One of the two men, a young lad Dorin didn't recognize, spoke up. "What the hell was that?"

Cormac responded softly and with complete composure, "We need some peace for a little while. Tonight we make our fortune, lads. I have a plan, are you with me?"

The young fellow smiled, but the other swallowed nervously. It was Pyter, the one-armed boy Dorin had spared. Who had ratted him out. He eventually nodded. The assistant went back into the hall and returned with a box and butchers aprons for the three of them to wear. He set the box down and unpacked it. A litany of blades, pliers, screws, and strange, twisted tools lay on the ground. Dorin's breathing quickened.

"I'm surprised to see you, Cormac," Dorin said through gritted teeth.

"Are you?" he asked. "Well, you scared me good, son. Took me hours to come back to my senses, was just outside the city limits when I turned around." Cormac leaned in, his breath smelled like liquor and onions. Dorin scrunched his nose. "So much more to be gained in Alexandria, wouldn't you say?"

Dorin turned to the one-armed boy. "And you, Pyter? You really know how to show your gratitude." He spat.

Pyter's skin was shiny and glossy in the lantern light. He couldn't meet Dorin's gaze, from fear or guilt Dorin wasn't sure. His voice was high, still very much like that of a boy. "You shot my arm off."

"I let you *live,* you sniveling snake. More than you deserved. More than the rest got. Every day, every hour, every second you're breathing is my gift to you."

Pyter swallowed a dry throat. The assistant slapped him in the chest. "Pyter! Snap out of it." He shook himself and complied. They grabbed a power drill from the set.

Dorin tried to keep his breath steady but failed. "Starting a little strong, aren't we? Can't we start with waterboarding, the hobbling wheel, something less dramatic? Shouldn't you *work up* to the good stuff?"

"Hm?" Cormac muttered. He'd been studying Soot and hadn't been paying attention. He noticed all of the tools his assistant had laid out for him. "No, no, no," he said, his brown moustache bounced with every word. "We won't need any of that. Besides, don't want to leave many more marks on him." He turned back to Dorin. "You'll be unconscious when they find you, and Pompeii won't know what happened. That'll give me and these two young gentlemen enough time to slip out unnoticed and steal the bounty out from under her nose." He and his assistant laughed. They were clearly on the same page. Pyter was not.

Dorin took a deep breath. "What bounty?"

"The House of Serpents," Cormac said, "for anyone who can discover a way into Volthsheim undetected. An entire mountain of gold! Pompeii and any crime boss worth their salt has been searching high and low for a solution. They've been scavenging for any information they can find—it's been months and still nothing. Now Pompeii thinks you're her ticket, but I think we'll get there first." He smiled again; his teeth crooked as his mind. He scooted the stool right next to Dorin and held up Soot at eye level. "I knew this was an amazing piece, but my word, did it exceed my expectations. Not only pierced, it *burnt* straight through Velkan plate. Haven't the faintest idea how to take it apart. You said you found this on the moon, right? Where, young man?"

"Pawnshop. On the cheap. You wouldn't believe what they just give away these days. Why? You moonlight as a smith or something?"

Cormac laughed. It was clear his day job as a gunsmith was nothing more than a front. His laughter turned to coughing, and he cleared his throat. "Funny," he said. His hoarse voice choked on the word. "I've always had the passion and talent for taking things apart to understand them. Technology, weapons, and people." He set the gun down and pulled out Dorin's Velkan knife. The blue edges burned bright in the dark cell. "Beautiful blade. This could cut through just about anything, couldn't it?" He eyed Dorin's metal arm. "And I remember this, all too well. I hope you don't mind if I take a peek." He held the knife with his palm on the haft, thumb and forefinger on the side of the blade. Like a scalpel. He began cutting through the thick metal of Dorin's right forearm. Dorin sucked air through his teeth.

Waste of time, Dorin thought. *Can't feel anything there! Unless I'm missing something? Piss, am I missing something?*

Pyter pried open a small panel with a pair of suspiciously stained pliers. The edges of the plate were rimmed in glowing orange from the blade. Where the plate had been removed was a steel aperture that resembled the radial bone and a dozen wires fastened to it like vines twisting up a tree.

Etkis had once forced Dorin to a doctor for an infected tooth. He'd gone kicking and screaming into the office. Although he'd been numbed at the time, he still remembered the feeling when the enamel was drilled away and all that was left with was a hole straight to an open nerve. He felt the same way at this moment. Like an open, gaping nerve.

"Amazing…" Cormac said. "You dented Velkan steel with one punch, yes? I saw the corpses you left upstairs—my, my. I look forward to learning from you, young man. But alas, now's not the time. Pyter, hand me the survival gauntlet." Pyter did as he was told, still not looking at Dorin. "Go stand watch lad," Cormac said. "Anyone comes by, we need to cover up our work and quick. Understand?" Pyter nodded and went to the cell door, but kept an eye on Dorin all the while. Cormac turned the knob on the back of the survival gauntlet and the lights on the knuckles turned red. "I've always wanted one of these. Perfect for the wilds. Fire setting, always useful." He turned the knob, the lights turned violet. "Gravity setting—Velkan tech, that is. You made some modifications, I see. So many little things with you, such a delight! Oh, and finally"—he turned the knob one last time. The lights turned blue— "electricity. My favorite. Now if I'm not mistaken, this metal arm of yours has wires that connect directly to your nervous system, yes?"

PISS FUCK I WAS MISSING SOMETHING DEFINITELY MISSING SOMETHING!

Dorin struggled against his restraints; the braces creaked against his strength, but his grunts and snarls were only met with laughter from the torturer. The assistant grabbed a leather strap and shoved it in Dorin's mouth and held it there. He couldn't talk if his teeth were shattered or if he bit out his tongue. Cormac put on the survival gauntlet—the sound of crackling air woven between his fingers. He touched the wiring.

A surge of electricity shot through Dorin's arm and into the rest of his body. His muscles engaged, and his tendons locked. All his nerves screeched at once, the pain receptors directly stimulated. No physical hurt could truly describe it because pain is only electrical signals interpreted by the brain. This was pure, unfiltered agony. Pyter's mouth hung open in horror, but he quickly closed it—he didn't want the others to see.

Cormac removed his hand, and the pain stopped instantly. The juxtaposition of searing pain and nothing made Dorin delirious. His head sagged, and the assistant took the leather strap out of his mouth.

"How do we get the gates of Volthsheim open?" Cormac asked. Dorin forced his head back up.

"Say please."

He got shocked again. He wanted to scream, but the nerves in his jaw were wired shut on the leather strap jammed back into his mouth. Pyter looked as if he were about to cry.

"How do we get the gate open?" Cormac asked again.

"…Have you tried knocking?"

Dorin got shocked a third time.

"How do we get the gate open?"

Dorin slurred his words. His faculties hardly functioned. "That's a no on the knocking, then?"

"This isn't going anywhere," Pyter muttered to the old torturer. "Maybe we should stop?"

"You need a stronger stomach, boy," he growled in response, his patience thinning. "We've barely just begun."

Dorin lost track of time. Every shock could've been a second or an hour for all he knew. He thought about it. Probably seconds. There was plenty of time left. He tried to spout as much nonsense as he could, sometimes coherent, mostly not. If they managed to break him, he'd hoped the overflow of misinformation would keep the truth hidden still. If Ash, the House of Serpents, or this lunatic learned about the microchips the House of Wolves injected into its human citizens, then it was possible they could steal or fabricate them and get into Volthsheim. He began to think about the last time he felt this magnitude of pain—Luna. He remembered the shredding pain and gnawing teeth on his arm, the same one that got shocked. Same, in a sense. He wondered if Ash would have resorted to this eventually. He couldn't think of a reason why she wouldn't. *Who knows,* he thought, *maybe she'll cut out my chip and use it to get into Volthsheim. Take something else from me. That'd be poetic or something.*

Another shock.

"What about the permits?" The torturer asked, frustrated. "Wolven merchants are given plaques of wood, what's special about them?"

Dorin could only mumble through his sobs. "I don't know."

Another shock.

"What are the plaques?" He asked again.

"…Nothing," Dorin muttered. He cried harder. He shouldn't have said that. He bit his lip until it bled.

"What do you mean 'nothing'?" Cormac asked, emphatic. He'd finally gotten something. He shocked Dorin again, longer this time. "What. Do. You. Mean. 'Nothing'?"

"Sir, we should stop! That's enough!" shouted Pyter. The torturer stood and hit the boy in the face. He fell, his good arm clutched his broken nose.

"This is not a business for the weak, boy! Don't like it? Leave! Otherwise, don't speak again!"

Dorin heard a familiar, sonorous voice trickle from the hallway just before he passed out. "There's no need for that."

He could only just make out a hazy silhouette, tall and broad. Arm in a sling. Luminescent blue eyes. Pyter had been distracted by the torture and fist to the face, and the assistant hadn't sounded an alarm or said anything at all. His chin was pointed as high as it could go in order to see the alien's helmeted face. The beast's arm was in a sling, but this did nothing to comfort the man. A mammoth with a broken tusk is still a mammoth, after all—perfectly capable of stomping a man into nothing.

The men stood still, trembling, as if in the presence of death itself. The goliath spoke again.

"Piss, it's dark in here. Hello, I heard shouting so I came over. I don't want to hurt you folks, I just need some information. I'm looking for someone. Black hair, short stubble, olive skin, brown eyes, metal arm."

Pyter nearly pissed himself. Cormac picked up Soot and held it impotently at the gigantic being. The heavy gun rattled in his hands. He could hardly keep it level.

"Ge-get back!" he shouted. "I'll shoot! I swear!" The alien put his hand up. Not in surrender, but in consolation. He wasn't threatened.

"It's all right, sir, I'm not interested in hurting…wait…that gun. Is that…" Etkis walked farther into the room. He saw Dorin strapped to the chair, unconscious, hole in his metal arm, his survival gauntlet on one of these other men. Power tools and knives strewn about the floor. His blood on the floor.

Etkis looked back to the old man, past the gun leveled at his chest, and to his wrinkled, mustachioed face.

"…Mr. Cormac?"

The air changed. The men all felt it. Like the moment a bomb is armed. A gun is drawn. A car crashed. A murder committed.

Any thought of "control" vanished from the Velka's mind.

"*Stop!*" Cormac shouted. He moved to fire, but Etkis read his movements perfectly. With an arm that spanned half the room, he snatched the assistant and hurled him toward the torturer as easily as a man would throw a pebble. Cormac panicked as his assistant flew straight at him.

CRACK.

Pyter pressed his hand to his ear in agony. The bolt passed straight through the assistant's belly, the soft tissue shredded to a boiled stew of viscera, and he rolled to the floor, leaving a red trail in his wake. The bolt had missed Etkis entirely and burned through the stone by his head, the rock bubbled to magma and dripped from the ceiling. Cormac screeched and dropped Soot, his hands mangled and purple from the recoil. Blood dripped from his fingernails. His broken knuckles poked out the back of his hand. Etkis crossed the room in a second and grabbed hold of Cormac by the entire breadth of his thin chest. Etkis smashed him into the wall, the cell shook, and dust rained from the ceiling. Pyter hadn't moved from the floor. He just watched Etkis slam the old man into the wall over and over and over again. Broken wall clattered to the floor with every blow. Blood and gray matter splattered to the floor in a flood, as if a dam had been broken and a river let loose. Soon nothing more drained out of the body. Etkis slammed it again and again until he held an unrecognizable strip of flesh in his blood-soaked hand. He dropped the corpse, and it sunk into a glob on the floor. There weren't any bones left to give it structure. One could hardly call it human.

Etkis turned his head. His flashlight-like eyes passed over Pyter. The boy made it to his hands and knees, bowed his head, and put his hand over his neck.

"Please!" He wept. "Mercy! I told them to stop, I did! I told them to stop hurting him!"

Etkis picked up Pyter by the scruff and held him at eye level. Etkis stared deep into the boy's face. He didn't recognize him. "Say that again," he whispered.

"I-I t-told them to s-stop hurting him!" Pyter spent the longest second of his life suspended meters off the ground, staring death in the face.

Etkis dropped him. He fell with a grunt.

"I believe you," he said. "Leave this place. Find a new line of work."

Pyter scrambled to his feet and ran as fast he could into the dark halls. Etkis crouched and snapped the restraints off Dorin's body. He shook his unconscious friend.

"Dorin? Can you hear me? Wake up!"

No response. Dorin's eyes were closed, but his chest rose and fell. Etkis didn't know what else to do. He reached around to the back of his belt and reached into a pouch. He pulled out one of his cylindrical liquid meals and uncapped the seal. The exposed, viscous liquid sloshed in the container. He held it to Dorin's nose.

"*Ah, sweet pissing Christ!*" Dorin screamed, suddenly and *horribly* conscious. His nostrils burned, he dove forward from the chair and retched onto the floor.

"Thank Okar." Etkis sighed and collapsed against the wall. Dorin vomited a few more times, the sweet coconut he enjoyed soured with regurgitation.

"It smells like Satan's bum." Dorin coughed. He slumped to his back, panting. "Thanks, buddy…"

"Yeah."

"So…it was a trap."

"Yup."

Dorin waved Etkis over and forced himself to a seated position. "I'm pretty sure my shoulder is dislocated. I need you to pop it back in place," he said.

"Are you sure? I don't want to snap you in half or anything."

"Just pretend you're pushing a baby."

"I—wha—have you pushed a baby?"

"No! Just, be *really* gentle."

Etkis grabbed Dorin's human arm between his thumb and forefinger. He had one eye closed, leaned away, and pushed. He felt a little pop, and Dorin screamed.

"*Sorry, sorry!*" Etkis shouted and pulled away. Dorin chuckled and rolled out his shoulder.

"Actually you did a pretty good job. Thanks. That was killing me." Dorin finally registered Etkis's own broken arm and got up as quickly as his body would allow. His voice was high. "What happened to you? Where's the rest of the unit? Where's Kya?"

"*This* is a courtesy of Jormar…would've killed me if it wasn't for Kya. She's fine, calling in the airstrike now, I hope. As for the rest…only three that I know of. Toa, an unconscious scout, and a lad you haven't met named Murray. They're deeper in the catacombs."

Dorin was covered in a cold sweat. He thought he'd be sick. "I'm sorry."

Etkis shook his head, his hand covered his visor. Dorin finally took stock of the room. The shattered wall. The two corpses. "I see you ran into Cormac…" he said.

Etkis's voice wavered. "Another mistake. He said he'd leave town. I believed him."

"He meant it when he said it. Changed his mind…" Dorin said, somber. "What you did to him though…that's not like you. Are you okay?"

"That?" Etkis pointed at his handiwork but refused to look at it. "That *is* me. Part of me at least…I don't know what happened, I just lost it. Lost control." Etkis slammed his fist into the wall and the entire cell shook as stone crumbled to sand beneath his rage. Dorin jumped for a second, an instinctual fear that Etkis noticed immediately. Shame flooded his spirit. "I'm sorry," Etkis whispered.

Dorin ran his human hand through his sweat and grime covered hair, "It's not your fault, none of it."

"Don't coddle me," Etkis responded, his voice bassy. Dorin thought better than to retort. Etkis hit the back of his head on the wall, eyes toward the ceiling, "But the ambush in the woods…how'd they know? I don't know what I did wrong."

"It was me…I never should have come," Dorin said.

"Don't say that. We'd never have even made it to the door if it wasn't for—"

"It's Ashton. She's Pompeii."

Etkis looked to Dorin in shock but didn't speak. He communicated only through the eyes. Dorin understood.

"No, I'm not. Thanks, though. The moment my name came up, I was screwed—but that's not the worst of it. She knew it was me, but she didn't know that I was working for the Wolves beyond being a simple guide. The Roarers' ranch? The kid I let live? He identified me. There was no way anyone would believe a simple guide would kill a whole group of freelancers. As soon as she put the pieces together, she must've had Serpents stalking the woods, just waiting for you all to show up."

"You couldn't have known. How could anyone?"

Dorin paused and turned back to the corpses in the room. Only two. "Wait—where is he? The kid? The one-armed rat!"

"One arm—oh…I let him go."

"*You what?*" Dorin shouted.

"I—he said he tried to stop them from hurting you! I believed him, so I let him live! I didn't recognize him."

"*Fuck!*" Dorin kicked the chair. Etkis bowed his head, unsure if what he had done was right or not. Dorin whispered, "I should've killed him when I had the chance."

"…Come on—we need to get out of here. Hopefully reinforcements will be here soon and—"

"No." Dorin said. He picked his survival gauntlet off of Cormac's remains.

"No?" Etkis asked.

"If the Wolves come here, it'll be a bloodbath. There are hundreds of freelancers in the main hall armed with Velkan tech, *and* they're ready. We need to clear them so Rother can acquire as much information out of this place as possible. And we need to catch Ash."

Etkis narrowed his eyes, "Dorin…this isn't a good idea. Don't let personal—"

"She's the mastermind of the entire human end of this insurgency! So unless you managed to grab Jormar…"

Etkis sighed. "No, I did not."

"Then we need her. We need what she knows."

Etkis stumbled to his feet and slapped his hand against his thigh. "But how do we clear a whole building of freelancers to get to her?"

"Actually, I have a few thoughts on that." Dorin fished in his pocket, begging for it to still be there. "*Ha ha!*" He pulled out a large lump of stone. Etkis waited for the punch line, but it never came.

"Your plan is a rock?"

"My captors thought it was just a rock too, otherwise I wouldn't still have it. It may look like it, feel like it, but it's not. How can you tell? The smell. Like burnt steak. This, my friend, is the only reason the Alexandrian economy functions. Useless to humans, but invaluable to Velkan technology. This is one hundred percent pure lunar ore from the moon's core. Also known as starship fuel."

CHAPTER 16

Wyrms, too many. Knives, useless. Davis tried plasma cutter. Had to beat them off with his arm. Out of ammo. Almost. One bullet left. They're squirming around outside, can't hear them in space but feel the vibrations growing stronger. Tell family I love them. That I didn't die like the rest. Won't be eaten in this cave.

—Carving found at the Tunglborg Mining Site, Luna, 6.18.1110
(commonly referred to as the Tunglborg Disaster)

Kya trudged through thigh-high snow. The wind blew against her bare body suit and armor, the metal seared her body with cold, and fresh snow pelted her visor. She'd left anything that could've kept her warm with Toa, and now the blizzard was at its peak. Every speeding spec of ice bore through her soul like a bullet. *Fuck me, it's cold.*

She couldn't see more than maybe two meters ahead, but neither could the Serpents. All she knew for certain was that she was hiking uphill. Soon she came to the hilltop. The spaceport was straight ahead, although she knew this more from memory than any visual indication.

Kya slung the Elo rifle over her shoulder and removed the flare gun from her belt. She told herself to fire it, but her fingers didn't move. She couldn't see the spaceport, but that didn't make it any less real. When she pulled the trigger, it would all be gone. Alexandria would lose the only livelihood it had. The only human superstructure left on Earth, gone. *Bankrupt. Starved. Would the city tear itself apart? Would they ever recover from this? Could they? Without the income from the spaceport, it would be unlikely the city would have a cash flow significant enough to fund rebuilding it. Millions of people would be left jobless, destitute, ruined.*

If there were any miners on the job right then, they'd likely die forgotten in the gray grikes and tunnels of Luna, doomed to die when they ran out of oxygen. Their corpses ripe for monstrous wyrms to tear apart. She pictured gaping maws and eyeless heads soaked in the blood of a father of four. Kya might as well put a bullet in his head herself. Not to mention any poor saps working the port itself tonight, crushed to death by shifting gravitational fields or incinerated by funneled atomic fission from the atmosphere. She wondered if she'd had any friends working there tonight, on that last transport that had come in, the one she and Etkis had seen.

She prayed, "Okar, take them with you, to…um…journey to a star? That's not right. May you die…ugh…honorably. Well. May you die—fuck…I'm sorry. I'm really sorry."

She pointed the flare to the sky and killed them all with a flick of the trigger.

Dorin and Etkis had made their way through the catacombs and prison cells when they heard the bombardment. Loud crashes of gun batteries and cannons slammed the earth with force that carried the vibrations kilometers away and nearly twenty meters underground. They picked up their pace. Time was short.

No one else was left in the cells, but the smell of blood and waste implied they'd been filled recently and often. Dorin stuck Soot, fully reloaded, back into his holster, his knife in the sheath. The hole the torturer had cut into the appendage didn't hurt, but Dorin couldn't stand the sight of it. The metal wound made his hair stand on end like nails on a chalkboard. He tore a red stained shirt from one of the corpses and wrapped it around his arm.

He wrapped another strip of shirt, cut like a bandana, behind his ears and over his nose. No one needed to see his face.

Etkis used another piece of his cloak to tie Dorin's survival gauntlet to the ore. He'd used so much of the cloth throughout the night that only a little nub near his neck remained. The lights on the gauntlet were purple, the gravity setting. Dorin carried Etkis's energy barrier. He hoped that the battery still had enough of a charge for what they planned to do. They navigated the winding tunnels until they began to hear the rabble from the main hall. It was straight ahead, on the other side of a steel door.

"Do you have everything you need?" Etkis asked.

"The G-spot, lubricant, and a hot metal rod to *penetrate* at fifteen thousand kilometers an hour to bring us to an explosive climax," Dorin said, holding up the ore, gauntlet, and Soot, respectively. Etkis cringed one last time. Dorin went on. "How much time do you need?"

"Two minutes? I can get out with the others by then." Etkis shuffled his feet and began to pace back and forth. "I don't like this."

"When has that ever stopped me?"

"Lunar ore…starship fuel. That reaction's supposed to take place in a gravitational prism that would fuse your body into solid lead…to do this in an exposed environment…"

"That *is* the point."

"Would you not—ugh—I don't know if your barrier will hold is what I'm trying to say. You could be *atomized*."

"Well not litera—"

"Literally. Atomized. Poof."

"Really? … Huh. Welp. Here's hoping!" Etkis squeezed his eyes shut. He'd seen his friend battered and broken today, emotionally and physically. He didn't appreciate the joke. Dorin shifted his tone, and pulled down is bandana such that Etkis could see his face. "I'll be okay, Etkis. I promise."

Etkis kept pacing. "Okay. Okay, okay. You're right. Don't start the reaction until you're on the third floor. Get as much distance as possible. And don't get shot. It'll drain the battery."

"Got it."

Etkis stopped and knelt. Dorin tapped his fist on the Velka's helmet. "Go. We've lost too much time as it is."

"Alright, going…good luck." Etkis hugged him and ran off back into the labyrinth. Dorin pulled the bandana back over his nose, walked over to the door, and pushed it open with the ore held under his human arm.

The air was frantic. All the freelancers prepared for battle until they got the word to move out. The long day they'd spent drinking kept a modicum of fear at bay, but their anxiety was still potent. Dorin could smell it. The bombardment left no question that the Wolves were on their way. Everyone was so panicked that they didn't notice him enter the room. He closed the door behind him and walked nonchalantly to the stairs. His metal arm was covered. None of the freelancers had seen his face, only his helmet, so he should have been unrecognizable save for his clothes. He sweated profusely but walked by unmolested. He made it to the stairs and the second floor. *Soon.* Dorin wondered if any of the freelancers would ask about the stone and gauntlet or the Velkan energy barrier attached at the small of his back. None of the others had such items, so surely he was suspicious. But none stopped him to ask. He made it to the next set of stairs and the third floor. *Very soon.*

As close to the target and as far from the source as possible, Dorin thought. There were plenty of marble pillars he could hide behind. He recited directions in his head. *Prime the gauntlet, drop it and the ore over the railing, and shoot it just before it hits the floor. From thirty meters away. Too soon, and I'll fucking *atomize* myself. Too late, and the ore will shatter on the floor and the whole thing is bungled. Simple. I got this. Easy peasy…I'm gonna fucking die here.*

Dorin walked over to the railing. Sweat dripped from his temple and off his chin. *Drop it. Just drop it.*

"Hey, are you all right?"

Dorin turned around and nearly had a meltdown. It was Catherine, head of the freelancers. The person who'd met him when he first entered. Dorin sweat bullets. She *had* seen him without his helmet.

But she didn't flinch.

Didn't move toward her gun.

Dorin remembered the bandana covered half his face, and the half that *was* exposed was beaten and swollen. To top it off, his metal arm was still covered. For once, he thanked Ashton for the sucker punch.

"Mhmm," Dorin squeaked. "Nervous."

"Well, don't be. We snagged that race traitor when he walked in here. Smooth sailing for the rest of the night!"

Dorin swallowed. He had no idea how to leave the conversation without sounding suspicious. "What about the Wolves?" he asked sheepishly.

"If they wanted to bomb us off the map, we'd already be a fucked-to-death pile of radioactive slag. They're gonna try and breach the compound, and that's when we'll have them! They have no idea we've got their own weapons to take them down. As long as we surprise them, we'll be able to hit them hard and escape. I was never really worried about that. I'm just glad we got that other guy, wasn't sure if *we* could manage…"

At the chance to inflate his ego, Dorin lifted a single eyebrow. "Other guy? I didn't think he was such a badass."

"Cocksucker with the metal arm boss told us to watch out for—any idea who he is?"

"Mmmmm, nope…is he a big deal or something? I thought he was just some schmuck. Is he…famous?" Dorin couldn't suppress his need for validation. "I'm very curious."

"Cyborg motherfucker. He and the boss ran jobs together back in the day—maybe it's all just stories, but you hear things, you know? The Ior bombing, the cull of Jinor, the Mercia massacre? He and the boss. Then, a few weeks ago, he slaughters a bunch of folk over in Lipel and turns Jarrod over to the Wolves. Never thought I'd see that blond bastard taken down. Who knows how much is true, but what's for sure not a story is here, tonight, he kills two Velka in close combat! One with his bare hands. Fuck, when I saw the corpse…that shit scares me. That's not normal. Not human. Thank God the boss was here."

"Yeah, she really saved our butts."

Catherine laughed but stopped herself. "Hey, I never said 'she.' You know… Pompeii's a woman? Who are you?"

God fucking damn it. "Didn't *you* say 'she'? Huh. Well, I think assuming Pompeii's a man is a little presumptuous, so I go back and forth between pronouns to keep the gender-neutral ambiguity equivalent! You know…like normal people do."

"…Have we met before? You seem really familiar. Because…even the voice. And your outfit." Her eyes narrowed. "And your…personality."

"Nope, no, can't say we have."

Catherine drew a knife and slashed.

Dorin leaned back just enough, and the blade shaved a few hairs off his chin. He grabbed her head and smashed her nose into the railing and threw her to the floor like a rag doll. He turned on the energy barrier, the gauntlet, and tossed the ore over. He drew and aimed carefully. One shot was all he got.

"Get him!" shouted Catherine through a bloody mouth.

Dorin could hear freelancers stomp toward him. It was now or never. He pulled the trigger. A line of crimson lightning rocketed from Soot straight to the asteroid. The stone lit up like an ultraviolet bulb burning violet radiance in the center of the ballroom. It was blinding. Like a miniature sun. Dorin ran for the nearest pillar to hide behind.

The Velka had crossed light-years through the vacuum of space to arrive at the Sol system. They reached near lightspeed through Alcubierre drives. They crushed space and time behind them and stretched it like putty at the bows of their gargantuan ships.

But at sub–light speeds, for tight maneuvers in battle, they needed something else. Something older, less eloquent, and far more volatile. Something explosive. Rocket fuel like humankind could only dream of.

Dorin didn't understand the mechanics behind it. No human did. The Velka had different, better mathematics, and they weren't keen on sharing their knowledge. All Dorin knew was that when a gravitational wave was run through refined asteroid ore, there was a reaction.

A violent reaction.

The kind that would usually take place in a starship's engine.

And now it was uncontained in a room full of squishy people.

There was a strong pull toward the center of the room down below. Dorin could feel it from the third story. His body was jammed against the pillar so hard he thought he might be forced straight through the marble. He held on. Screams echoed from the lower floors as people were drawn into the source.

They stopped. Dorin plugged his ears and shut his eyes tight, and the screams were replaced with a single roar.

The explosion incinerated everyone on the first floor. The building shook, and purple flames shot up and enveloped every pillar and stairwell, immolating everything. The fire was far weaker by the time it climbed up to the third floor, yet was still enough to burn a man to death. Dorin prayed his energy barrier would hold. He opened one eye, and the light nearly blinded him. He'd be seeing spots for at least an hour. The fire pressed against the barrier, clawing and gnawing to eat him alive. He couldn't see or hear anything through it. *Etkis—you'd better have made it out.*

The flames petered out. Patches all over the scorched floor still smoldered. The floor, pillar, stairs, and railing were all covered in ash except for a small white shadow Dorin had left. It was in the rough shape of a man, distorted slightly around the bevels of his shield. The marble there was pristine, as if it had just been mopped. The barrier shimmered blue a few times, then failed and died. Dorin stood, tore off his bandana, and removed the lifeless cylinder from the small of his back. He took stock of the carnage.

The doors on the second and third floors were horribly burnt but still stood. The first floor was obliterated. A crater in the center of the room. Every door had been blasted open.

There were no bodies near the blast. No bones, no blood, no dust. *Literally atomized.* It wasn't until the staircase of the second floor that Dorin began to see charred skeletons. On the third floor, people still had meat on their bones—if seared black. He heard an inhuman voice behind him.

"P-please."

He turned. Dorin only knew it was Catherine because that was where she'd fallen before the blast. Her hair was gone, her skin black and cracked. Her voice sounded like an old woman's, the eyes burnt out of her head. She wasn't even really talking to Dorin, merely pleading to an uncaring world.

"Kill me. Please."

Dorin started to leave but stopped. He cursed to himself. He walked over to her and knelt. He removed his knife. His jaw was tight, a lump of self-hate in his throat. He forced himself to stare at the consequences of his actions. He cradled her head and whispered, "I'm sorry…you were right to be afraid." He shoved the knife through the bottom of her jaw.

Dorin reloaded Soot and ran to the end of the hall, where the escape tunnel was.

That was where *she'd* be.

Etkis ran and slammed into the walls when he made tight turns in the stone labyrinth. His heart beat out of his chest. After an eon of twisting passageways, he made it to the entrance, where his soldiers were. They were exactly as Etkis had left them. Murray spoke up. "No contacts so far, sir. Did you manage to—"

Etkis hardly listened. He ran straight to the entrance of the cellars and kicked open the wood panels. They burst apart into tiny fragments of lumber.

"We need to leave, now."

Etkis walked over to Toa and picked her up as slowly as possible, he tried to be wary of her injury. Murray winced and stood when they heard a screeching explosion, the sound of shattering windows, and fire catapulting through the stone halls. Murray hobbled out, and Etkis grabbed the other wounded Velka and jumped out of the cellar just in time for a jet of purple flame to singe his backside.

"*Hot, hot, hot!*" He shouted, ran into the snow, and collapsed. The sound of vaporized snow fizzed beneath him. He lay there, tired but relieved that he'd made it and that his troops had made it. He'd never been so tired in his life. He ached and burned now that the suit's opioids had worn off. Etkis tasted blood and felt nauseous—he thought about falling asleep then and there. Amid the daze he felt sudden heart-wrenching panic and checked the two wounded Velka under his arms—both alive. *Thank Okar*, he thought.

"What was *that*, sir?" Murray asked. His eyes were on the compound. The windows on the first and second floor were blown open, and an otherworldly smell of ionized atmosphere rose out of the ruin.

"Dorin, succeeding where I failed. He's getting us the human leader and ensuring our troops encounter no resistance when they come to the compound."

"Your human friend? Huh. We'd best move out, sir."

"Yeah, yeah, we will. Just…just give me a minute."

Dorin bolted hard and fast, his feet felt numb on impact and his thighs warm and flush from the rush of blood through his legs. Lines of scorched marble pillars passed by him in a long tunnel, burnt flesh filled his nostrils with every breath.

He pumped his arms and rounded the corner into the lounge, breaking down the burnt door with his metal shoulder. Seven armed thugs were spread throughout the room. They were stumbling and struggled to rise from the explosion. But at the sight of his face, they managed to raise their guns. Dorin slid to the floor and inertia carried him out of the paths of streaming bullets. Chunks of floor rained down where his torso had been milliseconds before. He aimed Soot, the barrel hot and hungry for blood. He fanned the hammer and trigger in syncopation. Crimson lightning crashed into flesh over and over and all seven thugs burst into bubbles of magma and scarlet vapor. His ears hurt and rang from the echoing shockwave. The sound continued to bounce back and forth between the walls. This had all occurred in half a second. Dorin dug his heel into the floor and rolled back to his feet. He walked determined toward his true target. Right foot, left foot. Slow, methodical. Soot was trained on the target, its barrel smoked and radiated orange, like the mouth of a volcano. He brought the hand cannon closer and closer to Ashton until she was hardly a meter away. She raised her hands and surrendered. Her first surrender. Her eyes were bloodshot. Dorin's nostrils flared, and he narrowed his eyes as scalding tears poured down his face. His lips trembled so violently that he almost couldn't speak. It was the one-syllable question that haunted him more than anything else in his miserable life: "Why?"

Her mouth twitched between a trembling smile and utter fear. "Why what?"

Dorin pulled Soot's hammer back with an audible click.

Ashton bit her lip. "I was scared. I thought we were going to die. The pistols we had were just flares to the wyrms. And I knew that if you were…down, the beasts would come for you and I could escape. I could live. Otherwise we *both* would've died there."

"You don't know that—you couldn't have! You selfish fuck—you'd rather shoot me to make sure you live than take the chance together? What the hell? *You killed me!*"

"I thought I had, but here you are. Stronger than I ever thought. You saved me. You saved my life. Thank you. Thank you, my love."

Dorin laughed, his disbelief overwhelmed his fury. "'Thank you.' I can't… how…how can you say that to me? Don't you understand how fucking psychotic that sounds? Do you know what the right answer is? *I'm sorry! That's it. Why is that so fucking hard?"*

"…I'll make it up to you."

"*That's not an apology!*" Dorin screamed. "Our whole lives—every time you lost all our money, you said you'd make it up to me. When Mom died, you know what you said to me? Remember? Not 'I'm so sorry, I'll miss her too.' Not 'Everything will be okay.' You said, 'These things happen.' Took me years to realize how fucked up that was. And now, after you shot me in the back to save your own skin, you say *thank you.* No. Not again. I want a fucking apology." Soot was still pointed at Ashton but she began to walk toward him. "How could you do that to me? The things I did for—I killed for you. I *slaughtered* for you! I would've died for you."

She approached, slow, hands still up and out. "I know, that's why I—"

"*It's not the same you fucking psychopath!* Why can't you understand that…did you ever love me?"

Ashton put her hands on Soot, the orange metal seared her hands. Her cheeks flinched with the pain, and she lowered the gun. She whispered, "Always. Those days we spent together, in the wilds, hunting for gold, surviving on our wits and skill. The nights we spent charting the stars, the mornings we spent cooking meals. You'd build snow forts of what our ranch would look like. You'd talk about starting a family. I'd say we'd start with a dog…those were the happiest days of my life."

"Did you ever regret what you did?"

Ashton squeezed her lips tight, her brow bunched together. She couldn't look at him. "Every day." She rested her forehead on Dorin's chest and began to weep. He could hear the plummet of teardrops onto the floor.

"I-I'm so sorry, baby. I'm sorry. I was so scared. I don't—I'm sorry."

Dorin felt a vice release in his chest—he hadn't been aware of it until now. For years it had strangled him, and he didn't notice, or he chose not to notice. The release was the greatest euphoria he'd ever experienced. He wrapped his arms around her, and they cried together. They embraced, surrounded by blood and ash, and forgot everything. For a few seconds, he was happy.

She whispered, "I'm scared now too, D—"

"Why?"

"They're going to kill me—I'm not ready. There's so much more I want to do."

"They won't—"

"They'll kill me—I'm sure of it. Please. Run away with me. I want everything to go back to the way it was before I fucked it all up. I'm sick of being alone. Come with me."

Dorin felt every nerve and muscle shout yes. Everything he'd felt before, the anger, the betrayal, began to melt away. He bit his tongue. "I don't know…I don't trust you anymore."

"I know, I understand. But I'll do anything, whatever it takes to earn your trust back. Give me a chance."

All thoughts vanished. Dorin felt like he was trapped in a marionette. Words came out of his mouth without his permission. "I…I need to say goodbye to Etkis."

"Who?"

"The Velka I was with. I need to say goodbye. Then we can—"

Ashton whipped her head up to look at Dorin. "Why do you need to say goodbye to him?"

"He's my best friend. He deserves—"

Ashton scrunched her nose. "He won't let us—won't let *you* go! You can't talk to him."

"That's ridiculous! You don't know him like I do. If I talk to him, he'll support—"

"No. You're not talking to that disgusting cur anymore."

Dorin pushed her away. "Don't call him that! I know you have…concerns, but once you meet him, you'll see—"

"Dorin, I said no. I don't want you talking to him again."

"I'm not leaving without saying goodbye to him. Not with you, not with anyone."

Ashton shouted, her face beet red, "So you're going to give up your partner for that worthless friendship? *For that fucking cur?*"

Dorin felt his stomach sink. She panted. Air reached her brain, and her face changed from blood red to snow white. She knew what she'd done; she could read it on his face. "Dorin, I—"

"How dare you," he whispered.

"Dorin—just come with me, and we'll talk about this all somewhere safer. I have somewhere we can go. Once you've had some space and time, you'll see that talking to…to that Velka isn't what we want to do."

"What about what *I* want?"

She didn't respond.

"You just assume you and I want the same thing, but you didn't ask me. You never ask me. You tell me. You tell me what it is that I want because you know me *so well*. Etkis has been a better friend to me than you've ever been. He saved me. He saved me from monsters. He saved me from you. He saved me from myself. You're not taking that away. And the Wolves? They're my family now."

"You don't mean that."

"Don't I?"

"They're invaders!" she shouted. "This is our home, and we need to take it back."

"We don't deserve it. Earth was ours long before the Velka ever showed up, and look at what we did to it. A frozen waste. We can hardly live here. And what have we done since? We squabble and cheat and murder the same as we always have. Our time's over, and I say good fucking riddance."

Dorin stepped back, his voice wavering but absolute. "I get it now. You haven't changed. You're never going to change. You're still the same frightened, selfish, cruel person you've always been. I can't fix that, however much I want to. Your love and smile will always be paired with your violence and manipulation. You're a danger to me, to Etkis, to Volthsheim itself."

Ashton looked as though she'd been punched in the gut. Her face pale, eyes red—tears drew wet lines through the dirt and ash on her face. Her voice was small, defeated.

"Well…if that's what you think, you ought to shoot me. I'm not going to stop. I'm never going to stop until they're all buried and gone. It…it's not what you want. I understand. And I'm sorry you've never heard that from me sooner. But I can't just let it go. If you have to kill me, I understand. I'd rather it be you."

Dorin pointed Soot to her forehead. He could hear his heart beating in his ears, his face hot and scrunched in anger, hate, and loss. *Pull the trigger. She's never going to stop. Pull the trigger. You'll save so many lives. The war ends here. Pull the trigger.*

Ashton gave a gentle smile. She meant every word. "It's okay. I'm sorry. I love you."

Dorin screamed like a bullet had passed through his heart, and he shot his final bolt at the window on the north side. The hot metal blew open the bullet-proof glass. Dorin dropped Soot and collapsed to the floor in front of the couch. He hid his face. "Go. Don't ever let me see you again."

She looked at the escape and back to him. She choked on the words, unsure if they were right to say but still faintly hopeful. "Come with me," she begged. There was a long silence. Fresh tears tumbled down her face, her voice hoarse with emotion. "I—I can be better."

Dorin spoke with no emotion. Utterly empty. "No, you can't."

Ashton lingered for a moment. She stared at what all her glory had cost her. She turned, ran out, and jumped from the window.

Dorin leaned his head back on the sofa and exhaled. He felt release. Relief. He hadn't really breathed in years, and now he took his first breath. But beneath the euphoria was a yet unnoticed feeling. It itched in the back of his mind and crawled down to his neck, and he grew more and more aware of its presence. The old specter fastened its fingers around his neck, and all over again, he couldn't breathe.

CHAPTER 17

As with any invasion, eventually a resistance was mounted. The Velka had arrived in Sol silently, and were deeply entrenched by the time of first contact. Whether the alien scourge had engaged in a deliberate tactic of stealth or mankind's attention so divided by the Phantom Fire that it paid them no heed, it did not matter. It should still be noted that the cause and effect are unknown. Regardless, by the time we had united, there was no contest. They crashed upon us as a great tidal wave surging over a rowboat. No human force could stand against them for longer than a month. Loss after loss, they engraved it into us. They made sure we knew that the power to take something, rather than birthright, inheritance, or endogeneity, is the power to own it. Although we were born here, by the second of their arrival, this star system belonged to the Velka.

—*A History of Our Invaders*, VOLUME 1, BY CORNELIUS VALUM,
CHIEF HISTORIAN OF THE LIBRARY OF ALEXANDRIA

A patch of thick snow broke Ashton's fall. The burns on her hands from touching Dorin's gun stung horribly in the cold. She dug herself out of the snow and made her way around the compound. The storm threatened to strip away her sense of direction, so she clung to the walls and pulled herself forward, into the slowly weakening, abating winds. The whirling blizzard was calming, but she could barely see through the gale and night. Dawn approached, and the night became even darker as the pitch blackness heralded the sun.

She didn't know how she felt. Foreign emptiness filled her chest. Weightless and heavy at the same time. She'd never felt so powerless. Her jaw hurt. Her cheeks were sore. She'd been walking in delirious haze for a few minutes when she paused at the sound of voices ahead of her in the blizzard. Lightly digitized. Velka.

Jormar? she thought. She listened.

"Feeling better, sir?"

"No, but I'm ready, let's go. Okar, I could sleep for a week…we need to rendezvous with Dorin, then Kya."

Ash stopped and squeezed her blistered fists. *Wolves.*

The powerlessness she felt turned to rage. Fury. She drew her pistols. She heard the Wolves draw closer. Several pairs of luminescent eyes pierced the veil of night and snow. Two eyes, high above her, burned so bright that their searing blue reflected off the snow. The demon was enormous, as tall as Jormar.

There was only one Wolf it could be.

…Your fault.

She steadied her aim, and the snow crunched beneath her feet.

Your fault!

Etkis spoke.

"Murray, did you hear something? …Dorin? Is that you—"

YOUR FAULT!

Ashton fired and the bullet passed straight through the visor.

The giant stood for a second before he went down with a booming thud.

"*Etkis!*" Murray screamed. Bullets flew toward her, but Murray had no point of reference, nothing but a faint direction to shoot at. He fired his gun into nothingness until it was empty. Ashton shot at the glowing eyes but missed, she heard the bullets deflect off his helmet. Murray tracked the sound and tackled her, and her pistols flew out of her hands. She fell to the snow and felt armored hands grip her throat. Blood pumped in her temples, and her eyes bulged out of her head. She could finally see the alien clearly. She struggled against his hands, but his grip was unyielding. She tried to push him off from under his chin, but he was too tall, his arms too long. She felt her faculties failing, her vision failing.

Something caught her eye—there was blood on his thigh. She kicked there as hard as she could. Murray screamed and his grip loosened. Ash broke his hold and kicked him with both legs in the chest, and he flew off—she coughed so hard it shook her entire body. She heard her foe grab his gun and the telltale *chunk* of

Velkan slugs slotted into the firing chamber. Ashton searched frantically in the thick snow and fished for one of her guns. Her burnt palm stung against the grip. She closed her fingers around the weapon, spun, and let loose three rounds.

Murray's gun was leveled straight at her heart but never had the chance to fire. Three holes pumped blood out of his neck, and he collapsed, his hands pressed around the gushing red geysers. He'd bleed out soon. Ashton stood and caught her breath. The blizzard had dissipated completely, but she didn't notice. She stepped over Murray as his writhing slowed and slowed until his twitching turned into gentle spasms on the ground. She inspected the crumpled Velkan forms. Murray was done with. The other one was covered in plasma burns and unconscious. She unloaded a bullet beneath its jaw. Now to Etkis.

She couldn't tell if it still breathed.

The Wolf was enormous. She wondered if the bullet had penetrated through to the brain or not. Ash couldn't fathom why, but her stomach churned, her jaw hurt anew. She thought back to what Dorin had said, how he talked about this filthy filter breather. The look on his face when she insulted him. She sucked in air through her teeth and forced back tears and leaned her forehead on Etkis's shoulder. Ash bit her lip hard and banished her moment of doubt back to the tomb where it belonged. *No. This is for our own good.*

She put her gun to his ear.

A hand grabbed her foot, and she jumped. Ashton looked down. A female Velka. It muttered weakly.

"No, stop." Etkis had sheltered her beneath his bulk when he fell, his last act of consciousness. Ashton put her foot on the alien's neck and whispered.

"No. I will never stop. You curs can count on that."

Toa whimpered. She prayed to herself, "Okar, Callva, Kior, Treya, protect my house. Accept me, to journey through the stars—"

Ashton pulled the trigger twice. The muzzle flash illuminated her for a split second like the beam of a lighthouse passing over ships in harbor. She lifted her foot, and Toa didn't move. The roar of the gunshots was louder than Ash had expected, and she finally clocked that the blizzard had settled. She had further exposed her position. An uneasy feeling gripped her throat and she examined the hillside. The moon and the stars were gone, and the sun only just peeked over the horizon. Every color was muted, near impossible to see.

There was a dark figure so far away that she had to squint to make it out.

Bang.

The electric bolt caught Ashton straight through the shoulder, cracking through flesh and burning bone. She screamed and dropped her gun. She didn't think, she just ran toward the forest, a trail of blood in her wake. Elo bolts whizzed by into the snow. Ashton had no idea who the shooter was, but they were good. Very good. A shot grazed her leg, another her back. One made proper impact through her forearm before she made it to the edge of the woods. She kept running, and bolts crashed into trees. She hid in the dark and panted. She waited and listened to the sound of rapidly crunching snow. It didn't get closer.

Ash peaked from behind her tree and saw Kya sprint toward the carnage she'd left behind. Ash gritted her teeth. *Kya, you lying bitch...I'll skin you for this.*

Kya fell to her knees beside Etkis and shook him with all her might.

"Etkis? Etkis, get up—come on. You're okay, you're okay! Toa, Murray? Are you—fuck!" Kya's voice broke with violent feeling. She grabbed a pistol from her belt and fired a flare into the air. Ash felt a gust of wind trample the forest. Something massive had changed direction hard and fast. Ashton's heart raced. She stumbled back and tripped and fell. The clouds over the hillside bulged and parted to reveal the bow of a Wolven Caelicraft. It's shadow covered the valley like the alien doom Ashton knew it to be. The leviathan floated down to the ground the way only Velkan ships could. Landships flooded out of the Caelicraft's hangars mounted on its belly and headed to her compound like scavengers swarming a fresh corpse. Wolves would be there in seconds. Ash stumbled up and ran deeper into the forest, clutching her bleeding arm.

She ran until she couldn't hear the Wolven warships but no farther. The blood flowed heavily down her arm, shot twice, and it kept dripping down to the fresh snow. The ice swallowed it like paint on a canvas. Light began to bud more over the horizon. The forest turned from a haunting visage to a vibrant and colored battlefield, like an ancient painting of man's wars long past. Ash could now see the corpses she'd been walking by this whole time, Wolf and Serpent alike, coated in the sun's yellow and orange glow. She tried to keep walking but her vision became blurry. The blood loss made her lose her balance. She fell hard and didn't move. Ashton laid in the cold dirt, snow stung her face.

I wonder...is this how you felt? she thought. *Rejected, wounded, alone, face in the dirt, waiting to die?* Ashton closed her eyes.

Someone called out.

"Who's there?"

Ashton opened her eyes to the barrel of a gun. She looked past it to a Velka with bright green eyes.

"Yui?" Ashton asked.

"Pompeii..." Yui's ears perked in surprise, but soon they bowed back and up in hate, and her eyes narrowed. She kept her gun right where it was. "You look like swine shit...did that pet of yours manage to get out?"

"Yes, but he didn't shoot me."

"Humph, serves you right. Should've killed him when you had the chance."

Ash curled her nose in rage but forced her tone to be civil. "Agree to disagree. You gonna help me up?"

Yui raised her head and looked around at the woods, as empty as a graveyard could be. "Where are all the others? The other freelancers?"

"Dead, I think...Dorin blew them up."

"Blew them up? Okar save me, you *really* should've killed him. Well, that explains the explosion we heard."

Ashton barely heard Yui. She squeezed her eyes and opened them again. Everything was blurry. It was getting harder and harder to think, and her wounds grew less and less tenable with each passing second. She reached out her good arm. "Take me to Jormar."

Yui tilted her head. Her tone was mocking. "Why?"

Ashton felt her heart thump in her chest, every beat pumped more blood out of her wounds, and her senses weakened. "Because I'm injured. Because you need me and my network. Or because I fucking said so. *Pick one.*"

"You just said all your men are dead. What good are you to us now?"

"Doesn't matter what you think, it's Jormar's decision—"

"Lord Jormar is too kind. He pities you. I don't. You're a self-serving rat. You'll shoot us in the back the moment it suits you. Why shouldn't I kill you now? Save me the trouble. No one needs to know. It's just you and me out here."

Ash grimaced and forced herself out of the dirt to her knees. She wove her words perfectly, without thought. "The spaceport is destroyed by the evil occupying power. Ten million of my people are now ruined and angry—they'll need a leader to rally behind to reclaim whatever remains of their shredded dignity. Not just the men and women in Alexandria. Human beings, *all of us*, are furious and humiliated. We need action—you know what I mean. When the Wolves crushed your house, what did *your* people need? What Jormar was to you, whatever he was, I can be to the human race. I can do it. You know I can. So what do you want? Ten million ants for cannon fodder? Or an organized militia as an ally?"

Yui mulled it over for a few seconds, her expressive green eyes contorted in frustration. Ashton thought that she would've spat in her face if it hadn't been for the helmet. Yui stowed her gun and made a point to pull on Ashton's injured arm when she helped the warlord to her feet.

"*Ah!*" Pain forced spots of light to block Ashton's vision. "Fuck you, Yui."

The Velka put Ash's arm around her own neck to support her. "I can still change my mind if you prefer?" Yui mocked her.

Ash bit her lip hard and said no more. They had walked for what felt like hours when she came to a camp of Serpents. Beta site. Tents were huddled near the trees. Dozens of Velka gathered supplies and huddled over tables to discuss strategy. Jormar sat on a log, his gaze fixed on a small bonfire before him. His wounds were tended to, his left hand missing. His visor was cracked, his helmet, pauldrons and chassis were all scarred, dented, and black with dirt. It looked like he had run headfirst into a speeding train.

Jormar raised his head and saw her. His voice was weary, deep, and gentle.

"Pompeii? Are you all right, child? We were worried."

"No, I'm not all right!" Ash screamed. Yui leaned her head away from her charge, ear twitching in pain. "You had one job, *one fucking job, and you screwed it up*! What happened? Why were there Wolves outside my house? *And why are you suddenly right-handed?*"

"Calm yourself, young one. Sit—we'll get you treated."

Yui dropped Ashton off far more roughly than she needed to. Ash groaned. Her head was fuzzy from yelling and blood loss. Two Velka came over and injected her with fluids she didn't recognize and bandaged her bullet wounds. She flinched at their touch, disgusted by their gloved hands and the sound of filtered breathing. Their pointed canine-like ears looked like horns, their black visors and glowing eyes like revenants stalking her. Peering into her heart. They were repulsive creatures. One of the medics tried to wrap Ashton's burnt hands, but she pulled them away, her nose curled in hate. "No," she said. The medic looked at her and Jormar in confusion.

"Are you sure?" Jormar asked. "Those look serious."

"*No.*" She turned to the medic. "*Piss off.*"

The medic left, still confused. Jormar analyzed Pompeii, searching for context. He leaned in. The log he sat on nearly splintered against his shifting weight. "What happened?" he asked. "You seem more…volatile than usual."

"My entire compound got blown up that's what happened."

"No, that's not it. You've never cared much about that place or losing men on the field. This is something personal…was it that man you wanted to capture? You came alone. I assume he won't be joining us."

Ashton clenched her jaw and fought to contain her anger, rejection, and sorrow. Jormar got up and went over to her and sat down. His legs were crossed as if in meditation. He leaned in.

"I'm sorry. It must be hard," he said. Ashton got up with great difficulty and put distance between her and him, showing him only her back. He bowed his head. "Apologies. At my age I should know better than to stick my fingers into a bleeding heart. I'll drop it."

Ashton reached into her pocket and pulled out a box of tobacco and small parchment. She smelled the ground leaves and let the thought of nicotine soothe her nerves. This single box cost her more than an entire month's supply of food. Being the king had its perks. She began to roll a cigarette, but it proved difficult with her burnt hands—the red and raw flesh screamed in protest with every twitch of her fingers. "How'd you lose to the Wolves?" she asked. "You had the drop on them, didn't you?"

"We had them all in a gravity field, pinned."

"You managed to get them in a perfect kill zone and you still fucked it up. Unbelievable." Ashton pulled a lighter from her pocket and lit her cigarette.

Jormar tilted his head. "You haven't been in many wars, have you? Hmm. It's true it should've ended there, but often it only takes the strength of one soldier, one Velka's valor, to turn the tide. And that's exactly what happened. A goliath, only a little smaller than I, withstood the gravity. He held a tomahawk over his head and threw it through the field and killed young Ito. I couldn't have done it—the strength and skill required was outstanding. I fought him and nearly won, but another Wolf interfered. Ah, I haven't felt the thrill of combat in so long."

"Thrill? He killed your man!"

"I bear him no ill will. He merely performed his duty." Jormar reached down his breastplate and pulled out a necklace with an obsidian star. Ashton spotted runes carved in the center of the star but had no idea what they meant. Jormar cradled it as if it were a songbird. "His duty is the same that I feel for my house, that you feel for your people. Just because he's on the other side of the wall doesn't make them different. A Wolf still hopes that days are bright and warm, that their crops grow green and full, the same way as any Serpent, or any man." Jormar squeezed his pendant in his hand. He looked as though he could be praying. "If we were perfect, there would be no division. But the shield walls of Volthsheim aren't the only barriers we Velka have erected between us. All the houses, mine included, have built the same palisades. Ours are made from pride, theirs from wood and metal and mortar. This is the only difference. And for that, we are doomed to slay our brothers and sisters in the endless hunt for that which is scarce. Show more empathy for your foes, child. One day you might need it in return."

Ashton rolled her eyes. Jormar shook his head, disappointed.

"I hope to meet that Wolf again, off the field. He seemed like a genuine fellow."

Ashton spat on the floor. "I shot him."

"…Pardon?"

"Giant Wolf, right? Name's Etkis. I shot him in the head."

"Oh…I see. Is he—"

"Not sure, got shot myself before I could make sure the job was done."

"Mm…at any rate, my jarl has committed more troops, and we're to meet them down south. Should we gather your men?"

"Most at the compound are dead and the rest are all over the planet. I need to recruit more now. Alexandria's fucked, so plenty of idiots with guns will be needing work. Buy me time."

"How?"

Ashton scoffed and squeezed her hands. She snarled from the pain of her burns. "*How?* you ask. And you lecture *me* about war."

"I meant what did you have in mind?"

She smoked the cigarette down to the nub, tossed it on the floor, and stomped it out. "We're a known contact now. The Wolves are aware I'm working with you, and your scouts are being culled all over the planet. Enough with the shadows. It's time to break things. Burn villages. Raid supplies. Bomb transports. Kill Wolves. *That's how.*"

CHAPTER 18

Open file > Human Allies > Sanctioned Freelancer > Dorin—no family name. 23 years, 178 cm, 84 kg (with prosthetic), hair black, olive skin. Alexandrian Born. Orphaned age 14. Previous criminal freelancer. Discovered WIA, 3.12.1121, by then pilgrim Etkis Terra near Tsukichi Mining Site. Past crimes absolved by Jarl Tarkus Lupine for outstanding services conducted for the House of Wolves. Citizenship status: refused.

—Volthsheim database, restricted access for head of military fields only.

Special Notes: Metal arm (personalized prosthetic model-base: Volthsheim Armory HRA05), unique firearm (human technology of unknown origin, hyper lethal, ongoing covert study).
Latent threat level: alpha

—Volthsheim database, restricted access for first scout and jarlship only.

I always forget there's no sound on the moon. I hear blood pumping in my ears, feel it pulsing through the veins in my neck, her breathing through the radio in my helmet, but nothing else. Not even the slightest whisper from the hunters in the dark lunar mines. We're both careful to be silent even though it doesn't matter. The fear compels us to fall back on age-old instincts. Instincts in the face of death, I suppose. I see two beasts with long bodies and six legs, articulated like primordial insects. The archaic form was forgotten on the frozen Earth but all too real among Luna's dunes. Wyrms. They pass us by—five of them now. Each of the six pikes stab the gray sand

236

in a steady rhythm. I feel the vibrations run up my thighs. I pray—first time for everything—that they don't stick their eyeless heads into the crag we're hiding in. Like hammerhead sharks, pits near their gaping mouths would light up near our ambient electromagnetic fields, and they'd suss us out in a second. Darkness or not. That's *not* the last thing I want to see…their enormous maws, a trash compactor of teeth, gray flesh like Luna itself, wrinkled and tough. Could I push at least one off and give her time to escape? On Earth maybe, but here? I doubt it. I might as well try. She's hiding behind me, crushing herself into the deepest recess of the cave. There just wasn't enough room. My nose was nearly out of the shadows and into the tunnel. Out of the feeble protective electromagnetic interference the Lunar walls were giving us. If they find us, I'll be dead first anyway.

I squeeze my pistol for comfort, but it's like holding a cross in a foxhole and hoping it'll stop a mortar shell. It's a Velkan weapon, and an Elo weapon at that. To the beasts, the stream of electrons it fires would be a neon sign to a fast-food restaurant. They'd find us instantly. A direct hit would burn and blind a wyrm but not stop it. Utterly useless. There's a reason the House of Wolves let humanity do all the mining for them. If cave-ins and solar flares weren't enough trouble, wyrm legs could pierce deep into the gaps of Velkan plate armor. Why bother when they could have someone else do it?

Throwing the guns would be just as useful, maybe more so, without the electrical flare. We have no grenades. And human knives? What a fucking joke. Fighting's a bust, but if we stay here, we'll run out of oxygen, eventually.

Maybe if we keep hiding, we can find some of the wyrms' more recent…meals, and steal any oxygen they still have on them! That would work! We could stay hidden for hours longer if we needed to! Yes! Now all we need is…tools to prevent all the oxygen getting sucked into the vacuum of space. Which we don't have. Piss. Beneath the ruins of one of humanity's ancient lunar cities, we're surrounded by dozens of corpses with "potential" air and no way to get it. Nothing decays on the moon. It just stays there, grotesquely preserved at the moment of death. I've seen so many bodies wearing space suits from a bygone era on our way down here, and I didn't think twice about it. I've desecrated a few graves in my day, but this is the first one I might actually regret.

Funny, we'd bought these guns in case we came across any miners protecting their haul of ore, but we haven't seen a single one. Enough lunar ore here to buy and sell *half of Alexandria, just sitting here for the taking. Or so we thought. Well—now we know why the tunnel's deserted.*

Can't fight, can't hide. Piss.

I whisper, again on instinct, "We have to make a break for it."

Her voice is distorted by the radio. She crackles into my helmet. "Are you stupid? They'll see us!"

"It's our only chance. Five have passed us by, we might have a clear shot at the surface. As soon as I get out, set your booster to maximum and run straight for the entrance. I'll cover our backs."

"This won't work."

"I don't have any better ideas, do you?"

"..."

I lean out of the crevice and look down the tunnel. They're all over the floor, walls, and ceiling. Heads scanning every which way. It's only luck we haven't been found yet.

"It's now or never," I say. "Ready?"

"D…I'm really scared. I don't wanna die here."

"We're not gonna die, okay? We'll be just fine. Ashton, look at me—I love you."

"I love you too."

It's too dark to see her face, but I can make out the shadows of her red hair through her gilded visor. I smile. Thank God it's dark in here—she can't see how scared I am. She's right—this probably won't work. Wyrms are faster than us, even with the rocket boosters on our backs. But it's our only chance. Our only shot. I lean forward again and look back toward the wyrms.

"When I say go, run. Okay?"

"Okay."

I take a deep breath, maybe the last I ever take. "Go!"

I run out, and—

No sound. No pain either. But I do see a flash of blue light. It slams into my shadow, against the wall in front of me, and the light swallows the shadow whole. The shot punctures my suit and leaves a blast of charred skin in my right shoulder, and I fall to the ground. The actuators in my space suit gurgle as liquid sealant pool around the gaping hole. The ragged edges on my wound burn as the chemicals heat then harden into a seal.

I don't understand. What happened?

I turn my head and see her run and blast her boosters in my face. I feel vibrations in the ground. The wyrms are stampeding toward me. They run straight for where they sensed the blast of electrons and, in a second, one of them clamps its circular mouth on my arm. This I feel. Hundreds of teeth shred my flesh, and the vacuum of space obliterates whatever's left. I scream. I beg for help. I can still hear her breathing through my radio. She can hear me. I beg her to help me—to save me. I apologize—I don't know what I did wrong. Did I mess up again? It's my fault, it must be. But I can be better, just please save me!

I don't understand.

Her panting stops—the connection died. She's out of range. Now no one can hear me. No one can hear me dying. The gnawing flesh stops. The wyrms actually start fighting each other for the kill. I dig my fist into the gray sand to cope with the pain. Just let me pass out.

I'm next to one of the dead—a broken helmet and eaten face stare up at me. Teeth marks are carved into the skull, thousands of rake lines crossed in hatches that knurled the bone surface of the spaceman's face. That'll be me soon. There's something strange about this corpse. I don't know why, in this moment of betrayal and seconds before death, I'm taken in by the person whose grave I'm about to share. Burn marks cover the suit, and a dozen knife wounds surround a patch of a flag I don't recognize. The wyrms got to him postmortem, and whoever killed this person *really* wanted him dead. The limbs were missing, but instead of bone and flesh, all that remained was a steel aperture and wires spooling into the dust. Never seen anything like this. There's a holster, and there's something in it. I stretch to reach it. I don't know why I bother. There's no way it'll fire, I'm not lucky, but I do it anyway. There's nothing else to do. I scream—pulling my shredded arm from the wyrm's maw. I grab the enormous revolver, turn, point, and shoot.

A flash of deep red paints the tunnel. The wyrm eating my arm glows orange, swells, and bursts into a million pieces. Black blood splatters my legs, and I feel it burn my skin through my suit. I pull the hammer back and fire again and again, and each time a wyrm explodes into superheated flesh.

The recoil is brutal—more than anything I've ever shot before. And I've shot a lot of guns. My fingers are definitely broken.

They're all dead. I stagger up—more will come. To eat me and their brethren. I walk as fast as I can until I make it to the surface, and I keep walking. No sign of her. Nothing on the radio. All I hear is my own breathing.

Earth is bright and blue overhead—it must be a full moon down there. All the land blue with ice broken by thin veins of scattered green. A desolate home, to be sure.

I've walked for a minute before I even look at my arm. The bone is white, and the blood is red, but the remaining flesh is dead black. I want to throw up. I wanna pass out. Let me die in my sleep—please. I can't see much anymore. I just keep walking. I don't know where. Not that it matters.

I'll be dead soon anyway. Tears well up in my eyes and roll down my face and into my mouth. Salty and bitter.

I finally process what happened.

What did I do wrong? What? Please—I don't understand. My fault. It must be. Otherwise she wouldn't have.

My fault.

My fault.

I don't understand.

A large shape enters my failing vision. I have no idea what I'm seeing. Something picks me up and takes me somewhere, and suddenly my helmet's off. I'm not dead? I'm on a ship…

I can only look up—a Velka. From the House of Wolves. He towers over me, not just big but fucking enormous. Easily twice the size of the monsters that had just eaten the better half of my limbs. Good. Just step on my head, and it'll be over.

His lupine ears perk up, and two glowing blue eyes shine back at me.

"Okar…must've been wyrms. Don't worry, mister, everything's going to be okay. You're safe now."

Dorin let the vibrations from the landship's engine rock him into a barely conscious lethargy. Kya sat across from him in the landship, Etkis was lumped in a large stretcher between them. Dorin stared at Etkis, his armor removed and his wounds seen to. The little doll that the Roarers had made him still hung from his belt, now splattered with blood and grime. His helmet remained, a crudely patched hole in the visor where his right eye had been. Red had stained half of the white helm as if a brush had smeared paint onto it with a single stroke.

Kya studied Dorin, a lump in her throat. In the short time she'd known him, Kya could count on one hand the number of times he'd managed to shut his mouth for longer than a minute.

Dorin hadn't spoken in thirteen hours.

The rest of the regiment were in different landships, Etkis took up too much room in this one. Most were covered in white sheets. The few that survived were past death's door and were waiting in the lobby, ready to see the reaper.

Just like Etkis.

Kya tried to think of something to say to Dorin but came up short. What could she say? She didn't know him all that well, but she felt it was wrong not to reach out. To at least try.

"Are...are you okay?" she asked, uncharacteristically timid.

Dorin just shook his head. He wasn't crying. He wasn't breathing hard or shaking. He was still, his face vacant. Empty. Along with the cuts and bruises scored across his face and body, it made him look like a corpse.

Another hour went by, and the caravan of landships they rode with made it to the gates of Volthsheim. The steel walls creaked loudly and opened to the garage, where a medical team was waiting to receive their patients. Etkis, being the ranking officer and about twice the size of every other surviving soldier, was unloaded first and rushed to the Velkan hospital. The few survivors followed in short order. The rest were off to be honored by the state in a ceremony. Pyres would light the city for the remainder of the day, and then life would go on.

Dorin and Kya got off and found Rother waiting for them. Kya crossed her arms across her chest to begrudgingly salute her superior. He nodded in recognition, and she rested. Rother cast his gray eyes on Dorin.

"Dorin. Scout Wallace. Can't say I ever thought I'd be happy to see either of you, but here we are. My congratulations. Are you both well?"

Kya side-eyed Dorin, hoping for some kind of reaction, but she was left disappointed. He just stared at the floor. He didn't acknowledge Rother's presence. No "thank you," but also no quip. No biting remark. Rother noticed. His half ear twitched. Kya spoke up. "We were just luckier than most, sir. Thank you for your concern."

Rother grunted. He eyed Dorin—still nothing. "The jarl wishes to speak with both of you. The amount of information at the compound was staggering, we're still going through it all. Incinerated or otherwise. Soon we'll begin eliminating human insurgents all over the planet. Jormar and Pompeii may have evaded us, but regardless this was a tremendous victory for the House of Wolves. The entire troop is to be honored. Posthumously or otherwise. As the only two members of the operation capable of standing, you're to both go to the Great Hall immediately. Kya, your...compatriot arrived yesterday morning. He's been placed in a comfortable dwelling in the human neighborhoods, toward the eastern wall."

Kya placed her hand to her chest and breathed an enormous sigh of relief. Technically unprofessional in front of her superior officer, but she didn't care. Rother allowed it.

"Thank you. Thank you," she said in a near whisper.

Rother nodded. "You may see him once you see the jarl and have submitted your report. Dismissed."

Kya saluted again and had begun to walk away with Dorin when Rother placed his hand on the human's shoulder. "Dorin. A moment," he said. Kya thought to wait but a look from Rother told her to go.

Dorin finally met Rother's gaze. The Velka's calm voice betrayed no intent. "Dorin—I owe you an apology."

Dorin scrunched his eyebrows in dumbfounded confusion.

"Believe me, no one is more surprised than I am. The reports aren't in yet, but my scouts told me about what you did, the explosion, and that many of the freelancer remains had Velkan weapons. If we had stormed the compound, we would've lost dozens of our brothers and sisters, not to mention the information in the compound. I can't imagine it was an easy decision, but you made the right one. And for that you have my respect. And my thanks."

Rother reached out a hand. A human custom. Dorin shook it without thinking. He processed this praise, and a fire rose in Dorin's throat. His skin felt hot. His stomach sick.

"I…don't…" Dorin muttered. He couldn't finish the sentence.

Rother put his hand on Dorin's shoulder. "Etkis will survive. He's too strong to ascend with Okar just yet. But I understand. I've been where you are, many times. You replay every choice, every action you took and wonder if there was something you could've done differently. It's rarely so simple."

Dorin's face didn't twitch or contort, but tears tumbled down his cheeks all the same. "And when it *is* so simple?"

Rother's voice slipped to a timbre of compassion. "I'd say don't blame yourself, but then I'd be a hypocrite. You need time. Etkis will be in surgery, and you have much to be proud of tonight."

"Okay," Dorin muttered. He started to walk away. Rother tilted his head, unsettled.

"Dorin," he said, his voice emotionless again, "my scouts said they found you in the study on the top floor, surrounded by corpses. But Pompeii escaped. What happened?"

Dorin's mouth went dry, his throat lumped. He didn't turn around. *Can't show my face, can't let him see…* "They bought her enough time to get away. She broke through the window and jumped while I dealt with them."

"You didn't give chase? Unlike you."

Dorin's teeth chattered so loud he was afraid Rother could hear. "It was a long night."

Rother didn't respond. Dorin felt the silence cut into him like a knife. Rother's voice returned to the slightest edge of compassion. "Go. The jarl wishes to give you a reward. You deserve it."

THE END

Lightning Source UK Ltd.
Milton Keynes UK
UKHW020830300123
416164UK00014B/2392